"A STUNNING ... BLACK LIST"

"Another eye-opening thriller . . . one of her most brilliant and chilling books yet."
—The Washington Post

". . . . . Warshawski . . . . in . . . .
. . . . I . . hope it's not another . . . .
. . . . before we find out."
—Chicago Tribune

HARD TIME
Sara Paretsky

"V.I. WARSHAWSKI IS BACK . . . AND BOY,
WAS IT WORTH THE WAIT. . . .
This is Warshawski at her black-and-blue best."
—*The Miami Herald*

"In a crowded field of female detectives,
V.I. Warshawski rules."
—*Newsweek*

"REMARKABLE . . . ONE OF THE BEST
CRIME WRITERS IN THE BUSINESS . . .
a good old-fashioned thriller . . .
No major writer has done more to bring modern
Chicago lovingly to life on the page. In all its
brashness and chaos the city lives and breathes in
Paretsky's remarkable series of novels."
—*The Baltimore Sun*

"WELCOME BACK, V.I. WE MISSED YOU."
—*Chicago Sun-Times*

"THIS IS THE BEST WARSHAWSKI NOVEL
EVER AND WELL WORTH WAITING FOR.
Brilliantly plotted, full of heart-wrenching emotion,
packed with fast-paced action, and peopled with
richly complex characters, *Hard Time* packs a
powerful, unforgettable punch."
—*Booklist*

"HARROWING."
—*The Seattle Times*

*Please turn the page for
more extraordinary acclaim. . . .*

A V. I. WARSHAWSKI NOVEL

SARA PARETSKY

HARD TIME

A DELL BOOK

Published by
Dell Publishing
a division of
Random House, Inc.
1540 Broadway
New York, New York 10036

This novel is a work of fiction. Names, characters, places, and incidents either are the product of the author's imagination or are used fictitiously. Any resemblance to actual persons, living or dead, events, or locales is entirely coincidental.

If you purchased this book without a cover you should be aware that this book is stolen property. It was reported as "unsold and destroyed" to the publisher and neither the author nor the publisher has received any payment for this "stripped book."

ISBN: 0-440-29578-5

Reprinted by arrangement with Delacorte Press

Printed in the United States of America

May 2000

10   9   8   7   6   5   4   3   2   1
OPM

For Miriam

The footnote Queen, without attribution,
in the year you weren't writing,
(Oh, except for this essay on Shanghai, that one on
Benjamin, a little piece on theory)

In the year you're writing,
Let me have one back

THANKS

As always, many people provided help in creating this story. Dr. Robert Kirschner of the University of Chicago gave me much helpful forensic advice—even if his facts forced me to abandon an early draft of the manuscript and start over. Professor Shelley Bannister of Northeastern Illinois University explained much about Illinois prisons to me, including the law regarding prison manufacture. Attorney Margaret Byrne was helpful with specifics on treatment of inmates in the Illinois prison system. She also suggested the unique structure of my mythical prison in Coolis. Angela Andrews kindly and bravely shared her personal experiences with me.

On other technical matters, Sandy Weiss of Packer Engineering gave me much useful information, especially on the various cameras V.I. makes use of in this story. Jesus Mata provided Spanish translations for me; Mena di Mario did the same for Italian. Rachel Lyle suggested what became the main impetus to writing this novel. Jonathan Paretsky as always was most helpful with details on legal matters.

This is a work of fiction, and no resemblance is intended between any characters in it and any real people, whether living or dead or never known to me. The combined prison-jail complex at Coolis in this novel does not exist in reality anywhere in America as far as I know, but I believe it is a plausible one. However, details on treatment of prisoners in Coolis were drawn from the Human Rights Watch report *All Too Familiar: Sexual Abuse of Women in U.S. State Prisons.*

CONTENTS

1   Media Circus   1

2   The Woman in the Road   12

3   House Call   21

4   Searching for Wheels   31

5   Diving into the Wreck   41

6   Signor Ferragamo, I Presume   49

7   Habeas Corpus?   61

8   Poolside Chat   71

9   Out of the Mouths of Babes   83

10 Found in Translation   93

11 Clean—On the Outside   100

12 The Lion's Den   109

13 Saturday at the Mall   118

14 Crumbs from the Table   127

15 Family Picnic   140

16 A Friend of the Family   149

17 Spinning Wheels, Seeking Traction   158

18 These Walls Do a Prison Make   168

19 Power Dining   181

20 Child in Mourning   191

21 We Serve and Protect   205

22	Night Crawlers	216
23	A Run to O'Hare	226
24	Annoying the Giants	233
25	Reaching Out To—A Friend?	242
26	If You Can't Swim, Keep Away from Sharks	255
27	Hounding a Newshound	264
28	Friendly Warning	271
29	Help Me, Father, for I Know Not What I'm Doing	283
30	The Mad Virgin's Story	295
31	A Day in the Country	305
32	Midnight Caller	319
33	Thrown in the Tank	330
34	Fourth of July Picnic	340
35	A Little Game on a Small Court	348
36	Bail? Why Leave Such Cool Quarters?	359
37	In the Big House	365
38	Prisoners in Cell Block H	377
39	An Audience with Miss Ruby	384
40	Sewing Circle	394
41	Photo Op	404
42	Slow Mend	412
43	Planning Session	423
44	Diving in with the Sharks	433
45	Fugitive	446
46	In the Church Militant	460
47	For Those Who Also Serve	470
48	Meet the Press	473
49	Scar Tissue	486

HARD
TIME

Media Circus

LACEY DOWELL CLUTCHED her crucifix, milky breasts thrust forward, as she backed away from her unseen assailant. Tendrils of red hair escaped from her cap; with her eyes shut and her forehead furrowed she seemed to have crossed the line from agony to ecstasy. It was too much emotion for me at close quarters.

I turned around, only to see her again, red hair artlessly tangled, breasts still thrust forward, as she accepted the Hasty Pudding award from a crowd of Harvard men. I resolutely refused to look at the wall on my right, where her head was flung back as she laughed at the witticisms of the man in the chair opposite. I knew the man and liked him, which made me squirm at his expression, a kind of fawning joviality. Murray Ryerson was too good a reporter to prostitute himself like this.

"What got into him? Or more to the point, what got into me, to let him turn my bar into this backslapping media circus?"

Sal Barthele, who owned the Golden Glow, had snaked through the Chicago glitterati packed into her tiny space to find me. Her height—she was over six feet tall—made it possible for her to spot me in the mob. For a moment, as she looked at the projection screens on her paneled walls, her relaxed hostess smile slipped and her nose curled in distaste.

"I don't know," I said. "Maybe he wants to show Hollywood what a cool insider he is, knowing an intimate bar they never heard of."

Sal snorted but kept her eyes on the room, checking for trouble spots—patrons waiting too long for liquid, wait staff unable to move. The throng included local TV personalities anxiously positioning themselves so that their cameras could catch them with Lacey Dowell if she ever showed up. While they waited they draped themselves around executives from Global Studios. Murray himself was hard at it with a woman in a silver gauze outfit. Her hair was clipped close to her head, showing off prominent cheekbones and a wide mouth painted bright red. As if sensing my gaze she turned, looked at me for a moment, then interrupted Murray's patter to jerk her head in my direction.

"Who is Murray talking to?" I asked Sal, but she had turned away to deal with a fractious customer.

I edged myself through the crowd, tripping on Regine Mauger, the *Herald-Star*'s wizened gossip columnist. She glared at me malevolently: she didn't know who I was, which meant I was no use to her.

"Will you watch where you're going, young woman?" Regine had been tucked and cut so many times that her skin looked like paper pulled over bone. "I'm trying to talk to Teddy Trant!"

She meant she was trying to push her bony shoulders close enough for Trant to notice her. He was the head of Global's midwest operations, sent in from Hollywood when Global acquired the *Herald-Star* and its string of regional papers a year ago. No one in town had paid much attention to him until last week, when

Global unleashed its television network. They had bought Channel 13 in Chicago to serve as their flagship and brought in Lacey Dowell, star of Global's wildly successful romance-horror flicks, to appear on the first "Behind Scenes in Chicago" segment—with host Murray Ryerson, "the man who turns Chicago inside out."

Global was launching a "Behind Scenes" feature in each of their major markets. As a hometown girl made good and a Global star, Lacey was the perfect choice for the Chicago launch. Crowds of teenagers as excited as my generation had been by the Beatles lined up to greet her at O'Hare. Tonight they were waiting outside the Golden Glow to catch her arrival.

With the excitement of television and movies on hand, no one could get enough of Edmund Trant. Where he dined, how his mediagenic wife decorated their Oak Brook mansion, all were avidly covered by columnists like Regine Mauger. And when invitations were issued for tonight's party, everyone in Chicago's small media pond was anxious to find the silver-edged ticket in the mail.

Regine and the other gossip columnists weren't of much interest to Trant tonight: I recognized the Speaker of the Illinois House and a couple of other state pols in the group close to him and had a feeling that the man he was talking most to was another businessman. Regine, peevish at being stiffed, made a big show of inspecting the hem of her black satin trousers, to show me I'd torn them or scuffed them or something. As I pushed my way through the melee toward a corner of the bar I heard her say to her counterpart at the *Sun-Times,* "Who is that very clumsy woman?"

I edged my way to the wall behind Sal's horseshoe mahogany bar. Since my assistant, Mary Louise Neely,

and her young protégée Emily Messenger had come
with me, I knew I was in for a long evening. In her
current manic state Emily would ignore any pleas to
leave much before one in the morning. It wasn't often
she did something that made her peers jealous and she
was determined to milk the evening to the limit.

Like most of her generation Emily was caught up in
Lacey-mania. When I said she and Mary Louise could
come as the guests my ticket entitled me to, Emily
turned pale with excitement. She was leaving for France
next week to go to a summer language camp, but that
was bore-rine compared to being in the same room with
Lacey Dowell.

"The Mad Virgin," she breathed theatrically. "Vic,
I'll never forget this until my dying day."

Lacey got the nickname from her lead in a series of
horror flicks about a medieval woman who supposedly
died in defense of her chastity. She periodically returned
to life to wreak vengeance on the man who tormented
her—since he kept reappearing through time to menace
other young women. Despite the pseudofeminist gloss
on the plot, Lacey always ended up dying again after
defeating her agelong foe, while some brainless hero
cuddled a vapid truelove who had screamed herself
breathless for ninety minutes. The films had a cult
status among Generation X-ers—their deadly serious-
ness turned them into a kind of campy self-satire—but
their real audience was Emily and her teenage friends,
who slavishly copied Lacey's hairstyle, her ankle boots
with their crossed straps, and the high-necked black
tank tops she wore off the set.

When I got to the end of the bar near the service
entrance, I stood on tiptoe to try to spot Emily or Mary
Louise, but the crowd was too dense. Sal had moved all

the barstools to the basement. I leaned against the wall, making myself as flat as possible, as harassed wait staff rushed by with hors d'oeuvres and bottles.

Murray had moved to the far end of the bar from me, still with the woman in silver gauze. He seemed to be regaling her with the tale of how Sal acquired her mahogany horseshoe bar from the remains of a Gold Coast mansion. Years ago when she was starting out, she got me and her brothers to climb through the rubble to help her haul it off. Watching the woman tilt her head back in a theatrical laugh, I was betting that Murray was pretending he'd been part of the crew. Something about the shape of his partner's face or the full-lipped pout she gave when she was listening was familiar, but I couldn't place her.

Sal stopped briefly by me again, holding a plate of smoked salmon. "I have to stay here till the last dog dies, but you don't—go on home, Warshawski."

I took some salmon and explained morosely that I was waiting on Mary Louise and Emily. "Want me to tend bar? It would give me something to do."

"Be better if you went in the back and washed dishes. Since I don't usually serve food here at the Glow my little washer is blowing its brains out trying to keep up with this. Want me to bring you the Black Label?"

"I'm driving. San Pellegrino is my limit for the evening."

Murray maneuvered his way across the bar with his companion and put his arm around Sal. "Thanks for opening up the Glow to this mob scene. I thought we ought to celebrate at some place authentically Chicago."

He kept an arm around Sal in a protective hug and introduced her to his companion. "Sal Barthele, one of the truly great Chicago stories. Alexandra Fisher, one of the truly great Chicago escapees. And you know V. I. Warshawski."

"Yes, I know Vic." Sal extricated herself from Murray. "Stop showing off, Murray. Not all of us are swooning because you sat in front of a camera for fifteen minutes."

Murray threw back his head and laughed. "That's what makes this a great town. But I was talking to Alex. She and Vic were in law school together."

"We were?" The name didn't ring a bell.

"I've changed a little." Alex laughed, too, and squeezed my hand in a power shake.

I squeezed back, hard enough to make her open her eyes. She had the muscle definition of a woman who worked seriously with weights, and the protruding breastbone of one who survived on lettuce leaves between workouts. I have the muscles of a South Side street fighter, and probably matching manners.

I still couldn't place her. Her hair, dyed a kind of magenta, was cut close to her skull at the sides and slicked back on top with something like BrylCreem, except no doubt pricier. Before I could probe, a young man in a white collarless shirt murmured a few apologetic words to Alex about "Mr. Trant." She waggled her fingers at Murray and me and followed the acolyte toward the power center. The wizened gossip columnist, still hovering on the perimeter, stopped her for a comment, but Alex was sucked into the vortex and disappeared.

"So—what did you think, V.I.?" Murray scooped half the salmon from Sal's platter and downed it with a mouthful of beer.

It was only then that I realized he had shaved his

beard for his television debut. I had watched the beard go from fiery red to auburn to gray-flecked in the years he and I had collaborated and competed on financial scandal in Chicago, but I'd never seen his naked jaw before.

Somehow it made my heart ache—foolish Murray, anxiously decking himself for the media gods—so I said brusquely, "She has beautiful deltoid definition."

"Of my show, Warshawski."

I kept my eyes on the mahogany bar. "I thought you brought the same attention to Lacey that you did to Gantt-Ag and the Knife grinders and all those other stories we worked together."

"Sheesh, Warshawski, can't you ever give a guy a break?"

"I wish you well, Murray. I really do."

My glance flicked to his face. Whatever he saw in my eyes made him look away. He gave Sal another exaggerated grin and hug and headed in his companion's direction. As I watched him walk away I realized someone had been pointing a camera at us: he'd been embracing Sal for tape.

"Something tells me Murray picked the Glow to show all those Hollywood types he hangs around with black people," Sal said, frowning at his retreating back.

I didn't want to admit it out loud, but I thought sadly she was probably right.

"That Alex Fisher is part of Global's legal team," Sal added, her eyes still on the room. "They brought her out from California to mind the shop here. I had to deal with her a few times on liability questions about Lacey —I actually had to buy insurance to cover the event tonight. The studio wasn't even going to cover the cost of that until I told them the city health department was raising so many questions about food in the Glow that I'd have to shut down the event."

"Why'd they care? They could go anywhere."

"They're paying for the catering, and I only told them this morning. I hear they say in Hollywood that no one kicks Global's ball, but they're out-of-towners here." She laughed and disappeared into the minute kitchen.

Around midnight there was a flurry at the door. I hoped it was Lacey making her dramatic appearance so that I could collect Emily and leave, but it was only a couple of Bulls players—bore-rine to Emily Messenger and her friends. As the crowds shifted for them I made out Mary Louise and Emily, stationed where Emily could get an autograph as soon as Lacey cleared the entrance. Emily was in Mad Virgin uniform: the black tank top, stretch pants, and platform shoes that were sold through the Virginwear label Global owned.

Mary Louise must have worked something out with one of the officers assigned to cover the event. She had been a cop herself for ten years, and when she quit the force two years ago she'd done it in a way that didn't lose her any friends. The guy on duty tonight had placed Emily behind the velvet ropes set up to create the illusion of an entrance hall. He'd even found a barstool for Emily to perch on. I was envious—my calves were aching from hours of standing.

"Are you waiting for Lacey, too?"

I turned to find a stranger addressing me, a compactly built man several years younger than me, with curly brown hair and the hint of a mustache.

"I'm a friend of the groom," I said, "but I have a young guest who won't leave until she gets Lacey's autograph."

"A friend of—oh." His eyes twinkled in appreciation. "And I'm a friend of the bride. At least, we grew up in the same building, and she squeaked with excitement when she told me she was coming back to Chicago."

"Is she really from here? When actors say they're from Chicago, they usually mean Winnetka and New Trier, not the city."

"Oh, no. We grew up in Humboldt Park. Until we were twelve we hung out together, the only nerds in our building, so that the bigger kids wouldn't pick on us. Then she got a role on television and whoosh, off she went like a rocket. Now all those kids who used to corner her in the stairwell are trying to pretend they were her buddies, but she's not a fool."

"She remembered you?" I wasn't really interested, but even idle talk would help get me through the evening.

"Oh, sure, she sent me one of her fancy cards to this event. But she won't meet with me alone." He reached across the bar for a bottle of beer and shook himself, as if shaking off a train of thought. "And why should she? Which groom are you a friend of? Do you work for the television station?"

"No, no. I know Murray Ryerson, that's all."

"You work for him?" He grabbed a plate of tiny sandwiches from a passing waiter and offered it to me.

I don't like to tell people I'm a private investigator—it's almost as bad as being a doctor at a party. Everyone has some scam or some time that they've been robbed or cheated that they think you'll sort out for them on the spot. Tonight was no exception. When I admitted to my occupation, my companion said maybe I could help him. Something rather curious had been happening in his plant lately.

I stifled a sigh and dug in my evening bag for a business card. "Give me a call if you want to talk about it in a place where I can give you my full attention."

"V. I. Warshawski?" He pronounced my name carefully. "You're on Leavitt and North? That's not so far from me."

Before he could say anything else there was another stir at the entrance. This time it was Lacey herself. The waters parted: Edmund Trant extricated himself from his crowd and appeared at the door to kiss Lacey's hands as the cameras began to whir again. Murray used his bulk to barrel his way next to Trant in time for Lacey to kiss him for the cameras. The policeman at the door greeted Lacey and directed her to Emily. I watched while she hugged Emily, signed her book, and flung herself into the arms of another Global actor on hand for the event.

While I worked my way along the wall to the front to collect Mary Louise and Emily, Lacey moved her entourage to the center of the room. The guy I'd just been speaking to managed to position himself behind the waiter bringing her a drink. I stopped to watch. Lacey greeted him with enthusiasm, so he must have been telling the truth about their childhood. But he seemed to be trying to talk to her seriously about something—a mistake in a gathering this public. Even under the soft rainbows of Sal's Tiffany lamps I could see Lacey's color rise. She turned away from him in hauteur and he made the mistake of grabbing her shoulders. The off-duty cop who'd gotten Emily her seat muscled his way through the crowd and hustled him out the door. When we followed a few minutes later, the man was standing across the street staring at the Golden Glow. As we came out he hunched his hands down in his pockets and walked away.

"Vic, you've made me *blissfully* happy," Emily sighed as we walked past the line of Lacey's fans. "There they are, waiting for hours just to get sight of her, and she actually kissed me and signed my book, maybe I'll even be on TV. If someone told me two years ago that every girl in Chicago would be jealous of me, I'd never have believed them in a million years. But it's come true."

2

The Woman in the Road

EMILY CHATTERED WITH excitement all the way to the car, then fell deeply asleep in the backseat. Mary Louise leaned back on the passenger side and slipped out of her high heels.

"I stayed up all night to watch poor Diana marry Prince Creep when I was that age," she commented. "At least Emily got to touch Lacey."

I had wanted to go to O'Hare to join the vigil for Ringo and John, but my mother was desperately ill by then; I wasn't going to worry her by riding around on buses and L's after curfew. "Some guy was trying to get next to Lacey as we left. He said they grew up together in Humboldt Park. Is that true?"

"I'm glad you asked." In the sodium lights on the Inner Drive I could see Mary Louise's grin. "I have eaten and drunk Lacey Dowell facts for the last two weeks, ever since you called with the invite, and it's high time you shared the treat. Lacey's birth name was Magdalena Lucida Dowell. Her mother was Mexican, her father Irish; she's an only child who grew up in Humboldt Park and went to St. Remigio's, where she starred in all the school plays and won a scholarship to Northern Illinois. They have an important theater program. She got her first break in film twelve years ago, when—"

"All right, all right. I'm sure you know her shoe size and her favorite color, too."

"Green, and eight-and-a-half. And she still likes the chorizo from her home neighborhood better than any trendy food in L.A. Ha, ha. Her father died in an industrial accident before she started making real money, but her mother lives with her in Santa Monica in a nice oceanfront mansion. Supposedly Lacey gives money to St. Remigio's. They say she kept the cardinal from closing the school by shoring up its scholarship fund. If that's true it's worth something."

"A lot." The light at Lake Shore Drive turned green, and I swung into the northbound lanes.

"Come to think of it, you should have picked up some of these gems from Murray's interview. Didn't you watch?"

I grimaced at the dashboard. "I think I was so embarrassed to see him doing it at all that I couldn't focus on what he was saying."

"Don't be too hard on him," Mary Louise said. "Guy has to live on something, and you're the one who told me the Global team axed his biggest stories."

She was right. I knew Murray had been having a tough time since Global bought the paper. They hadn't stopped any of his digging, but they wouldn't print any stories they considered politically sensitive. "We have to pay attention to the people who do us favors in this state," Murray quoted to me bitterly when management killed a story he'd been working on for months about the new women's prison in Coolis. He mimicked his editor one night at dinner last winter: *Americans*

*have grown accustomed to sound bites. Sex, sports, and
violence are good sound bites. Skimming pension funds
or buying off the state legislature are not. Get the picture, Murray?*

What I'd somehow forgotten was how much of a
survivor Murray was. No one was more surprised than
me to get one of those prized tickets to Global's
postlaunch party—and maybe no one was more surprised to read on it that we were celebrating Murray's
debut as Chicago's "Behind Scenes" reporter. What
Murray had done to land the job I preferred not to
contemplate. He certainly wasn't going to tell me that—
or anything else. When I called to ask, I spoke to an
assistant who politely assured me she would give him
my messages, but he hadn't come to the phone himself.

I knew Murray had put out discreet feelers for reporting work around the country. But he was a couple
of years older than me, and in your forties companies
start looking at you as a liability. You need too much
money, and you're moving into an age bracket where
you're likely to start using your health insurance. Also
against him was the same thing that made it hard for
me to operate outside the city: all his insider knowledge
was in Chicago. So he had looked long and hard at
reality, and when reality stared back he blinked first.
Was that a crime?

At two on a weeknight, traffic on the drive was
sparse. To my right, sky and lake merged in a long
smear of black. Except for the streetlights coating the
park with a silvery patina, we seemed alone on the edge
of the world. I was glad for Mary Louise's presence,
even her monologue on what the sitter would charge
for looking after Emily's young brothers, on how much

she had to do before summer session started—she was going to law school part time besides her part-time work for me—was soothing. Her grumbling kept me from thinking how close to the edge of the world my own life was, which fueled my hostility to Murray's decision to sell himself on the air.

Even so, I pushed the car to seventy, as if I could outrun my irritability. Mary Louise, cop instincts still strong, raised a protest when we floated off the crest of the hill at Montrose. I braked obediently and slowed for our exit. The Trans Am was ten, with the dents and glitches to prove it, but it still hugged corners like a python. It was only at the traffic lights on Foster that you could hear a wheeze in the engine.

As we headed west into Uptown, the loneliness of the night lifted: beer cans and drunks emerged from the shadows. The city changes character every few blocks around here, from the enclave of quiet family streets where Mary Louise lives, to an immigrant landing stage where Russian Jews and Hindus improbably mix, to a refuse heap for some of Chicago's most forlorn; closest to the lake is where Uptown is rawest. At Broadway we passed a man urinating behind the same Dumpsters where a couple was having sex.

Mary Louise glanced over her shoulder to make sure Emily was still asleep. "Go up to Balmoral and over; it's quieter."

At the intersection a shadow of a man was holding a grimy sign begging for food. He wove an uncertain thread through the oncoming headlights. I slowed to a crawl until I was safely past him.

Away from Broadway most of the streetlights were gone, shot out or just not replaced. I didn't see the body in the road until I was almost on top of it. As I stood on the brakes, steering hard to the left, Mary Louise screamed and grabbed my arm. The Trans Am spun across the street and landed against a fire hydrant.

"Vic, I'm sorry. Are—are you okay? It's a person, I thought you were going to run over him. And Emily, my God—" She unbuckled her seat belt with shaking fingers.

"I saw him," I said in a strangled voice. "I was stopping. What could yanking my arm do to help with that?"

"Mary Lou, what's wrong?" Emily was awake in the backseat, her voice squeaky with fear.

Mary Louise had leapt out of the car into the back with Emily while I still was fumbling with my own seat belt. Emily was more frightened than injured. She kept assuring Mary Louise she was fine and finally climbed out of the car to prove it. Mary Louise probed her neck and shoulders while I fished a flashlight out of my glove compartment.

Assured of Emily's safety, Mary Louise hurried to the figure in the road. Professional training pushed the four beers she'd drunk during the evening to the back of her brain. Her stumbling gait on her way to the figure was due to the same shock that made my own legs wobble when I finally found the flashlight and joined her—we hadn't been going fast enough to get hurt.

"Vic, it's a woman, and she's barely breathing."

In the light of my flash I could see that the woman was very young. She was dark, with thick black hair tumbled about a drawn face. Her breath came in bubbling, rasping sobs, as if her lungs were filled with fluid. I'd heard that kind of breathing when my father was dying of emphysema, but this woman looked much too young for such an illness.

I pointed the light at her chest, as if I might be able to detect her lungs, and recoiled in horror. The front of her dress was black with blood. It had oozed through the thin fabric, sticking it to her body like a large bandage. Dirt and blood streaked her arms; her left humerus poked through the skin like a knitting needle out of a skein of wool. Perhaps she had wandered in front of a car, too dazed by heroin or Wild Rose to know where she was.

"Vic, what's wrong?" Emily had crept close and was shivering next to me.

"Sugar, she's hurt and we need to get her help. There are towels in the trunk, bring those while I call an ambulance."

The best antidote for fear is activity. Emily's feet crunched across broken glass back to the car while I pulled out my mobile phone and called for help.

"You take the towels; I'll deal with the emergency crew." Mary Louise knew what to say to get paramedics to the scene as fast as possible. "It looks like a hit-and-run victim, bad. We're at Balmoral and—and—"

I finished covering the woman's feet and ran to the corner for the street name. Glenwood, just east of Ashland. A car was about to turn into the street; I waved it on. The driver yelled that he lived there, but I took on the aura of my traffic-cop father and barked out that the street was closed. The driver swore at me but moved on. A few minutes later an ambulance careened around the corner. A squad car followed, blue strobes blinding us.

The paramedics leapt into efficient action. As they

attached the woman to oxygen and slid her smoothly into the ambulance, a crowd began to gather, the mixed faces of Uptown: black, Middle Eastern, Appalachian. I scanned them, trying to pinpoint someone who seemed more avid than the rest, but it was hard to make out expressions when the only light came from the reds and blues of the emergency strobes. A couple of girls in head scarves were pointing and chattering; an adult erupted from a nearby walk-up, slapped one of them, and yanked them both inside.

I took the flashlight and searched the street, hoping to find a wallet or paper or anything that might identify the woman, but was stopped by one of the patrolmen, who led me over to Mary Louise with the comment that searching the accident scene was police business.

Mary Louise kept a protective arm around Emily while we answered questions. The officers joined me in an inspection of the Trans Am. The fireplug had popped the hood and bent the front axle.

"You the driver, ma'am?" one of the cops asked. "Can I see your license?"

I dug it out of my wallet. He slowly copied the information onto his report, then typed in my name and plate numbers to see how many outstanding DUI's I had. When the report came back negative, he had me walk a line toe-to-toe—much to the amusement of the pointing, snickering crowd.

"Want to tell me how this happened, ma'am?"

I glared at Mary Louise but went through my paces: no streetlights, didn't see body until almost on top of it, swerved to avoid, impaled on fireplug.

"What brought you down this street to begin with, ma'am?"

Normally I don't let the police make my business their business, but normally I don't have a white-faced sixteen-year-old in tow. Poor Emily, her thrilling adventure in ruins around an accident victim—I didn't need to prolong her misery by fighting with cops over the Fourth Amendment. I meekly explained that I was running Mary Louise and Emily home and that we were taking a shortcut through side streets. A long cut as it turned out, but who could have known that? And at least our stumbling down this street might give the young woman a fighting chance at survival. All I really grudged was my damaged car. I felt ashamed: a young woman lay close to death and I was worrying about my car. But major repairs, or even a new vehicle, were definitely not part of this summer's budget. I thought resentfully of Murray, rolling with the punches and coming up roses.

"And where had you been with the young lady?" A narrowing of the eyes, what were two grown women doing with a teenager they weren't related to.

"We had an invitation to the Lacey Dowell event downtown," Mary Louise said. "I'm Emily's foster mother and I don't let her go to events like that alone at her age. You can call Detective Finchley in the First District if you have any questions—he was my commanding officer for four years and he knows how Emily and I came together."

After that the atmosphere thawed: one of the men knew Finchley, and besides, if Mary Louise was one of them she couldn't possibly be involved in anything criminal. The officers helped me push the Trans Am away from the hydrant so that it wouldn't be ticketed. They even gave us a lift home. I didn't mind being squashed between the cage and the backseat: it beat

waiting for a slow ride down Clark Street on the number twenty-two bus.

As we pulled away from the curb the people on the
street watched happily: a satisfactory end to the outing
—three white women carried away in the squad car.

3

House Call

MY FATHER WAS lying in the road in the wasted final stage of his illness. He had left his oxygen tank on the curb and was gasping for breath. Before I could get into the street to pick him up, a squad car rounded the corner and ran over him. You killed him, you killed him, I tried to scream, but no sound came out. Bobby Mallory, my father's oldest friend on the force, climbed out of the car. He looked at me without compassion and said, You're under arrest for creating a public nuisance.

The phone pulled me mercifully out of sleep. I stretched out an arm and mumbled "Is it?" into the mouthpiece.

It was my downstairs neighbor, his voice rough with anxiety. "Sorry to wake you, cookie, but there's some cops here saying you was involved in a hit-and-run last night. They was hanging on your bell and the dogs were going crazy so I went to see what was going on, and of course Mitch bounces out to see who it is, and the one guy, he starts carrying on about Mitch, don't I know there's a leash law in this town, and I says, last I heard you don't need to keep a dog on a leash in your own home and who are you, anyway, disturbing the peace like this, and he whips out his badge—"

"Did he really say hit-and-run?" I demanded, pushing my sleep-sodden body upright.

"He holds out his badge and demands you by name, not that he could pronounce it right, of course. What happened, doll? You didn't really hit someone and leave them lay, did you? Not that I haven't told you a million times not to drive that sports car so fast around town, but you stand up to your mistakes, you wouldn't leave no one in the street, and that's what I told the one twerp, but he starts trying to act like Dirty Harry, like I'm scared of some tin-pot Hitler like him, when I beat up guys twice his size at—"

"Where are they?"

Mr. Contreras is capable of going on for a day or two once he's in full throttle. He's a retired machinist, and even though I know he worked some fancy lathe in his days at Diamondhead Motors, I can really only picture him with a hammer in his hand, out-driving John Henry, along with any mere mechanical device. "They're downstairs in the lobby, but I think you better get out of bed and talk to them, doll, even if they're pissers, pardon my French, not like the lieutenant or Conrad or other cops you know."

It was heroic of him to include Conrad Rawlings in the same breath as Lieutenant Mallory. Mr. Contreras had been unhappy about Conrad's and my affair, his usual jealousy of the men I know compounded by his racial attitude. He'd been relieved when Conrad decided things weren't working between us, until he saw how deep the feelings had gone with me. It's taken me a while to recover from the loss.

I hung up and shuffled to the bathroom. A long shower used to be enough to revive me after short nights, but that was when I was thirty. At forty-plus the only thing that revives me is enough sleep. I ran cold water over my head until my teeth were chattering. At least my blood was flowing, although not as much to my brain as I needed for an interview with the police.

While I was toweling myself I heard them leaning on the bell at my third-floor door. I looked through the spy-hole. There were two, a short one in a brown polyester suit that had been through the dryer a few too many times, and a tall one with an acne-scarred face.

I cracked the door the width of the chain and poked my head around so they couldn't see my naked body. "I'll be with you as soon as I get some clothes on."

The short one lunged forward, trying to push the door open, but I shut it firmly, taking my jeans into the kitchen to dress while I put my stove-top espresso-maker on to boil. It's one of those cheap metal ones that can't foam milk, but it makes strong coffee. I scrambled into my clothes and went back to the door.

The short one in brown polyester bared tiny teeth in a circle like a pike's. "V. I. Warshki? Police. We have some questions for you."

"Warshawski, not Warshki," I said. "My neighbor said you were with the police, which is why I opened the door, but I need to see some proof. Like your badges. And then you can tell me why you've come calling."

The tall one pulled his badge out of his coat pocket and flashed it for a nanosecond. I held his wrist so that I could inspect the badge. "Detective Palgrave. And your companion is? Detective Lemour. Thank you. You can sit in the living room while I finish dressing."

"Uh, ma'am." Palgrave spoke. "Uh, we don't mind talking to you in your bare feet. We have a couple of questions about the female you came on last night."

A door thudded shut at the bottom of the stairwell. Mitch and Peppy began to race upstairs, followed by Mr. Contreras's heavy tread. The dogs barreled past the detectives to get to me, squeaking as if it had been twelve months instead of twelve hours since we were last together. Lemour kicked at Mitch but only connected with his tail. I grabbed both dogs by the collars before anything worse happened.

When they finished jumping up and kissing me, the dogs, especially Mitch, were eager to greet Lemour. Peppy's a golden; Mitch, her son, is half black Lab and enormous. Like all retrievers, they are incurably friendly, but when they're pawing the air and grinning they look ferocious to strangers; our visitor wasn't going to try to muscle his way past them.

Mr. Contreras had reached the doorway in time to see Lemour kick at Mitch. "Listen here, young man, I don't care if you're a detective or a meter maid, but these dogs live here and you don't. You got no call to be kicking them. I could have you up before the anticruelty society, policeman kicking man's best friend, how'd your ma and your kids like to read that in the paper?"

The detective wasn't the first person to be rattled by Mr. Contreras. "We're here to talk to the lady about a hit-and-run she was involved in last night. Take your animals downstairs and leave us alone."

"It so happens, young man, that the lady owns the golden. We share looking after them—not that it's any of your business—so if she wants them up here it's fine with me. And as for whatever questions you got, you're way off base if you think she was involved in some hit-and-run. I've known her twelve years, and she would no more run over someone and leave 'em lay in the street than she'd prop up a ladder to climb to the moon.

So you got some accident victim claiming otherwise, you been totally misinformed. Be a good idea if you called your boss and made sure you got the right address or license plate or whatever, otherwise I guarantee you'll feel foolish wasting your time and everyone else's on this—"

"Uh, sir." Palgrave had been trying to cut the flow short for some minutes. "Uh, sir, we're not accusing her of hitting someone. We only want to ask her some questions about the incident."

"Then why didn't you say that?" Mr. Contreras demanded in exasperation. "Your buddy here was carrying on like she ran over the pope and left him to bleed in the street."

"We need to ascertain whether the Warshki woman hit the woman or not," Lemour said.

"Warshawski," I said. "Have a seat. I'll be with you in a minute."

I went back to the kitchen to turn the fire off under my pot; fortunately it had just reached the point where it sucked water up through the filter into the top, not the point where it started filling the house with the stench of scorched metal. Lemour, apparently fearing I might be going to hide or shred evidence, perhaps my car, followed me to the kitchen.

"It makes two cups," I said. "Want one?"

"Listen, Princess Diana, don't get smart with me. I want you to answer some questions."

I poured out coffee and looked in the refrigerator. I'd been in Springfield testifying at Illinois House hearings into contracting scams the last few days. The only thing close to food was a dried heel of rye. I looked at it dubiously while Lemour foamed at the mouth behind me. I ignored him and took my coffee into the living room. Detective Palgrave was standing stiffly at attention while Mr. Contreras sat in my good armchair, holding Mitch's collar.

"Detective, is there any word on the woman I stopped to help last night?" I said to Palgrave.

"She was taken to Beth Israel, but—"

His partner cut him off. "We ask the questions, Warshki; you give the answers. I want a complete description of the encounter you had in the road last night."

"It's *Warshawski*. It may be a sign of dyslexia when you can't pronounce all the syllables in a long word, but you can get over it with speech therapy, even as an adult."

"Uh, ma'am," Palgrave said, "could I just ask you to describe what happened last night? We're trying to investigate the incident, and we need to find someone who can tell us what happened."

I shook my head. "I don't know anything about the woman—she was lying in the road. The streetlights are out on that stretch of Balmoral, so I didn't see her until I was about ten feet from her. I stood on the brakes, swerved, hit a fireplug, but did not hit the woman. My passenger, who's a ten-year veteran with the Chicago police, summoned an ambulance. We could see that the woman had a broken arm, and her breathing was labored; the front of her dress seemed bloody. I don't know anything else about her. I don't know her name, how she came to be there, or whether she's still alive."

"How much did you drink last night?" Lemour demanded.

"Three bottles of mineral water."

"You're sure you didn't hit her and are trying to dress it up as a Good Samaritan act?"

"Uh, Doug, why don't we talk to the passenger. Get some confirmation of Ms. Warshki's—sorry, ma'am, what is it? Warshouski?—anyway, of her story."

"She took so long answering the door, she was probably calling to feed the other woman her lines," Lemour grumbled.

"You can talk to Ms. Neely," I said, "but the officers on the scene took a complete report last night. They even breathalyzed me. Why don't you look at that?"

Palgrave's face became more wooden. "Uh, ma'am, did your passenger witness the breathalyzing? Because we were told it didn't take place, that you refused."

I stared at him. "I signed that report, and it included a statement that I had not been drinking. Let me see it."

Palgrave shifted uncomfortably and said they didn't have the report with them. Lemour was all in favor of arresting me for manslaughter on the spot; I was trying to weasel out of a DUI charge, he said. Palgrave told him to tone it down and asked if it was really true that Mary Louise was a ten-year veteran with the force.

"Yes, indeed. You can talk to Bobby Mallory—Lieutenant Mallory—at the Central District. She was under his command for quite a few years," I said. "I'll get him on the phone for you now. Or Terry Finchley. He was her immediate superior."

"That won't be necessary, ma'am," Palgrave said. "We'll talk to this Neely woman, but if she witnessed your—uh—breathalyzing that's probably good enough. To be on the safe side, we'll take a look at your car, make sure it wasn't involved in the accident."

"Who is the woman I stopped for, anyway?" I demanded. "Why does it matter so much to find someone to take the fall for her injuries?"

"We're not trying to make you take a fall," Palgrave

said. "She's an accident victim and you were on the scene."

"Come on, Detective," I said. "I happened on the scene after someone left her lying in the road. I didn't put her there, didn't hit her, didn't do anything but wreck my car swerving to miss her."

"In that case a look at your car will get us out of your hair," Palgrave said. "We'll tow it to the police lab and get back to you about when you can pick it up. Where is it now?"

"It wasn't drivable. It's where the accident took place—you can look up the address on the report when you get back to the station."

That made Lemour start to boil over, but Palgrave calmed him down once more. When they finally left I felt limp. Who could the woman be to merit this much aggravation? But I couldn't worry about that until I dealt with my car. If the cops were determined to find a perpetrator, I wanted the Trans Am to have a clean bill of health before it got into police hands.

I called the mechanic I go to when I have no other choice. Luke Edwards is one of the few guys out there who still knows what a carburetor does, but he's so depressing I try to avoid him. He came to the phone now with his usual drooping tones. He identifies so totally with machines that it's hard for him to talk to people, but our relations have been particularly strained since a car of his I borrowed got totaled by a semi. Before I could finish explaining what I needed, Luke cut me off, saying he didn't want to hear my tale of woe, he'd known since I trashed the Impala that I couldn't be trusted behind the wheel.

"I spent three months getting every bearing on that engine purring in unison. I'm not surprised you wrecked your Trans Am. You don't know how to look after a car."

"Luke, forget that for a minute. I want a private lab to inspect my car and certify that it didn't hit a person. I'm not asking you to work on it today, just to tell me the name of a good private lab."

"Everyone thinks they come first, Warshawski. You gotta wait in line along with all the working stiffs."

I tried not to scream. "Luke, I need a civilian lab before the police get to my car. I ran into a fire hydrant swerving to miss an accident victim, and some cop is taking the lazy way out instead of running an investigation. I want to have a lab report to wave in his face in case he doesn't do the rest of his homework."

"Police after you, huh? About time someone called you on your reckless driving. Just kidding you. Calm down and I'll help you out. Cheviot is the lab you want, out in Hoffman Estates. They're pricey but they got a rock-solid rap in court. I and my friends have used 'em a couple of times—I can call for you and set it up if you want. Tell me where your baby is and I'll send Freddie out with the truck, get him to take the Trans Am out to Cheviot. He sees a cop, should he run over him?"

Luke being funny is harder to take than his depression. I pretended to laugh and hung up. Mr. Contreras, watching with bright anxious eyes, told me I'd done the right thing but wanted me to do more.

I didn't think there was much else I could do except call Mary Louise. She was trying to dress one of Emily's young brothers, who was protesting loudly. When she realized what I was saying she let the kid go and gave me her full attention.

"I don't know anyone named Lemour, but I'll ask

Terry," she promised. "I read that report last night before I signed it, and it made crystal clear the fact that we had not hit that poor creature. There shouldn't be a problem. I'll certainly tell them that when they come around here. I have to get Nathan to day camp, but I'll call Terry as soon as I get back."

Mary Louise could make that phone call more easily than I. Terry Finchley, her commanding officer her last four years on the force, was a rising star in the violent crimes unit. When Mary Louise resigned, she was careful to do it in a way that left him on her side.

I'd actually met Mary Louise on cases where Terry Finchley and I had crossed paths. I'd always liked him, but since the end of Conrad's and my affair he's been rather stiff with me. He and Conrad are pretty close; even though it was Conrad who broke things off, Terry thinks I treated his friend shabbily. Still, he's too honest a person to extend his stiffness to Mary Louise simply because she works for me.

"You gonna call the lieutenant and make a complaint?" Mr. Contreras asked, meaning my father's old friend Bobby Mallory.

"I don't think so." Bobby was much more likely to chew me out for interfering with a police investigation than he was to phone the Rogers Park station and complain about Lemour. He would probably say, If I wanted to play cops and robbers, I'd have to be ready to take the heat that comes with it.

4

Searching for Wheels

So whatcha going to do next, doll?" Mr. Contreras asked.

I frowned. "I'd like to find out who that woman is, so I can try to understand why the cops are so eager to find someone to take the fall for hitting her. In the meantime, I need to get hold of a car. Who knows how long it'll be before the Trans Am is fit to drive again, especially if it ends up as police exhibit A."

I called my insurance company, but they were useless. The Trans Am was ten years old; the only value it had to them was as scrap. They wouldn't help me with a tow, the repairs, or a loaner. I snarled at the agent, who only said blandly that I shouldn't carry property damage on such an old car.

I slammed down the phone. What was I doing sending good money to this idiot and the company of thieves he represented? I checked a few rental places, but if the Trans Am were tied up for weeks I'd be shelling out hundreds, maybe even a thousand, to rent something I'd have no equity in.

"Perhaps I should scrape together a few grand and buy something used. Something good enough that I could resell it when my car comes out of the shop. Or a motorcycle—you know—we'll see the world from my Harley!"

"Don't go buying a Harley," Mr. Contreras begged. "One of my buddies, before your time, old Carmen Brioni, he used to ride a big old Honda 650 around town, thought he was a teenager all over again, until a semi run him off 55 down by Lockport. After that he never talked again, lived like an eggplant for seven years before the good Lord was kind enough to pull the plug."

We studied the ads in the paper together, which left me more discouraged: anything roadworthy seemed to run three or four thousand. And would take a good day out of my life to hunt down.

"Why don't you leave car-hunting to me?" Mr. Contreras said. "I sold mine when I moved here because I figured I couldn't afford all that extry for insurance and whatnot on my pension. In fact, you know that's why I moved out of the old neighborhood when Clara died, besides, most of my friends had got scared and left the city, so it wasn't like I was missing my pals. Here I figured I'd be close by the L and walking distance to the stores. And of course it saves me all that parking aggravation, but I still can tell whether an engine runs good or not. What do you have in mind?"

"A Jaguar XJ-12," I said promptly. "There's one here for only thirty-six thousand. Standard shift, convertible, the old body before the Ford engineers got their hands on it."

"That ain't practical. Those ragtops don't have any backseat to speak of, and where would the dogs sit?" He startled me into laughing, which made him beam with pride.

"Oh, yeah, the dogs," I said. "You know, it's going

to have to be a beater. Unless I decide to junk the Trans Am. But I only want to buy something if it's a reasonable alternative to renting."

He started running a black fingernail down the page, whispering the words under his breath as he read, his eyes bright with interest. He has his own friends, and he tends a garden in our tiny backyard with painstaking care, but he doesn't really have enough stimulation in his life—it's why he gets overinvolved in my affairs.

I skimmed the news sections, trying to see if our accident victim had made the morning edition, while Mr. Contreras worked the ad pages. Commonwealth Edison's inability to provide the city with power got a tiny mention, as did wildfires in Florida, but Global's television debut took up most of the front page.

Murray had a byline, describing his interview with Lacey Dowell. It was the first time he'd been on the front page in ten months. First time in the paper in three. "Just haven't been covering the right stories until now, Murray," I muttered. First the paper spends four days hyping Global's new television network. Then the network makes its debut. Then they write up what they showed on television. It made a neat loop, but was it news?

Even Regine Mauger's column had been moved to a prominent spot because she was covering the television launch. *Teddy Trant was glowing last night, and not only from the soft lights of Sal Barthele's original Tiffany lamps,* she cooed. *With House Speaker Jean-Claude Poilevy on one side and Lacey Dowell on the other he has every right to be pleased with the impression he's making on Chicago.*

Regine went on to describe the other players, including members of the Illinois Commerce Commission, the mayor and his wife, whom I'd missed in the throng, and of course the denizens of the town's TV studios, whose feelings get hurt if they're overlooked.

Murray Ryerson, whose trademark red beard disappeared for the occasion, took to the camera like a duck to water. His chosen escort—or did she choose him?—was Alexandra Fisher from Global's front office, stunning in an Armani evening ensemble. But don't let that cleavage fool you: when she puts on her power suits she's as invincible as Dick Butkus.

Of course some problems always erupt at occasions like this. A bird tells us that Lucian Frenada, from Lacey's old neighborhood, finagled an invitation in the hopes of holding Lacey to a boy–girl romance, but Officer Mooney, on loan from Chicago's finest, muscled him outside before he could make a full-scale scene. Lacey had no comment, but Alex Fisher says the star is troubled by the misunderstanding. Other hangers-on, like Chicago investigator V. I. Warshawski, who used to be an item with Ryerson, probably were hoping for crumbs to drop from one of the richest tables to be set in town for years.

That last sentence jolted me out of my chair so fast that Peppy barked a warning. Damned scrawny bitch with her fifty face-lifts, annoyed because I'd tripped on her Chanel trousers. Me, hoping for crumbs from a Hollywood table? And still pining for Murray? I didn't know which suggestion offended me more.

It's true Murray and I once had a fling, but that was history so ancient there weren't even any archaeological remains to look through. Far from pining over him, I'd realized after a few weeks that going to bed with someone that competitive had been a colossal mistake. Who the hell had even cared enough to tell Regine Mauger? Murray, out of spite toward me for not being enthusiastic enough about his debut? "Took to the camera like fleas to a dog," I said savagely.

The story reminded me that Alexandra Fisher said she'd gone to law school with me. While Mr. Contreras continued his slow study of the ads, I went to the hall closet and pulled out the trunk where I keep bits and pieces of my past. On top, wrapped in cotton sheeting, was my mother's concert gown. I couldn't resist taking a moment to pull back the sheet and finger the silver lace panels, the soft black silk. The fabric brought her to me as intensely as if she were in the next room. She wanted me to be independent, my mother, not to make the compromises she did for safety, but holding her gown I longed to have her with me, guarding me against the great and little blows the world inflicts.

I resolutely put the dress to one side and rummaged through the trunk until I found my law-school class directory. We'd had a Michael Fisher and a Claud, but no Alexandra. I was snapping the booklet shut when I saw the name above Claud's: Sandra Fishbein.

The photograph showed a petulant, wide-mouthed face with a mop of wild curls a good six inches thick. She'd been number two in our class and what the faculty called a rabble-rouser. I remembered her chewing me out for not joining her proposed sit-in over women's bathrooms at the law school.

You're a blue-collar girl, she harangued me with a speech she'd used before, *you should know better than to let the establishment stand on your face.* I remembered the scene vividly—she came from the kind of family where children got European travel as high-school graduation presents. For some reason the fact that I was a blue-collar girl, maybe the only one in my class, made her feel she needed my support or approval or respect, I was never sure which.

It's your establishment, and your face, I'd replied on that occasion, which only wound her up tighter. *If you're not part of the solution, you're part of the problem,* she'd snapped. Oh, all that old-time rhetoric. She'd applauded my going to the public defender, while she went off to clerk for a judge on the tony Sixth Circuit.

Well, well. Girl radical had gone to Hollywood, cut her halo of wild hair close to her head, changed her name—and conducted surgery on her politics. No wonder she'd given me that challenging stare last night.

I put away the directory. Emphysema had forced my father onto long-term disability when I was in law school. His illness affected everything about me then, from my decision to marry in the hopes I'd produce a grandchild for him before he died to my lack of interest in campus politics. I'd taken the public defender's job so I could stay in Chicago and be with him. He died two years later. My marriage hadn't survived much longer. I'd never had a child.

The dogs were pacing restlessly, a sign that they badly needed a walk. I carefully rewrapped the silk dress and pushed the trunk back into the closet. I promised the dogs I'd be with them as soon as I checked my appointments on my Palm Pilot. I had a one o'clock with one of my few really important clients—translate that to read big retainer, big billing, prompt payment. Thanks to Lemour and the ruckus he'd stirred up, it was after eleven now. I barely had time to run the dogs and get something to eat. Since my refrigerator held only an orange besides the stale bread, I leashed up the dogs and went out with my backpack to forage for food.

A cool spring had given way overnight to the oppressive mugginess of midsummer. There aren't any parks close to our building, but I couldn't make the dogs do three miles to the lake and back in air that covered us like a sock. By the time we reached the grocery store, even Mitch had stopped pulling at the leash and was glad to rest in the shade of the building. I pulled a collapsible drinking bowl out of my pack and bought a bottle of water for them before buying my own food, along with a cappuccino from the coffee bar across the street.

As we ambled home in the heat, I kept wondering about the woman in the road. In the dark street I couldn't tell what had happened to her, but that humerus sticking up like a branch from a swamp told some terrible tale of violence. The tall stolid detective had let out that the woman was sent to Beth Israel. That was fortunate, because Max Loewenthal, the executive director, was the lover of one of my oldest friends. With dogs in one hand and coffee in the other, I couldn't very well whip out my cell phone to call the hospital. I urged the dogs to a trot, bribing them with some bread.

As we rounded the corner at Racine, a brown Chevy bristling with antennas slowed down. Detective Lemour rolled down his window and called out "Warshki." I kept going.

He turned on his loudspeaker and broadcast to the neighborhood that those dogs better not be let off their leash. "You think you're smart, Warshki, flaunting your friends in the PD, but I'm going to be on you like your underwear this summer. If you so much as run a stop sign I'll be there, so watch your step."

A woman with a toddler in tow looked from me to the police car, while two kids on the other side of the street stared, slack-jawed. I stopped and blew Lemour a kiss. His face darkened with fury, but his partner seemed to restrain him; he took off with a great screeching of rubber.

Why did the cops care so much about the injured woman? Maybe it was only Lemour who cared, but his threat made me almost as nervous as he intended. I urged the dogs up Racine to my apartment. I was beginning to think having an outside lab look at the Trans Am was the smartest thing I'd done this year.

Mr. Contreras had left a note in his large unpracticed hand to tell me he was down in his own place, making phone calls to a few likely prospects, and would I drop the dogs off with him on my way downtown. I showered again to wash the sweat from my hair, then called Max Loewenthal's office while I dried off.

Max was in some meeting or other, which didn't surprise me. Fortunately his secretary hadn't gone to lunch and was glad to check on a Jane Doe for me. I gave her my cell-phone number and dressed at a record-setting pace, in a wheat-colored pantsuit, black top, and silver earrings. I could slap on a little makeup in the L.

I didn't have time now for breakfast. I grabbed an apple from my groceries, stuffed my pumps into a briefcase, and ran back downstairs with the dogs. Mr. Contreras stopped me with a status report, although I told him I was on my way to Darraugh Graham's.

"You'd better get going then, cookie," he said, following me to the hall and hanging on the door. "It don't do to keep the one guy who pays his bills on time waiting. I got a lead on a Buick Century with ninety-seven thousand on it, and a Dodge with some less, but maybe a whole lot more rust. What time do you think you'll get back? Want me to take a look at these without you, or what?"

"You the man, Mr. C. Pick out the car of our dreams and I'll drive you downtown to the Berghoff for dinner."

The dogs were convinced I was going to the lake and tried to leave with me. I shut the door on them firmly. Running the four blocks to the L got me sticky and sweaty again. I could have made time for breakfast by skipping the second shower.

I climbed the platform for the Red Line going south. The Red Line. In some moment of hallucination a few years back, the city had color-coded the trains. You used to know what train to take by where you wanted to go. Suddenly the Howard L, which I'd ridden all my life, became red and the O'Hare Line turned blue. It made Chicago look like Mister Rogers's neighborhood instead of one of the great cities of the world. And what if you're color-blind? Then how do you know whether you're even on the Brown or the Orange Line? And then, to make it worse, they'd installed these ticket machines. You have to buy a round-trip ticket even if you're only going one-way, the machines don't give change, and there aren't any human beings to assist you if you climb onto the wrong platform by mistake.

And the final insult: when a train finally arrived, the air-conditioning wasn't working. I melted into my seat, too hot to bother with makeup. I folded my jacket on my lap and tried to sit absolutely still for the fifteen-minute trip. I was riding the escalator up at Randolph Street when Cynthia Dowling called back from Max's office. "Vic, I'm afraid it's bad news about your Jane Doe. She died in the operating room."

5

Diving into the Wreck

A DR. SZYMCZYK had been the surgeon on call. With the broken arm and severe contusions on both legs, they couldn't be sure what the main locus of her problem was, but when Szymczyk saw the X rays he'd decided her abdominal injuries were the most critical.

Cynthia read to me from the surgeon's dictation: *"She had advanced peritonitis: the entire abdominal cavity was filled with fecal matter. I saw already it was late, very late for helping her, and as it turned out, too late. The duodenum had ruptured, probably sometime previous to the broken arm, which looked very fresh. Forensic pathology will have to answer questions of time and manner of inflicting wounds.* Is that what you wanted, Vic?"

Not what I wanted, that death, those wounds. Poor little creature, to meet her end in such a way. "I take it they didn't find anything on her to identify her? Do you know what time she was sent to the medical examiner?"

"Umm, hang on . . . yes, here it is. Dr. Szymczyk pronounced death at seven fifty-two. The operating-room administrator called the police; your Jane Doe was picked up and taken to the morgue at ten-thirty."

So she was my Jane Doe now, was she? I came to a

halt in the middle of the sidewalk. I'd made a vow a few years back to stop diving into other people's wrecks: I only got battered on the spars without getting thanks—or payment. I didn't feel like jumping overboard one more time.

A woman hurrying toward State Street banged into me, jarring the phone and breaking the connection. "Do you think a cell phone gives you ownership of the streets?" she yelled over her shoulder.

Sidewalk rage, the new hip form of urban rudeness. I tucked the phone into my briefcase and went into Continental United's building. On the outside, the curved glass walls reflected the city back to itself; inside, it cooled the inhabitants with arctic efficiency. The sweat on my neck and armpits froze. I shivered as I rode the elevator skyward.

During a meeting to discuss the background of a candidate to head the paper division, and the unrelated problems dogging delivery trucks from the Eustace, Georgia, plant, I wondered what special insight fasting brought people. The apple I'd snatched on my way out the door was all I'd eaten since the snacks at last night's party. Far from feeling a heightened consciousness, all I could think of was food. I tried to keep a look of bright attention on my face and hoped the general chatter would cover my growling stomach. Fortunately I've sat through enough similar sessions that I could interject a cogent-sounding question or two, laugh at the human-resources vice president's dull jokes, and agree to turn around the investigation in three days, unless I had to go to Georgia.

When we finally broke, at four, I encountered Darraugh Graham himself in the hall. Civility—need—required me to chat with him, about his son, about the political situation in Italy where he had a major plant, about the assignment I'd just been handed. I was lucky that Darraugh continued to come to me, instead of turning all his business over to one of the big outfits like Carnifice. Of course Carnifice supplies the armed guards Continental United needs for transporting payroll. I think they handled Darraugh's security when he visited Argentina last winter. But he still gives me a significant chunk of work requiring more analysis than muscle; it behooves me to pay attention to his private chitchat.

He clasped my shoulder briefly and gave a wintry smile of farewell. I hurried to the elevator and fell into the frozen yogurt stand in the lobby. Extra-large chocolate and vanilla with nuts, fruit, and little waffle chips. Breakfast and lunch in one giant cup. I sat in one of the spindly chairs in the lobby to pry dress pumps off my swollen feet and slip back into my running shoes. Happiness lies in simple things, after all—a little food, a little comfort.

When I'd eaten enough to raise my blood sugar to the functioning point, I called Luke to get the word on my car. My better mood deflated rapidly: he estimated repairs at twenty-nine hundred.

"Freddie towed it to Cheviot for you, but he took a look at the damage when he unloaded it. You bent the front axle and stove in the radiator for starters. And when Freddie got there he found the neighborhood helping themselves to the battery, the radio, and a couple of tires, so I'll have to repair the dash. And before you squawk, let me tell you that a big shop would charge at least a thousand more."

I slumped in the hard chair. "I wasn't squawking. That gurgling noise was the last of my pathetic assets being sucked into the Gulf of Mexico. Does this estimate include the kind of professional courtesy I gave you when I drove those creeps away from your yard?"

"You didn't do anything for me I couldn't do myself, Warshawski, but I know you don't know what it takes to fix this car."

I bit back an acid rejoinder. "What about your forensic buddies? What are they saying about inspecting the front end?"

"The earliest they can get to it is tomorrow afternoon. And I have a note here from Rieff at Cheviot. He says they need the autopsy report on the hit-and-run victim. And they ideally need the clothes she had on when she died. Their analysis is going to run you another grand, easy, probably more. Of course I won't start repairs until after they've finished. And until you give me the go-ahead. But tell you what, Warshawski, being as you helped me out with those kids, I won't charge you for the tow."

"Luke, you're a prince."

Irony was wasted on him. "One good turn deserves another."

I pressed the END key before I let my temper get the better of me. I'd spent three nights in his alley, nabbed a group of teenagers, put the fear of God into them sufficiently to make sure they didn't return, and then stupidly gave Luke a courtesy discount in the belief he would reciprocate on future repair bills.

Twenty-nine hundred in repairs plus another grand for a forensic inspection. And yet another thousand or two for a replacement? Maybe I'd be better off renting by the week. Of course, I could let the Trans Am go for scrap and buy a used car with more oomph than the ones Mr. Contreras was investigating, but I loved my little sports car.

I smacked the tabletop in frustration. Why can't I ever get ahead of the game financially? I work hard, I pay serious attention to my clients, and here I am, past forty and still scrambling at month's end. I looked with distaste at the melted remains in the cup. Soggy waffle and lumps of berry floated in beige sludge. It looked like an artist's depiction of my life. I stuffed the cup into an overflowing garbage can by the door and went out to catch the Blue Line to my office.

Since it was rush hour a train came almost as soon as I climbed onto the platform. Not only that, it was one of the new ones, air-conditioned and moving fast. It didn't make up for everything that had gone wrong today, but it helped. In ten minutes I was at Damen and back in the wet heat.

A new coffee bar had opened, I noticed, making three, one for each of the three streets that came together at that corner. I stopped for an espresso and to buy a *Streetwise* from a guy named Elton who worked that intersection. Over the months I'd been renting nearby we'd struck up a relationship of the "Hi, how's it going" kind.

When I moved my operation to Bucktown two years ago, the only liquid you could get by the glass was a shot and a beer. Now the bars and palm-readers of Humboldt Park are giving way to coffee bars and workout clubs as Generation X-ers move in. I could hardly criticize them: I'd helped start that gentrifying wave.

The Loop building where I'd rented since opening my practice had fallen to the wrecker's ball more than a year ago, taking with it not just inlaid mosaic flooring

and embossed brass elevator doors, but the malfunc-
tioning toilets and frayed wiring that had kept the rent
affordable. After the Pulteney's demise I couldn't find
anything even close to my price range downtown. A
sculpting friend convinced me to rent space with her in
a converted warehouse near North and Damen, on
Leavitt. I signed before the area started to be trendy and
had been savvy enough—for once—to get a seven-year
lease.

I miss being downtown, where the bulk of my business lies, but I'm only ten minutes away by L or car.
The warehouse has a parking lot, which I couldn't offer
clients before. And a lot of the queries I used to have to
do on foot—trudging from the Department of Motor
Vehicles to Social Security to the Recorder of Deeds—I
can handle right in my office by dialing up the Web.
The one thing I don't automate is my answering service:
people in distress like a real person on the line, not a
voice menu.

Inside my office I sternly turned my back on the
futon behind my photocopier and powered up my computer. I logged on to LifeStory and submitted the name
and social security number of the man Darraugh
wanted to put in charge of his paper division.

Most investigators use a service like LifeStory. Data
on things you imagine are private, like your income,
your tax returns, those education loans you welshed on,
and how much you owe on that late-model four-by-
four—not to mention your moving violations in it—are
all available to people like me. In theory you have to
know something about the person, like a social security
number and perhaps a mother's maiden name, to get
this information, but there are easy ways around that,
too. When I first went on-line two years back, I was

shocked by how easy it was to violate people's privacy. Every time I log on to LifeStory I squirm—but that doesn't make me cancel my subscription.

The menu asked me how much detail I needed. I clicked on FULL BACKGROUND and was told that it would be a forty-eight-hour turnaround for the report—unless I wanted to pay a premium. I took the slow cheap route and leaned back in my chair to look through my notes. The rest of the assignment would keep until tomorrow, when I'd be—I hoped—more alert. I checked with my answering service to see if anything urgent had come in and then, before calling it a day, phoned over to the morgue.

Dr. Bryant Vishnikov, the medical examiner and the only pathologist I know personally, had left at noon. When I explained that I was an investigator working for Max Loewenthal over at Beth Israel and wanted to know about the Jane Doe we'd sent in this morning, the morgue attendant tried to persuade me to wait until morning when Vishnikov would be in.

I could hear the television in the background, loud enough to make out Chip Caray's patter about the Cubs. It's amazing how little actual information about the game in progress sportscasters give—I couldn't even tell who was at bat.

"The Cubs will still be here tomorrow, and maybe you will be too, but I can't wait that long," I told the attendant.

He sighed loudly enough to drown out the squawk of a chair scraping back from the desk.

"They haven't done the autopsy yet," he announced, after I'd held for four minutes. "She came in too late for the doc to start on her, and he didn't want anyone else working on her, apparently."

"What about her ID? Did the cops have any luck with AFIS?"

"Uh, yeah, looks like we got an ID."

He was making me pay for forcing him to work while on shift. "Yes? Who was she?"

"Nicola Aguinaldo."

He garbled the name so badly I had to ask him to spell it. Once he'd done that he came to a complete halt again.

"I see," I prodded. "Is she so famous I should recognize the name?"

"Oh, I thought maybe that was why you were so anxious—escaped prisoner and all."

I sucked in an exasperated breath. "I know it's hard, having to work for a living, but could you pretty please with sugar on it tell me what came in with the print check?"

"No need to get your undies in a bundle," he grumbled. "I only got four people waiting to look at their loved ones."

"As soon as you tell me how long Aguinaldo's been running, you can turn your charm on the public."

He read out the notes in a fast monotone and hung up. Nicola Aguinaldo had slipped out of a hospital in Coolis, Illinois, on Sunday morning, when the shift changed. The women's correctional facility there had taken her in to treat what they thought might be an ovarian abscess, and Aguinaldo had left with the laundry truck. In the next forty-eight hours she'd made it back to the North Side of Chicago, run into some villain, and gotten herself murdered.

6

Signor Ferragamo, I Presume

THE ATTENDANT HADN'T included Aguinaldo's last known address in his summary, but that might not have been in the report, anyway. I looked in the phone book, but no one with that name lived anywhere near where Mary Louise and I had found her. Not that that meant anything—if she'd fallen afoul of some pimp or dealer, she might be far from home. It's just that someone escaping from jail usually heads for relatives.

I sucked on a pencil while I thought it over and went back to my computer. None of the usual software turned up an Aguinaldo. I'd have to find her through the arrest-and-trial report, and they're not easy to locate. Since I don't have access to the AFIS system, it would mean searching trial records one at a time, without even a clue on an arrest date to guide me. Even with a Pentium chip that could take me a few weeks. I called Mary Louise again.

"Vic! I was going to get back to you after dinner, when I can hear myself think, but hold on while I get the boys their pizza."

I heard Josh and Nathan in the background shouting over whose turn it was to choose a video, and then Emily, with adolescent disdain, telling them they were both stupid if they wanted to see that bore-rine Space

Berets tape one more time. "And I don't want any pizza, Mary Louise, it's too fattening."

"I suppose Lacey Dowell never eats pizza," Josh yelled.

"No, she eats the blood of obnoxious little boys."

Mary Louise called sharply to Emily to hang up the phone when she got the bedroom extension. In another moment the fighting in the background was switched off.

"I was out of my ever-lovin' mind the day I thought fostering three kids would be a simple management problem," Mary Louise said. "Even with Fabian paying enough for good home help, it's relentless. Maybe I'll switch from law to social work so I can counsel teen-agers on how grueling it is to be a single mom.

"Anyway, the news on Lemour is kind of disturbing. Terry says he has a bad rap, even among cops, that there've been around a dozen complaints against him over the years for excessive violence, that kind of thing. But what's more troubling is that Rogers Park lost the incident report. Terry asked them how they knew to come to you if they didn't have the report, and they didn't have a good answer for that. I didn't get the names of either of the officers on the scene last night, did you?"

I felt ice start to build around my diaphragm. No, I hadn't done anything that elementary. We could track down the paramedics—they should have a copy of the report. That would be another time-consuming search, but an uneasy impulse was making me think I'd better make the effort.

"Before you go, there's one other thing," I said. "The woman we found is dead—poor thing had some kind of advanced abdominal injury. She was on the run from Coolis. Could you find out when she was arrested, and why?" I spelled *Aguinaldo* for Mary Louise.

I didn't want to dive into Nicola Aguinaldo's wreck, but it felt as though someone had climbed up behind me on the high board to give me a shove.

Even after Detective Lemour's idiotic hints that I'd been driving drunk this morning, it hadn't occurred to me to call my lawyer. But if Rogers Park had lost the incident report I needed Freeman Carter to know what was going on. If a lazy detective decided to slap a manslaughter charge on me, Freeman would have to bail me out.

Freeman was on his way out of the office, but when I gave him a thumbnail sketch of the last twenty-four hours, he agreed it was too serious to turn over to his intern. After I told him Rogers Park claimed to have lost the incident report, he had me dictate a complete account into his phone recorder.

"Where is your car, Vic?" he asked before hanging up.

"The last I saw it, it was hugging a fireplug in Edgewater."

"I'm late. I don't have time to play games with you. But if the State's Attorney demands it when I talk to him in the morning, I expect you to produce it. And for Christ's sake don't get on your charger and gallop around town confronting the cops. You've turned this over to me and I'm promising to take care of it. So don't do anything rash tonight, okay, Vic?"

"It all depends on your definition, Freeman, but I think the most I'm up to is trying to find something to drive around town in."

He laughed. "You're doing okay if you can keep your sense of humor. We'll talk first thing."

After he hung up I tried to think what further steps to take. I called Lotty Herschel, whom I've known since my undergraduate days. She's in her sixties now, but still works a full schedule both as a perinatalogist at Beth Israel and running a clinic for low-income families on the west fringe of Uptown.

When I told her what was going on she was horrified. "I don't believe this, Vic. I'll ask Max what happened to the young woman when she got to us, but I don't think that will shed any light on why you're being harassed in such a way."

Her warmth and concern flowed through the line, making me feel better at once. "Lotty, I need to ask a favor. Can I come over for a minute?"

"If you can hurry. In fact, Max and I are going out in half an hour. If you don't have a car can you take a cab to me?"

It was close to seven when a cab decanted me on north Lake Shore Drive. For years Lotty lived only a short walk from her clinic, on the top floor of a two-flat she owned. When she turned sixty-five last year, she decided that being a landlord was an energy drain she didn't need and bought herself a condo in one of the art nouveau buildings overlooking the lake. I still wasn't used to dealing with a doorman to see her, but I was glad she'd moved into a place more secure than the fringes of Uptown—I used to worry about her, small woman alone in the early-morning darkness, every user on Broadway knowing she was a doctor.

The doorman was beginning to remember me, but he still made me wait for Lotty's permission before letting me pass. Lotty was waiting for me when the elevator reached the eighteenth floor, her dark, vivid face filled with concern.

"I'm on my way out now, Victoria, why don't we ride down together and I'll give you a lift home while you talk."

Driving with Lotty is almost more adventure than I wanted at the end of a difficult day. She thinks she's Sterling Moss and that urban roads are a competitive course; a succession of cars with stripped gears and dented fenders hasn't convinced her otherwise. At least the Lexus she was driving now had a passenger-side air bag.

"The paramedics would have filed a report at the emergency-room admitting station," I explained as we drove across Diversey. "I want a copy of that—I'm hoping it will include the names of the officers on the scene, and maybe even a copy of the police report, which the Rogers Park station says has disappeared."

"Disappeared? You think they lost it on purpose?"

"That ape Lemour might have. But reports get misfiled every day; I'm not going to be paranoid about this —yet. Could you keep your hands on the wheel even if you're alarmed or annoyed?"

"You can't come to me for help, Vic, and then start criticizing me," she snapped, but she looked back at the road in time to avoid a cyclist.

I tried not to suck my breath in too audibly. "The other thing is, I'd like the dress Aguinaldo was wearing when she died. Cheviot Labs needs to inspect it to see whether there are signs of any car—especially my car— in the fabric. They wouldn't tell me at the morgue if her clothes came over with her, but I'm betting they're still at the hospital, assuming they're not in the garbage. Could you get Max to track them down? Or ask him for permission for me to call the ER staff? It'd have to be tonight, I'm afraid—the longer we wait, the more likely the clothes will be pitched."

She turned left at Racine after the light had changed —in fact after the eastbound traffic had started to roar through—but I didn't say anything, in case she became cranky enough to cut in front of a bus or a semi.

"We can do it by phone in Max's car. If I can get his attention away from Walter Huston and his horse." Her tone became sardonic: Max has a passion for old Westerns which seems utterly at odds with his other passion, Chinese porcelains. It's also at odds with Lotty's tastes.

"So you're off to watch a Western just because your man likes them." I grinned at her as she pulled up in front of my building. "Well, Lotty, it's taken you over sixty years, but you're finally learning to be graciously submissive to male authority."

"Really, Vic, must you put it like that?" she snorted, then leaned across the seat to kiss me. "Please don't move rashly on this investigation. You're in a swamp, my dear; it's important that you test each step before putting your full weight on it. Yes?"

I held her for a moment, drawing comfort from her embrace. "I'll try to move cautiously."

"I'll call you in the morning, my dear, after I've spoken to Max." She squeezed me briefly and put the car into gear again. "Remember, you're coming to dinner at my place on Monday."

Mr. Contreras was waiting for me on the front stoop. He had spent the day on the phone tracking down cars and badly wanted to talk about them. He'd located an old Buick in Park Ridge that he thought would be the best bet and arranged with the seller for us to look at it tonight—which meant a nice long ride on public transportation, since a cab to the suburbs would run at least forty dollars.

When Lotty roared through that intersection, it had occurred to me I probably left skid marks on the road. Just in case, and just in case no one had obliterated them, I wanted to get up there to photograph them while some daylight remained. Mr. Contreras, always eager for a piece of real detection, called the car owner to say we'd be a little late so that he could help me inspect. I took the dogs for a quick walk around the block and collected my camera and a magnifying glass.

We rode the Red Line up to Berwyn, which was only five blocks from the accident. The golden light of a summer sunset made the streets appear less tawdry than they had in the middle of the night. A group of boys pedaled by, some sitting two to a bike, and we passed a few skateboarders, but no Rollerbladers—in-line skates belong to the yuppie world further south.

At the corner of Balmoral a group of girls was jumping rope. I noticed two Mad Virgin T-shirts on girls whose dark hair was pulled back under fringed scarves. Global Entertainment's tendrils reached even into the immigrant communities.

When I inspected the street I realized I'd wasted time on a fool's errand. The fireplug I'd hit was slightly bent, and even after almost eighteen hours you could still see a trace of rubber in the road where I'd stood on my brakes. But there was no sign of where Nicola Aguinaldo had lain. She hadn't been dead when we found her: no one outlined her body in chalk. I photographed the tread marks and the fireplug, using a flash since the light was dying.

The girls stopped their jumping to stare at me. "You know Morrell, miss?" "Take my picture too, miss?"

"Put me in the book too, miss. Morrell talk to me, not to her."

They began posing and shoving each other out of the way.

"Who's Morrell?" I asked, wondering if a cop had come around pretending to be writing a book.

"Morrell, he's a man, he's writing a book about people who ran away from jail."

I stared at the speaker, a girl of about nine with a braid that reached to the top of her shorts. "Ran away from jail? Does that mean—did he come here today?"

"No, not today, but most days. Now will you take my picture?"

I took shots of the little girls alone and together and tried to get them to tell me about Morrell. They spread their hands. He came around, he talked to some of the parents, especially Aisha's father. They didn't know who he was or where to find him. I gave it up and went back to inspecting the street, getting down on my hands and knees with the glass while Mr. Contreras stood over me to make sure no one hit me.

"You lose something, miss?" "You trying to find your ring?" "Is there a reward? We can help."

I sat back on my heels. "You know a woman was hit here in the road last night? I'm a detective. I'm looking for any clues about her accident."

"You really a detective? Where's your gun?" one demanded, while another said, "Women can't be detectives, don't be a fool, Sarina."

"Women can be detectives, and I am one," I announced.

The girls started inspecting the area around the curb for clues. I found something like dried blood on the asphalt where I thought Nicola Aguinaldo had lain and photographed the spot from several different angles, then scraped a bit onto a tissue. It wouldn't be very convincing if I had to talk to a judge or jury, but it was the best I could come up with.

The girls decided this meant Sarina was right—I must be a detective, they'd seen someone do the very same thing on television. After that they offered me a variety of items, from an empty Annie Greensleeves bottle to a Converse high-top. I solemnly inspected their findings. In the midst of the detritus, a piece of metal caught my eye as it had theirs: "This is gold, isn't it, miss, is it valuable? Do we get a reward?"

It wasn't gold but heavy plastic. It was new, and its shine had attracted the girls—it clearly hadn't lain long in the gutter. It was shaped like a Greek omega, but it wasn't a charm, more like some kind of signature from a handbag zipper, or maybe a shoe. I thought I should recognize the designer, but I couldn't place it off the top of my head.

Mr. Contreras was getting restive: he really wanted to get out to Park Ridge to look at the car he'd picked out. I pocketed the emblem and put the rest of their findings in the garbage.

"Who is the oldest?" I asked.

"Sarina's twelve," they volunteered.

I handed a girl in a fringed scarf one of my cards and three dollars. "The money is for all of you to share; it's your reward for helping me hunt for clues. The card is for your friend Morrell. When he comes again, will you give it to him? It has my name and phone number on it. I'd like him to call me."

The girls clustered around Sarina. "What's it say?" "Ooh, Sarina, she is a detective, it say so right here."

"She going to arrest you, Mina, for talking back to your mama."

Their comments faded as we rounded the corner to the L. Mr. Contreras filled me in on the Buick Skylark we were going to see. "He's asking seventeen hundred, but it's got ninety-eight thousand miles. You can probably bring him down a couple a hundred, but maybe you want your buddy Luke to go over a car before you buy it—all these computers and whatnot it ain't so easy to tell what's going on inside an engine these days."

"Yeah, my buddy Luke." I thought bitterly of our conversation this afternoon. "He's likely to demand the mortgage on my apartment before he lifts a finger to help. After getting my estimates from Luke I'm beginning to think I should rent something for a few weeks. Even fifteen hundred seems way more than I can afford for temporary wheels, and if it's that beat up I'll have trouble reselling it."

The old man deflated visibly: he'd spent all day on the project and politely deferred pushing it while he helped me on my silly Sherlock Holmes imitation. Guilt is not an adequate reason for bad business decisions, but I couldn't bear to see him so woebegone. We picked up falafel sandwiches and Cokes at a storefront underneath the L tracks and trudged up the stairs for the first leg in our journey.

By the time we got to the seller's apartment, I was so fed up with public transportation I was ready to pay almost any price to get rolling again. The Red Line to Howard. The old Skokie Swift—now the Yellow Line—and then the real time-eater, the wait for the suburban bus to take us five miles further west, to a stop close enough to the guy's place that we could walk.

"You know, if we don't buy the car and take possession tonight, we may end up camping in that forest preserve we passed," I told Mr. Contreras as we started walking. "The sign says the last bus leaves the Gross Point depot at nine-thirty, and it's a quarter of now."

"Cab." He was puffing a little from the heat and the walk. "I'll treat you to a cab back to the L, cookie."

When we finally reached the seller's apartment, we saw the car wasn't as bad as I'd feared. Rust over most of the driver's door and around the trunk made it look depressing, the tires were worn, but a ten-mile drive to the airport and back didn't reveal anything amiss in the engine. The seller was a kid who'd graduated from Champaign in engineering this spring. He bought the Skylark used when he started school, drove it hard for five years, and wanted to unload it now that he'd landed a real job with serious money. All the time we talked about his beater, he couldn't stop looking at the Ford truck he'd bought to celebrate entering the job market at a hundred thousand a year. Without much real haggling we got the Skylark for twelve hundred.

Mr. Contreras overwhelmed me by pulling twenty carefully folded twenties from his inside pocket: "My contribution to the family car," he insisted, when I tried to demur. I offered to let him drive home, but he refused.

"I don't see so good at night anymore, cookie. Matter of fact, I been worrying about it some."

"Then let's get you to the doctor," I said. "You can't neglect your eyes. If you need new glasses or have cataracts or something, now's the time to take care of them."

"Don't make me out to be an old man," he snapped, locking the seat belt. "You're as bad as Ruthie, wanting to push me into an old-age home. I can still see good enough to make out that gizmo you took from them girls on the street. What was it, anyway?"

I'd forgotten about it during our long ride and pulled it out of my shirt pocket for his inspection. He couldn't place it any more than I could, but when we got home —in twenty minutes versus the eighty-seven we'd spent on the way out—I dug a copy of *Mirabella* out of the stack of papers in my recycling box. I went through it page by page studying the ads and on the inside of the back cover struck gold—or painted plastic. A pair of Ferragamo loafers were standing back to front against a rose silk scarf, and a pair of omegas like the one the girls had found were stitched into the strap across the instep.

"*Va bene*, Signor Ferragamo," I said aloud. A horse-shoe, not an omega. The Ferragamo logo. I'd recognized it because I tried on some Ferragamo pumps a few weeks ago: my beloved red Bruno Magli's had finally become so worn that not even old Señor Delgado out on Harlem could patch the sides enough to attach new soles.

I'd decided I couldn't afford shoes that cost almost three hundred dollars this summer—a wise decision, considering the expenses I was racking up right now. It was hard to imagine that the immigrants living along Balmoral and Glenwood could afford them either. I suppose someone might have gone into debt for an up-scale logo, but I went to bed wondering where in the metropolitan area someone was looking in annoyance at a shoe or handbag with a damaged strap.

7

Habeas Corpus?

MARY LOUISE CALLED me early in the morning. "Vic, I'm running to get Nate to day camp, so this'll be quick: there isn't much, anyway. Aguinaldo was working as a mother's helper for someone named Baladine out in Oak Brook. She'd been there two years when she stole a gold necklace worth forty or fifty thousand dollars—it had gems in it too, bitty diamonds or rubies. They pressed charges—"

"The Baladines?" I interrupted. "As in the Robert Baladines?"

"Robert, Eleanor, and their three children. Do you know them?"

"No, darlin', he's so big I don't even think of him as competition. He runs Carnifice—you know, the billion-dollar PI firm, only when they get that big they're called 'Security Providers,' or something."

"Well, be that as it may, Mrs. Baladine loved that necklace—Robert gave it to her when little Robbie was born, blah, blah, so she pressed charges in a serious way. The defense tried to plead Aguinaldo's blameless previous life and the fact that she was the sole support of a mother and two kids of her own, but we were being tough on immigrants that month and Aguinaldo got five years. She'd been a model prisoner for fifteen months, had worked her way into the clothes shop, which is a premium gig at Coolis, when she escaped. Last known address on Wayne, about two hundred yards from where we found her." She read out addresses and phone numbers both for Aguinaldo's home and the Baladines.

"Now I've got to scoot—Natie's frantic he'll miss the opening ceremony, and he's gotten real into raising the flag and playing reveille. Who knows—maybe he'll want to join the army or be a cop when he grows up."

"Or maybe play the bugle. I'll get him one for his birthday."

"You dare, Vic, and he'll practice under your window every morning at six!"

It wasn't quite eight when she hung up. Too early to expect a report from Freeman. I thought I'd give Vishnikov a chance to take off his jacket and finish his coffee, or whatever his morning office ritual was. I did a full workout in my living room, including a session with my weights. I even took the trouble to put the weights back in the closet before trying the morgue. Vishnikov was in the dissecting room and didn't want to be interrupted. I left a message and took the dogs out.

The air was still thick with humidity, but it was early enough that the heat wasn't unbearable. I ran the dogs to Lake Michigan and back, a nice three-mile stint. The cops have started a major roundup of leash-law violators, even ticketing people whose dogs are swimming from the rocks along the lake, but I managed to get Mitch and Peppy in and out of the water without a citation.

"Lemour may be on me like my underwear, but he's

apparently not an early riser," I told the dogs on the way back.

I tried Vishnikov as soon as I got in, but he still wasn't taking calls. I wanted to go out to Oak Brook and talk to Eleanor Baladine about Nicola Aguinaldo, and I wanted to get up to Aguinaldo's home in Uptown, so the faster I got to my own office and did some work that would generate income, the faster I could get to an investigation that might help save my hide. The only thing more important than doing my real work was getting hold of the dress Aguinaldo had been wearing. As soon as I got to my office I called Lotty.

"You were in luck, Vic: the administrator in charge of the ER in the mornings is so meticulous a follower of regulations that he's wasted on Beth Israel's small protocols. He bagged and labeled the clothes. Do you want to pick them up?"

"No. I don't want anyone claiming I could have tampered with them. I want him to messenger them over to Cheviot Labs. With a note on where they've been since coming off poor little Ms. Aguinaldo's body yesterday. Shall I call Max and ask for that? Or can you?"

She said it would be quicker if she handled it. "And on the other matter, the report the paramedics filed, Max is asking Cynthia to fax you a copy." She hung up on my thanks: she was in the middle of a ferocious patient schedule.

One of the things I invested in when I moved to my new building was a set of detailed maps of most of the states and an art-supply cabinet for storing them. I pulled out the counties of rural Georgia where one of Continental United's trouble spots lay, hoping that I wouldn't have to go there in person to see why so many tire punctures occurred on County Road G. As I drew a line on the map from Hancock's Crossing, where Continental's warehouse sat, to the intersection of County G and Ludgate Road, Freeman Carter's secretary called.

"Freeman wants to talk to you, Vic. He has an opening at twelve-fifteen if you can stop by his office."

I thanked her and turned back to my maps. I was betting either a driver or a dispatcher owned a service station on that corner: it had to be someone who could make sure trucks used a particular route which they probably strewed with nails. The drivers then had no choice but to hike up the road to the station for their tires. I called the director of human resources whom I'd met with yesterday, and asked him to fax me copies of the repair bills. It would be annoying to have to go down and confront these people in person; I hoped I could figure it all out from the paper trail.

Vishnikov returned my call as I was getting ready to leave for my appointment with my lawyer. "Vic! What's up? Need help hiding a body?"

"It may come to that, if a police ape named Lemour harasses me any further. But this is about a body you already have—Nicola Aguinaldo. She died yesterday at Beth Israel in the OR and came in too late for you to work on."

There was a pause on the other end. "That's funny: I remember now, she came in at the end of the morning. I took a quick look at her—there was something unusual about her, so I wanted to do the autopsy myself, but she wasn't—hold on while I check."

He put the phone down. I heard chairs scraping, a murmur of voices, and then a door shutting. I waited a good five minutes before Vishnikov came back.

"Vic, this is one of the more infuriating moments in

my tenure here. Some jag-off released the body last night. I can't even find out who—a form was filed but not signed."

"Released to the family?" I was puzzled. "When I called last night, they didn't have a next of kin listed."

"The form says the girl's mother claimed it. How the hell they released it—well, that's neither here nor there. I've got to go. I need to—"

I spoke quickly, before he could hang up. "What was it about her body that made you want to look at it yourself?"

"I don't remember now. I'm too goddamned angry to think about anything except getting hold of the bastard who let this body out of here without authorization." He slammed the receiver in my ear.

This was the first time I'd heard Vishnikov blow up in the four or five years I've worked with him. I wondered if Lemour had somehow engineered removal of the body, before an autopsy proved I hadn't hit her, or maybe proved she hadn't been hit by a car at all. I began to wonder if Lemour had killed her himself and was trying to find someone else to blame. When he couldn't pin it on me he got a buddy in the morgue to quietly let the body go.

The Beth Israel fax had come in while I was talking to Vishnikov. I stuffed it into my briefcase and dashed out to the L to ride down to Freeman Carter's office in the Loop.

Freeman rented a suite that held the requisite mahoganies and objets d'art of lawyers in the financial district. He rose to greet me when his secretary sent me into his inner office. His summer suit had been tailored to fit his tall body and even to make him look a little broader through the chest, and his white-blond hair had been cut as carefully as the suit. He makes a good impression in court, which I like, and has the brains to back it up, which I like even more.

"Vic, I talked to Drummond at the State's Attorney and he made some calls." He perched on the corner of his desk. "Rogers Park has lost the incident report but they asked the officers who came to the scene to reconstruct it. They say you refused to take a sobriety test—"

"That is an outright lie." I felt my cheeks flush. "They didn't ask for blood, but they breathalyzed me and I walked a line and did all that stuff for them. Freeman, I don't drink and drive, and all I had all night long was three Pellegrinos."

"They got to the scene too late to witness the accident, so they're not accusing you of hitting the Aguinaldo woman. But the State's Attorney is saying if you'll own up to the hit-and-run they won't jeopardize your PI license or standing with the bar by a criminal prosecution."

I was so furious the blood drummed in my ears. "This is so outrageous I can't even comment on it. I will not perjure myself because a couple of cops are too lazy to conduct a proper investigation."

"Whoa, there, Vic. I don't blame you for being angry, but let me finish. I told Drummond that was unacceptable—but if they're claiming you refused a blood test, I need to be one hundred percent sure of the ground I'm on."

"When I'm stupid, careless, or criminal I don't walk away from it, but in this day and age where presidents and senators lie as a matter of course, I don't expect anyone's word of honor means much." I tried to regain my composure. "However, I am telling you the unvarnished truth about Nicola Aguinaldo. Not a courtroom truth. Talk to Mary Louise. She's not under my thumb, and she was at the scene."

He reached behind him to push the intercom button. "Callie, Vic's going to give you some phone numbers when she leaves. Mary Louise—what is it?—Neely. I need her to come in ASAP to give me something like a deposition. Go over my schedule with her and find what fits."

He turned back to me. "It would be very helpful if you produced your car for forensic inspection. Where is it, Vic?"

I gave a tight smile. "It's over at the Cheviot Labs. When they've done all their tests and taken pictures, the police can have it. You know, yesterday morning when Lemour and his partner came over, at first it seemed pretty much like a routine inquiry, following up to a manslaughter. For which the cops usually just go through the motions if there isn't a witness to ID the car. I had my car towed because Lemour seemed so aggressive it got me worried. Half an hour later he threatened me on the street, which told me I was right to be concerned."

Freeman gave a twisted smile. "Vic, this is so like you, to take matters into your own hands. The police are claiming your car as evidence in a manslaughter investigation. Can you do me, your long-suffering counsel, a huge favor and produce it by the end of the day? I would be most grateful. Tell Callie—she'll arrange with Drummond for police technicians to pick it up from Cheviot Labs. And for God's sake, don't start a vendetta against Lemour. You can make better use of your time. I've got to run now: I have a conference at the federal building and I want to grab a sandwich."

As he headed for the door I said, "Before you go, Freeman, did you know the dead woman was a nanny out at the Baladines' in Oak Brook before her arrest? I presume it's the same Baladine who heads Carnifice Security. Is he pushing on the State's Attorney in some way?"

"Can you tell Callie that, too? She'll add it to your file."

"Also, which is really interesting, the dead woman's body was released from the morgue in the middle of the night last night. Before Vishnikov could do the autopsy. Who better than a police detective to arrange something like that?"

"Vic, don't go on a witch hunt after Lemour. Whoever this woman was, and whatever Lemour or even Baladine is doing with her, she is not worth your career. And not to be crude, you haven't got the resources, either financial or in muscle, to take on someone Baladine's size, let alone the Chicago cops. Got it?"

I tightened my lips but followed him to his outer office, where he stopped to rattle off a string of instructions to Callie—most of them about other clients. He finished with my affairs.

"Vic has a few things for you—and she's going to tell you where her car is so you can call Gerhardt Drummond over at the State's Attorney and let him in on the secret—isn't that right, Vic?" He gave me a malicious grin and trotted out to the elevator.

When I finished telling Callie Mary Louise's phone number and the rest of the stuff, I headed out. Down in the building lobby I stopped to call Mary Louise myself, to explain what Freeman wanted, but only got her machine. She was on the go a lot, between the kids, her work for me, and her classes. I gave as concise an explanation as I could and told her to call me on my cell phone if she had any questions.

I frowned at the fast-food stalls in the lobby. You used to be able to get a bowl of homemade soup or a deli sandwich in the mom-and-pop diners that dotted the Loop. The new buildings had moved all their shops inside, to so-called plazas, where they control the take, then brought in chains that drove the coffee shops out of business. I picked up something called a Greek salad —I guess because it had two olives and a teaspoon of feta on it—and went back to my car.

Mary Louise had given me the Baladines' home number this morning. I sat in my car, trying not to spill oily lettuce on my lapel, and phoned Oak Brook. If Robert Baladine broke my legs or bombed my office I'd let Freeman chant "I told you so" over my hospital bed a few hundred times.

A woman with a heavy accent answered. After some prodding she put me through to Eleanor Baladine. "Ms. Baladine? This is V. I. Warshawski. I'm a Chicago detective. Did you know that Nicola Aguinaldo had escaped from prison?"

The silence at the other end was so complete, I thought for a moment the connection had gone. "Escaped? How did she do that?"

It was such a strange answer that I would have paid good money to know what went through her mind in the seconds before she spoke. "I'll tell you what I know when I see you. We need to talk as soon as possible. Can you give me directions to your house? I have your address, but the suburbs are a mystery to me."

"Uh, Detective—uh, does it have to be this afternoon?"

Bridge club? No, not for the contemporary rich woman. Tennis, or something more recherché. Her Artist's Way group, I bet.

"Yes, it does. The faster I get information, the sooner I can figure out where she was headed when she left Coolis. I understand she was with you for two years. I'd like to find out what you knew about her . . . associates."

"She was a maid. I didn't gossip with her about her associates."

"Even if all you ever said to her was, 'Change the baby's diaper,' or 'Make sure you vacuum under the beds,' you must have had some references before you hired her." I tried to sound reasonable, not like an irritable old leftist.

"Oh, very well." She sighed mightily but gave me detailed instructions: the Eisenhower all the way to the end of the expressway, out Roosevelt Road to the winding side streets of one of the area's most exclusive small communities.

8

Poolside Chat

Half an hour later, as I turned onto Gateway Terrace, I thought that *community* was a strange word for a collection of houses that isolated people so thoroughly. Each house—if that's what you call something with twenty rooms and four chimneys—was set so far back behind trees and fences that you saw only fragments of facades or gables. There weren't any sidewalks, since no one could possibly walk to town—or rather, mall—from this distance. I passed a handful of kids on bikes and was passed in turn by a Jaguar XJ-8 —top down to showcase a woman with blond hair whipping behind her—and a black Mercedes sedan. That was all the street life Gateway Terrace offered me before I reached number fifty-three. Quite a contrast to the crowded, littered streets of Uptown.

I stopped the battered Skylark at the gate and looked for a way in. A large sign told me the premises were protected by Total Security Systems (a division of Carnifice Security) and that the fence was electrified so not to try to climb over it. I wondered if one of those spikes at the top had caused the damage to Nicola Aguinaldo's abdomen. She ran away from Coolis to this house, seeking help from her old boss, impaled herself, and they dumped her near her apartment, waiting for someone like me to come along who could take the fall for her injuries.

As I was scanning the property I became aware that someone on the other side was inspecting me. A round-faced boy of ten or so stepped forward when he realized I'd spotted him. He was wearing jeans and a T-shirt with the Space Berets—Global's big action toy—on it.

"Hi," I called through the fence. "I'm V. I. War-shawski, a detective from Chicago. Your mother is expecting me."

"You're supposed to phone the house," he said, coming closer and pointing to a recessed case with a phone in it.

The steel case was so sleek I'd overlooked it. As my hand moved toward the cover it slid back with a whisper, but before I could reach for the phone inside the boy opened the gates for me himself.

"I'm not really supposed to do this, but if you're with the Chicago police I guess it's okay. Is there something wrong with Nicola?"

I was startled, and wondered if his mother had complained to him. "What makes you think that?"

"The only time the cops were here before was when Mom had them arrest Nicola. Or does she want you to take Rosario this time?"

I asked him to wait a second while I moved my car away from the middle of the entrance. He said he'd ride up to the house with me and hoisted himself into the passenger seat. He was a plump boy, rather short for his age—which was somewhat older than I'd first guessed—and he moved clumsily, as children do when they've been teased about their size.

"This doesn't look like much of a cop car." It was an observation, delivered in a flat voice.

He had a forlorn dignity that made me unwilling to lie to him. "I'm not a cop. I am a detective, but a private one, a PI. And I have come with some questions about Ms. Aguinaldo. It sounds as though you liked her?"

"She was okay." He hunched a shoulder. "Has she done something else wrong?"

"No. Not that I know of, anyway, and even if she has it doesn't matter, or not to me."

We had reached the top of the drive. It forked so that you could go to the garage—big enough for four cars—or the house—big enough for forty residents. I pulled over to the edge, behind a Mercedes Gelaendewagen, the $135,000-dollar model. The vanity plate read GLOBAL 2. I wondered what GLOBAL 1 was attached to. Maybe a Lamborghini.

I wanted to ask the boy about Aguinaldo, but it didn't seem right to question him without his mother's knowledge. And without telling him that she was dead. Or maybe I was being chicken—who knew how a sensitive child would react to the news of his ex-nanny's death.

"So why are you out here?" he demanded.

I made a face to myself. "Ms. Aguinaldo escaped from prison last week. Before she could—"

"She did?" His face brightened. "Cool! How did she do it? Or do you think I'm hiding her?"

On the last question he turned sullen. Before I could answer him, a girl came running from the garage side of the house, yelling "Robbie" at the top of her lungs. She was seven or eight, with water plastering her hair and bathing suit to her body. Where her brother was chunky and blond, she had dark hair and was slim as a greyhound.

My companion stiffened and stared straight ahead. The girl saw the car and ran over to us.

"Robbie! You know Mom will have a fit if she sees you in there." To me she added, "He's supposed to walk instead of riding. You can see he has a weight problem. Are you the Chicago cop? You're supposed to go around back; Mom's waiting for you there. She sent me to tell Rosario to open the gate when you got here, but I suppose Robbie already let you in."

Robbie left the car while she was piping out her report. The girl was young enough to parrot adult comments without editing; the Baladines must have reported Robbie's weight problem to strangers so often that it seemed natural to her to tell me about it. I wanted to say something reassuring to him, but he had slipped around the other side of the house.

"You know, there are worse things in life than being overweight," I pointed out as I followed the girl past the garage.

"Yes, like stealing and getting sent to jail. That's what Nicola did, so we had to get Rosario instead. I was only six when they arrested Nicola, so it was still all right for me to cry. I cried when Fluffy got hit by a car, too."

"You are sensitive, aren't you," I said in admiration.

"No, that's for crybabies. I don't do it anymore, but Robbie cried over Nicola and he was almost eleven. He even cried when Fluffy killed a bird. That's only nature. Mom! She's here! She gave Robbie a ride from the gate to the house!"

We had arrived on the far side of the garage, where a four-lane twenty-five-meter pool and a tennis court offered the Baladines a chance to unwind after whatever rigors a day might hold for them. The pool and court were fringed with trees that created pleasing shade against the heat.

Two women were leaning back on padded chaises, eyes shielded by outsize sunglasses. Their swimsuits showed off bodies made perfect by total devotion to their care. They looked up when the girl and I appeared, but continued a desultory conversation with each other.

A third woman, also showing the kind of body that wealth and leisure afford, stood in the shallow end of the pool. She was coaching two little girls who were splashing along the lane next to her. Twin boys were jumping into the water at the deep end, chasing each other with plastic weapons. Several had been dropped at the edge of the pool. Space Berets action figures. I'd seen them at Mary Louise's—both her boys collected them.

"Not so much motion with your kicks, Utah," the woman in the pool commanded. "Rhiannon, don't lift your arms so high coming out of the water. One more length, both of you, with less wave action. Jason and Parnell"— here she raised her voice to a shout—"if you don't stop making so much commotion you're getting out until we're done here."

She stood with her back to me while Utah and Rhiannon did another twenty-five meters, working hard to keep their splashing to a minimum. My guide watched critically.

"Utah's my sister. She can do better than me when I was her age, but my form is improving. I'm definitely better than Rhiannon. Want to see?"

"Not today," I said. "If Utah's your sister, are you Wyoming or Nevada?"

The girl ignored me and dived into the pool, so

smoothly that she barely caused a ripple. She surfaced a third of the way down her lane. Her form was definitely better than mine.

The woman boosted Utah out of the pool, then hoisted herself out with one smooth push from her upper arm. A fourth woman, dark and round as a Gauguin portrait, came out of the shadows and wrapped a towel around the smaller girl. She silently handed another towel to the mother, then walked off with Utah.

"I'm Eleanor Baladine. I hope this is important, because you're interrupting my training program."

"The Sydney Olympics?" I asked.

"I know you think you're being funny," she said coldly. "Robert and I don't know how good our girls may get, but they could have a shot at a team in ten years. Especially Utah—although Madison is looking better all the time. And Rhiannon Trant is shaping up fast, even though she only started last summer."

Rhiannon Trant? Daughter of Edmund, Murray's new owner? That explained the Global plate out front —I'd thought it stood for Baladine's plans for world domination. "That's good. It would be a shame if they only swam for fun."

"No one swims for fun. You either compete or you aren't motivated enough to get in the water. I missed an Olympic spot by six-tenths of a second. I don't want my girls to lose out like that."

She broke off to call out an instruction to Madison. One of the women in the chaise longues, feeling Rhiannon was being neglected, sat up to call encouragement to her. If she was Edmund Trant's wife, no wonder gossip columnists like Regine Mauger were slobbering over her. It wasn't just her gold hair and tan, but the way she moved, even in a beach chair, and the little twitch of humor at her mouth, as if laughing at herself for caring about her daughter's ability to compete in a neighborhood pool. She made me feel as wide and clumsy as young Robbie.

"I'm V. I. Warshawski." I approached the pair in the chaise longues. "I'm a detective who has some questions for Ms. Baladine about Nicola Aguinaldo."

Eleanor Baladine rushed over. "My children's old nanny, you know, the one we had to send to Coolis for robbery—"

"Burglary, wasn't it?" I interrupted. "Or did she break in and use a weapon?"

"Excuse me, Detective." Baladine poured rich sarcasm over her words. "Not being used to the criminal element, I don't understand these distinctions."

"How did you hire Ms. Aguinaldo to begin with?" I asked.

"Through an agency. We all use it—Help Across Borders—they're usually utterly reliable. They assured me Nicola's immigration status was in order and vouched for her references. She was very good with the children, which I suppose wasn't surprising since she had one of her own—"

"I thought it was two," I interrupted.

"Maybe you're right. This was several years ago; the details are vague to me now. Madison! Work with the kickboard and concentrate on your hips! You're using way too much leg motion. You're a seal with little flippers: let's see them move."

"She lived here? With her children?"

"Certainly not. I'm not running a day-care center, and the person who works here has to concentrate on that: work."

"So how often did she see her own family? And how did she get to them?"

"I always gave her Sundays off, even though it was often inconvenient for us. Except when we traveled, when I had to have her along. Do you have children, Detective? Then you don't know how hard it is to travel with three little ones. The girls are always getting into something, and my son tends to be secretive and wander off where no one can find him. In an effort to avoid anything approaching exercise." Her eyes stayed on the pool; she was moving her hands up and down like little seal flippers, as if trying to get Madison to move properly.

The other two women threw in their own murmured complaints about how hard it is to manage children on the road. "They need their own little routines and friends," one explained.

And pools and ski slopes and who knows what else. "And to see her children every Sunday, someone drove her to the train?"

Mrs. Baladine took her eyes from her daughter long enough to stare at me in some hauteur. "Since the robbery for which Nicola was arrested was over two years ago I can't imagine what bearing her transport has on the situation."

"I'd like to know who could have picked her up when she fled Coolis. She can't have walked all the way to Chicago from there. Did some man fetch her on her days off? Or a woman friend? Or did you or Mr. Baladine drive her to the train?"

"We couldn't take that kind of time. Sometimes Robert gave her a lift if he was going into Oak Brook for a meeting, but she usually picked up the Metra bus at the bottom of Gateway Terrace. Once or twice he drove her all the way home, when he had to be in the city. I knew it was a long trip for her, so I let her spend the night in town and took on getting the kids ready for school myself Monday mornings."

"That was quite a sacrifice on your part." I tried to conceal my contempt, since I wanted information from her, but she wasn't stupid, and she bristled at my words.

I continued hastily. "She'd never stolen anything before she took that necklace, is that right? Did you ever get any sense of what drove her to do that?"

"She was poor and we were rich. What other reason would there be?" She was watching the pool again, but a stiffness in her posture made me think she knew more than that.

"I'm trying to find out who was in her background. If some man who badly needed money was controlling her, or if she had started to use drugs . . ." I let my words trail away suggestively.

"Yes, that's it, Eleanor," the third woman put in eagerly. "She must have known a lot of guys who could have attacked her. Didn't one of them come out here one weekend?"

"Attack her?" I asked. "Who said anything about that?"

The woman looked toward Eleanor Baladine, or at least moved her dark glasses toward her, and mouthed, "Boo-boo," then jumped to her feet, squeaking, "Jason and Parnell are getting much too rambunctious. It's time I got them out of the pool and home. You're a *saint*, Eleanor, to let them come over here when you're trying to coach."

"What was a boo-boo, ma'am?" I asked. "Letting

me know you'd already heard about the attack on Ms. Aguinaldo, even though it hasn't been made public?"

She laughed. "Oh, me and my big mouth. My husband says he can't ask me the time of day because I'll give him a dinner menu instead. I have no idea why that came floating out."

"And what do you say?" I asked Eleanor Baladine. "Did she tell you about the attack on Ms. Aguinaldo? Or did you tell her?"

"Listen here, Officer Whoosis, I've had about all the snooping into my private affairs I'm going to tolerate. Nicola turned out to be the worst kind of immigrant, lying, stealing, filling my son's head with superstitions. I was frankly glad to see her go to jail. If she escaped and got hurt, well, I hate to say it, but she probably had it coming."

"I don't think anyone had these injuries coming. She was murdered. In an extremely foul way. Someone kicked or punched her hard enough to perforate her small intestine, then left her in the road. She died when fecal matter filled her abdomen. It was an unbelievably painful death. If you knew about this before I got here, well, it makes me want to know a lot more about relations between you and your husband and Ms. Aguinaldo."

The children had climbed out of the pool. The girls were huddling within range of their mothers, but the twin boys were pelting each other with the Space Berets. The dark woman reappeared to drape Madison in a towel. The child grabbed her hand.

Mrs. Trant put her arms around Rhiannon. "The injuries sound dreadful, Detective, but maybe we could discuss them some other time."

Eleanor was made of sterner stuff. "I want the name

of your captain, and your name, too, Officer Whoosis. Just because we live in the suburbs doesn't mean my husband doesn't have powerful connections in Chicago."

"I'm sure he does, Ms. Baladine, head of Carnifice and all. As I've said a number of times, my name is V. I. Warshawski." I pulled a card from my handbag. "And I'm a detective. But private, not with the Chicago police."

Eleanor's eyes blazed and her chest expanded enough that she could have crossed the pool without stopping for air.

"Private detective? How dare you? How dare you insinuate your way onto my property to ask impertinent questions? Leave at once or the police will be here. Real police, who will have your behind in jail for trespassing so fast your head will spin."

"I'm not trespassing: you invited me onto your property."

"And now I'm uninviting you. Get out of here. And don't give my son a ride anywhere or I'll have you charged with kidnapping. You are undermining my efforts to get him to lose weight."

I couldn't keep back a laugh. "You are a mighty strange woman, Mrs. Baladine. Your former nanny is murdered and what you care about is your son's waistline. So he's not as addicted to lettuce and workout machines as you and your pals—but he seems like an attractive boy. Don't keep running him down in front of strangers. And do keep my card. Whether I'm public or private, Ms. Aguinaldo is dead and I'm investigating. If you change your mind about letting me in on what you know about her personal life—give me a call."

Eleanor dropped my card on the pavement, started

to grind it with her bare heel, then thought better of it. She clapped her hands and turned to the girls. "Madison, Rhiannon, back in the pool. I want to see a two-lap race. Winner gets a bowl of frozen yogurt."

As I passed the corner of the garage I heard Mrs. Trant say, "I think Rhiannon's had enough for one day, haven't you, darling?"

9

Out of the Mouths of Babes

As I was fumbling with the release mechanism to the gate, Robbie emerged from the shrubbery. His mother might inveigh against his lack of athletic ability, but he knew how to snake through the undergrowth like Natty Bumpo.

I stopped the car and got out. We faced each other in silence. All I could hear was the birds telling each other about choice worms or approaching cats. The house was so remote I couldn't make out even a faint echo of Eleanor Baladine's coaching, or the shrieks from the boys in the pool.

The longer the silence lasted, the harder it would be for him to break, so I spoke first. "I'm sorry I didn't have a chance to tell you about Nicola's death before your sister showed up."

He flushed a painful red. "How did you—you didn't tell Mom I was listening, did you?"

I shook my head. "I didn't know you were there—you're much too skilled in the undergrowth for a city slicker like me to hear."

"Then how did you know I heard you talking to her?"

I smiled. "Deduction. They teach us that in detective

school. It must be hard to live with three such determined athletes as your mother and sisters. Is your father
a mad swimmer, too?"

"Tennis. Not that he was ever a champion like Mom
—she has a gazillion trophies, just never anything from
the Olympics, so we're supposed to do it for her. I tried,
I really did, but—but when they keep calling you butter
—butt—"

"Nicola didn't do that, did she?" I cut in before he
embarrassed himself by bursting into tears.

He gave a grateful half smile. "Nicola, she didn't
speak much English. Some Spanish, but her real language was Tagalog. That's what they speak in the Philippines, you know; that's where she came from. She
always said it was better to read and know many things
from books than be able to swim. Without an education she could only be a nanny or clean houses. She
taught me how to know the stars so I could track at
night. I got a book of constellations in Spanish and
English, which made Mom crazy; she thought Nicola
should learn English instead of me Spanish. Maybe Nicola called me butterball in Tagalog."

That seemed to be an attempt at a joke, so I laughed
a little with him. "Who were the women who were
there today?"

"Oh, they're friends of Mom's. Mrs. Trant, her
daughter and Madison are in the same grade. And Mrs.
Poilevy. Parnell and Jason Poilevy. I'm supposed to play
with them because their father is important to my father, but I can't stand them."

Poilevy. The Speaker of the Illinois House. He'd been
standing next to Edmund Trant at the party Tuesday
night.

"Tell me about the necklace," I suggested to Robbie.

"What about it?"

"Do you know if it was really valuable? Do you think it was really missing?"

"You mean, did Mom only pretend it was gone so she could make a scene about Nicola?"

Say what you will about today's children—all those crime shows they watch make them understand the double-cross young. "Something like that."

"You don't know how tough Mom is. If she wanted Nicola gone, *phht,* out the door she'd go. No, Nicola took it all right." He frowned. "She sold it at a place near where she lived. When Mom raised the roof and called the cops and everything, the Chicago police found it at this—some kind of jewelry resale shop."

"Pawnshop," I suggested.

"Yeah, that's what it was. Pawnshop. And the man from the pawnshop picked out Nicola from a photograph. And I remember Dad saying"—here he flushed painfully again—"'Stupid spick only got twelve hundred dollars for a fifty-thousand-dollar necklace.'"

"Do you know why she stole the necklace to begin with?"

"Her little girl had asthma and it got real bad, she had to go to the hospital, only Nicola couldn't pay the bill, I guess. I heard her asking Mom for a loan, and, well, it was thousands of dollars, I guess Mom couldn't possibly loan her that much money, it would be years before Nicola could pay it off. I gave her five hundred dollars—the money I've saved from my grandparents' birthday checks—only then somehow Dad found out, he stopped the checks, that was when he and Mom made me—"

He pulled at his T-shirt, so that the Space Berets

stern faces distorted into sneers; when he spoke again it was in such a rapid monotone I could barely make out the words. "They made me go to this camp for fat kids where you had to run all day and only eat carrots for dinner, and by the time that was over, Nicola was arrested and on trial and everything. I never saw her again. I thought if she ran away from jai . . . only now she's dead. Who killed her? Did you tell Mom she got kicked to death?"

If I'd known this sensitive boy was listening I wouldn't have been so graphic with Eleanor. "The doctor who tried to save her life at the hospital said he thought she'd been punched or kicked, but no one knows who did it. I'm hoping I can find that out. Did she ever talk to you about any of the people in her life, anyone she was afraid of, or owed money to?"

"It's only that she was—she wasn't very big and she was afraid of people hitting her; once she thought Mom was mad enough to throw something at her, she —it was horrible, she was begging her not to hurt her. I wish—" His face crumpled and he began to cry. "Oh, shit, oh, shit, only crybabies cry, oh, stop."

Before I could offer any words of comfort he vanished into the shrubbery. I got back in my car, then, wondering if he might be lurking within earshot, got out again.

"I'm going to leave one of my business cards behind this post," I said loudly. "If anyone finds it who wants to call me, my number's on it."

The grounds were so carefully groomed there were no pebbles or branches to weight the card. I finally tore a twig from the shrubbery and placed it behind the gate-release post with my card. As I released the gate I heard a motor revving behind me. The Mercedes Gelaendewagen appeared, going fast. It overtook me before I finished turning onto Gateway Terrace. Mrs. Trant was at the wheel. She and Mrs. Poilevy still had on their heavy glasses, which made them look like the menacing action toys at the pool's edge.

The Skylark huffed after them but couldn't keep pace. Before I reached the first intersection the Mercedes had disappeared.

In a few minutes I was back on the main roads, where strip malls and office towers made the Baladine home seem a remote Eden. Buildings of unrelated size and design are plunked haphazardly on the prairie out here, as if their haste to fill the vast space makes developers dig it up at random. It reminded me of a giant box of chocolates, where someone had eaten bits off dozens of pieces in a greedy desire to consume the whole thing at once.

In the distance the orderly Chicago skyline appeared. I swung onto the expressway—Arthur seeing Avalon through the mists and eagerly returning. Not that the pockmarked apartments and burned-out lots lining the inbound Eisenhower were any more delightful than the western suburbs.

A roar in the Skylark's exhaust made it hard for me to think about the Baladines. I hadn't gotten what I'd gone out there for: the name of anyone who might have hurt Nicola Aguinaldo. And what had I learned? That the very rich are different from you and me?

Certainly they're different from me. The neighborhood where I grew up was a lot more like Uptown than Oak Brook. Every kid on my block knew what a pawnshop was: we were often the ones our parents sent with the radio or coat or whatever was going up the spout to pay the rent.

By the same token I didn't know what life with a full-time nanny was like. Did they talk about their private lives to their young charges? You couldn't live intimately with people for two years without sharing many intimacies, I suppose, if you found a language in common.

Had Nicola preyed on young Robbie's sympathies? A sensitive overweight boy would be an easy mark in this house of obsessed athletes. Maybe Nicola got tired of Mom—I certainly had after twenty minutes—and decided to steal both her son's affections and her jewelry. Not that I was investigating this long-gone burglary, but I wondered if Nicola Aguinaldo really had an asthmatic daughter.

And what about Dad? Robbie had been awfully quick to get the implication of Eleanor Baladine making an excuse to fire Nicola. And those friends of the Baladines knew something—there was a whiff of concealed knowledge in the stiffening, the glances. Had Robert started playing with the help on those days off when he drove her to Chicago? When she ran away from prison did she think he would come to her rescue —leave Eleanor for a Filipina immigrant? Could he perhaps have killed her to keep her from messing with his happy home?

The rush hour was building. The drive home took almost twice as long as the one out, and the exhaust got louder in the long backup off the Eisenhower to the northbound Kennedy. By the time I pulled up in front of my apartment, my bones were vibrating from it. Definitely not a car I wanted to spend the rest of my life in.

Mr. Contreras was out back with the dogs, working

over his tomatoes. I called from my back porch and Peppy came up to see me. Mitch was gnawing on a tree branch and barely lifted his head.

As I changed into jeans Peppy followed me around the apartment, making it clear she expected to come with me. "I'm going to Uptown, girl. What if someone assaults me and you're left in the car for days? Not that a car on that block gets left for long. And I'd have to leave the windows open—anyone could come by and steal you or hurt you." I couldn't withstand the longing in her amber eyes. After taking my gun from the safe and checking the clip and the safety, I leashed her up and called down to my neighbor that I was taking her with me on an errand.

As I parked between a rusted Chevy and an empty pickle jar, I wondered what went through Nicola Aguinaldo's mind when she made that long trip home on Sundays. Suburban bus to train, train to Union Station, walk to State Street, L to Bryn Mawr, the six blocks over to her apartment on Wayne. Over two hours, even if all connections went smoothly. And when she got home, instead of a pool and manicured grounds for her children, she'd find a tiny glass-strewn square of hard-packed dirt in front of her building. If she had fallen in with some scheme of Baladine's, maybe it was in the hopes of buying her children's way out of Wayne Street.

The girls who'd helped me canvass the street last night were jumping double-dutch when I pulled up. I picked the pickle jar out of the gutter before someone could run over or throw it. I didn't see a garbage can so I tossed it into the open rear window of the Skylark. Peppy stuck her head out, hoping that meant I wanted her. The girls caught sight of her and stopped jumping.

"Is that your police dog, miss?" "Does he bite, miss?" "Can I pet him?" "Will he stay in the car?"

"It's a girl dog who is very gentle; she'd love to say hi to you. Shall I let her out?"

They giggled nervously but approached the car. Peppy has perfect manners. When I let her out of the back, after dancing for a minute to show her pleasure at being released, she sat and extended a paw to the girls. They were enchanted. I showed them how she would take a dog biscuit from my mouth, our noses brushing gently.

"Can I do that, miss?" "Did you raise her from a baby?" "Ooh, Derwa, she likes you, she licked your hand!" "Mina, that police dog going to bite you!"

"Do any of you remember Nicola Aguinaldo?" I asked as casually as I could. "I'd like to talk to her mother."

"Did she steal that gold thing we found?"

"Don't be stupid," another girl with thick braids and a head scarf snorted. "How could she steal something when she was already in jail?"

"That's right, the missus didn't like the way the mister looked at Sherree's mother, that's right, so she pretended Sherree's mom stole something," a third put in.

Someone objected that Sherree's mom really had stolen a necklace and she was a thief, but one girl said, "That's dirty talk, about Sherree's mom and the mister; you shouldn't be saying stuff like that."

"Well, it's only the truth! It's not saying that Sherree's mom did something dirty, not like Mina's mom, you know—"

A hand reached across and slapped the speaker. Before the fight could escalate, I snapped at them to be quiet.

"I'm not interested in what anyone's mother thinks, says, or does—that's her private business. I need to talk to Sherree's grandmother. Will one of you show me where to find her?"

"They moved," Sarina, the oldest, said.

"Where?" I asked.

They looked at each other, suddenly wary. In the world of illegal immigrants, detectives who ask questions about the family are never benign. Not even Peppy or the beat-up Skylark could make me seem less than an educated Anglo—and hence attached to authority.

After some dickering they agreed that I could talk to one of their mothers. Mina was nominated: she'd lived across the hall, and her mom had looked after Sherree when the baby died.

"What baby?"

"Sherree's little sister," a small girl who'd been silent before spoke up. "She coughed and coughed, and Señora Mercedes took her to the hospital; that was when—"

"Shut up!" The big girl with the long braid smacked her. "I told you you could play with us if you kept quiet—well, here you are blabbing your big mouth off, same as always."

"I am not!" The little one howled. "And Mommy says you have to look after me anyway."

"Mina!" I cut in, not sure which one I was addressing. "Let's go talk to your mother and leave these two to sort out their problem."

A girl with short curly hair looked at me. During the discussion she had hovered on the edge of the group, an outsider with the in crowd.

"I guess you can come up." She wasn't enthusiastic.

"But my mom's afraid of dogs; you can't bring your dog inside."

Half a dozen shrill voices promised to look after Peppy, but I thought it would be more prudent to return her to the car. Even a beautifully mannered dog can turn fractious with strangers, and childish strangers also couldn't control her if she decided to follow me—or chase a cat across the street.

10

Found in Translation

"My mom doesn't speak much English," Mina warned me as she took me inside.

"Neither did mine." I followed her up the narrow stairs, where the smell of old grease and mold vividly brought back the tenements of my own childhood. "We spoke Italian together."

"My mom only speaks Arabic. And a little English. So you'll have to talk to me unless you know Arabic." As we climbed the stairs she took a fringed scarf out of her jeans pocket and tied it around her curls.

Mina's mother—Mrs. Attar to me—received me in a living room that I also knew from my childhood. I used to sit in places like this when my mother took me with her on social calls in the neighborhood: overstuffed furniture encased in plastic, a large television draped in a piece of weaving from the Old Country, a thicket of family photos on top.

Mrs. Attar was a plump, worried woman who kept her daughter planted firmly next to her. Even so, she insisted on offering me hospitality, in this case a cup of thick sweet tea. Hers might be a seat of poverty, but her manners sure beat those in Oak Brook.

I drank the tea gratefully: the heat outside became overwhelming in the overstuffed room. After thanking her for the tea, and admiring the weaving on the television, I broached my subject. I hoped Mina would do an accurate job with the translation.

"I have some bad news about Nicola Aguinaldo. She ran away from prison last week. Did you know that? She died yesterday. Someone hurt her very badly when she was on her way to this apartment building, and I would like to learn who did that."

"What? What you are saying?" Mrs. Attar demanded.

Mina snapped off a string of Arabic. Mrs. Attar dropped her hold on the girl and demanded information. Mina turned back to me to translate. That role was familiar to me as well. My mother's English became fluent with time, but I could still remember those humiliating meetings with teachers or shopkeepers where I had to act as interpreter.

"The girls say you looked after Sherree when the baby was in the hospital. Was that after Nicola was sent to jail? I know the baby was sick before."

When Mina translated, first for me and then for her mother, she said, "My mother doesn't remember Sherree staying here."

"But you remember, don't you?" I said. "You agreed with your playmates when they brought it up."

She looked at me slyly, pleased to be in control. "There are so many kids in this building they probably got confused. Sherree wasn't here."

Mrs. Attar ripped off a question to her daughter, probably wanting to know what our side conversation was about. While they talked I sat back on the crinkling plastic and pondered how to get Mrs. Attar to talk to me. I didn't care whether she'd ever looked after Sherree Aguinaldo. What I needed was the address where the grandmother had moved with Sherree, or the names of any men Mrs. Attar might have seen with Nicola Aguinaldo.

I looked Mrs. Attar in the eye, adult to adult, and spoke slowly. "I'm not with the government. I'm not with Children and Family Services. I'm not with INS."

I opened my handbag and spread the contents on the cluttered coffee table. I laid out my credit cards and my private-eye license. Mrs. Attar looked puzzled for a moment, then seemed to understand what I was showing her. She scrutinized my driver's license and the PI license, spelling out my name from card to card. She showed it to her daughter and demanded an explanation.

"You see?" I said. "There is no badge in here."

When Mrs. Attar finally spoke to me, she said in halting English, "Today is?"

"Thursday," I said.

"One ago, two ago, three ago is?"

"It'd be Monday, Ma," Mina cut in in exasperation, adding something in Arabic.

Her mother put a light hand over her daughter's mouth. "I tell. Men comes. Early early, first prayers. Is —is—"

She looked around the room for inspiration, then showed me her watch. She turned the dial back to five-thirty.

"I wake husband, I wake Mina, I wake sons. First wash. Look outside, see men. I afraid. Woman here, have green card, I find."

"Derwa's mom," Mina put in, sulking because she wasn't controlling the drama any longer. "She's legal; Mama got her to ask the men what they wanted. They were looking for Abuelita Mercedes, so Mama went and woke her—they're not Islam, they don't have to get up at five-thirty like we do."

"Yes, yes. Abuelita Mercedes, much good woman, much good for Mina, for Derwa, take with Sherree when I working, when Derwa mother working. All childrens call her 'Abuelita,' meaning 'Grandmother,' not only own childrens. I take him—"

"*Her*, Mama; if it's a woman it's her, not him."

"Her. I take her, I take Sherree. Men coming here"—she stabbed at her chair, to indicate this very room—"I say, she my mother, these my childs all."

"And then?"

"Leave. No good stay here. Men go, more men come, no good."

I assumed she meant Abuelita Mercedes had to move before more INS agents showed up looking for her. "Do you know where she went?"

A sigh and a shrug. "Better not know. Not want problem."

I asked Mrs. Attar if she knew of any men Nicola had dated. Mrs. Attar only shrugged again—she couldn't help. When I asked about Mr. Baladine—the boss who sometimes drove her home—Mrs. Attar lifted her palms in incomprehension. Nicola was a good mother—it was the only reason she went out to work among rich strangers, to make money for her two little girls. She came home every week to see them; she was never late, she never had time for men. Mina smirked a little at this, which made me wonder if the kids would tell a different story.

"America no good place. Baby sick, mother no money, mother go jail. Why? Why peoples no help?"

She turned to Mina to put her ideas more completely. In Egypt a mother could take her sick baby to a clinic where the government would care for it, then there was no need for the mother to steal to pay the bills.

"Now mother dead, and why? Only want help baby. America very no good."

I couldn't think of a convincing rebuttal. I thanked her for her time and tea and let Mina take me back outside. Her friends had vanished. I tried to ask her about Nicola Aguinaldo, whether Mina had ever noticed any men visiting her or knew of talk on the streets about her, but the child was hurt at her friends' defection. She hunched her shoulder angrily and told me to mind my own business. There didn't seem to be much else I could do, so I got into the rattling Skylark and drove off.

I stopped in the park at Foster to give Peppy a walk. The police were sweeping the area in their three-wheeled buggies, slowing when they passed anyone with a dog, so I kept her on her leash. She didn't like it —especially since the squirrels weren't similarly constrained—but unlike her son she doesn't yank my arm off when she's tied up.

Aguinaldo had run away from Coolis without knowing that her mother had fled their apartment. And then? Had she come home, found her mother gone, and called Baladine for help, only to be beaten up? Or met up with some old boyfriend in the neighborhood with the same disastrous results?

"Those women around the pool knew something, but what? About Aguinaldo's escape, or her injuries, or her relations with Robert Baladine? We're no closer to having anything on Aguinaldo's private life than we did this morning," I said, so severely that Peppy flattened her ears in worry.

"And that smirk Mina Attar gave, when her mother said Nicola had no time for men, it could have concealed anything—the other kids implied Mrs. Attar had plenty of time for men, so Mina might have been smirking at her mom. Or maybe Mina knew something about Nicola that she wasn't saying. It was the look of someone who felt she knew someone else's guilty secret, that's for sure."

And what about this guy Morrell whom the kids had mentioned, the one interviewing people who had escaped from prison? Could he have played some role in Aguinaldo's escape, or in her death?

Who had claimed Aguinaldo's body? Abuelita Mercedes, the neighborhood grandmother? If so, how had she learned that Nicola was dead? From Morrell? Who was he—a social worker? A journalist? I didn't think he could be from INS. And I didn't think he was a cop—he'd been coming around before Nicola's death.

I jerked Peppy away from a dead gull. I wished Vishnikov had done the autopsy when Nicola's body arrived on Wednesday. If she'd gone to the hospital in Coolis for an ovarian cyst, maybe that had caused her internal problems, although the Beth Israel surgeon thought she'd been hit or kicked. The external injuries had been fresh when I found her, and that broken arm looked as though it had just occurred, as if she'd been struck by a car. If so, was there a boyfriend who beat her up? My mind circled back to Robert and Eleanor Baladine.

I could imagine a lot of scenarios where a man might have sex with the live-in nanny, from unregulated desire through hostility toward his wife or rivalry with his son. But would he have prosecuted Nicola for theft as a way to protect himself? Would she have turned to him for help when she escaped from prison? And then—and then what?

He was clearly friends with Edmund Trant, the head of Global Entertainment's media division, or at least the two wives were friends. Along with the wife of the Illinois House Speaker. That was cozy for a couple of important businessmen, to know their wives schmoozed with the wife of the state's key power broker.

I wondered what Murray knew about relations between Edmund Trant and Robert Baladine. Or Trant and Speaker Poilevy, for that matter. I bundled Peppy into the backseat of the Buick and went home.

11

Clean—On the Outside

I CAUGHT MURRAY at home. "Murray, hi, V.I. here. Quite a job you did Tuesday night—I saw even *The New York Times* condescended to notice Chicago and give you a couple of lines."

"Thanks, Vic." His tone was cautious.

"Even I got a little mention," I persisted. "Was it you who talked to Regine Mauger about me? Crumbs from the Global table would sure be tasty. Maybe it would only take one Global crumb to replace my car."

"Christ, Vic! Give me a break. Do you think I suggested something like that to Regine? Someone gets under her skin and she goes after them like a horsefly. I don't know what you did to annoy her—maybe you called up and persecuted her in her own home. She huffed up to me at the Glow, demanding to know who you were and who got you an invitation."

"I wonder who told her about that eons-old fling you and I had." I sounded earnest and puzzled; when he stammered over a response, I added, "Sorry, I didn't call to tease you. I'm glad you got a good response to your gig. I really called because of something odd I stumbled on—just about literally—on my way home from the party."

I gave him a brief summary of my accident. "I

haven't seen a mention in the papers, even though she broke out of Coolis on Sunday. But I learned something curious today. She was an illegal Filipina immigrant. Who used to be Robert Baladine's nanny—his kids' nanny, anyway—before she went to jail. Don't you think that's worth a line or two of type, Baladine being head of Carnifice Security and all?"

"Illegal immigrants who escape from prison and die aren't the kind of story I cover, Vic. I can mention it to the City Desk, but if it happened Sunday—well, today's Thursday, after all."

I ignored the coldness in his voice. "You know Eleanor Baladine is a mad swimmer? She missed a chance to swim in the Olympics and is determined her children will do it for her. I went out there this afternoon and watched her lashing kids around the pool. Besides her own they included Edmund Trant's daughter and Jean-Claude Poilevy's sons. By the way, if you heard the names Utah and Madison, would you imagine you were being given street directions or hearing about two little girls?"

"If you're trying to imply that Edmund Trant and Jean-Claude Poilevy got together with Robert Baladine to kill Baladine's ex-nanny, you're so far over the edge that no one can pull you back, Warshawski. I have to run—I'm going to be late for dinner."

"Sandy Fishbein or Alexandra Fisher or whoever it is can wait five minutes without hurting your television prospects. The Rogers Park police lost the incident report and now they're saying I was driving drunk and refused a blood test. They want me to take a fall on a hit-and-run in exchange for immunity from prosecution. Don't you think that's queer?"

He was silent for a long moment. "It's unusual. But

it doesn't make me think Baladine is in a conspiracy with Trant and Poilevy to get you."

I fidgeted with the phone cord. "I don't think anyone's out to get me—I mean, not because I'm me. But I do think someone with a heavy hand is leaning on Rogers Park and the State's Attorney to make a tidy end to the case. Because I happened along and called an ambulance I was nominated for the tidy ending—they couldn't know housekeeping has always been my weakest point. Poilevy could be leaning on the State's Attorney as a favor to Baladine, you know, to keep anyone from asking questions about his relations with his kids' ex-nanny. Stranger things have happened in this town. They might have rushed in to charge me, except I'm a detective, my passenger was an ex-cop, and I sent my car to a private lab for forensic work. Along with the clothes Aguinaldo was wearing when she died."

"Vic, it's not that I don't love you, but I'm late, and I don't have a clue why you're telling me all this."

I suppressed a sigh of impatience. "What do you know about Trant and Poilevy's working together, or Poilevy and Baladine, that would tell me whether it's Poilevy pulling this particular lever?"

"Nothing. And I'm not stirring up water around Edmund Trant. For any consideration you can think of. Not even the chance to watch Eleanor Baladine chase him around the pool with a whip."

"Because you know he's Mr. Clean? Or because you're squeamish about taking on your great-grandboss?"

"My great-grand—oh." When he spoke again, it was without the irritation he'd shown before. "Look, Vic. Maybe I'm being chicken. Okay, I am chicken. But you know how hard I tried to peddle my ass after Global bought the *Star*. In nine months I got three offers, and they weren't for serious journalism: hardly anyone's doing that now. I'm forty-six. If I start bird-dogging Trant or his friends I could find myself on the street—with no one wanting to hire a guy who guns for his own boss. So you think I'm a sellout for going on the tube. You want to lord it over me, o queen of the incorruptibles, be my guest, but—there's plenty to investigate in this town without my taking on Trant."

"I don't want to lord it over you. But—here's one thing I've been worrying about. What if Baladine was sleeping with the help and set her up—initially, I mean. Maybe he gave her the necklace, then pretended she stole it."

The more I said, the stupider it sounded, so the faster I talked. "Then she runs away, she needs money, she calls the one person with money she knows—Baladine—"

"Do you have one shred of evidence for this?"

Embarrassment made me hug my knees to my chest, but I bluffed past it. "Well, the three women in Oak Brook sure knew something about Aguinaldo—they knew she'd been assaulted before I mentioned it, and you guys hadn't printed a line of type about her. Not only that, her body disappeared from the morgue before Vishnikov could do the autopsy."

"Vic, this isn't like you. You haven't done your homework," Murray said dryly. "Carnifice runs Coolis for the State of Illinois. So Baladine knew Aguinaldo had escaped, because he heads the company that runs the prison. And he probably got an ID on her from the morgue same as you, only faster. So it's not surprising the ladies already knew. Sorry, Vic. This is a nonstarter. Although I could talk to Trant—I hear the Hollywood operation can use a boost, and that story has Keanu Reeves and Drew Barrymore written all over it. Unless someone's paying you a big fee for fishing in this pond, I'd pull my line in."

He hung up before I could respond. My cheeks were stained crimson. Anger or embarrassment? Or both. Running opposite the how-dare-he track in my mind was his uncomfortable final remark. Why the hell was I taking time to ask questions when I had no fee, no client, and a wrecked car to add to my overhead?

I'm only a few years younger than Murray. I couldn't blame him for not wanting to take on his boss —especially on the insubstantial grounds I'd suggested. It's true Murray has a condo in Lincoln Park and a new Mercedes convertible, compared to my spartan four rooms and beat-up Buick, but you feel fifty coming toward you and start getting nervous about how you're going to afford old age. At least, I do at times.

Murray's scoffing nettled me, but it embarrassed me, too. In the morning I went soberly about the business I was being paid to conduct, taking time only to call Cheviot Labs for a report on the Trans Am. They were giving my car a clean bill of health. I was nervous enough about the pressure from the State's Attorney to ask them to messenger over a copy of the report before they gave the car to the cops, and I found an empty folder for the paramedics' report Max had faxed to me. It was labeled *Alumni Fund,* from when I'd agreed to help raise money for my law school class. I'd done it mostly to help build connections among firms that might need a professional investigator, although when I automated, I'd discovered that most of the information was out of date. I'd type a proper label later, but for now I would attend to my own business. I would not pursue any other ideas, including a thought I'd had about going down to the Ferragamo boutique to see if they knew what garment that little logo had come from.

I printed the LifeStory report on the job candidate I was investigating for Darraugh Graham. I called banks and previous employers and put together a nice little dossier. I went back to my maps of rural Georgia.

At two a messenger arrived from Cheviot with their forensic report on my car. A man named Rieff had signed it. After a thorough inspection of the Trans Am's front end, he said he found no traces of organic matter in the paint, wheels, or grille except for insect carcasses. Rieff was willing to stand up in court and pronounce the Trans Am clean outside, if not in. For this work the lab asked the modest fee of $1,878.

I wrote out a check, then faxed the report to my lawyer's office with a crisp note telling him to get the State's Attorney off my back. Freeman called a little later to tell me that privately the state was persuaded by the Cheviot report, but they weren't going to admit that publicly because, as Freeman said, "You were such a pain in the ass about turning the Trans Am over to begin with. The cops are going to make you pay by holding on to your car."

Rogers Park still hadn't found the incident report, but Freeman thought he'd persuaded them to back away from harassing me about Nicola Aguinaldo's death. Mary Louise had helped, by having Finchley call over to the station and letting them know I essentially had a police witness on my team.

"Thanks, Freeman. Out of curiosity, are the cops doing anything else to find who killed Nicola Aguinaldo, now that they've decided I'm not an easy arrest? And are they doing anything to find her body? No one at her old address knows where her mother is living these days."

"Vic, that's none of your business. I told the State's Attorney that we had no compelling interest in her death and that if they let you alone you'd leave her alone. I don't know what got that bee buzzing in their brains to begin with, but I don't think you have anything else to worry about on this. So leave Aguinaldo's death to the cops. You know the story on hit-and-runs as well as I do: with seven hundred murders a year in this town, manslaughter has to take a backseat. You don't need to stand there like Aimee Semple McPherson haranguing sinners if they don't put round-the-clock teams on finding who hit her."

He paused, as if inviting my response; when I didn't say anything he added, "I'm going to Montana for the weekend to do some fly-fishing with a client, so try not to get arrested until Tuesday, okay?"

"I guess that's funny, so I'll laugh, but next time you make a promise in my name to the SA, talk to me first." I hung up with a snap.

So all that excitement with Detective Lemour and my car had been a tempest in a teapot? But someone had killed Nicola Aguinaldo. And those women in Oak Brook knew she was dead before I told them. Okay, Murray was right: one of them was married to the head of the company that ran Coolis for the state, and the woman had been his kids' nanny. So probably he had been notified ahead of the rest of the world. But in the absence of an autopsy, and with no news reports on Aguinaldo, how had those women known she'd been assaulted?

"Don't touch it, Vic. Leave it alone or it will come back and bite you," I admonished myself.

I went back to the Georgia problem with a dogged intensity. I was deep in a reverse directory on the computer, looking for people who lived near the garage that was outfitting Continental United's trucks with new tires, when the phone rang.

It was a woman, with a low smooth voice like cream. "I'm calling from Mr. Baladine for I. V. Warshawski."

So Aguinaldo's death was going to bite me without my touching it. My stomach tightened. I shouldn't have discounted the mad swimmer's threat to tell on me to her powerful husband.

"I. V. Warshawski was Isaac Bashevis Singer's pen name when he wrote for the *Daily Forward* in the thirties. I'm V. I., the detective. Which of us do you want?" Even at forty-plus, nervousness still makes me mouth off.

The cream didn't lose any of its smoothness. "Is this Ms. Warshawski? Mr. Baladine wants to see you this afternoon. Do you know where our offices are?"

That sounded like a command; if nervousness makes me flippant, commands make me ornery. "I know where your offices are, but I don't have time to drive to Oak Brook this afternoon."

"Can you hold, please."

I put the speakerphone on so I could hear her when she returned and obstinately went back to my reverse directory. Dance music wafted to me from Carnifice's on-hold program, followed by a description of Dr. Jekyll and Mr. Hyde. "When you're not home, is your children's nanny Dr. Jekyll or Mr. Hyde? Carnifice Security's Home Security Division can show you how to monitor your nanny on the job. We can trace her references before you hire her, too. Call us for an estimate." They added an 800 number.

The dance music returned, followed almost immediately by the cream. "Mr. Baladine can see you at five today."

"I could be free at *my* office at five if he wants to sit on the Eisenhower all afternoon. Unfortunately I don't have time to do that. How about tomorrow?"

"Mr. Baladine has to be in Washington tomorrow. Can you tell me a time that you could get to Oak Brook today?"

I didn't want to make that long drive just to be chewed out, but I'd love to meet the guy, as long as I didn't have to face rush-hour traffic to do so. "How about seven?"

She put me on hold again, this time only long enough for the start of a spiel on Carnifice's bodyguarding service. If I could make six-thirty, Mr. Baladine would appreciate it.

I said I'd do my best to earn the big man's appreciation and turned thoughtfully back to my computer. Before going on with this dull problem in Georgia, I logged on to LifeStory and asked what they had on file about Robert Baladine. Yes, I told the machine, I was willing to pay a premium for short turnaround.

12

The Lion's Den

CARNIFICE HEADQUARTERS WERE what you wanted in your security provider if you were a rich parent or wealthy multinational: enormous Persian carpets floating on polished parquet, desks and cabinets that a lot of rain forest had been hacked down to provide, doors opened by magnetic card or guard only, a beautiful young woman who took you from the guard in the lobby to your destination. It was quite a contrast to Warshawski Investigations, where the lone PI or her part-time assistant brought you into a converted warehouse.

My young escort smiled politely when I commented on the ambience, but when I asked how long she'd been at Carnifice, she said that company policy forbade her answering any questions.

"Not even to tell me the time or the weather?"

She only smiled again and opened Baladine's door for me. She mentioned my name, perfectly pronounced, to the woman who sat enthroned in the antechamber, then left, although not, to my disappointment, walking backward.

"Ah, Ms. Warshawski. I'll let Mr. Baladine know you're here." The woman's skin and hair matched her smooth rich voice; the bias-cut dress she wore would have paid the Trans Am's repair bill and left something over for gas.

The great man kept me waiting twelve minutes—exactly the amount of time that I was late. A perfect system of punishments, no doubt learned in running private prisons around the country. I wandered around the room while I waited, looking at photographs of a lean, tanned man with various sheiks and presidents, and at the exhibits of memorabilia, ranging from a Presidential Medal of Freedom to a mock-up of the women's correctional facility at Coolis. I was particularly interested in that, since it made escape seem impossible. The back abutted the Smallpox Creek, but there were no windows or gates on that side. Three layers of razor-wire fencing looped around the front.

"Are you interested in prison security, Ms. Warshawski?"

The lean, tanned man of the photos was standing behind me. I turned and shook his proffered hand. He was fifteen years older than his wife, as I'd learned from my afternoon's research, but looked well able to keep up with her in the pool, or any other arena.

"Only at Coolis, Mr. Baladine—I wondered how a small person like Nicola Aguinaldo could circumnavigate all those fences and guard boxes and so on."

"Ah, yes, poor Nicola. I understand she faked an illness and was taken to the Coolis Hospital, where it was easier to escape. An unhappy life and, I gather, an unhappy death." He put a hand on my shoulder and shepherded me toward his own office. "Claudia, can you bring us something to drink? I understand you like Black Label, Ms. Warshawski."

"Not when I'm negotiating the Eisenhower. Mineral water will be fine, thanks." Since I'd investigated him I shouldn't have been surprised that he'd done the same to me.

His private office was filled with more photographs and trophies—and exotic hardwoods and carpets and art. A diploma issued by the Naval Academy held a prominent place near his desk, next to a photograph of a much younger Baladine on board a destroyer, shaking hands with Nixon's Secretary of Defense.

"Yes, I was in Vietnam in the sixties. And then had my own ship for a few years."

"That was before you joined Rapelec's defense division, wasn't it?"

I said it without looking at him: I didn't want to overplay my hand by scanning his face for any surprise at my research into his life—which had not garnered his drinking preferences. Still, I'd learned that at Rapelec he had moved rapidly from a job in systems procurement to managing their submarine division, and then to heading the manufacture of all rapid-deployment weapons, before the end of the Cold War shrank the importance of the unit. Carnifice brought him in as CEO five years ago. Their private prison business was one of the divisions that had grown the most rapidly under his command.

Claudia brought a bottle of Malvern water and poured for both of us, with a murmured reminder that his conference call with Tokyo would be coming through in half an hour.

"Thanks, Claudia." He waited for the door to shut. "A picture like that probably doesn't inspire you in the same way as it does me, since I gather you and I were on opposite sides in Vietnam."

Okay, he had a staff of three thousand plus to go looking at everything from my drinking habits to my college protest activities, but it still made me uncomfortable. I knew I would have to work hard to keep my temper—since his research had probably also told him that was a vulnerable spot on my heel.

"I was on the side of Washington and Jefferson," I said, "perhaps the side of naïveté and idealism. And you?"

"Certainly I've never been naive. Either about America's external enemies or her internal." He gestured me to a seat next to a coffee table made out of some kind of gold burl.

"And so it was a natural progression for you. To move from killing Zimbabweans to incarcerating Americans. Although exactly why Zimbabwe was an American enemy I'm not sure."

At that his face did twist in brief surprise: Rapelec's arming of the South African secret forces' raids into Zimbabwe during the eighties had been the most deeply buried item I'd found in my afternoon's research. I didn't think it had anything to do with Nicola Aguinaldo's death, but it did shed some insight into Baladine's character.

"Unfortunately, in matters of national security it's not possible to be idealistic. I always think that's a luxury for people who aren't willing to dirty their hands. But perhaps we should move to matters of more immediate importance. My wife was most upset by your questioning her yesterday under pretense of being a detective."

I shook my head. "No pretense. I am a detective. I'm licensed by the state of Illinois and everything."

He smiled condescendingly. "You know you're splitting hairs: she never would have admitted you, let alone spoken to you, if she hadn't believed you were with the Chicago police."

I smiled back. "You should be pleased with me, Baladine—it shows I'm not afraid to get my hands dirty."

He frowned briefly. "I'd prefer you demonstrated that someplace other than with my family. Particularly with my son, who has an unfortunate streak of naïveté of his own and is an easy prey for anyone willing to take advantage of his vulnerability."

"Yes. I suppose one always thinks one's own family ought to be off-limits, no matter how much one claims to inhabit the world of real politik. It's what makes it so confusing, don't you think? Everyone has a family, even Gadhafi, that they think should be off-limits. Everyone has a point of view, and who is to judge which point of view is more reliable or more worthy of protection?"

"And what point of view were you trying to protect by harassing my wife?"

He kept his tone light, but he was upset that I'd one-upped him in a philosophy discussion—he controlled his hands, but he couldn't control a pulse in his temple. I made sure that the breath of relief I exhaled went out very softly indeed.

"My own, Mr. Baladine. With all the money you spent finding out about my whisky preferences, I'm sure you must have put a dollar or two into learning about the State's Attorney's attempt to arrest me for a hit-and-run involving your former nanny. Or was he doing that at your and Jean-Claude Poilevy's request?"

He laughed with a practiced humor that didn't reach his eyes. "I'm honored you have that much respect for my power, but I don't think Nicola's death was anything but an unfortunate accident. She ran away from jail; she got hit by a car. I can't even say I'm sorry: she was a liar and she was a thief. My strongest feeling is annoyance, because my hyper-emotional son is having another tiresome episode over her death."

"Poor Robbie," I said. "Not the son for a manly man. Maybe he was swapped at birth with an artist's child."

Irony was wasted on him; he made a face. "I sometimes think so. His kid sister is twice the man that he is. But you didn't bother my wife to find out whether J.C. and I were framing you, because you didn't know we were friends until you ran into Jennifer out there."

He was rattled by my investigation, or he wouldn't have the chronology so pat in his mind. "I had hoped your wife could tell me something about Ms. Aguinaldo's private life, but she apparently had no interest in a woman who was the most intimate caregiver of her children. Maybe you delved deeper?"

"What's that supposed to mean?" He picked up his water glass but eyed me over the rim as he spoke.

I crossed my legs, smoothing out the crease in the silk—I'd taken time to go home to change before trekking out here. "Carnifice provides in-home surveillance and a reference service for nannies. I assume you employed it when you hired Nicola Aguinaldo."

"It's the old truth about the shoemaker's children, I suppose: we relied on the credentials of the agency we had used in the past. It didn't occur to me that Nicola was illegal. And I knew about her children, of course, but I wasn't interested in any private life she might have had on her days off, as long as it didn't spill over into my family." He forced a smile. "Into my private point of view."

"So you don't know who she would have run to for

help when she escaped last week? No lovers, no one who might have beaten her up?"

"Beaten her up?" he echoed. "I understood she was hit and killed by a car. One other than yours, of course."

"Funny," I said. "Your wife and her friends knew she'd been attacked. If they didn't learn it from you, where did they hear it?"

Once again I could see the pulse jump at his temple, although he put his fingers together and spoke condescendingly. "I'm not going to try to untangle a game of who said what to whom. It's childish and not good investigative work, as I often tell our new operatives. Perhaps I spoke to my wife before I had all the information from the Cook County State's Attorney and the Chicago police. The latest word from them is that she was killed in a hit-and-run."

"Then you should get your team to talk to the doctor who operated on her. Even though her body has disappeared, so the medical examiner can't perform an autopsy, the ER doctor at Beth Israel saw that she'd been killed by a blow that perforated her small intestine. Inconsistent with being hit by a car."

"So all you wanted from Eleanor was a lead on Nicola's private life. I'm sorry we can't help you with that."

"Woman worked for you what—two years?—and you know nothing about who she saw on her days off, but in one afternoon you nail down my whisky preferences? I think you care more about your children's welfare than that."

He chuckled. "Maybe you're more interesting to me than a diaper-changing immigrant."

"She seemed to make a deep impression on your son. That didn't concern you?"

Again his mouth twisted in slight distaste. "Robbie cried when the cat caught a bird. Then he cried when the cat had to be put to sleep. Everything makes a deep impression on him. Military school might help cure that."

Poor kid. I wondered if he knew that lay in his future. "So what did you want with me that entailed my making the journey all the way out here?"

"I wanted to see whether you would make the trip."

I nodded but didn't say anything. His point: to prove he was big and I was small. Let him think he had made it successfully.

"You've been an investigator for sixteen years, Vic." He shifted deliberately to my first name: I was small, he could patronize me. "What keeps you going when your annual billings barely cover your expenses?"

I grinned and stood up. "Idealism and naïveté, Bob. And curiosity, of course, about what happens next."

He leaned against the padded leather of his armchair and crossed his hands behind his head. "You're a good investigator, everyone agrees with that. But they say you have a funny kink in you that keeps you picking up stray dogs and that stops you from making a success of yourself. Haven't you ever thought about giving up your solo practice and coming to work for—well, an outfit like mine? You wouldn't have to worry about overhead. You'd even have a fully funded retirement plan."

"This isn't a job offer, by any chance?"

"Something for you to think about. Not an offer. What would you do if outfits like Continental United stopped tossing you their small jobs? We handle their big ones already; they might agree to roll everything into one package with us, after all."

My constant nightmare, but I made myself laugh, hoping the smile reached my eyes. "I'd cash in my CD's and go live in Italy for a while."

"You don't have enough CD's to live on."

"Your people have been thorough, haven't they? I guess I'd hang out in the alley and share a bone with the rest of the strays. Maybe chew on your old shoes—you know, if you've got a Ferragamo loafer missing its little tag and you're thinking of throwing it out anyway."

He stared at me without speaking. Before I could poke any deeper, Claudia came in to say that his Tokyo call was waiting for him.

I smiled. "Catch you later, Bob."

"Yes, Ms. Warshawski. I can guarantee our paths will cross."

The young woman who'd brought me up was waiting in the hall to escort me back down. To keep me from getting lost? Or to keep me from filching some of Carnifice's high-tech gadgetry and using it to steal their clients? I asked her, but of course company policy forbade her telling me.

13

Saturday at the Mall

THE LAST DREGS of light were staining the western sky pink when I got home. I took the dogs for a walk, then sat chatting in the backyard with Mr. Contreras until the mosquitoes drove us inside. All the time we were discussing whether the Cubs could stay alive in a race for the playoffs, whether Max and Lotty would ever get married, if a lump on Peppy's chest required a trip to the vet, I kept wondering what the real story of Nicola Aguinaldo's death was.

Something about it worried Baladine enough to pull me out to Oak Brook and alternately threaten and bribe me. Maybe his only agenda was to flex his muscles in my face, but I thought he was too sophisticated for simple acts of thuggery. Had my last idle remark, about his shoes, really caught him off guard, or was it my imagination?

And who had claimed Nicola Aguinaldo's body so pat? Was it her mother—or had it been Baladine, trying to prevent Vishnikov from performing an autopsy? That seemed hard to imagine, since the body wasn't claimed until late Wednesday night, and Vishnikov might well have made his examination as soon as Aguinaldo's remains arrived.

"Whatcha thinking about, doll? I asked you three

times if you wanted any grappa, and you're staring into space like there was UFO's flying past the window."

"That poor young woman in the road," I said. "What is so important about her? You'd think she was a fugitive Iraqi dissident or something, the way she's become the focus of so much attention."

Mr. Contreras was glad to talk it over with me, but after an hour of thrashing out the events of the week I didn't feel I had any more insight into what was going on. I finally told him I'd have to sleep on it and stumped slowly up to bed. It wasn't even ten o'clock, but I was too worn out to do anything but sleep.

Saturday I woke so early that I was able to get a proper run in before the heat settled on the city. I even took the dogs swimming and still was out of the shower by eight.

Of the women around the Baladine pool two days ago, the most approachable seemed to be Global magnate Teddy Trant's wife. Maybe I could catch up with her someplace in the morning.

It was a pain having all my computing capability at the office. If Carnifice took over my little operation, I suppose Baladine would pay me enough to install a terminal at home. Until then I had to trundle down to Leavitt to look up the Trant family. I didn't want to spend the time or money on the kind of search I'd done on Baladine yesterday—all I wanted was Mrs. Trant's name and home address. Her first name was Abigail, she used her husband's last name, and they lived four miles northwest of the Baladines with their nine-year-old daughter, Rhiannon. I packed binoculars, picked up a couple of daily papers and a copy of *Streetwise* from Elton, and once again pointed the Rustmobile toward the Eisenhower and the western suburbs.

As soon as I got to Thornfield Demesne I realized the Skylark was badly suited for surveillance. For one thing it stood out hideously against the Range Rovers and other all-terrain vehicles needed to navigate the perilous ground between mansion and mall. More to the point, you can't park on these leafy winding roads in front of the gated communities out here. The demesne's entrance was protected by a guard station that would have put the old Berlin Wall to shame. Not only that, a private security patrol—probably from Carnifice—periodically sent out a cruiser, no doubt to pick riffraff like me up and throw us back across the border.

I drove to a curve in the road about fifty feet from the entrance and pulled my maps out—I could probably pretend one time to the security patrol that I was lost. With the maps propped up on the steering wheel, I tried using my binoculars, but all I could see were tree leaves. If I was really going to survey the place, I needed a horse, or maybe a bicycle. I was on the point of driving to the nearest mall to see if I could rent one—preferably a bike, since I'd never been on a horse—when I had a bit of luck. The great wrought gates of the demesne opened, and the Mercedes Gelaendewagen with the GLOBAL 2 plates shot out.

I wrenched the Buick into a clumsy U-turn and followed at a discreet distance. Once we got onto a main road I let a few cars get in between me and Abigail. To my relief she drove past all the entrances to the Oak Brook shopping mall—I couldn't imagine trying to engineer a meeting with her in there. We'd gone south a couple of miles when the Mercedes turned at a sign announcing the Leafy Vale Stables. It looked as though I could get my wish for a horse after all.

Fortunately, the leafy vale lay on the far side of the

stables and house; I could see the Mercedes clearly from the road. I parked on the verge and watched as the little girl from the Baladine pool jumped out of the passenger seat. Abigail Trant climbed out and escorted her toward one of the buildings. The child was wearing riding clothes, but the mother had on knee-length shorts and a body-hugging top. Mother seemed to be giving directions to a woman who cocked her head deferentially. Abigail Trant kissed her daughter and climbed back into her sports utility tank. I drove a little further and backed the Rustmobile onto the verge where I could turn in either direction. The Mercedes turned toward Oak Brook.

My heart sank when she headed into the mall. It's one thing to strike up a conversation over the produce counter, quite another in the middle of the couture salon at Neiman Marcus. I followed her gamely, parking a few cars beyond the Mercedes on the east side of the mall, and trailed behind her to the Parruca Salon. Parruca had a grand set of double doors. They were lined on the inside with red leather. I was able to detect that when a doorman opened them and greeted Abigail Trant by name. The doors closed as she asked after him with the graciousness of the true grande dame.

Short of pretending to be the new shampooer, I could hardly follow her while she had her weekly hair appointment. I wondered how long beautification took. At least long enough for me to wander into the maze of shops in search of a bathroom and a tall iced tea.

After half an hour I came back outside and waited with my newspaper. There wasn't anyplace to sit, since you're not supposed to be outside a mall—you're supposed to be inside buying. As the sun rose toward the middle of the sky, the shade cast by the buildings became a thin wedge. I pushed my shoulders against the stone wall separating Parruca from the sportswear shop to its south and tried to pay attention to the problems besetting Kosovo.

Teenagers swarmed past me, chattering about hair, clothes, boys, girls. Solitary shoppers strode past, their faces set in grim lines, as though buying were an onerous duty. Every now and then the doorman opened Parruca's red leather doors to decant a client or admit a new one. Finally, when my shirt was so soaked with sweat that I thought I'd have to slip into the sportswear shop to get a fresh one, Abigail Trant came out.

"We'll see you next week, Mrs. Trant," the doorman said, gracefully pocketing her tip.

I unglued my shoulders from the wall. Her honey-streaked hair was carefully combed into the right suggestion of windblown disorder, her makeup painted on with a subtle hand, her nails a gleaming pearl. To approach her in my sweaty sunburned state seemed almost sacrilegious, but I did it anyway.

She was startled but didn't run shrieking for a security guard. Yes, her pleasant face showing no disdain, she certainly remembered my visit to Eleanor Baladine's pool two days ago. But it was all she could do to keep track of her own daughter's nanny—she certainly didn't know anything about Eleanor's.

"And you know, Teddy and I didn't move back to the Chicago area until eighteen months ago, so that girl who was killed the other day wasn't even around then. I'm afraid I can't answer any questions about her."

"Can you take ten minutes for a cup of coffee and answer a few other questions?"

A dimple appeared briefly at the corner of her

mouth. "I've never been interrogated by a detective—maybe it will help me understand how to respond to the girls I'm sponsoring for the You Can Do It Foundation. Many of them seem to have been arrested before reaching high school, although usually for shoplifting." She looked at her wrist. "I have just about fifteen minutes before my next engagement."

The coffee bar was so mobbed we didn't bother waiting for drinks but perched at the high counter. Mrs. Trant readily stepped me through a few basics—she had grown up not too far from here, gone to school with Jennifer Poilevy, had been thrilled when Global sent her and her husband back from Los Angeles to the Midwest.

"L.A. is a difficult place to raise a child. Everyone is on perpetual display, and the kids get sucked into that precocious environment far too young. Out here Rhiannon can simply be a child."

With her swimming exercises, her horse, and all those other accoutrements of the simple life. But I wanted help, so I kept my sardonic observations to myself.

"It doesn't seem as though Eleanor Baladine's children have that same freedom," I said. "Although I guess the girls are following her swimming regimen pretty enthusiastically."

"I admire Eleanor, I really do. She's lucky to have a gift that absorbs her so completely. And she's wonderful to take Rhiannon under her wing, especially since Rhiannon's started to outperform Madison. But I think it's a mistake to push children too hard. When they get to adolescence that can come back to haunt you, you know."

I grunted noncommittally. "You said that you grew

up with Jennifer Poilevy. Was Eleanor Baladine part of your childhood as well?"

Looking briefly at her watch, Abigail Trant explained she'd gotten to know Eleanor before they moved to Oak Brook when their husbands started doing business together four years ago. "BB was solving a lot of Global's security problems, and the two of them seemed to hit it off. And of course, Jean-Claude Poilevy has been incredibly helpful to us since we moved out here."

I could imagine how helpful the Illinois Speaker could be to someone with money to fling in his direction—zoning regulations bent, tax breaks for Global, a special deal on the mansion in Thornfield Demesne. "I know the prison notified Baladine as soon as Nicola Aguinaldo got away, so Eleanor knew all about her death before I showed up. Do you have any hunches about why she was so rattled?"

Abigail shrugged. "It's hard when violence comes close to your children, and the girl had been her children's nanny."

I smiled in a way I hoped invited bad-girl chat. "But really—I know she's your friend and you've known her for years—watching her with her son, she doesn't strike me as the warmly concerned mother."

Abigail smiled back but refused to play. "BB is such an athletic man, and his naval service was the most important part of his life. It's understandable he wants his only son to follow his path, and that may blind him and Eleanor to how hard they are on him. And it's a tough world for a boy these days, it would be better if he could develop the ability to compete in it. If that's all you need to know, I have to get going. We have twenty people coming to dinner and the caterer is going to need directions from me."

She slid from her stool; I followed and said, "BB called me out to his office last night to threaten to put me out of business for asking questions about how his kid's old nanny died. Do you have any idea why?"

She paused next to her stool. A teenager demanded to know whether we could make up our minds—were we going or staying—other people are waiting for seats, you know. The rudeness made Abigail Trant lean a hand on her stool and say we'd be through in a minute. The teenager gave an exasperated sigh and swung around, deliberately hitting Trant with her bag.

"Mall brats," Abigail Trant said. "Why Rhiannon is not allowed to hang out here—I don't want her acquiring these manners. Tell me a little about your business. I gather you're not as big as Carnifice."

Thank heaven for mall brats—Trant would be in her Mercedes by now if she hadn't wanted to stomp on the kid. I gave her a thumbnail sketch of the difference between Warshawski Investigations and Carnifice Security. Something about it piqued a genuine interest from her—she forgot about the time and asked me how I'd gotten into detection, what special training I'd needed, how long I'd been doing it.

"Do you enjoy having your own business? Doing all the work yourself, do you ever have time for a private life?"

I admitted a private life was hard for me to maintain. "Since I have to work for a living, I'm happier working for myself than I would be in a big outfit like Carnifice. Anyway, I like knowing that it's my work that's solved a problem."

"Do you think BB could put you out of business?"

I hunched an impatient shoulder. "I don't know. But I'm curious to know why my asking questions about his kid's old nanny makes him want to."

She tapped the wooden counter with one pearl-colored nail. "I don't think there's any special mystery about the dead girl. I think it has to do with BB's personality. You came to his house, you interrogated his wife and his son, and it makes him feel that you proved he was vulnerable. He's threatening you so he can feel better about the fact that a private detective with a very small company could penetrate his security systems." She looked at her watch and gave a little gasp. "The time! I really have to run now."

She threaded her way expertly through the crowds of shoppers. Everything about Abigail Trant depressed me —her polished good looks and manners, the fact that she had stiffed me half a dozen times with perfect good manners, and the possibility she could be right about Nicola Aguinaldo. She was only thirty-five, but she could dance rings about me—no wonder she was entertaining important guests in Oak Brook and I was taking my sweaty body back to my un-air-conditioned car.

14

Crumbs from the Table

WHEN I GOT back to the city I was too worn out by the heat to go to my office. I'd been planning on buckling down on my project for Continental United, but I went home and showered and lay down.

As I dozed through the midday heat my conversation with Abigail Trant kept coming into my dreams. In some of them she was sweetly commiserating because my work interfered with my social life. In others she was standing on the sidelines as BB Baladine threatened me. I woke for good from a nightmare in which Baladine was choking me while Abigail Trant said, "I told you he didn't like to be threatened."

"But I wasn't threatening him," I said aloud. "It was the other way around." And what was I supposed to do, back away from Baladine because he interpreted any approach as aggression? Anyway, maybe Abigail Trant was right about Baladine's character, but I thought there was more to the story than that—some issue about Nicola Aguinaldo, either her life or her death. Perhaps when she escaped from prison she approached Baladine and he interpreted that as a threat, knocked her out, then ran over her. As he got back into his car the emblem came off his loafer. My research said

he was a Porsche man. I wondered if his Carrera had
been in a body shop lately.

It was all a load of speculative nonsense. Except for
the fact that Nicola Aguinaldo was dead. I wished I
could talk to her mother. Why had Abuelita Mercedes
disappeared so suddenly just at the time her daughter
died? Maybe if I went back to Aguinaldo's neighborhood I could find the mysterious Mr. Morrell, the man
asking questions about people who escaped from jail. I
made myself an espresso to cut through the dopiness I
felt from dozing in the heat, and got dressed again.

I dumped my sweaty jeans in the hamper and chose
my outfit carefully—Abigail Trant had made me feel
like a grubby hulk. I laughed at myself, a little shame-
faced, but still put on clean linen slacks with a big white
shirt, even dabbing on lipstick and powder. The result
didn't approach Ms. Trant's perfection: a polished appearance is like any other skill—you have to work at it
a lot to be good. Maybe weekly visits to Parruca's
would help, too.

Saturday is errand day in Uptown just as in Oak
Brook, but the girls here were doing chores, not taking
riding lessons. When I rang Mrs. Attar's bell, a sullen
Mina, huffy at having to dust, came to the door. The
girls had mentioned someone named Aisha; it was Aisha's father Morrell was talking to. After some grumbling, Mina directed me to the other girl's apartment,
two doors up the street.

Aisha's father was home, looking after a small boy
who was wearing only a diaper. The man greeted me
with unsmiling reserve and didn't move out of the doorway. In stilted but passable English he demanded to
know what business of mine it was whether he had a
daughter named Aisha? When I explained my errand,

the man shook his head. He was afraid the neighborhood girls liked to tease strangers. He didn't know anyone named Morrell. His wife might have known a woman named—what was it? Abuelita Mercedes?—but she was at the market; the name meant nothing to him. And now if I would excuse him he was very busy. I handed him a card, with a request to call me if he ever heard from Mr. Morrell. It fluttered to the floor in front of him, where I left it.

It was humiliating to be mistaken for an INS officer. Or an agent of a foreign secret-police force. I didn't know which would be worse.

There might have been something more profitable I could have done with the rest of the afternoon, but I went home and worked on personal projects, matting some prints I'd picked up at a flea market. One of the pictures showed a young woman about Aguinaldo's age. She was partly dressed, in a kind of camisole, and was staring at a window; what I liked about the picture was the reflection of her face in the glass.

I started wondering about the shirtdress Aguinaldo had been wearing. The lab's report had explained only how they'd tested the outside of the fabric for automobile traces. Maybe the inside of the shirt could tell me something about how Nicola Aguinaldo had died.

I was actually feeling edgy enough to try the lab. Of course no one was answering on a Saturday afternoon. I worked my way through the voice menu and left a message in the mailbox of the guy who had signed the report on the Trans Am.

Sunday morning I went out with the dogs for another early swim, keeping an eye open for Lemour. Back home I told Mr. Contreras I would take Peppy to the office with me for company. I assured him I'd be back by four: he and the dogs and I were joining Mary Louise and her foster sons for a picnic. Mary Louise and I get together once a week to go over work; this week we'd decided to combine it with a family outing.

"Okay, doll, okay. You got a water dish down there? It's too hot for the princess to go all day without drinking."

I bit back a sharp retort. "Her comfort is my main object in life. And my office is air-conditioned. I hope no animal-rights people are out throwing yellow paint on her today, because she just won't give up that big old fur coat, not even in June, will you, girl?"

Peppy grinned in happy agreement and clattered down the stairs with me, her tail waving a pointed put-down at Mitch, left at home with my neighbor. At my office she ran first to Tessa Reynolds's studio. Tessa is a sculptor. These days she was working with marble; the dust made her short dreadlocks glitter under her bright lights. She waved a muscular forearm at me, gave the dog a quick scratch, but was too deep in her work to take a break.

If Tessa wouldn't stop to talk I had no choice but to go to work myself. While my computer came up I pulled out my phone books and started calling everyone in the metropolitan area named Morrell. I didn't try anything smart—just the unvarnished truth: V. I. Warshawski, private investigator, looking for the man asking questions of immigrants in Uptown. Of course half the people weren't home, but those who were either didn't know what I was talking about or affected not to.

"Enough, Warshawski, get to the stuff you know you need to do," I muttered, inserting a CD-ROM with a cross-directory for Georgia phones and addresses.

Checking phone numbers was mindless work; my thoughts kept creeping back to Aguinaldo. Baladine said she'd faked an illness to get sent to the hospital. Mary Louise said the prison had reported an ovarian cyst. Did Baladine know that was faked? Or that the report was a fake?

When I was with the public defender, my clients found it impossible to get medical care. One man with lymphoma had a tumor constricting his diaphragm and died in solitary for causing a disturbance when he tried to summon help. It was hard to believe that Coolis was so tender of their charges that Aguinaldo could have faked an illness. And once she'd fled the hospital, how had she gotten to Chicago so fast?

I put down my notes on Georgia and went to the cupboard to pull my Illinois county maps. Peppy, lying under a table, half-sat up to see whether I was leaving. She lay down again when I returned to my desk.

The hospital in Coolis sat on the northwest end of the town, the prison side, where growth was fastest. If Aguinaldo had left in a supply or laundry truck, they would have gone out the service road, which followed Smallpox Creek. I squinted through my magnifying glass to bring up the details. Assuming she'd hopped off the truck before it reached the town center, she had limited choices—she could follow Smallpox Creek on foot north to Lake Galena or try to hitch a ride on Route 113, which led from the hospital past the prison as well as northeast away from the town.

There was only one crossroads between the hospital and the prison, Hollow Glen Road, which intersected again with 113 a mile north and another state road a mile south. It might be worthwhile to see if someone picked her up—assuming Robert Baladine hadn't been waiting at Hollow Glen Road in his Porsche. Those queries were ones that only the police or state marshals had the resources to undertake. I put the map down in frustration.

I went back to my paying client's work and forced myself to stay with it, copying numbers into a file, then laying them across a blowup of the area where Continental United's trucks were coming to grief. I was hard at it when Tessa popped her head around my door.

"Your friend Murray is outside—he rang my bell by mistake. Shall I let him in? He's brought some talent with him."

My brows shot up in surprise, but I followed her to the front door. Murray was outside with Alex Fisher. She had on skintight jeans and a big mesh shirt, which revealed not only her Lycra tube-top but the sharp points of her breastbone. As she and Murray came in, I glanced at Alex-Sandy's feet, but of course if she owned Ferragamos with a missing emblem she wouldn't have them on.

Murray stopped to talk to Tessa. "Sorry you couldn't make it to the Glow Tuesday night. You missed a great evening."

Tessa gave him the kind of polite brush-off she'd learned from her years jetting around the world with her wealthy parents. I always envy someone who doesn't have to go to the jugular. As I promptly did.

"Sandy—sorry I didn't recognize you right away Tuesday night. You looked a lot different when you were urging us all to the barricades back in law school."

She flashed an empty smile. "I'm Alex now, not Sandy—another one of the changes in my life."

She surveyed my office with frank interest. I'd divided my share of the warehouse into smaller spaces with pasteboard partitions, not because I need a lot of rooms but because I wanted some human scale to the place. Aside from that and good quality lighting, I hadn't invested heavily in furnishings.

Alex-Sandy seemed to be preening herself, perhaps imagining her own office by contrast, when her eyes widened at a painting on the partition facing my desk. "Isn't that an Isabel Bishop? How did you come by it?"

"I stole it from the Art Institute. Do you want to sit down? Would you like something to drink?" An elderly woman whose grandson had been stripping her assets gave me the Bishop in lieu of a fee, but that didn't seem to be any of Alex-Sandy's business.

"Oh, Vic, you always had a bizarre sense of humor. It's coming back to me now. Do you have Malvern water? It's hideously hot out—I'd forgotten Chicago summers."

"Malvern?" I stopped on my way to the refrigerator. "Did you introduce BB Baladine to that, or the other way around?"

"I didn't know you knew Bob. I think it's something we probably both learned from Teddy Trant. He spends a lot of time in England. Do you have any?" It was said smoothly, and it was even plausible.

She sat on a stool next to the table where Peppy was lying. The dog had gotten up to greet her and Murray, but something in my tone must have sounded a warning, because she crawled under my desk.

I offered Alex-Sandy a choice of tap water or Poland Springs, which is cheap and no different from the foreign imports as far as I can tell. Murray took iced tea, which Tessa makes fresh and drinks by the gallon when she's working. We share a refrigerator out in the hall and write scrupulous notes about who's taken what from whose shelves.

"Murray says you've become a private investigator," Sandy said when I'd sat at my desk. "It seems like strange work for someone with your education. Did you get tired of the law? I can totally understand that, but my own fantasies run more to retiring to a ranch."

"You know how it goes, Sandy—Alex—middle age comes on and you revert to your roots. You left the barricades for the boardroom; I couldn't stay away from my cop-father's blue-collar work." I turned to Murray. "Sandy was always on my butt for not joining protest movements with her. She kept telling me that a blue-collar girl—whatever that is—should be in the forefront of organizing struggles."

"You have to learn to move on from those old battles. These are the nineties, after all. Anyway, Murray suggested your name when we were mulling over how to help Lacey with a sticky situation."

A crumb from the Global table. Maybe Murray had been as embarrassed as I by our conversation the other night and was trying a subtle amend. I could see him at dinner with Alex-Sandy. At the Filigree, or perhaps Justin's, the hot new hole on west Randolph, Murray leaning across the table toward Alex's modest cleavage: *You know, V.I., you know what a prickly bitch she's always been. But she did the legwork on a couple of the stories that built my reputation and I hate to leave her standing in the dust. Isn't there something Global needs that would give her a break?*

"Global has a gazillion lawyers, detectives, and strong-armed types to protect their stars." I wasn't hungry enough yet for a crumb, I guess.

"It's a little trickier than that," Murray said, "at least as I understand it. Since you were at the Glow on Tuesday, maybe you saw the problem."

"Lucian Frenada," Alex said briskly. "He and Lacey had a boy–girl kind of understanding twenty years ago, and he won't accept that it's over, that Lacey's moved on and he has to also."

I stared at her blankly. "And?"

"And we want you to make that clear to him, clear that he has to stop harassing her, calling her, or hunting her out in public." Alex spoke with an irritability that definitely hadn't changed from her old harangues.

"I don't do bodyguard work. I'm a one-woman shop. I have people I call on for support, but if you want guaranteed protection you need to go to an outfit like Carnifice."

"It's not a bodyguard kind of situation." Alex looked around for a table and put her drink on the couch next to her. "She says she's not afraid of him, but that he's embarrassing her."

I made a face. "Murray, if this was your idea of a favor, take it somewhere else. If she's not afraid of him, she can talk to him. If he's bugging her, the studio has the muscle to make him back off."

"You didn't used to be stupid in law school," Alex snapped. "If it was that simple we'd be doing it. They were childhood friends, stood up for each other when the rest of the street harassed them for being geeks. She can't bear for his feelings to be hurt, because he rescued her at least once from some serious bangers in the stairwell. Beyond that, the guy is a kind of model enterprise-zone leader. If it looks like a big corporation is persecuting him, we'll have a lot of hostility in the

Spanish press, and of course that would be damaging for Lacey's image."

Murray was fidgeting with his glass. Something about the picture was making him ill at ease, whether Alex's condescension or my snappishness or the assignment as a whole I had no way of knowing.

"He owns a business?" I asked. "What kind?"

"Gimmicky clothes," Murray said. "Uniforms for kids' teams, specialty T-shirts, that sort of thing. He started out doing the soccer uniforms at St. Remigio's and moved on. He employs a lot of people right there in the neighborhood. On their old street he's the second-biggest hero, right behind Lacey."

"So what do you want me to do? Burn down his factory so that he has so much to worry about he leaves Lacey alone?" To my annoyance, Alex-Sandy seemed to be considering this smart-ass suggestion. "Lacey's going back to Hollywood, he's staying here, it's not a problem."

"It's image, Vic," Alex snapped. "Lacey's going to be in town for eight weeks—they're shooting *Virgin Six* here this summer. We can't have him harassing her, and we can't put him down hard. Why don't you look into his affairs, see if he's cut some corners someplace, see if we can't offer him a little quid pro quo: leave Lacey alone and we won't report you. If you turned up something, Global would be very grateful, and they have the resources to express their gratitude."

I leaned back in my chair and studied them. Murray had stopped playing with his glass in favor of mutilating his napkin. Gray balls of wet paper were falling on his jeans. Alex was staring at me with an arrogant impatience that I found exasperating.

"I'm not manufacturing evidence of a crime or misdemeanor, even if it means so much to Global they give me the residuals for *Virgin Six*."

"Of course not, Vic." Alex bristled. "I'm not asking for that—but for you to fish. What's your usual fee?"

"A hundred an hour plus nonoverhead expenses."

She laughed. "I'd forgotten how honest you always were. Most people double or triple a number when a studio lawyer comes to visit."

Meaning a hundred was so low it had to be the truth.

"We'll double your fee if you'll make this a priority. And throw in a high five-figure bonus if you come up with something we can use. Here are Frenada's addresses and phone numbers."

"Not so fast, Sandy." Like Aisha's father this morning, I let the proferred paper fall between us. "I need to think it over, and I'd have to talk to Ms. Dowell to see if she has the same take on the story you do."

Alex-Sandy pursed her lips. "We'd rather Lacey wasn't involved."

My jaw dropped. "If she's not involved, then what on God's green earth is all this fuss about?"

Murray coughed, a deferential sign so out of his normal character that my irritability increased. "Vic, let me put it bluntly. You can talk to Lacey, of course, and get her read on Frenada. What we're trying to avoid, or what Global is trying to avoid, is any hint that they're beating up on Lacey's old friends.

"No one wants you to manufacture anything. And no one who knows you would imagine that you ever would. As I made clear to Alex when we were talking about this last night. But if you do find something that the studio can use as a bargaining chip with Frenada, then we'd—they'd—prefer Lacey didn't know it was because of Global that things got resolved. And we don't want it in the papers."

"Seems to me Teddy Trant can decide that," I said, not trying to keep sarcasm out of my voice.

"Teddy only controls one paper and one television station, and anyway, the business side doesn't dictate to the editorial," Alex-Sandy said.

"Yeah, and the pope has no effect on the parish churches around here. I'll think about it and let you know. Of course, if I agree to work on it, Global signs the contract. Not you. And not Murray as your front man." I barely kept "your stooge" from popping out.

"Come on, Vic, you know me. And Murray's a witness."

"We're going to flap our little Phoenix neckties and shout the Chicago fight song to prove our loyalty to each other? We went to law school on the South Side of Chicago, not to Eton. Maybe the South Side has stuck to me more than the law, but one of the things Professor Carmichael pounded into our heads was the importance of written contracts for business agreements."

Her wide mouth flattened into a hard line, but at last she said, "Think it over. I'll call you tomorrow morning."

"I'm not making a decision that fast. I have some urgent projects in hand that I have to finish before I can consider yours. Which is why I'm working on a Sunday. By the way, Murray, what made you drop by here today? You can't possibly have expected to find me in."

Alex answered for him. "Oh, we stopped at your apartment first, but the old man said you were here. I'll call you tomorrow."

"I can't wait to hear his description of you. As

Murray can tell you, it's likely to be colorful and unstinting."

Why did I have to show hackle every time my fur was ruffled? No sooner had I asked myself that pointed question than I called to Murray, who was following Alex-Sandy through the door, "Was it Justin's or Filigree where you cooked this up?"

He turned and cocked a sandy eyebrow at me. "You wouldn't be showing some jealousy there, would you, Warshawski?"

15

Family Picnic

I STARED AT the computer for a while, but I couldn't summon any enthusiasm for the Georgia trucking problem. Murray's last remark rankled. Which meant there might be a grain of truth to it. Not that I was jealous of women he dated, danced, slept with. But we'd worked together for so long we had the shared jokes and short-cuts of old comrades. It did hurt to see him more in tune with someone like Alex Fisher-Fishbein than me. I had character, after all. All she had was power, money, and glamour.

Murray was an investigative reporter. He had the same sources I did—sometimes even better ones—for uncovering dope on entrepreneurs around town. Maybe he was offering Frenada to me as a chance to make some real money. Or because he felt guilty for selling himself to Global. Maybe I should be grateful, but all I felt was queasy.

Alex's reason for coming to me instead of the studio's usual security detail made a kind of sense, but not enough. When I'd talked to Frenada briefly at the Golden Glow, he'd seemed personable, quiet, not a masher. Still, one is forever reading about serial killers who seemed quiet and normal to their neighbors. And it's true, I myself had watched Frenada accost Lacey in the middle of the Golden Glow. If he was really a stalker, then Alex was being pretty cavalier about danger to Lacey. If he wasn't, then Global had some agenda that was going to get me in a pack of trouble if I took on their dirty work.

Frenada had said at the party that maybe I could help him—that something odd was happening in his office. My own upheaval around Nicola Aguinaldo had driven my conversation with him far from my mind. Now I wondered if Global was already doing something to discredit him. If he'd stumbled on their plan, and Global realized it, Alex might be trying to bring me in as fresh bait on the line.

I logged on to LifeStory and requested a check on Frenada, not so much because I'd decided to take the job as to look for some context around the guy. To understand his character, I'd do better to talk to the people who knew him, but I couldn't afford to spend time with his employees or his priest or whoever in Humboldt Park if I wasn't going to take the job.

As I tried to make up a list of tasks for Mary Louise and me to split on the Georgia inquiry, I couldn't help thinking of Alex's remark, that if I did the work she wanted, Global had the resources to express their gratitude. A bonus in the high five figures. I wondered how high. Fifty thousand would not only get me a new car but let me build a cushion, maybe hire someone full-time instead of relying on Mary Louise's erratic hours. Or what if it were seventy or eighty thousand? Murray was driving a powder-blue Mercedes these days; I could pick up that red Jaguar XJ-12 I'd seen in the ads on Wednesday.

"And that's how they catch their fish," I admonished

myself out loud. "If you can be bought for the price of a used car, V.I., then you're not worth owning."

I worked hard for another couple of hours, stopping only once, to go out for a sandwich and to let Peppy relieve herself. After that I didn't look up until Tessa came in around three-thirty.

"Mary Louise hasn't been in for a while," she commented, perching on the couch arm.

"You keeping an eye on the premises?"

She grinned. "No, doofus. You aren't the only detective around here: when Mary Louise comes in she always tidies up the papers. I'm taking off. Want to go for a coffee?"

I looked at the clock. I told her I'd have to take a rain check so I could get back to pick up Mr. Contreras. I started my system backup program and began hunting through the heap on my desk for the report Max had faxed over from Beth Israel: I wanted to discuss it with Mary Louise. I'd forgotten stuffing the papers into the folder labeled *Alumni Fund* but came on it by the sophisticated method of going through all the folders I'd stacked up lately.

I pulled out the report the paramedics had filed with the hospital. It described where they'd found Aguinaldo, what steps they'd taken to stabilize her, and the time they'd delivered her to Beth Israel (3:14 A.M.), but not the names of the officers who'd talked to Mary Louise and me in Edgewater. I wondered if I needed to know badly enough to pay for Mary Louise to talk to the ambulance crew and see if they remembered the guys. But I didn't know how else to start finding out whether Baladine or Poilevy had been pulling the strings that made the cops come after me.

"I'm going to take a shower. And neatly put away

all my tools," Tessa added pointedly as I dropped the folder back on the heap of papers: if Mary Louise were working on it she'd have typed up a label on the spot and stuck it in the drawer with other pending cases.

"Yeah, you always were teacher's pet. It ain't going anywhere, but I am." I shut down my system for the day and stuffed a second copy of the backup program in my briefcase. It was the second thing my old hacker friend had taught me—always keep a copy of your programs off the premises. You never think your office is the one that will be burgled or burned to the ground.

Tessa, her hair heavy from her shower, was locking her studio when I came into the hall. She had changed into a gold sundress of some kind of soft expensive cotton. I wondered if a ten-thousand-dollar wardrobe could make me look as good as her or Abigail Trant. The two came from similar worlds—fancy private schools, fathers successful entrepreneurs. Probably the only difference was their mothers—Tessa's had broken through the white male barricades into a major law career.

"Not to be a feline, but I always thought Murray liked softer women than that bionic specimen he brought in today," Tessa remarked as she set the alarm code. "He was kind of preening when he introduced us, so I take it they weren't making a business call?"

"Not the Bionic Woman—a Space Beret." When she looked puzzled, I said, "I can tell there aren't any small boys in your life. That's Global Studio's movie-cartoon-comic-book and megabillion-dollar action figure. The woman is one of their lawyers. When we were in school together she was Sandy Fishbein and led sit-ins. Now that she's Alexandra Fisher and sits on boards, I get confused about how to think about her or what to call her. She's seduced Murray, and now they're trying for a ménage à trois with me."

"I never trust a woman who gets all her muscles at the health club and only uses them as an accessory to her wardrobe," Tessa announced, flexing her own arms, sinewy from years of hammering on stone and metal.

I laughed and waved at her as she climbed into her pickup—one of those fancy modern ones with leather seats, air-conditioning, and perfect suspension. Seen next to it, the Skylark looked more decrepit than ever. I felt another unwelcome twist of jealousy. I wouldn't have traded either of my parents for the wealthiest tycoons in the West, but every now and then I wished my legacy had included more than the five-room bungalow whose sale after my father's death barely covered his medical bills.

The thought of Abigail Trant made me wonder if she'd played a role in sending Alex and Murray to me. Something about my operation had roused her full interest. Maybe she'd gone to Teddy. Playing with his tie as they dressed to receive their important guests: *Teddy, you know that woman that BB is so riled about? I think she's worth helping. Let's send her some work.* So maybe I should think about the offer more carefully. At least find out if Frenada really was harassing Lacey Dowell.

When I got to the apartment I ran upstairs to call Mary Louise's house. Emily answered, saying Mary Louise had already left for our picnic.

"That's okay. It's your expertise I want right now. Do you know where Lacey Dowell is staying while they're shooting *Virgin Six*?"

"You're not trying to prove she committed some kind of crime, are you?" Emily demanded.

"No. Someone was saying an old friend of hers was harassing her. I want to talk to her doorman and see if it's true."

She thought it over and decided it was an innocuous enough reason to reveal her heroine's whereabouts: a suite at the Trianon, a luxury hotel on the tip of the Gold Coast that overlooks the cardinal's residence on one side and Lake Michigan on the other. A nice change from the corner of North and California, where Lacey had grown up.

"Thanks, honey. You're not coming out with us this afternoon? Mr. Contreras is going to provide the food."

She mumbled something about having to see her father. "He's got a new girlfriend. He wants us to be friends before I leave for France."

"You don't have to do it if you don't want to," I reminded her.

"Yeah. I guess. Anyway, I'm flying on Wednesday, so I might as well tell him good-bye."

I don't suppose you ever outgrow the hope that your parent, however vile and violating he may have been, will magically turn into someone who cares about you. I turned sadly to join Mr. Contreras and the dogs in my car.

In the event, I had a pleasant outing. We joined Mary Louise and the boys in a forest preserve on the northwest side. Over a meal Mr. Contreras had created with boys in mind—fried chicken, potato chips, chocolate cupcakes, and marshmallows—Mary Louise and I went through the list of jobs that had come in this week. I had a half dozen background checks that were her main contribution to my work and a few other odds and ends, but I really wanted to talk to her about Alex-Sandy's offer and my meeting with Baladine.

"You don't need me to tell you not to touch that Global assignment," she said. "I hope your pal Murray isn't signing on for some real sleaze with them: that job sounds pretty bogus. As far as I can tell, your only reason for taking it on is to see what Murray is up to—and that's not enough reward for maybe getting hung out to dry by one of the biggest laundries in America."

I sat back on my heels, blushing—I didn't know I was that transparent. "It's not only that. What if Abigail Trant stuck an oar in to try to keep Baladine from swallowing me up?"

Mary Louise snorted. "What if she did? Are you supposed to fall over and slobber on her manicured toenails? Come on, Vic. This isn't a job, it's a setup. You know that as well as me."

She was right. Probably right. I didn't need the aggravation of being spun around by an outfit as slick as Global.

"But the Aguinaldo business is different," I said. "That's having a direct effect on me, what with that creep Lemour, and the State's Attorney panting for me to take a fall. Will you check with the paramedics to see if they can remember the officers who came to the scene that night?"

"I can do it, but it's a question of money, Vic. You pay me, remember, so even if it's pro bono for you, it's not for me. I think it's an unnecessary detail right now, given your budget. You have plenty else going on. You told me the evidence from Cheviot Labs on your car got the SA to back off. Let it go for now. I'll make those Georgia phone calls for you in the morning, but you know as well as I that there's a trip south of the Mason–Dixon line in your future: I can't leave town with those two monsters on my hand." She gestured toward Nate and Joshua, playing Frisbee with the dogs.

She bit her lip, the way people do when they're deciding to say something you don't want to hear, then burst out, "Vic, there's a kernel of truth in what Baladine said to you. About you going after strays all the time—only I call them wild-goose chases. You gnash your teeth over how you're always hard up for money, but you've got the contacts and the skills to build a big agency. It's just there's something in you that doesn't want to go corporate. Every time it's about to happen you get involved in a story like Aguinaldo's, and *phht,* there goes your chance to grow your business."

"Grow my business?" I faked a punch at her. "You sound like a business-school manual."

She started shadowboxing me, and pretty soon we were chasing each other around the park, the dogs in hot pursuit and the two boys screaming with excitement from seeing grown-ups act like children. When we flopped back on the grass, gasping for breath, the conversation moved in a new direction.

Nonetheless, her wisecrack felt as though it were coming close to some truth that I wasn't willing to face in myself. I wondered about it as I was driving home with Mr. Contreras and the dogs. Maybe Alex Fisher was right, that my blue-collar roots defined me. Would it make me feel guilty to enjoy a material success that my parents hadn't achieved? In fact, that might have saved my mother's life? She had died of cancer, a uterine cancer that metastasized because she hadn't sought treatment when her symptoms first appeared.

Mr. Contreras's conversation made it possible to defer any more serious self-examination. "Those two boys are awful cute, and the little one might make an athlete. They see anything of their old man?"

"Meaning that growing up with only a foster mother may make him a sissy?" I asked, but when he started coughing with embarrassment I let him off the hook and told him that Fabian was not exactly the athletic type. "He's got a new girlfriend, some student half his age. Maybe she's idealistic enough to think she wants to take on his first wife's children, but I don't know that they'd be better off."

16

A Friend of the Family

THE SUN WAS still well above the midsummer horizon when we got back to the city. It was early enough and light enough to go down to the Trianon to check on Lacey. I knew Mary Louise was right, that touching anything Global was involved in was an invitation to disaster, but I needed to find out if they were actively trying to set me up. I dropped my neighbor and the dogs at the apartment and went south, first to my office to tack together a letter authorizing me to make inquiries, then on to the Gold Coast.

The doorman at the Trianon sent me to the head of the hotel's security detail, since he was in checking his duty rosters for the upcoming week. I couldn't believe my luck when I was ushered into the office: Frank Siekevitz had been a rookie who rode with my dad for a year right after my mother died. With the ethnic insularity of some Chicagoans, Siekevitz had clung to a mentor named Warshawski. That made him doubly delighted to see me; we spent a half hour catching up not just on our lives, but on the contemporary situation in Poland.

"You didn't lose that big diamond tiara of yours at our reception for the French president, did you, Vicki?" he asked with a wink.

I'd forgotten the tiresome way my father's colleagues all use a nickname I hate. "I wish. No, I'm an investigator, private, not public."

"Yeah, private, that's where the money is. You're smart to do that. Plus you don't face the hours or the dangers you do on the force. I'm a hundred percent happier now that I'm doing private security."

Yep. That was my life. Filled with money and safety. I explained frankly that Global had hired me to keep Lucian Frenada from harassing their big star and that I wondered how much of a pest he really was. After consulting with the doorman, Siekevitz said that Frenada had been around once, on Thursday, but Lacey had brought him to her suite, where he stayed for over an hour. He had phoned twice, and she had taken both calls. Their switchboard kept a list of the people phoning her just in case a question of harassment arose.

Siekevitz actually let me look at the phone log—he knew Tony would want his little girl to get all the help she needed. "Not that you were very little when I met you, Vicki, playing forward on that high-school team of yours. My, my. Tony was that proud of you. He'd love to know you walked in his footsteps."

I gave a sickly smile, wondering what my father would really make of the life I was leading these days, and bent over the log. Teddy Trant called every day. Sometimes Lacey spoke to him, sometimes she told the operator to say she was in the health club. Regine Mauger, the *Herald-Star*'s gossip columnist, was the only person whose calls she absolutely refused to take. I felt meanly pleased by that.

When I asked if I could speak with the star myself, Siekevitz shook his head regretfully. "She went off to California for a few days, since they weren't ready to

start shooting. She'll be back Thursday, from what I
hear. Of course the studio is keeping the suite for her.
It's only eight thousand a week. For Hollywood that's
the same as a buck for you or me."

We chatted another few minutes about his private
life. No, he'd never married. Never met the right
woman, he guessed. He escorted me to the entrance,
where I gave the doorman a ten for his pains. I walked
across the park to my car: I hadn't wanted to raise
doubts in the hotel staff's minds by letting them see the
wreck I was driving.

As I drove home through the soft purple of early
night, I thought sourly that Alex was trying to set me
up. But why? Lacey Dowell clearly didn't feel bothered
by Frenada. As for Murray's role in the errand, he was
in so far over his head that my exasperation was tem-
pered by sadness. Even though I wanted to see him and
tell him what I'd learned from Siekevitz, I didn't want
to go looking for him: it would be too painful to find
him with Alex Fisher. Anyway, I didn't know where
Chicago's movers shook these days—or nights. Murray
used to be a regular at Lucy Moynihan's place on
Lower Wacker, but that was a journalist's watering
hole; television personalities drink elsewhere.

Cruising around town looking for him would really
waste time I didn't have. I went virtuously home and
bundled my dirty clothes into the washing machine in
the basement. The phone was ringing as I let myself
back into my apartment.

"Ms. Warshawski?" It was a man and a stranger.
"My name is Morrell. I understand you want to talk to
me."

An hour later I was sitting across from him at Drummers, a wine bar in Edgewater. Morrell was a slender

man about my height, with light curly hair. That was as much as I'd been able to tell from watching him walk up the street toward me.

At the fringe of the pavement an older couple ate a late dinner, hunching toward each other to talk across the noise of the tables full of boisterous young people. I felt a twinge of envy for the woman, white-haired in the streetlight, her hand resting on the arm of the old man. Meeting a stranger for a drink because of an investigation made me feel very lonely.

I had tried to explain what I wanted to know over the phone when Morrell called, but he said he would only answer my questions if he could see me in person. He was calling from Evanston, the first suburb north of Chicago; Drummers was a halfway point between us.

"You're really a private investigator?" he asked when the waiter had brought our drinks.

"No, it's my hobby," I said, getting cranky. "My day job is wrestling alligators. Who are you, besides the man talking to people who've run away from jail?"

"Is that what the children said?" He laughed softly. "What I really want to know is who is paying you to ask questions about Nicola Aguinaldo."

I took a swallow of cabernet. It was vinegary, as if it had sat open in the bar too long. Served me right for ordering pricey wine in a neighborhood that only three years ago had been proud to serve Mogen David by the bottle.

"I'd be a mighty poor confidential investigator if I told a complete stranger who was hiring me to do a job. Especially a stranger who is asking questions about an immigrant who died in an unpleasant and, as it turns out, suspicious way. Perhaps you're an undercover INS

agent? Perhaps even an agent of the Iraqi secret police
—what are they called? Ammo or something?"

"Amn," he corrected. "Yes, I see the problem."

He tapped a finger on his coffee cup and finally decided he'd have to reveal something if I was going to
talk. "My interest is in political prisoners. I've written
on that subject off and on in various places for over a
decade. My work has appeared in places like *The New
Yorker,* but a lot of what I write is for organizations
like Americas Watch or the Grete Berman Institute.
They're the ones who commissioned this particular
book."

I'd vaguely heard of the Grete Berman Institute—a
man whose mother died in the Holocaust had endowed
it to help torture survivors recover. "This particular
book being about?"

He ate some of the nuts on the table. "I'm curious
about the life political refugees can make, whether they
find unusual obstacles or sources of strength in starting
out fresh in a new place. If a man—or woman—was a
professional in their home country, they're often wel-
comed by an academic institution, here or in Europe.
Anyway, professionals are the kind of people who most
often have the resources and contacts to emigrate once
they've been released from prison. But what of someone
outside that professional milieu who leaves home?
What happens to him then?"

The waiter stopped with the stock inquiry; I asked
him to take the cabernet away and bring me a glass of
Black Label, neat. "I see. Aisha's father."

"Yes. Aisha's father. What led you to him?"

I smiled. "I grew up in an immigrant neighborhood
much like Aisha's and Mina's. There's no such thing as
a secret among the children, especially if it involves

someone like you—or me—coming in from the outside."

"Yes, I always worry about who the children will talk to, but if you swear them to secrecy it only makes them behave more suspiciously to strangers. I heard about you from them. That you were a cop who came around with a police dog. Looking for Señora Mercedes."

I took a sip of whisky. "If you came home with me I'd introduce you to the police dog. She's an eight-year-old retriever with the incurable friendliness of all goldens. I wasn't trying to sniff out Señora Mercedes with her. Or I was, but not with deportation in mind. Her daughter ran away from the prison wing of Coolis Hospital a week ago today and ended up dead a few hundred yards from her old front door."

"And what's your interest in the young woman?"

"I found her lying in the road Tuesday night. She died a few hours later in the operating room at Beth Israel, of advanced peritonitis caused by a severe blow to the abdomen. I'd like to know how she got from Coolis to Balmoral and who inflicted that desperate injury on her."

"Are you usually this quixotic, Ms. Warshawski? Spending your life investigating deaths of poor immigrant prison escapees?"

His mocking tone nettled me, as perhaps he intended. "Invariably. It makes a nice change from wrestling alligators, to meet people as uniformly civil and helpful as you."

"Whoof." He sucked in a breath. "I apologize: I earned that. I'm not often in Chicago. Who could I talk to who knows your work?"

That was fair. Why should he give confidential information to a stranger? I gave him Lotty's name and
asked him for a reference in return. He knew Vishnikov
from forensic work the pathologist had done in South
America for the Berman Institute.

The older couple behind me paid their bill. They
strolled across the street to the car, their arms around
each other. I felt more forlorn than ever.

"If you know Vishnikov, maybe you can remind him
about Nicola Aguinaldo's body. It's disappeared from
the morgue. Tomorrow I hope to find out what it would
cost to do an analysis of Aguinaldo's clothes, if the private lab that looked at them still has them, but it would
be so much easier if I knew where her body was. If her
mother has it, how did she learn her daughter was
dead? She left the old apartment the morning of the day
I found Nicola. Some official-looking men came around
and scared the neighborhood, as I'm sure you must
know."

I paused and finally Morrell gave a grudging half
nod.

"So who were the men?" I continued. "State marshals sent by the prison to look for Nicola? INS agents,
as the neighbors suspected? Private agents of a large
security firm? At any rate, since Señora Mercedes vanished, the men haven't been back. So they were looking
either for Señora Mercedes or her daughter. If one of
your contacts in that neighborhood would tell you the
mother's whereabouts, maybe you'd be the man to talk
her into getting the autopsy done."

Morrell didn't say anything. I became aware of the
waiter and bus crew hovering around our table. It was
eleven o'clock; the only other people still at a table were
a young couple buried in each other's necks. I fished a

ten out of my wallet. The waiter swooped on it while the crew quickly cleared the table.

Morrell handed a couple of singles to me. We walked down the street together toward Foster, where we'd both parked. Drummers was only seven or eight blocks from where I'd found Aguinaldo's body, but it might as well have been seven or eight miles.

"I wish I knew someone who could tell me about Aguinaldo's life before she was arrested," I burst out as Morrell stopped at his car. "Did she have a boyfriend who beat her up when she came home, then left her to die in the street? Or was it her wealthy employer—she thought he would help her when she ran away from jail, but he hurt her instead? Someone in that building on Wayne knows, at least knows who she was sleeping with."

He hesitated, as if debating whether to speak. Finally he pulled out a card and gave it to me.

"I'll talk to Aisha's family and see if they know anything about Señora Mercedes. I've never met her personally. If I learn anything that may be helpful to you I'll call you. And you can reach me through the number on the card."

It was the local number for the press agency that represented him. I put it in my hip pocket and turned to cross the street.

"By the way," he said casually, "who *is* paying for you to ask these questions?"

I turned to face him again. "Are you asking in a more subtle way if INS is bankrolling me?"

"Just wondering how quixotic you really are."

I pointed across the street. "See that late-model wreck? I'm quixotic enough for that to be the car I can afford to drive."

I climbed into the Skylark and turned it around, with a roar of exhaust that made me sound like a teenage boy. Morrell's Honda moved sleekly to the intersection ahead of me. He must make some money writing about torture victims; the car was new. But what did that prove? Even a person with strong principles has to live on something, and it wasn't as though he was driving a Mercedes or a Jag. Of course, I had no idea what his principles were.

17

Spinning Wheels, Seeking Traction

IN THE MORNING I went to my office early: I had a meeting with potential new clients at eleven, and I didn't want my personal searches to make me late. I looked Morrell up on the Web.

He had written a book about psychological as well as physical torture as a means to suppress protest in Chile and Argentina. He had covered the return to civilian government in Uruguay and what that meant for the victims of torture in a long essay in *The Atlantic Monthly*. His work on SAPO forces in Zimbabwe had won a Pulitzer prize after its serialization in *The New Yorker*.

Zimbabwe? I wondered if he and Baladine had met there. Although Baladine probably hadn't actually gone to southern Africa. He would have directed operations from the Rapelec tower on east Illinois Street, or perhaps met their South African customers in London.

The *Herald-Star* had interviewed Morrell when the Chile book came out. From that I learned he was about fifty, that he'd been born in Cuba but grew up in Chicago, had studied journalism at Northwestern, and still followed the Cubs despite living away from home most of his adult life. And that he only went by his last name; the reporter hadn't been able to dig his first name out of him. Although they had his initials—C.L.—he wouldn't divulge the name.

I wondered idly what his parents had called him. Maybe he'd been given some name commemorating a great battle or economic triumph that was so embarrassing he dropped it. Was he Cuban, or had his parents been there with a multinational or the army when he was born? Maybe they'd named him for some Cuban epic, like the Ten Years War, and he'd shed it as soon as he could. I was tempted to hunt through old immigration or court records to come up with it, but I knew that impulse was only frustration at not being able to get a sense of direction.

To change sources of frustration, I turned to the LifeStory report I'd requested on Frenada. I'd invested in a priority turnaround—not the fastest, which sets you back a few grand, but overnight, which was expensive enough. I saved the report to a floppy and printed it out.

Frenada's personal finances were simple enough for a child of eight to decipher. He had an interest-bearing checking account, where his expenses more or less equaled the thirty-five hundred dollars he took home from his business each month. The business, Special-T Uniforms, was nine years old. It had grown from annual receivables of six thousand to over four hundred thousand.

Frenada was writing regular tuition checks to St. Remigio's Catholic school for two children—not his own as far as I knew. At least there was no record of a marriage, or any indication of a child-support agreement. He averaged seven hundred dollars a month each on his American Express and MasterCard, for the ordinary business of living. He held a certificate of deposit for twenty thousand dollars. He was paying a mortgage on a $150,000 two-flat in the Irving Park neighborhood, and he had a life-insurance policy worth a hundred thousand dollars, with three children named Caliente listed as the beneficiaries. Besides that munificence, he drove a four-year-old Taurus that he'd just about paid for.

No holdings in the Caymans, no portfolio of stocks or options. No residue of the drug trade, no unusual income of any kind that might indicate blackmail. Frenada was either extremely honest, or so clever that not even LifeStory's paid informants could track his holdings.

So what did Murray and Alex-Sandy think was buried here? If it was a juvenile crime, I wasn't interested in digging that far into his past. Maybe he'd done a quasilegal deal to get preferred treatment in orders or to obtain financing. That didn't seem any different from Baladine and Rapelec in Africa, except the scale was smaller.

I reached Murray in his office. "I can't take on this Frenada assignment. Since you came along with Alex to try to hire me, I assume I can tell you without needing to talk to her."

"Yeah, I'll tell her. Any particular reason?"

I stared at the floor, noticing the dust bunnies that had gathered around my copier. "I'm busy these days," I said after too long a silence. "An inquiry like this would take more resources than I have."

"Thanks for trusting me, Vic. I'll tell Alex you're too busy."

His anger, more hurt than rage, made me say quickly, "Murray. You don't know what Global's real agenda is here, do you?"

"Alex talked the situation over with me on Friday," he said stiffly. "If it sounds incredible to you, then it's because you don't understand the way Hollywood operates. Everything is image for them, so the image becomes more real than the actual world around them. Lacey's success and Global's image are intertwined. They want—"

"I know what they want, babe," I said gently. "I just don't know why they want it. In the matter of the actual world, I talked to the house dick at the Trianon. I don't know if he'd be as forthcoming with you as he was with me, but you might check him out."

We hung up on that fractured note. Poor Murray. I didn't think I could bear to witness his vulnerability if Global took him to pieces.

Mary Louise came in around ten, after she'd gotten Nate and Josh off to day camp. She was going to make phone calls to Georgia for me while I pitched my wares to a couple of lawyers who were looking for a firm to handle their investigations. Such meetings often lead nowhere, but I have to keep doing it—and with enough enthusiasm that I'm not defeating myself walking in the door.

"You call this Alex woman to say you weren't playing Global's game?" Mary Louise asked as I gathered presentation materials into my briefcase.

"Yes, ma'am, Officer Neely." I saluted her smartly. "At least, I told Murray."

The phone rang before I could leave; I hovered in the doorway while Mary Louise answered. Her expression became wooden.

"Warshawski Investigations . . . No, this is Detective Neely. Ms. Warshawski is leaving for a meeting. I'll see if she can take your call. . . . Speaking of the devil," she added to me, her finger on the HOLD button.

I came back to the desk.

"Vic, I'm disappointed that you won't take the job for me," Alex said in lieu of a greeting. "I'd like you to think it over—for your sake as well as Lacey's—before I take your no as final."

"I've thought it over, Sandy—Alex, I mean. Thought it over, talked it over with my advisers. We all agree it's not the right assignment for me. But I know the house detective at the Trianon; you can trust him to look after Lacey for you."

"You talked to Lacey after I expressly asked you not to?" Her tone was as sharp as a slap in the face.

"You're piquing me, Sandy. What would Lacey tell me that you'd rather I didn't hear?"

"My name is Alex now. I wish you'd make an effort to remember. Teddy Trant really wants you to take this job. He asked me personally to offer it to you."

So maybe Abigail was putting a finger in my pie. "I'm excited. I didn't think the big guy knew I was on the planet. Unless BB Baladine told him?"

That made her huffy. "He knows about you because I recommended you. After Murray gave you a glowing buildup, I might add."

"I'm grateful to both of you, but the answer is still no."

"Then you're making a big mistake. Think it—"

"That almost sounds like a threat, Sandy. Alex, that is."

"Friendly advice. Although why I bother I don't know. Think it over, think it better. I'll leave the offer open until noon tomorrow." She broke the connection with a snap.

"Murray can do better for himself than that" was Mary Louise's only comment when I repeated the conversation before taking off.

My presentation went well; the lawyers gave me a small job with the prospect of bigger ones to follow. When I got back at four, Mary Louise had completed her calls and typed up a neat report for me to send over to Continental United in the morning. Altogether a more productive day than I'd had lately.

I finished my share of the report and went over to Lotty's. We try to get together once a week, but tonight was our first chance for a relaxed conversation in over a month.

While we ate smoked salmon on her tiny balcony, I caught Lotty up on the little I knew of Nicola Aguinaldo's story. When I told her about Morrell, Lotty went into her study and brought out a copy of *Vanishing into Silence,* his book on the Disappeared in Chile and Argentina. I looked at the photograph on the jacket flap. Of course I'd only seen Morrell by candlelight, and he was seven or eight years younger in the picture, but it was obviously the same man. He had a thin face and was smiling slightly, as if mocking himself for posing for a photograph.

I borrowed the book from her—I wanted to get an idea of how Morrell thought, or at least what he thought. After that, Lotty and I talked idly about other matters. Lotty's is an intense, sometimes stormy presence, but in her home, with its polished floors and vivid colors, I always find a reassuring haven.

Lotty's workday starts at six. I left early, my mood benign enough to take on dull household tasks: I put my laundry away, cleaned the mold out of the bathtub,

washed down the kitchen cabinets and floor. The bedroom could use a vacuuming, but my domesticity
spreads only so far. I planted myself in front of the
piano and began picking out a fughetta with slow, loud
fingers.

It's possible, as the detective at the Trianon had said
yesterday, that my dad would have loved to see me follow in his footsteps, but I knew my mother would not.
She wanted me to live a life of erudition if not artistry,
to inhabit the milieu the second World War had destroyed for her—concerts, books, voice lessons, friends
who lived for music and art. She had made me learn
both piano and voice, hoping I would have the vocal
career the war had taken from her. She certainly would
have resented anyone who called me a blue-collar girl.

I moved from the fughetta to warming up my voice,
which I hadn't done for several weeks. I was finding my
middle range when the phone rang. It was Morrell.

"Ms. Warshawski. I'm in the neighborhood. Can I
come up for a minute?"

"I'm not ready for company. Can't we do this on the
phone?"

"I'd rather not. And I won't be company—I'll be
gone so fast you almost won't know I was there."

I'd changed into cutoffs for my housework, and my
arms and legs were streaked with dirt. So be it. If he
wanted to drop in on me unawares, he had to take me
as I was. I went back to my middle voice and let Mr.
Contreras and the dogs answer the bell when Morrell
rang.

I waited a minute before going out to the landing.
My neighbor was interrogating Morrell: "Is she expecting you this late at night, young man? She never mentioned you before that I ever heard of."

I laughed a little but ran down the stairs in my bare feet before the woman who lived opposite Mr. Contreras came out to complain about the noise. "It's okay. He's got some information for a case I'm working on."

I introduced Morrell to Peppy. "This is the police dog. The big guy is her son. And this is my neighbor and good friend, Mr. Contreras."

The old man had been looking hurt that I hadn't told him about Morrell earlier, but my introduction appeased him slightly. He took the dogs back inside the apartment after only a very small discourse on how I needed to let him know what strangers to expect when the police were on my butt.

Morrell followed me up the stairs. "I suppose with a neighbor like that you don't need a security system. Reminds me of the villages in Guatemala, where people seem to look out for each other more than we do here."

"He drives me crazy half the time, but you're right: I'd feel mighty lost without him."

I ushered Morrell to the stuffed armchair and sat astride the piano bench. In the lamplight I saw that his thick hair was streaked with white and the laugh lines around his eyes were more deeply grooved than in his book-jacket photo.

"This really will take only a minute, but my years in South America make me nervous about giving confidential information over the phone. I managed to find Nicola Aguinaldo's mother. She didn't know her daughter was dead. And she definitely doesn't have her body."

I looked at him narrowly, but there's no real way to tell whether people are lying to you or not. "I'd like to talk to Señora Mercedes myself. Can you tell me where you found her?"

He hesitated. "She's not likely to confide in a stranger."

"She confided in you, and last night you assured me you'd never laid eyes on her."

His mouth twitched in the suggestion of a smile. "I've talked to a couple of people about your work, and they were right: you are a very astute observer. Can you please take my word for it, that Señora Mercedes doesn't have her daughter's body?"

I picked out a minor triad in the bass clef. "I'm getting fed up with people pushing me toward Aguinaldo with one hand and pulling me away from her with the other. There's something wrong with how she died, but you seem to be joining the group of break-dancers writhing on stage, saying, 'Watch,' 'Don't watch.' I need to find someone who knows about Aguinaldo's private life. Her mother may not, but her kid might. Children know a lot about what their mothers get up to."

He drummed his fingers on the chair arm, thinking it over, but finally shook his head. "The trouble is, the more people who talk to Señora Mercedes, the riskier her position becomes."

"Riskier how?"

"Deportation. She wants to stay in America so that her surviving granddaughter can get an education and make something more of herself than being a nanny or a factory hand. I can try to find out something for you, if you'd like. . . ." His voice trailed away, leaving it as a question.

I agreed somewhat grumpily. I hate leaving a crucial piece of an investigation in someone else's hands, especially when I don't know anything about his skills.

He got up to leave but stopped to admire the piano.

"You must be a serious musician to keep a baby grand in your living room. I play some, but not on anything this nice."

"My mother was a serious musician. One of her old friends keeps this in shape for me, but I never made it past Thompson's fourth book." I loved action too much, even as a child, and my hours of practice were a misery when I longed to be running or swimming.

Morrell gave the same self-mocking smile he'd shown in his photo and sat down to try the piano. He ran through part of a Chopin nocturne with unusual feeling for an amateur. When he saw "Erbarme dich" on the music rack, he started to play and I began to sing. Bach produces a certain kind of balm. When Morrell got up to go, with an apology for showing off, I felt calmer but no more certain than I was earlier whether he was telling the truth about Nicola Aguinaldo's mother. But if she didn't have the body, where was it?

Perhaps those researchers who want you to listen to Bach or Mozart to boost your brain are right, because when he left I had an idea for the morning. It wasn't the best idea I ever had, as it turned out, but that wasn't really Bach's fault.

I went down to Mr. Contreras's when I heard the front door shut. As I'd expected, my neighbor was waiting up to see how long I kept a strange man in my apartment.

"How would you like to go on a wild-goose chase with me tomorrow?" I asked him before he could comment on Morrell. "Be a grieving grandfather whose darling baby ran away from jail and died a sad death?"

He revived instantly.

18

These Walls Do a Prison Make

THE NEXT MORNING, while Mary Louise sat at my desk organizing files, I collected my maps and set out with Mr. Contreras and the dogs for the long drive across the state to Coolis. The muffler was rumbling more loudly than ever. The air-conditioning didn't work, so we had to ride with the windows open and our teeth rattling.

"That muffler wasn't this bad when we picked up the car," Mr. Contreras observed when we stopped at the Elgin toll plaza to throw in our quarters. "Guy must have stuck it on with duct tape to sell this heap."

"Let's hope the thing holds together until we're back in Chicago."

The dogs kept their heads out the windows, periodically switching sides as we moved into the real country and they picked up the scent of the river. West of Rockford we pulled over at a rest area for lunch. Mr. Contreras was a willing but uncertain partner in the outing; while the dogs swam in the Fox River we went over his lines until he felt confident enough to fly solo.

Even with that long break, by keeping the Rustmobile roaring at its top speed—around seventy—we managed to get to Coolis a little after twelve. It was a pretty town, built in a valley of two small rivers feeding the Mississippi: the big river lies ten miles to the west. Coolis had been a lead-mining hub in the 1800s, but was close to death when the state decided to build its new women's prison here.

I'd never known who in Coolis had enough money or clout to grease Jean-Claude Poilevy's wheels, but as we drove through town to the prison, we passed Baladine Hardware, followed by Baladine Lincoln–Mercury. I could see BB as a boy at Baladine Hardware, playing with the combination locks and fantasizing about someday playing with really big locks and keys. As a friend of Poilevy's, Baladine would have had the inside track anyway on where the legislature awarded the prison contract, but the decision to build in his family's town must have taken a major contribution to the Republican party coffers.

Illinois seems like a large place when you look at a map, stretching four hundred miles from Wisconsin to Missouri, but it's really just a cozy little hometown, where everybody knows everybody else and nobody tells secrets outside the family. Businesses pay money to politicians to get even greater amounts of money pumped back to them via state contracts, and while some of it may be scuzzy, none of it's illegal—because the guys who have their hands in one another's pockets are writing the laws.

The prison stood two miles west of town; scraggly strip malls had grown up along the route. Signs warned drivers against hitchhikers, since they might be escaped prisoners and should be considered dangerous. Women like Nicola Aguinaldo, for instance, might bleed all over you; that would be bad.

Even Mr. Contreras grew quiet when we passed the front gate. Three layers of high fencing, with razor wire along the tops and current running through the outermost, separated us from the prison. It looked in some ways like a modern industrial park, with its low white buildings laid out in a kind of campus—except that the windows were mere slits, like the arrow holes in a medieval castle. Also like a castle, watchtowers holding armed guards covered the perimeter. A kind of reverse castle, where the guards thought the enemy lay within rather than without.

Although the land around the prison was dotted with wildflowers and trees, inside what wasn't concrete had become hardscrabble from too many marching feet and too little care. In the distance we could see some women playing what might be softball; as they ran they kicked up dust eddies.

"Umph." Mr. Contreras let out a grunt after I turned around and headed back into town. "If you wasn't desperate before you landed in that place, you sure would be after you'd been there a day or two. If that didn't cure you of a life of crime nothing would."

"Or it would get you feeling so hopeless you'd feel you didn't have any choices." My neighbor and I do not think as one on most social issues, but that doesn't stop his wanting to be involved in helping me tilt at whatever windmill I'm charging on a given day.

The hospital lay inside the town boundary, off the main road leading to the prison. Behind it ran Smallpox Creek, flowing northwest to the Mississippi, although not at any great pace. We let the dogs out again to cool off in the water, then checked the side roads around the hospital. Just as my maps had shown, you could either go directly to jail or into town from the hospital, but you didn't have any other choice for escape than the creek. After driving the route long enough to memorize it we returned to the hospital and parked.

Coolis General had started as a small brick building. With the arrival of the prison and wealth, two enormous wings had been attached, giving it the appearance of a dragonfly. We walked up a long path, past beds of summer flowers, to the entrance, which was in the old part, the body of the insect. Signs directed visitors to the Connie Brest Baladine Surgicenter, to radiology, and to patient information.

"Howdy," Mr. Contreras said to the bored woman at the information desk. "I need to talk to someone about my granddaughter. She—well, she was a patient here up to last week, and things didn't turn out too good for her."

The woman braced herself. I could see *what to do if family threatens a malpractice suit* running through her mind as she asked Mr. Contreras for his granddaughter's name.

"Nicola Aguinaldo." He spelled it for her. "I ain't saying we blame the hospital or anything, but I sure would like to know how she come in and how she left and all. She—well, she got herself in a little bit of trouble up in Chicago, and she was over here in Coolis, in the jail, when she took sick."

Once he got past his initial nervousness, he was in full stride. I began to believe that Nicola Aguinaldo really had been his granddaughter, with the family that worried about her, but you know how it is with today's young people, you can't ever tell them nothing. The woman at the desk kept trying to interrupt him—she wanted to explain that she couldn't talk to him about patients, especially not when they were prisoners, but she finally gave up and summoned a superior.

In a few minutes a woman about my own age showed up. If she'd been sprayed with polyurethane she couldn't have been glossier or more untouchable. She introduced herself as Muriel Paxton, the head of patient affairs, and invited us to follow her to her office. The back of her crimson suit barely moved as she walked, as though she'd figured out how to use her legs without involving her pelvis.

Like all modern hospitals, Coolis General had spared no expense on their administrative offices. Radical mastectomies may be done now as outpatient procedures, but heaven forbid that management skimps on any attention to comfort. Muriel Paxton enthroned herself behind a slab of rosewood that clashed with the red of her suit. Mr. Contreras and I, feet sinking to our ankles in the lavender pile on the floor, sat in faux-wicker side chairs.

"Why don't we start with your names." Ms. Paxton held a pen like a dagger over a legal pad.

"This is Nicola Aguinaldo's grandfather," I said, "and I'm the family lawyer."

I spelled my last name slowly. As I hoped, the presence of a lawyer kept Ms. Paxton from demanding Mr. Contreras's name—he didn't want to call himself Aguinaldo, and he'd told me on the way over if he was going to take part in this scheme he didn't want his name taken down.

"And what seems to be the problem?" The administrator's smile was as bright as her lipstick, but no warmth came with it.

"The problem is, my little girl is dead. I want to know how she could have got out of here with no one the wiser."

Ms. Paxton put the pen down and leaned forward, a

motion learned in media training school: lean forward forty-five degrees to show concern. It wasn't reflected in her eyes.

"If a patient wants to check out, even if it's not in her best medical interest, there's little we can do to stop her, Mr. Uh—"

"Huh, that's a laugh. She come over from the jail, in chains like as not, and you say she can check herself out if she wants to? Then I bet the waiting list from the jail over to here must be five miles long. How come we never was told she had female problems? How come when she called home she never said nothing about that, that's what I'd like to know. You tell me you can let someone waltz away from this hospital without their family knowing they was even in here to begin with?"

"Mr. Uh, I assure you that every precaution—"

"And another thing, who even did the diagnosis— some prison warden? She didn't have nothing wrong with her that we ever heard of. Not one person from this hospital got in touch with us to say, 'Your baby is sick, do we have your permission to do surgery?' or whatever it was you was planning on doing. What happened—did you mess up on the surgery and—"

I had briefed Mr. Contreras as best I could over lunch, but I needn't have worried: with the bit in his teeth not much short of a bullet can stop him. Ms. Paxton kept trying to interrupt, growing progressively more angry at each failure.

"Now, now," I said soothingly. "We don't know that they did surgery, sir. Can you look up Ms. Aguinaldo's record and let us know what you did do?"

Ms. Paxton jabbed her computer keys. Of course, without a subpoena she shouldn't tell us anything, but I was hoping she was angry enough to forget that part of her training. Whatever she saw on the screen made her become very still. When she finally spoke it was without the fury that I had been counting on to push her to indiscretion.

"Who did you say you were?" she demanded.

"I'm a lawyer and an investigator." I tossed my card onto her desk. "And this is my client. How did you come to let Ms. Aguinaldo out of the hospital?"

"She ran away. She must have feigned her illness as an excuse for—"

"You calling my baby a liar?" Mr. Contreras was indignant. "If that don't beat the Dutch. You think because she was poor, because she went to jail trying to look after her own little girl, you think she made up—"

Ms. Paxton's smile became glacial. "Most of the prisoners who seek medical care either have injured themselves on the job or in a fight, or they are malingering. In your granddaughter's case, without the permission of the doctor in charge I am not at liberty to reveal her medical record. But I assure you she left here of her own free will."

"As my client said earlier, if anyone can walk out of here of her own free will, you must have a prison full of people trying to injure themselves in order to get moved to the hospital."

"Security is extremely tight." Her lips were opened only wide enough to spit the words out.

"I don't believe you," Mr. Contreras huffed. "You look at that machine of yours, you'll see she was just a little bit of a thing. You brung her over in a ball and chain, and you telling me she sawed it off?"

In the end, he got her angry enough that she phoned someone named Daisy to say she had a lawyer here who needed proof that you couldn't get out of the prison ward. She swept out of her office so fast that we almost had to run to keep up with her. Her high heels clicked across the tile floors as if she were tap dancing, but she still didn't move her hips. We trotted past the information desk, down a corridor where various hospital staff greeted Ms. Paxton with the anxious deference you always see displayed to the bad-tempered in positions of power. She didn't slow her twinkling tapping across the tiles but did nod in response, like the Queen of England acknowledging her subjects.

She led us behind the hospital to a locked ward separated from the main hospital by three sets of doors. Each was opened electronically, by a man behind thick glass, and the one behind you had to shut before the one in front of you could open. It was like the entrance to the Fourth Circle in Dante. By the time we were in the prison ward I was pretty much abandoning hope.

Like the rest of Coolis General, the ward was built out of something white and shiny, but it had been created with the prison in mind: the windows once again were mere slits in the wall. So much for my idea that Nicola had jumped out a window when the staff's back was turned.

A guard inspected Mr. Contreras's pockets and my handbag and told us to sign in. Mr. Contreras cast me an angry look, but signed his name. When I filled mine in below his, I doubted whether any state employee could have found him by his signature—it looked like *Oortneam*. Ms. Paxton merely flashed her hospital badge—the guard knew her by sight.

Inside the third door we were met by Daisy—Nurse Lundgren to us—the ward head. She looked coldly at Ms. Paxton and demanded to know what the problem was.

"These people are concerned with the escape of that color—that girl, that young person who got away last week." Ms. Paxton's realization that the colored girl's grandfather and lawyer were present flustered her. "I want them to see that this ward is very secure. And that however the girl got away it wasn't through any negligence on our part."

Nurse Lundgren frowned. "Are you sure you want me talking to them? The memo from Captain Ruzich was very clear on the subject."

Ms. Paxton smiled with more menace than a mere frown could convey. "I'm relying on your discretion, Daisy. But the grandfather has driven all the way from Chicago. I'd like him to see that we do take proper precautions when prisoners are entrusted to our care."

"Very well," the nurse said. "I'll take them onto the ward. I expect you have enough work of your own without needing to come with us."

Ms. Paxton seemed to be of two minds whether to fight Lundgren in front of us but finally swiveled on her motionless hips and stalked away.

"How many escapes have you had from the hospital?" I asked as we followed the nurse into the locked ward.

"Five," the nurse said. "But that was before this wing was built. It used to be fairly easy to jump out a window, even if it had bars, because the girls knew how to finagle their way into the cafeteria or some other place they weren't meant to be."

I glanced in a room as we passed. It was empty; Lundgren didn't object when I asked to inspect it. It had the tiny arrow holes of the prison, and no bathroom: Lundgren said the women had to use a bathroom in the hall, which was kept locked and was opened by a correctional officer. The hospital couldn't afford to have hiding places in the room where an inmate could either lie in wait to attack—or kill herself in private.

In the next room a woman was lying in bed, sleeping heavily, wasted as my mother had been by her cancer. Across the hall a young woman with dark curly hair was watching television. It was only when I looked closely that I saw she was handcuffed to the bed.

"How are you feeling, Veronica?" Lundgren called as we passed.

"I'm okay, Nurse. How's my baby?"

Veronica had given birth early that morning. She'd be returned to the prison in another couple of days, where she could keep her infant for four months. Coolis was progressive that way, the nurse explained, releasing the lock on the door that separated the nurses' station from the ward. She cut short a flirtation between one of her subordinates and the corrections officer assigned to guard the hall, telling her junior to pay attention to the ward while she talked to us.

"It's hard for them to work here—it isn't like real nursing, and then they get bored when the ward is as empty as it is right now."

She led us into a tiny room behind the nurses' station that held a table, a microwave, and a small television. It was the one room on the floor with actual windows, but as these were made of wire-enforced glass they didn't offer much of a view.

Lundgren took us through the statistics of the floor without any hesitation. There were twenty beds, but they never had more than eight or ten of them filled, except one disastrous occasion when there was a major food-poisoning outbreak at the jail and some of the patients with heart trouble came close to dying.

As to how easy or hard it was for an inmate to get to the hospital, she wasn't privy to prison decisions, but in her experience, women were pretty sick before they were brought over. "Girls are always trying to get over here. The hospital food is better and the routine is easier to take. In jail there are counts every six hours, and lockdowns and all the rest of it. For someone serving a long sentence the hospital can seem like a vacation. So the prison makes it hard for anyone to malinger."

"And Nicola Aguinaldo? How sick was she when she came here?"

Her lips tightened, and her hands moved uneasily in her lap. "I thought she was quite ill. So ill I was surprised that she was able to move enough to leave."

"What was the problem?" Mr. Contreras demanded. "Was it some kind of woman problem? That's what the cops told me, but she never said nothing about that to her ma—"

"A doctor didn't actually examine her before she left. I was told by the prison nurse that they suspected an ovarian cyst. But before a doctor could see her, she was gone."

"How did that little bit of a thing get away from you and the guard and everyone?" Mr. Contreras demanded.

Lundgren didn't look at us. "I wasn't on duty when it happened. I was told she used her small size to follow behind the laundry cart, on the side away from the guard, and that she probably concealed herself in the cart when the janitor stopped to talk to someone. In theory the laundry would be inspected before leaving this ward, but in practice they probably let it go through without poking at it: no one wants to touch soiled linens. A number of the women have AIDS."

"And you believe Aguinaldo escaped that way?" I asked, keeping my voice neutral. "Wasn't she cuffed to the bed?"

Lundgren nodded. "But these girls have nothing to do all day long except figure out how to use a hairpin on their handcuffs. It happens now and then that one of them gets loose, but since the ward is locked it doesn't do them much good. I don't think there's anything else I can tell you. If you'd like some time alone in the chapel before you set out, I can have an orderly show you to it. Otherwise he'll escort you to the main entrance."

I left my card on the table when we got up to leave. "In case something else occurs to you that you'd like me to know about, Nurse."

On the way out, Mr. Contreras exploded with frustration. "I don't believe it. A laundry cart, huh? Things ain't bigger than a minute, and not even Nicola was that tiny. I want you to sue them. Sue them for—what was it you said—not taking due something?"

Veronica, the woman who'd had the baby, managed to be in the hall, cuffed to the orderly, who was escorting her back from the bathroom. "You know Nicola? What happened to her?"

"She's dead," I said. "Do you know why she was in the hospital?"

Nurse Lundgren appeared next to us. "You can't be talking to the patients, ma'am. They're inmates even if they're in the hospital. Veronica, you're well enough to parade the hall, you're well enough to get back to the house. Jock, you can take these visitors out to the main entrance. Show them where the chapel is before you come back."

Veronica looked momentarily furious, then, as if her

powerlessness were something she'd just remembered, her shoulders sank and her face crumpled into despair.

Jock gave permission to the man behind the glass wall to release the doors. At the entrance to the main hospital wing, he pointed down a hall to the chapel.

19

Power Dining

So what do you think, doll?" Mr. Contreras asked as he buckled himself into the seat. "That nurse seemed mighty uneasy. And how would a little thing like that girl was get out of a place like that?"

I didn't have an answer. Nurse Lundgren seemed competent, and even, for the setting, compassionate. I agreed she'd seemed uncomfortable, but it would be easy for me to read into that what I wanted to. Maybe she was troubled at the loss of a patient rather than covering up special knowledge of Aguinaldo's escape.

We drove over to Smallpox Creek to let the dogs cool off again before the drive home. Mr. Contreras, suddenly seeing Nicola Aguinaldo as a person, not an illegal immigrant or a criminal, was subdued during the ride. We got home a little before six. Mary Louise had shoved a packet underneath the locked inner door with a report on her day's work. She had delivered our report to Continental United; the human resources vice president had called to say they were delighted with our work, but that they thought they would have to send someone down to Georgia to check on things in person. And that someone would likely be me—unless Baladine persuaded the company to turn all their work over to Carnifice.

I didn't want to hang about the back roads of Georgia, waiting for someone with a tire iron to hit me on the head. On the other hand, if I stayed in Chicago I might start doing unlucrative things like tailing Morrell, to see if a man worried about committing himself on the phone might drive to Nicola Aguinaldo's mother's home.

A man named Rieff phoned from Cheviot Labs at eleven, Mary Louise had written in her round schoolgirl hand. *He says he can provide a printout of what is on Aguinaldo's dress, but he does not know how meaningful it is. It was a long T-shirt with Lacey Dowell as the Mad Virgin on it. A label said it was a specialty shirt but did not identify where it was manufactured. There are traces of sweat, which are presumably Aguinaldo's, but without a DNA sample he couldn't say. There is a trace of cigarette ash around the inside of the neck. He is not charging for that information because the analysis was already done when they inspected the dress last week, but if you want to know what brand of cigarette, that will cost around two hundred extra.*

Cigarette ash around the inside of the neck? I wondered if Aguinaldo was a smoker, and how hard or easy it was to drop ash down your own neckline if you smoked.

I turned back to Mary Louise's notes. *At two o'clock Alex Fisher phoned. She wanted to know if you had thought over her offer any more. I said you were out of town for the day and would get back to her in the morning; she urged me to push you to take the job, it would mean a lot for your agency one way or another however you decided. Vic, what does this woman want?*

She'd underscored the question several times. I was

with her there: what did Alex want? What was Teddy Trant going to do to me if I didn't dig around in Frenada's affairs? Put a V chip in my TV so I was forced to watch nothing but Global programs? If Abigail Trant had persuaded her husband to give me some work, was that enough reason for him to be surly at my refusal to accept it?

Of course the other connection to Global was Lacey Dowell. She, or at least her face, kept cropping up. Now she was on the shirt Nicola Aguinaldo had on when she died. Was Global's big star involved in something so ugly the studio wanted to pin it on Frenada? But there was nothing to link Lacey with Nicola Aguinaldo, at least as far as I could tell.

Maybe I should try to see Lucian Frenada. I had entered the phone numbers Alex Fisher gave me into my Palm Pilot. When I called his home, a machine told me, in Spanish and English, that Frenada regretted not answering my call in person, but that he was perhaps at his factory and would get back to me if I left a message.

I thought it over, then got up abruptly and went downstairs. If Frenada was perhaps at his factory I could see him in person. My back was stiff. A nagging sensible voice—-Mary Louise's or Lotty's—told me if I had to poke at this wasp's nest at all to do it in the morning. Or at least to take my gun, but what was I going to do with it—pistol-whip him into telling me what secret Trant wanted me to find?

There is no direct route from my place to Frenada's factory. I snaked south and west, through streets filled with small frame houses and four-plus-one's, past boys skateboarding or in small gangs on their bikes, now and then crossing pockets of lights around bars and pool halls. As I passed the fringes of Humboldt Park, the streets revved up with boom boxes and low-riders but died away again at the seedy industrial corridor along Grand Avenue.

A freight line cuts northwest through the area, making for oddly shaped buildings designed to fill odd lot sizes right up to the embankment. A train was rumbling past as I pulled in front of a dingy triangular building near the corner of Trumbull and Grand.

Lights blazed through open windows on the second floor. The outer door was shut but unlocked. A naked bulb glared just inside the entrance. Drunken letters in a notice board listed a wig manufacturer and a box maker on the ground floor. Special-T Uniforms was on two. As I climbed concrete steps slippery with age, light glinted on long falls of hair in a display case. It was like walking behind the guillotine after dark.

The noise coming down the stairwell sounded as though fifty guillotines were all whacking heads in unison. I followed light and sound along a metal walkway and came to Special-T's open door. Even though it was nine at night, nearly a dozen people were working, either cutting fabric at long tables in the middle of the floor or assembling garments at machines along the wall. The racket came partly from the sewing machines, but mostly from the shears. Two men positioned layers of cloth at the end of the tables, clamped them in place under a pair of electric shears, then wielded a control box to release the blades.

I watched, fascinated, as the shears whicked through the fabric and the men carried pieces over to the sewing-machine operators. One person was sewing letters to the backs of shirts, another attaching sleeves. At least half the crew was smoking. I thought of the cigarette ash smudged into the neck of Nicola Aguinaldo's dress.

Maybe it had come from the person who made the garment, rather than from Aguinaldo herself.

Lucian Frenada was standing at one of the cutting tables next to a stocky man with thin black hair. They seemed to be discussing the proper placement of a pattern stencil. I walked over to stand in his range of vision —if I touched him to get his attention he might be startled into landing under one of the fabric scythes.

Frenada looked up, frowning. *"Si? Le puedo ayudar en algo?"*

I held out my card. "We met at Lacey Dowell's party last week," I shouted over the noise of the machinery.

The man next to him stared at me with frank curiosity: was I a girlfriend so enamored that I would pursue Frenada into his shop? Or was I with INS, about to demand that all hands produce their papers? Frenada touched his arm and said something in Spanish, then pointed at the floor, ankle-deep with scraps of cloth. The man passed a command on to one of the cutters, who stopped his work to start sweeping.

Frenada took me to a cubbyhole at the rear of the floor, which was protected enough from the floor noise to allow conversation. Fabric samples and patterns festooned the top of a metal desk; production schedules were taped to the door and the sides of an old filing cabinet. The only chair had a motor on it. Frenada leaned against the door; I perched gingerly on the edge of the desk.

"Why are you here?" he demanded.

"You mentioned Tuesday night that something odd was happening at your shop."

"Do you usually sell your services like this, door to door?"

My cheeks and neck grew warm with embarrassment, but I couldn't help smiling. "Like encyclopedias, you mean? A reporter I know has been asking questions about your business. And I remembered what you said, so I wanted to see Special-T for myself."

"What reporter? What kind of questions?"

"Wondering what secrets you were hiding here at Special-T." I watched him steadily, but he looked only puzzled, and somewhat scornful.

Another freight train began to thunder behind the building, drowning Frenada's reply. While I waited to be able to hear him, I looked around the office. On his desk, underneath one of the fabric swatches, I saw a glimpse of a slogan I knew from Emily Messenger's wardrobe: *The Mad Virgin Bites*.

The train passed, and Frenada said, "Secrets? I can't afford such things. I thought you meant—but it doesn't matter. My business runs on a shoestring; if something a little strange happens, then I have to accept it as an act of God."

"Lacey reassured you when you saw her on Thursday?"

"Did she—who told you—"

"No one. It was a deduction. That's what I do—get facts and make deductions. They teach it in detective school." I was babbling, because of the Mad Virgin T-shirt.

Frenada looked around his office and caught sight of the shirt. He got to his feet and moved me toward the door.

"My business has nothing to do with Lacey. Nothing at all. So keep your deductions to yourself, Miss Detective. And now, by another gracious act of God, I have a large order to get out, the largest I have ever been blessed with, the uniforms for a soccer league in New Jersey, which is why you find me here so late at night." He hustled me out through the shop floor to the metal walkway, waiting until I reached the stairwell landing before he turned back inside.

I put the Rustmobile into noisy gear and started for home. My route took me past St. Remigio's church and school, where Lacey Dowell and Frenada had been students twenty years ago. Lacey had learned acting there, and Frenada had started his business by making the school's soccer uniforms. I slowed down to read the times for daily mass from the signboard, wondering whether I might go in the morning, meet the priest, learn something about Frenada. But if Frenada had told his confessor why he had a Mad Virgin T-shirt half-buried under his fabric samples, I didn't think the priest would share it with me.

Was that the secret that Trant wanted me to find? Was Frenada making bootleg Virginwear clothes in his little factory and selling them in the old 'hood? In that case, it was a legitimate inquiry. Although I expected Trant used something like Burmese or Honduran slave labor for his own production, in which case I was just as happy for Frenada to sell pirated shirts employing local workers at living wages.

Sal had called while I was at the factory, wanting to see if I'd like to catch Murray's second program and get some dinner. I took the L down to the Glow so I could drink: it had been a long day and I didn't want to drive anymore, anyway. The usual crowd of tired traders was drinking, but they let me switch from the Sox on GN to Global—after all, it was only the third inning and the Sox were already down four runs.

After his debut with Lacey Dowell I wondered what

Murray could find to titillate the viewers, but I had to agree with Sal: the second show at least nodded in the direction of respectable journalism. He'd taken a sensational local murder, of a prominent developer, and used it as the springboard for a look at how contracts are awarded in the city and suburbs. Although too much of the footage showed the man at Cancun with three women in string bikinis, Murray did wedge in fifty-seven seconds on how contracts get handed out in Illinois.

"Some of it was respectable, but he was too chicken to mention Poilevy by name," I grumbled when the show ended.

"You want egg in your beer?" Sal said. "Guy can't do everything."

"I wish he'd covered the women's prison at Coolis. That'd be a great place to showcase a cozy pair of dealmakers. I'm surprised it's not called Baladine City."

"Vic, this may make sense to you, but it's Greek to me."

"Ever since that wretched party you threw here last week, I've been running around in circles. Like my dog Mitch chasing his tail, come to think of it—exhausting and about as meaningful." I told her what I'd been doing. "And don't tell me it's none of my business, because it is, even if no one is paying me for it."

"Get off your high horse, St. Joan." Sal poured me another finger of Black Label. "It's your time and money; do what you want with it."

That encouragement didn't cheer me as much as it might have, but dinner at Justin's in the west Loop—where the owner knew Sal and whisked us past a dumbfounded line of beautiful Chicagoans—made me much happier. At least until I caught sight of Alex Fisher halfway through my tuna in putanesca sauce.

I couldn't help staring. Alex was at a table with Teddy Trant and a bald man with the kind of shiny face all Illinois politicians take on after too much time snuffling around in the public trough. Jean-Claude Poilevy in person. If Trant would rather eat with him and Alex than the exquisite Abigail, there was something seriously wrong with his taste.

When we got up to leave, Alex and her convoy were still talking over coffee. Sal tried to dissuade me, but I went to their table. Trant was as perfectly groomed as his wife, down to the clear polish on his manicured nails.

"Mr. Trant," I said. "V. I. Warshawski. I wanted to let you know I appreciate your willingness to send me some work. I'm sorry I couldn't take it on for you."

Alex gave me a look that could have done laser surgery on my nose, but Trant shook my hand. "Global tries to do business with local firms. It helps us anchor ourselves in cities we're new to."

"Is that why you've been talking to Lucian Frenada?" It was a guess, based on the Mad Virgin decal I'd glimpsed at Special-T earlier in the evening, but everyone at the table froze.

Poilevy put down his coffee cup with a clatter. "Is that the guy you were—"

"Lucian Frenada is the man who's been harassing Lacey." Alex cut him off quickly and loudly.

"Sure, Sandy, sure. It's not a bad story, even if it has a few holes around the edges. Alex, I mean. She changed nicknames in the last twenty years," I added to Trant. "We were such good pals when she was Sandy, I keep forgetting she's Alex now."

"What do you mean, holes around the edges?" Poilevy asked.

"I did a little looking. I talked to Lucian Frenada. I talked to the head of security at Ms. Dowell's hotel. Maybe the studio is overreacting to the scene between Frenada and Ms. Dowell at the Golden Glow last week —understandable with an important star—but I can't find any evidence that Frenada's been hanging around her."

"That isn't what I asked you to investigate," Alex snapped.

"No, but you haven't been asked to pay me anything either, have you."

Sal came up behind me and put a hand on my arm. "Let's go, Vic. I've got to get back to the Glow—it's my night to close."

I reminded Alex and Trant that they knew Sal from last week's party. We all said meaningless nothings, about Murray's debut, about Sal's bar, but I would have given a month's billings to know what they said when Sal and I moved out of earshot. I turned to look when we got to the door; they were bent over the table like the three witches over a pot.

20

Child in Mourning

WHAT WITH THE drive to Coolis and the long night hopping around town, I was glad to crawl into bed. I read a little of Morrell's book on the Disappeared in South America, stretching my legs between clean sheets to pull the kinks out of my spine.

The phone rang as I was drifting off. I groaned but stuck out an arm and mumbled a greeting. There was a pause on the other end, then someone garbled my name in a hurried voice just above a whisper.

"Yes, this is V. I. Warshawski. Who is this?"

"It's—This is Robbie. Robbie Baladine. I was at the gate, you know, when you came last week, you know, when you talked to my mom about—about Nicola."

I came fully awake in a hurry, turning on the light as I assured him that I remembered him well. "You're the expert tracker. What can I do for you?"

"I—It's not for me, but Nicola. I want—want to go to her funeral. Do you know when it is?"

"There's a problem about that," I said carefully. "The morgue seems to have lost her body. I don't know how that happened, but until they find it there can't be a funeral."

"So he was right." His young voice was filled with a

kind of bitterness. "I thought he was making it up to—to tease me."

"Your dad?"

"Yeah, old BB." He was forgetting to whisper in his anguish. "Him and Eleanor, they've been so mean about Nicola. Since she died and all. When I said I wanted to go to her funeral, they said why, so I could stand around with all the emotional spicks and bawl to my heart's content, and then finally BB said there wouldn't be a funeral because no one could find the body and to—to shut the fuck up."

"I'm sorry, honey," I said inadequately. "I guess your dad worries about whether he's a tough enough man, and so he's always on guard against any strong feelings. I don't suppose it's much comfort to you now, but can you imagine him as someone who is incredibly weak and scared so he acts like a bully to keep other people from guessing how scared he is?"

"You think that could really be true?" There was wistfulness in the young voice, a hope that his father's meanness wasn't due to his own failings.

I thought of Baladine, casually helping with the dismemberment of African newborns, getting his hands dirty, and wondered if my diagnosis had any basis in reality. Maybe he was someone who enjoyed torture for its own sake, but I gave Robbie a hearty assurance I didn't feel.

"Your father is a cruel man. Whatever the reason for his cruelty, will you try to remember that his sadism is about him, about his needs and weaknesses, and not about you?"

I talked to him for a few more minutes, until he'd recovered enough equilibrium for me to turn the conversation. There were two questions I wanted to put to him before we hung up. The first was about Nicola's smoking. Oh, no, Robbie said, she never smoked, not like Rosario, their nanny now, who was always sneaking off behind the garage for a cigarette, which made Eleanor furious, because she could still smell the smoke on her breath even after Rosario swallowed a zillion peppermints. Nicola said she had to save all her money for her children; she couldn't waste it on cigarettes or drinking.

My second question was whether his dad owned any shoes with horseshoe emblems—and if he did, were any of the emblems missing. Robbie said he didn't know, but he'd look.

It made me feel like a creep, asking Robbie to spy on his own father—but I suppose it also made me feel like I was paying BB back for his frothing over his son's masculinity. If he'd been proud of his sensitive child I might not have done it. But if he could be proud of a sensitive child, he wouldn't be doing other stuff.

Before Robbie hung up I asked, as casually as I could, how he'd gotten my unlisted home number: it wasn't on the business card I left him last week.

"It was in BB's briefcase," Robbie muttered. "Don't tell me I'm a criminal to go snooping in his case, it's the only way I know when he's planning something awful, like that camp for fat kids he sent me to last summer. I checked it out, and he had this whole file on you, your home number and everything."

My blood ran cold. I knew Baladine had done research on me—he'd made that clear enough on Friday—but it seemed worse, somehow, his carrying the information around with him.

"Doesn't he keep his case locked?"

"Oh, that. Anyone with half a brain knows all you

have to do is plug in his ship's ID, the biggest number in his life."

I laughed and told him he was plenty smart enough to keep up with his dad if he could remember not to let BB get under his skin. In case I ever needed to burgle Baladine's briefcase myself, I got Robbie to give me his father's ship number. On that note he seemed to feel calm enough to hang up.

I finally went to sleep, but in my dreams Baladine was lugging Nicola Aguinaldo's body through Frenada's factory, while Lacey Dowell leaned heavy breasts forward, clutching her crucifix and whispering, "Her hands are dirty. Don't tell her anything, or the vampire will get you."

In the morning I had a call from the operations manager at Continental United, asking me to come in to discuss my report. He thanked me for writing so clearly that everyone could understand it: too many firms cloak the obvious in meaningless jargon, he said. Maybe it was my ability to write a clear English sentence that kept Continental coming to me, rather than my superior analytic skills.

They didn't want to fire the dispatcher without concrete evidence, the operations manager added, or without knowing whether the plant manager was in on the scam.

"If you want to spend the money you'll have to have someone on the spot doing surveillance," I said. "It'll take two people. One to handle the truck, one to operate a camera. And it has to be people who aren't at the plant, because you don't know how many employees on the ground are involved, or at least aware."

As I'd feared, they nominated me as the one to handle the camera. And they figured their fleet manager in

Nebraska could pose as a truck driver, as a walk-on for someone out sick. They were losing so much money on that route, not just from replacing tires but from lost delivery time, that they wanted me to "do what it takes, Vic; we know you're not going to pad a bill for the heck of it."

I was sort of flattered, although, remembering Alex-Sandy's scorn for my low fees, I wondered if it was more a description of a low-rent outfit than a compliment. My man made a call to Nebraska; the fleet manager would meet me in Atlanta tomorrow night. A nice bonus for me if we wrapped it up quickly.

From Continental United's offices I went to the Unblinking Eye. They carry surveillance matériel as well as running a more prosaic film and camera business. I talked to the surveillance specialist about the kind of equipment I ought to use. They had some marvelous gadgets—a still camera that fit in a button, one that was disguised in a wristwatch, even one in the kid's teddy bear if you wanted to watch the nanny. Too bad Eleanor Baladine hadn't trained one on Nicola Aguinaldo. Or maybe she had—the Baladines probably had every up-to-the-moment security device you might want.

I settled on a video camera that you wore like a pair of glasses, so that it followed the road as you drove. You needed two people to operate it, since it required a separate battery pack, but that was okay: the Continental fleet manager would wear the glasses while I operated the equipment. I saw no need to plunk down four grand of Continental's money to own the camera, but took it on a week's rental.

The Unblinking Eye is on the west edge of the Loop. It didn't seem that far out of the way to drive the extra

fourteen blocks to the morgue to see if Nicola Aguinaldo's body had turned up. Since Vishnikov starts
work at seven I wasn't sure he'd still be there this late in
the afternoon, but he was actually walking to his car
when I pulled into the lot. I ran over to intercept him.

When he saw me he stopped. "The girl who died at
Beth Israel. Is that why you're here?"

Her body hadn't turned up; he had lost track of the
inquiry in the press of other problems, but he'd get
back to it tomorrow. "As I recall, the release form
wasn't signed. It's the trouble with these job sinkholes
the county runs. Most of our staff is good, but we always have some who are there because their daddies
hustle votes or move bodies for the mob. I've turned her
disappearance over to the sheriff for an investigation,
but a dead convict who was illegal to begin with
doesn't rank very high—family isn't in a position to
make a stink, and anyway, if they've been able to conduct a funeral they're not going to want to."

"I don't think this family has held a funeral. I
haven't seen them myself. In fact, I don't know where
they are, but a guy named Morrell has been interviewing immigrants in Aguinaldo's old neighborhood. He
says you know him, by the way."

"Morrell? He's a great guy. I know him from my
work on torture victims in the Americas. He pulled me
out of one of the worst traps I ever walked into, in
Guatemala. Nothing he doesn't know about the Americas and torture. I didn't realize he was in town. Tell him
to call me. I have to run." He climbed into his car.

I leaned in before he could shut the door. "But, Bryant—Morrell talked to Aguinaldo's mother. She didn't
even know her daughter was dead, so she definitely
doesn't have the body."

He stared at me in bewilderment. "Then who does have it?"

"I was hoping you could help on that one. If the form wasn't signed, is there a chance the body is still in the morgue? Maybe the tag got taken off or changed. The other possibility is that a Chicago police officer named Lemour got the body. Do you think there's any way to find out?"

He turned the ignition key. "Why would—never mind. I suppose it could have happened. I'll ask some more questions tomorrow." He pulled the door shut and shot past me out of the lot.

I walked back slowly to the Rustmobile. I wished Vishnikov hadn't turned the investigation over to the sheriff's office. If anyone was covering up for the disposal of Nicola's body, the sheriff's office was probably knee-deep in how it was done. But I had enough going on without trying to run an inquiry at the morgue.

I went home to take the dogs for a swim and to let my neighbor know I'd be in Georgia for a few days. I also called my answering service, telling them to hand any problems over to Mary Louise until Monday.

I drove up to O'Hare with Mary Louise and the boys to help put Emily on the plane to France. She was scared and excited but trying to cover it with a veneer of teen cool. Her father had given her a camcorder, which she used with a studied offhandedness. At the last minute, when he saw she was really leaving, four-year-old Nate began to bawl. As we comforted him and his sniffling brother, I thought again of poor Robbie, unable to express his grief over his dead nanny without his father tormenting him.

We took the boys out for an evening show of *Captain Doberman*—another Global moneymaker. Over ice cream afterward, Mary Louise and I discussed odds and ends.

"Emily wanted me to promise I wouldn't let you get Lacey in trouble while she was away." Mary Louise grinned. "I think it was more like a subtle hint that she wanted every word of any conversation you and Lacey have."

"I haven't seen Lacey, only her old childhood friend Frenada. Over at his Special-T—" I broke off. "Mary Louise, you left me a note about the report from Cheviot on that shirtdress they found on Nicola's body. You wrote down that the label said it was a specialty shirt. Could it have been *Special-T*?"

I spelled out the difference. Mary Louise looked chagrined and said she would check with the engineer at Cheviot Labs in the morning. She asked if I wanted her to go over to Frenada's shop and talk to him while I was away, but we decided that could wait until I got back from Georgia.

It was past ten when I got home, but I wanted to pack my gun before going to bed. It's a time-consuming business, and in the morning I'd be too rushed to get it done to FAA specs. I laid packing and cleaning materials on the dining room table and took the gun apart, placing two empty magazines in the carton—the cartridges have to be packed separately. I was cleaning the slide when the phone rang.

It was Rachel from my answering service. "I'm sorry to call so late, Vic, but a man named Lucian Frenada is trying to get in touch with you. He says it's really urgent and he doesn't care if it's midnight, if you don't call him he's going to get the police to find you and bring you to him."

I blinked—that was a curious coincidence. When the

phone at the factory didn't answer, I reached him at home.

He was so furious he could hardly get out a coherent sentence. "Did you plant this story? Are you behind this effort to defame me?"

"Do you know that I have no clue what you're talking about? But I have a question for—"

"Don't play the innocent with me. You come to my plant with insinuations, and twenty-four hours after I refuse to hire you, this—this slander appears."

"Which slander? Innocent or not, I don't know what it is."

"In the paper, tomorrow's paper, you thought I wouldn't see it? Or not so early?"

"Okay, if we have to do it by twenty questions, let me guess. There's a story about you in tomorrow morning's paper, is that right? About you and Lacey? You and that Virgin T-shirt? Do you want to tell me, or do you want to hold while I go out and find a newsstand with the early edition in it? I can be back in half an hour, probably."

I don't know whether he believed me or not, but he didn't want to wait for me to call him back. He read me from Regine Mauger's column in the early edition of the *Herald-Star:* "*A little bird at the State's Attorney says Lucian Frenada, who's been hanging around Lacey Dowell all week like a sick pit bull, may be using his T-shirt factory to smuggle cocaine into Chicago from Mexico.*"

"Is that it?" I asked.

"Is that it?" he mimicked bitterly. "It is more than enough. She calls me a sick pit bull, which is a racist slur anyway, and then accuses me of being a drug dealer, and you think I shouldn't be angry? My biggest order of my life, the New Jersey Suburban Soccer League, they can cancel if they think I'm a criminal."

I tried to stay patient. "I mean, is that the only story on you in the paper? Regine Mauger can print anything as a rumor. A little bird told her. I don't know if anyone at Global—I mean the *Herald-Star*—fact-checks her. But if they ran a news story, that means they have actual evidence."

"No one could have evidence of this, because it isn't true. Unless they made it up." He was still angry, but calmer. "And I am thinking you could have been a little bird yourself, out of revenge."

"Then you aren't thinking at all," I snapped. "If I want to stay in business the last thing I'll do is run smear campaigns on people who spurn my services. That word gets around fast. The next thing I'd know, all my clients would have left me for Carnifice."

"So if you didn't plant that story, who did, and why?"

I let out a compressed breath. "You want to hire me to find out, Mr. Frenada, I'll be glad to talk it over. Otherwise, since I'm leaving town in the morning, I need to get to bed."

"That would be funny, wouldn't it—I call to chew you out and end up hiring you. The trouble is, I am so vulnerable, I and my small company." His voice trailed away.

I knew that feeling. "Do you feel like telling me the odd thing you mentioned last week, or why you had a Lacey Dowell shirt in your plant?"

"I—they came—I made a couple on spec." He floundered for words. "It didn't get me anywhere. Global uses offshore labor, it's much cheaper than anything I can produce."

"Why didn't you want to tell me last night?"

He hesitated. "For personal reasons."

"To do with Lacey?" When he didn't say anything I added, "You didn't make the shirtdress Nicola Aguinaldo was wearing when she died, by any chance?"

He became totally quiet, so much so I could hear the tree toads croaking from the back of the house. Frenada gave me a hurried good night and hung up.

So he did know something about Nicola Aguinaldo's death. That was a sad and startling thought, but it wasn't as urgent for me at the moment as my own fury with Murray. Was that what he told Alex Fisher-Fishbein I would do—plant evidence of a cocaine ring at Special-T Uniforms? And then, when I didn't jump at their offer, he and Alex decided to move matters on by putting a rumor in the paper?

I called Murray. He wasn't at home—or at least he wasn't answering, and he wasn't at the office. I tried his cell phone.

"Vic! How in hell did you get this number? I know damned well I never gave it to you."

"I'm a detective, Ryerson. Getting a cell phone number is child's play. It's the grown-up stuff that has me baffled. What was the point of that charade you and Alex Fishbein acted out in my office last week?"

"It was not a charade. It was a serious offer to give you—"

"Some crumbs from Global's richly spread table. But when I didn't snatch the bait you took an easier tack and planted a story in that prize bitch Regine Mauger's ear. The last time she checked a source was probably 1943, but it doesn't matter if a column devoted to innuendo gets the facts wrong."

"How do you know they're wrong? How do you

know he isn't smuggling coke in through his shirt factory?"

"So you did plant the story with her!" I was so furious I was spitting into the receiver.

"No, I didn't," he shouted. "But I read my own damned paper to see what they're printing. And yes, I usually get the early edition as soon as it's out. If you've made yourself the guy's champion you are going to have egg all over your smug face. And I for one will not be sorry to help plaster it there. My story will run on Friday, and it will sizzle."

"What are you talking about?" I demanded. "Did going on TV make you feel checking facts was for little people? I looked into Frenada's finances when you and Sandy Bitchbein came around last week. He's clean as a whistle."

"Clean as a whistle? One that's been in the sewer for a week. I did a priority check on Frenada when I learned Regine was running this little tidbit. Guy's got money parked all over the globe."

"Bullshit," I screamed. "I looked him up on Life-Story on Sunday and he doesn't have a dime except the pittance that little T-shirt factory makes for him."

"No." Murray was suddenly quiet. "You didn't. You couldn't have. I just ran a check on him, a priority-one, two thousand bucks to turn it around in ten hours, and it's not true. He's got three accounts in Mexico that are worth a million five U.S. dollars each."

"Murray. I ran the check. I did at the deepest level of numbers. That's why I turned down Bitchbein's offer."

"Her name is Fisher. Why you have a knot in your ass about her—"

"Never mind that. Don't let her wave so many

Golden Globes in front of you that you're too blinded to see the facts, Murray. And by the way, if you're planning on leading your story with, 'There was egg all over smug V. I. Warshawski's face,' don't, because there won't be. I'm leaving town in the morning, but as soon as I get back I'll fax you a copy of that LifeStory report. If I were you, I'd hold off running your sizzle until you've seen it."

I hung up smartly and went back to packing my gun. I'd been feeling irritable about going to rural Georgia, but taking on some punks putting nails under truck tires was beginning to sound downright wholesome compared to what I was looking at here in Chicago.

I was too tired, and too agitated by Murray to figure out what was going on with all these people. If Frenada manufactured the dress Nicola was wearing when she died, how had she gotten it? Had he given it to someone at Carnifice? Given it to Nicola herself? Or to Alex Fisher?

And then there was Global. They wanted me to expose Frenada, then miraculously came up with a rumor about him and cocaine when I wouldn't do the job. I wished I'd known that when I saw Trant and Poilevy last night. It could have made the conversation livelier, although I suppose Alex would have kept them from saying much.

My brain swirled uselessly. It was way too much for me to figure out with the minute information I had. I snapped the gun case shut and filled out the forms I needed for the airline. Put jeans and some sweatshirts in an overnight bag with the gun and a small kit of basic toiletries, then packed the surveillance camera, some blank cassettes, and a charger for the unit together with my maps in a briefcase. That should get me through a few nights away. A book for the flight. I was working my way through a history of Jews in Italy, trying to understand something of my mother's past. Maybe I'd get as far as Napoleon by the time I came home.

21

We Serve and Protect

I SPENT THE next several nights on the back roads of Georgia, sitting in the passenger seat of a fully loaded thirty-ton truck. The fleet manager, who looked authentic with a beer gut hanging over oil-stained jeans, had ambled in as a replacement for a sick driver; I was his girlfriend who hopped on board once the truck left the yard, but with plenty of people to see it happen. To make a long story short, it gave us the right veneer of venality, and we were able to rope in the dispatcher without much trouble. He fingered three buddies and the plant manager. And it was all on film, which made it tidy. Continental United promised an appropriate expression of gratitude—not the kind of bonus I might have snared from Alex Fisher, but enough to pay the Trans Am repairs and cover my mortgage for a couple of months.

When I got home Saturday afternoon, I felt refreshed, the way one does from executing a job well. And the job had been so straightforward, none of the tangled web of weirdness of Baladine and Frenada and Global Entertainment.

Despite my pleasure at being away from all those strange people, the first thing I did, after greeting Mr. Contreras and the dogs, was skim the *Herald-Star* for the last few days to see whether Murray's story on Frenada and the drug ring had run. To my relief it hadn't. Murray apparently still had enough journalism left to wait for the facts. I would reward this good behavior—or try to guarantee its continuation—by going down to my office right now to fax him the Life Story report on Frenada. I wanted to check my mail, anyway.

After taking the dogs to a pocket-size park in the neighborhood, I told my neighbor to fire up the grill, I'd be home for chicken and tomatoes in an hour. I picked up my briefcase, the camera and videocassettes still inside it, and drove the two miles south, humming "Voi che sapete" under my breath.

My happy mood disappeared as soon as I reached my office. I actually was halfway across the room before my brain registered the disaster. The deranged upheaval of papers on the floor wasn't because of me: someone had taken the place apart. Had dumped papers out of drawers with a wanton hand. Unzipped covers from the couch cushions and left them on the floor. Poured a cup of coffee over the papers on the desk. I gaped dumbly for a long moment, not moving, not thinking.

Street vandals. Druggies who'd seen I was away and taken advantage. But the computer and printer remained. Anyone looking for quick cash or the equivalent would have taken those, and anyway, the average druggie wasn't sophisticated enough to bypass the number pad on the front door.

I felt ill, an uncontrollable shiver rising along my back. The violation was too extreme. Someone had been in my space, had come in brazenly, made no effort to conceal it. Were they looking for something, or was this like smashing up hospitals in Zimbabwe—trying to terrify the civilian populace and destabilize the government?

My first impulse was like anyone's—call the cops, get away from the sickness as fast as possible. But if there was some signature in the mess that would tell me who had been there, I'd miss it if I let the cops look first. I sat on the arm of the couch, shaking, until I could control my legs enough to walk, then slid a bolt home on the inside of my office door. Someone— Baladine?—had proved he could get past the number pad on the front door without any trouble, but he'd have to break the inner door down to get past that bolt.

I zipped the cushions back into their covers. Even if I disturbed some vital piece of evidence, I needed to sit down. I wanted water too, but that meant going to the hall, to the refrigerator, and I didn't want to open my door until I felt safe inside my building.

What did I have that someone might want? Besides my computer, of course. My Isabel Bishop painting was the only valuable in the office. I got up and looked at the partition facing my desk. The painting had been tossed to the floor. I didn't touch it. The glass would show prints if any had been left.

Even Tessa absorbed in work would have responded to the racket made by this wantonness. Would the intruders have hurt Tessa? Again I wanted to run to the hall, run to look in her studio, but fear kept me locked inside.

I finally pulled my cell phone from my handbag and phoned Tessa's home. She lived with her parents in their Gold Coast duplex. Her mother answered, the rich contralto that worked magic in courtrooms around the country vibrating the airwaves.

"Victoria. How are you? I didn't recognize your voice."

"No, ma'am. I've had a bit of a shock. I just got in from out of town and found my office vandalized. I wanted to make sure Tessa was all right."

Mrs. Reynolds made the proper statements of alarm and concern but reassured me about Tessa. She had picked her daughter up at the studio for a cup of coffee around noon. Tessa was off for a weekend's sailing with friends, and Mrs. Reynolds, back from a busy week in Washington, had wanted to see her alone for a few minutes.

"When the police come, have them examine her studio to make sure nothing's wrong in there. I've never liked her being that close to Humboldt Park. I don't care how big her lats are, as she keeps telling me, or how good you are in a fight, you two young women need to be in a safer part of town."

"You're probably right, ma'am," I agreed, as the easiest way to end the conversation.

I leaned back on the couch and shut my eyes. Imagined lying in Lake Michigan with the sun overhead until my breath was calm enough for me to think about my situation. If this were Baladine's work it could be an attempt to terrorize me, but if he were also looking for something what would it be? I thought through my conversations during the last week, with Frenada, with Alex. With Murray. The last name came most reluctantly to mind.

I'd told Murray about my LifeStory report on Frenada, that I had proof he was clean. But this was not Murray Ryerson's work. It could not be. Murray was a journalist. The story and the chase, wherever the road led you, that was what mattered to him. Global couldn't have destroyed that in him in a few weeks, he was better than that. Really, he was.

I was saying the same thing over and over in my mind, as if standing in front of the bench pleading his case. I needed to find the hard copy, if it was still there, although with the leisure to search my absence had guaranteed them, the intruders could have turned over every piece of paper in the room.

I shut my eyes and tried to remember what I'd done with the LifeStory printout. I'd stuffed everything into a desk drawer, because I knew Mary Louise was going to be in using the desk, and unorganized stacks of files drove her mad. I opened the drawer. Many of the papers had been pulled out, exposing a box of tampons I kept there. They were rolling around in the drawer, and I automatically stuffed them back into the box. They wouldn't go in, so I picked up the carton, forgetting for the moment about evidence.

Inside was a plastic freezer bag filled with white powder. I stared at it, my numbed mind moving like a dog in quicksand. Cocaine. Maybe heroin—I wouldn't know one from the other. Someone wrecked my office and planted drugs in it. I didn't want to send it to a lab for testing, and I didn't want to explain it to the cops. I didn't want to explain it to anyone.

I leapt to my feet in a sudden frenzy and searched every drawer in the room, every light fixture, every crevice. I found two more bags—one taped inside the printer and the other tucked into a rip in the fabric underneath the couch.

I unbolted the door and ran down the hall to the bathroom, flushing and flushing until the powder was gone, until the bags—cut to pieces with Tessa's cuticle scissors—were gone, standing under the shower in my clothes, running hot water over me until I thought any treacherous trace of powder was gone. I got out and changed into a clean set of Tessa's work clothes. Hung my wet ones from a hook behind her studio entrance. A bubble of incipient hysteria made me want to leave a note on the refrigerator in our *I took* column. *I took one pair of cuticle scissors and a pair of khakis and a T-shirt. Will replace ASAP.*

Back in my office, I picked up the cell phone and called the cops. While I was waiting for them I put on a pair of latex gloves and looked gingerly through my papers. I had put the Frenada report in an old file, but I couldn't remember which. I could only remember thinking Mary Louise would have typed a fresh label at once. The squad car still hadn't shown when I came on the folder labeled *Alumni Fund*. The Frenada printout was still in there, along with the paramedics' report Max had faxed me from Beth Israel.

The police come slowly to this end of Wicker Park. On an impulse born of fear, I stuffed all the papers into a manila envelope, addressed them to Mr. Contreras, and went down the street to the mailbox at the corner of Western and North.

Elton was standing there with his usual ingratiating smile: *I will not hurt you, I am your friend, help me out.* He started his usual patter:

"*Streetwise,* miss. Get your update on hot bands in Chicago this weekend. Find a nice place for your boyfriend—oh, evening, Vic. You been away?"

I gave him a five and took a paper. "Been away. Someone broke into the office while I was gone. You notice anyone strange hanging out the last few nights?"

Elton scrunched up his face in earnest thought but shook his head regretfully. "But I'll be on the lookout

now, Vic, you can count on that. God bless you, Vic.
. . . *Streetwise,* sir. Now, how about a list of all the
hot new bands in this area, place to take your best
girl . . ."

Blue strobes were dancing toward me along North
Avenue. I hurried back up Leavitt and got to my office
as a blue-and-white pulled up. A young pair stepped
out, black woman, white man. The perfect TV cop-
show pair. I showed them mutely what I'd come on.

"You didn't touch anything, did you, ma'am?" the
woman asked, following me into the office.

"I—uh, I put the covers back on the couch." Somehow that seemed the worst thing. "I tried not to touch
any papers, but I'm not sure. Anyway, my prints are on
everything. Mine and my assistant's."

The male half of the team was on his radio sum-
moning additional troops. It's something cops love to
do. The work has so much tedium that when one of
them finds something, the others all get invited to look.
In ten minutes they had a whole battalion in place.

I was answering questions from the pair who took
the call—was anything missing, had the lock been
forced, how long had I been out of town—when a
plainclothes team arrived. A thin, triumphant voice demanded to know if the crew had searched the premises.

"I don't think the perp is on the premises, Sergeant,"
the woman said.

"Not for the perp, for drugs. We've got information
that Warshki is dealing."

Craning my neck, I saw Detective Lemour. He was
wearing the same brown polyester suit he'd had on the
first time I saw him, unless he'd bought a closetful on
sale at Wal-Mart.

I stood up. "Sergeant Lummox. What a coincidence. I didn't know you worked burglary."

"It's Lemour, and I don't work burglary, I work violent crimes. I told you I'd be on you like your underwear, but you went on across that line, Warshki, the one we knew you danced on, and we've got you dead to rights."

"What are you talking about, Lemming? Since when is it a crime in this town to be the victim of a major break-in?"

The woman on the team coughed to cover a laugh, while her male partner stood as solemnly as if he'd been embalmed.

"It's not a crime, if it really happened." He showed his row of little pike's teeth in a vindictive smile.

"If it really happened? Sergeant, I trust you have a tech unit on the way here to take prints, because if you don't I am going to be raising a serious complaint with the police review board. And if you accuse me in front of witnesses of dealing in drugs, then I will also sue you as a private citizen for slander."

"You do that, Warshki, but I have a red-hot tip that you've got a half kilo of powder right here on the premises. And you schmucks can stop grinning behind your hands and search this office. Now."

For the next twenty minutes, seven uniformed people turned my office over. The papers that the original invaders hadn't tossed joined the landfill in the middle of the room. I sat with my arms crossed, my lips tight with anger—and my heart thumping erratically. What if I had missed a niche? I hadn't climbed a ladder to deal with the ceiling fixtures—I'd only checked the lower ones, the spotlights and lamps that I'd installed when I moved in.

I was fuming with an impotent rage, wishing I could get him on film, when I remembered the surveillance camera in my briefcase. I picked it up from the floor next to the couch and pulled the glasses out. Lemour watched me closely, but when he saw I was only putting on glasses he turned his head away. In that brief moment I reached into my case and fumbled with the battery pack. After two nights in the dark roads of Luella County I could load it blindfolded. I put in a new tape and started recording, following the team's destructive swath through the room, but focusing mostly on Lemour.

Lemour himself went to my printer and pulled out the cartridge. When he didn't find the bag of powder he dropped the cartridge, leaving a sooty trail on the floor, and banged the printer on its side. Twelve hundred dollars of Hewlett Packard's best work. I hoped it would survive mauling.

Scowling with fury, he marched to the couch and yanked me to my feet. He ran a hand underneath, found the slit in the bottom, fumbled inside it. When he came up empty he bared his pike's teeth in an ugly grimace. He ordered two of the uniforms to turn the couch over. He ripped the fabric completely off the bottom and started prodding the interior.

At that point I pushed past him and went to the desk to beep my lawyer. "Freeman," I said to his machine. "It's V. I. Warshawski. The cop who was harassing me last week is in my office. I had a break-in; he came around accusing me of dealing drugs. And now he's ripped my couch and is wreaking havoc with my papers. If you get this message I'd appreciate your earliest possible response."

Lemour's thin lips were a line of rage. He shoved the

uniforms out of the way and yanked the phone from my hand, then slapped my face hard with his open palm. I kept my arms at my side through an effort of will so intense that my shoulders ached.

"You think you're smart, don't you, Warshki?" he hissed.

"Phi beta kappa my junior year at Chicago. That's usually for smart people, Lemming." I was taking singer's breaths, pushing air to the front of my mouth, keeping my voice light so that no cracks of fury showed in it.

He slapped the other side of my face. "Well, you're not as smart as you think you are. If I have to take this room apart brick by brick, I will find where you put that stash. I know it's here, you smart-assed broad. Cuff her while you finish searching," he added to the woman who'd answered my original call.

She couldn't look at me. Her dark face turned purply-black with shame as she locked my wrists together; she muttered, "I'm sorry," through lips that barely moved.

The glasses had slipped off my face at a cockeyed angle. She settled them back on my nose. My neck ached. Tension. Or maybe whiplash from the force of Lemour's blows.

The crew went through the room, then the hall and the bathroom. Brick by brick. Lemour watched, patches of red on his white cheeks, spittle forming around his mouth. I kept my video glasses on him as best I could with my arms hooked to a radiator coil.

When the team didn't find the drugs, I thought Lemour was going to go over the brink and choke me. He may have thought so too, but his cell phone rang before he could do it.

"Lemour," he snarled. "Oh . . . no, sir, it wasn't . . . we did, sir, all three places . . . bitch must've . . . I did, sir, but I couldn't be here twenty-four hours a day . . . I could still bring her in . . . I see. You can?" His pike's teeth showed in an unpleasant grin. "I'll look forward to that, sir."

He put the phone back in his pocket and turned to me. "Your lucky day, Warshki. My—boss says if you swallowed the evidence I can't hold you, although I'd like to bring you in and choke it out of you. You can go home. You—Holcumb, is it? Uncuff her and let her go."

While the officer undid the lock, she whispered that her mother was an upholsterer, that she'd bring her over in the morning and get her to repair my couch, no charge. I was too tired and too angry to do anything but nod my sore neck. I leaned against the wall, my arms crossed, until the last of the battalion had left. I barricaded the door from the inside and sat on the couch. The mess in the room was now so unbearable I couldn't imagine ever being able to work in this space again.

22

Night Crawlers

Mr. CONTRERAS ROUSED me from my stupor, calling on my office phone, his voice rough with anxiety: at four-thirty I'd said I'd be back in an hour for dinner, and here it was almost eight. When I told him what had happened he insisted on flagging a cab and coming to the office. Nothing I said could dissuade him, and in my fragmented state I didn't try too hard. When he knocked on the door fifteen minutes later, I shocked both of us by bursting into tears.

"This is terrible, doll, this is terrible. Who could've done such a thing? That cop, that creep that wanted to arrest you last week? And he hit you? You can't take that. You gotta tell someone. Call the lieutenant. Call Detective Finchley."

I blew my nose. "Yeah. Maybe. What I'd like is to get some kind of padlock for the doors. Whoever broke in bypassed the code on the front door. They can break down padlocks too, but they'll be more obvious from the street if they're doing that."

One of the chains had opened a big all-night home supply store not too far from my building. The old man rode over with me and helped pick out locks and tools. When we got back I was still so jumpy that I insisted on inspecting both my office and Tessa's studio to make sure no one had arrived in my absence.

While Mr. Contreras set to work installing the locks, I made a half-hearted effort to organize the wreck. The Isabel Bishop I handled with latex gloves, putting it in a plastic bag to give to Mary Louise on Monday. I wanted her to get it dusted for fingerprints and to have someone in the department run a check on AFIS. I also figured I could pay her to put files in order: it would be so much easier for her than for me, since she was not only more organized, but not so emotionally invested in the destruction.

I did restore the couch, screw in the light bulbs that the vandal cops had removed, picked up obvious garbage, scrubbed coffee stains from the little bit of carpet. My mother's engraving of the Uffizi Gallery had been knocked over and the glass cracked. I bit my lip but put it in the bag with the Isabel Bishop. I wasn't going to break down over this. The picture wasn't damaged underneath; the glass could be replaced.

The printer cartridge Lemour had dropped on the floor was leaking carbon. I threw it out, cleaned out the printer, and installed a fresh cartridge. I held my breath and turned on the machine. I hit the TEST button, and a page of beautifully executed font samples ran out the mouth. I felt better. One small vessel saved from the inferno.

When Mr. Contreras grunted with satisfaction that he'd got the place pretty well bolted down, my office still looked like the *Titanic* after the iceberg. Who would have thought the old room had so much paper in it?

Mr. Contreras praised my progress—more visible to

him than me—and I dutifully praised his handiwork, which was actually quite impressive. With a handful of inexpensive tools he'd installed a serious lock system. Nothing is impregnable, but this would take long enough to smash that Elton or someone might wander along and interrupt the intruders. I took time to call Tessa's mother to explain what I'd done and to leave a message for Tessa—I'd drop off a spare key before she got back from her sailing trip.

As we walked to the car, Elton popped out of the shadows. "Saw you had the cops with you, Vic. They find anything?"

"*Nada*. But the sergeant who came is in on the fix. If you see anyone—don't call 911, because the cops may be the perps. Call—can he call you?" I asked Mr. Contreras. "I'm not home enough."

My neighbor wasn't pleased at my involving him with a street person, but he grudgingly agreed that I could write his phone number on one of my business cards and hand it to Elton. "Call collect," I recklessly committed my neighbor. Illinois Bell charges thirty-five cents—it's even harder for the homeless to come up with correct change than for the rest of us.

When we got home I insisted first on inspecting the Rustmobile to make sure no contraband had been slipped into the trunk. Then I brought Mitch and Peppy up to the third floor with me while I made a circuit of my apartment. I was ashamed of my jumpy vulnerability, but every time I thought of those bags of white powder, the skin on the back of my neck crawled.

My neighbor put fresh charcoal on the grill outside his back door and started cooking chicken. Before going down I called Lotty, hoping for sympathy—and a prescription for my sore neck. She gave not just sympathy but alarm, trying to persuade me to spend the night in the safety of her eighteenth-story apartment. I thought I'd be happier in my own home, among my own things, but told her I'd keep the dogs with me until things simmered down.

"As far as your neck goes, my dear—aspirin and ice. Ice now and before you go to bed. And call me in the morning."

I felt irrationally bereft when she hung up. She'd offered me a bed—why did I want technical medicine instead of love? Ice, when the left side of my neck was sore to the touch? What did Lotty know about neck injuries, anyway. I stomped into the kitchen, filled a freezer bag with ice, and pressed it against the sore area, as if determined to prove her wrong. Instead, by the time Mr. Contreras phoned up to say the chicken was cooked, I could move my head more easily. Which made thinking more possible as well.

The cassettes that I'd made of Lemour in my office—I needed to do something with those. A copy for my lawyer, and maybe one for Murray. Would he run a story on the break-in? Was I testing him, to see whose orders he was following?

After dinner I went back upstairs and hooked the cassette pack up to my VCR and ran the tape. Knowing I had sat passively while Lemour grew ever more demented made me feel the violations of the afternoon all over again. My stomach clenched. I could hardly bring myself to keep watching. When I heard the call that made Lemour let me go, though, I sat up and played it back several times.

His caller kept cutting him off. Perhaps he didn't like

Lemour's thin nasal voice. But maybe he didn't want Lemour revealing too much on an open line. Lemour's evil grin, and the way he said he'd look forward to that —whatever *that* was—made it clear they had some more elaborate frame in store. Although what could be more elaborate than drugs planted in my office I didn't know. Maybe I should go to Lotty's after all.

I stopped the tape again when Lemour said it was my lucky day, I could go home. He paused before saying his "boss" had ordered my release. A cop does not refer to superiors as bosses; he calls them by title—lieutenants or watch commanders—whatever the highest rank happens to be. So who was on the phone? Baladine? Jean-Claude Poilevy?

Maybe a really sensitive machine could pick up the voice of the person speaking to Lemour. I could talk to the engineer at Cheviot Labs about that, but it would probably have to wait until Monday. Just in case the guy came in on weekends I left a message on his voice mail.

I locked the tape in my closet safe and went back downstairs to collect the dogs. With an aspirin on top of my long day—my long week—I was asleep as soon as I turned out the light.

Two hours later the phone pulled me up and out of a deep well of sleep. "Ms. Warshawski? Is that you?" The hoarse whisper was barely audible. "It's Frenada. I need you at once. At my plant."

He hung up before I could say anything. I held the receiver to my ear, listening to the silence at the other end. My mind had that deceptive clarity that the first hours of a sound sleep bring. Frenada didn't have my home phone number: when he called to scream about

Regine Mauger's blurb in the *Herald-Star*, he got me through my answering service. Perhaps he used caller ID and had picked up my number when I called his home.

I turned on my bedside light and looked at my own ID pad. *Caller unidentifiable.* The person had either blocked the call or was using a cell phone. I went into the living room. Mitch and Peppy had been sleeping next to the bed, but they followed me, crossing in front of each other so that I had a hard time moving.

I nudged them out of the way and found my briefcase where I'd left it, next to the television. I dug out the Palm Pilot and looked up Special-T Uniforms. When I phoned the plant, the number rang fifteen times without an answer. His home phone gave me only his bilingual message.

"So what should I do, guys?"

Mitch looked up at me hopefully. *Go for a run* seemed to be his advice. Peppy lay down and began methodical work on her forelegs, as if to say, *Take a bath and go back to sleep.*

"It's a setup, don't you think? Lemour's handler made him release me. So that they could trap me at the plant? Leaving me with egg all over my smug face, as Ryerson informed me Wednesday night? Or was this really Frenada, in serious trouble? In which case, why didn't he call the cops, instead of me?"

The dogs looked at me anxiously, trying to figure out my mood from my voice. Maybe Frenada's experience with the cops was the same one I'd had this evening, so that he didn't feel he could rely on them.

A wiser person would have followed Peppy's advice and stayed home. Maybe I am that wiser person now—experience does change you—but in the middle of the night, with that sensation of looseness that made me think I was still thirty and able to leap tall buildings at a bound, I pulled on my jeans and running shoes, put my gun back together and stuck it in a shoulder holster under a sweatshirt, put my PI and driver's licenses in my back pocket with a handful of bills, and made my cautious way down the back stairs. To their annoyance, I left the dogs behind—if I got involved in a shooting war I didn't want them complicating the battle.

Lemour thought he could get me, but I would make a monkey of him. That seemed to be the gist of my thinking, if acting solely on impulse can be called thinking.

I drove past the plant at Grand and Trumbull. A light was shining through one of the rear windows on the second floor. In case Lemour had set a trap, I didn't slow down but turned south at the next intersection. I parked three blocks away.

Saturday nights on the fringes of Humboldt Park are not quiet. The streets in this industrial section were empty, but sirens and dogs keened a few blocks away. I even heard roosters crowing. Someone was running a cockfight nearby. A freight train squeaked and hooted in the distance. As it drew near, its rackety *clank-clank* drowned out other sounds.

When I got to Frenada's building I scouted it as closely as I could in the dark. I paused outside an old delivery van, listening intently at the rear doors to see if it was a stakeout vehicle, although it was hard to hear anything above the thundering of the freight train.

I stood across the street from the entrance for ten minutes, waiting for some sign of life. Or was I waiting for my courage to build enough for me to enter a rickety building alone in the dark? The longer I stood, the more inclined I would be to go home without looking inside. And what if that really had been Frenada on the phone? And what if he really was in trouble, bleeding, dead? Then what? I took a deep breath and crossed the street.

The front door was unlocked. *It's a trap, Vic,* the sensible voice whispered, but I slid sideways through the opening, gun in hand, palm clammy against the stock.

Inside the entrance, the dark wrapped around me like a living cloak. I could feel it grabbing at my neck, and the soreness, which I'd forgotten, came back. I moved cautiously to the stairwell, fighting the impulse to turn tail and run.

I climbed the slippery concrete stairs, pausing on each riser to strain for noises inside. Outside, the freight thumped and squeaked into the distance. In the sudden stillness I could hear the sirens and car horns again, making it hard to focus on the building. I hugged the stairwell wall, trying to make no sound myself, hoping the hammering of my heart was audible only to me.

At the top landing I could see a bar of light under Special-T's door. I moved faster, as if light itself meant safety. At the door I knelt down to look through the keyhole but saw only the legs of the long worktable. I lay flat, trying not to think of the filth of decades against my face (how many men had spat on this floor when walking out at the end of the day?), my eye pressed against the thin slit of light. All I saw were bolts of fabric and some wadded-up paper. I waited a long time, watching for feet, or for a shadow to move. When nothing happened I stood up and tried the handle. Like the outer door, the one to the shop floor was open.

A clothes shop is probably always chaotic, but Special-T looked as though someone had tossed the place through a wind tunnel. Whoever had rampaged through my office had been here as well. The long tables in the middle where the cutting took place had been cleared; fabric, shears, and pattern stencils lay in a heap around them. Along the wall, the sewing machines stood with their covers unscrewed. A single light over one of the machines was the one that I'd seen from the street.

I moved fearfully toward a small room at the back, expecting at any second to come on Frenada's body. Instead, I found more signs of upheaval. The vandals had taken the room apart with a ruthless hand. The intruders had been looking for something: drawers stood open, their contents dangling over the side to spill on the floor. A piece of loose tile had been pulled up and tossed to one side. Invoices, dressmaking patterns, and fabric samples made a gaudy stew on the floor. The bulbs had been removed from the desk lamp.

I was certain that there must be bags of powder on the premises, but it wasn't a search I wanted to make alone and in the dark. I looked in Frenada's office for the Mad Virgin shirt I'd seen on Tuesday. When a quick inspection of the tangled heap of cloth and paper didn't reveal it, I moved to the hall. I'd see if Frenada was in the john or at the back by the freight elevator; if he wasn't on the premises I was out of Dodge.

The toilet was in the hall that ran outside Special-T's door. A supply closet was next to it; the freight elevator was at the end farthest from the stairs. I had looked inside the closet and found nothing more disgusting than a mop that needed a good bath in disinfectant, when I heard the scuffling sound of a door opening, of many feet trying to sneak silently up concrete stairs. A second later a train began to wheeze and crank its way up the track: if they'd waited only a heartbeat longer I'd never have heard them.

23

A Run to O'Hare

I SLID OUT of the supply closet. No cover there. Where? No way to scale the wall, no way up to those windows. I ducked into the freight elevator. The train rattled the walls, drowning any sound of my pursuit. If they'd started up the stairs, it wouldn't take them long to look in here. Even if I had a key to start the elevator, while it toiled downstairs a dozen men could wait outside the door and pick me off like a duck in a crate.

Fool. Damned cocky fool to plunge into this building when the whole evening was painted with red warning signs, stay away, don't touch. Someone knew me too well, knew that I'd weigh the risks and take them anyway. Set the tiger trap. If I was a real tiger I could have leapt from shop floor to window and been on my way.

I looked around the elevator cage. The service hatch stood open. I measured the distance: about four feet over my head. I wasn't a tiger, and I'd get only one chance on these forty-plus muscles. A light bounced off the hallway wall. I crouched, swung my arms, and jumped. My hands clawed at the edge of the opening. Left hand on a nail, grab hard with my right while I move the left, claw for purchase, fingers digging into splintery wood, biceps bulging as they hoist my weight.

The freight train screeching past covered my scramble through the hatch, my rasping breath.

Above me a skylight filtered in starlight, showing ghostly shapes of cables and the wooden slab that covered the hatch. I slid it across the opening. The cage shook with the thundering of the train but settled down as the noise receded. I started hearing voices, words muffled by the shaft, then one directly under me.

"She should be here."

My stomach heaved, felt as though it might split itself open.

"Did you see her leave home?" Lemour's unmistakable squeak.

"No, but her car's gone. She must have gone out through the alley before we thought of putting a watcher out back. And there's no answer on her phone."

"Then we beat her here. Maybe she stopped for help. I'll get someone into the broom closet, someone in Frenada's office. You wait here."

The voices faded. I was sitting on a piece of metal. Now that I knew I must not move, I became aware of every surface detail—an edge like a razor cutting into my left buttock, the cable under my right foot that would twang if my sore muscles buckled.

I took slow careful breaths, the air scraping against my dry throat. I was terrified that I might have to cough. I inched my neck slowly back so that I could see the skylight. Some rungs were bolted to the wall leading up to it. If I could get to them without the man in the elevator hearing . . . Tilting my head back increased the strain on my throat, and a large cough built in my lungs. I held it as long as I could, desperately swallowing but unable to produce enough saliva to coat it. Just as I could hold it no longer the cage began to shake again. For a brief flash of terror I thought the watcher was following me up the hatch, but as the cough exploded in my chest, another train began to rumble behind the building.

Grabbing the cable in front of me, I eased myself to my feet. My left thigh trembled. I'd been bracing myself with it, not realizing until I started to move that it held my weight. I flexed my leg cautiously; even with the train as cover I couldn't afford a loud noise here in the shaft.

As soon as the worst cramping subsided, I stepped to the edge of the cage and tugged on the rung above my head. It seemed secure. Holding it firmly I pushed with my right leg on the rung in front of me. It held as well. I stepped off the edge of the cage and began hoisting myself up. Like in Ms. McFarlane's gym class back in high school, when we had to climb ropes. *Why,* one of the girls had demanded, *we're never going to be firefighters.* If I got out of here—when I got out of here—I'd go back to South Chicago and tell today's know-all adolescents: *The day may come when you're as stupid as me, when you've backed yourself into an ambush and need to climb out of it.*

A short climb, only fifteen feet. Five rungs to the skylight. Step, hoist, and then a final yard into space to reach a tiny platform for the work crew to sit on. You couldn't be a very big machinist and work in this space. And why didn't the skylight open? Didn't they ever need to get out on the roof? I couldn't see a latch. Was this window simply decorative?

The train continued to rattle underneath. I pulled my gun from my shoulder holster and smashed the stock, hard, against the glass. It crashed down the shaft. No one could overlook that sound. I knocked the glass clear from frame. Pulled my sweatshirt over my head and erupted through the window as the watcher underneath me shouted for backup.

I scrambled onto the flat tar roof and ran to the edge. A cop car was parked on Trumbull, blue strobes inviting, warning bystanders. Another covered the west end of the building. I backed away and ran to the other side. The freight tracks curved behind the building. The train rocking slowly through the turn cut off any escape on that side.

In the middle of the roof a head popped through the broken skylight. "Freeze, Warshki!"

I fell to the flat tar as Lemour fired. Swung my legs over the side. Extended my body by my fingertips. Lemour ran toward me. I twisted as far to the right as I could and dropped.

Like falling off a bike. The boxcar moved forward underneath me; I fought to keep upright but landed hard on my left hip and forearm.

I lay that way, rocking with the train, so happy at my escape that I almost relished the pain in my side. A badge of the adventure. I wasn't too old to leap tall buildings after all. I grinned stupidly in the dark.

I lay that way for about ten minutes, watching streetlamps and tree branches rock past. As my euphoria at escaping died down, I began to worry about what to do next. I couldn't ride this train out of town. Or I could, but what would I do then? A stay in a cornfield overnight. Persuade someone to give a beat-up, disheveled specimen a ride to the nearest town. Some small-town Wisconsin cop finding me with a gun on me and not believing I had any right to it. Even worse was the possibility that Lemour was following the train. I stopped grinning and sat up.

I had no idea where I was. The city as familiar to me as the bones and markings of my face had changed into a mass of signal lights and looping tracks. I felt alone in the swirling dark. The train was gathering speed, hurling through strange seas toward strange land. A southbound freight rattled past, shaking me so hard I lay down again.

A plane floated over me, a giant grasshopper, its lights bulging eyes. Lying on my back I could see the belly light, the landing gear. O'Hare. So at least we were somewhere near the city.

The train suddenly braked, with a jolting screech that rocked me back again on my sore hip. I didn't take time to curse or feel my bruises but scrambled crablike to the front of the car, found the ladder and climbed down. The train was still moving, although slowly. I jumped free of the slicing wheels, rolling with the motion of the train, landing on grass, rolling downhill, my gun digging into my breast, until I came to rest against a concrete wall.

I got on my hands and knees, but when I heaved myself to my feet I felt a tearing in my side that took my breath away. I leaned against the wall, tears smarting in my eyes. Gingerly, I touched the area under my holster. An edge of pain cut through me. A broken rib? A badly torn muscle? If Lemour had persuaded someone to stop the train, I couldn't stand around waiting to heal. I had to keep moving.

When I started to walk the gun bore into the sore area. I used the wall as a brace and held my left arm up to unbuckle the holster. Checking the safety on the

Smith & Wesson, I stuck it in my pocket and fastened the holster loosely around my waist.

The sleeves of my sweatshirt had gaping tears from the glass in Special-T's skylight. The rest of me was covered with oily mud. Blood was caked along my neck and arms—cuts I hadn't known I was getting were starting to bother me. I hobbled along as fast as I could, straining my ears for sounds of pursuit above the rocking of the train.

Bright lights above the wall I was using for support showed me every detail of the ground—refuse of fast food tossed from cars, Coke cans, plastic bags, even shoes and clothes. I limped my way along the wall to the bottom of the embankment. The street sign said MONTROSE AVENUE. Lying on the boxcar, I had thought I'd been traveling an hour or more and pictured myself in some unknown suburban landscape, but I was still inside the city. The unknown landscape suddenly turned on its side in my brain and I knew it. The concrete wall was a barricade between me and the Kennedy expressway. The roar I was hearing didn't come from the train, which had moved on, but from traffic.

I followed the exit ramp up, looking nervously behind me but not seeing Lemour. Each step was now a prolonging of fatigue and pain. I made it across the expressway bridge to the L stop, where I fed singles into a ticket machine, then slumped onto a bench waiting for a train.

It was four-thirty now and the summer sun was beginning to turn the eastern sky a muddy gray. When a train screeched in twenty minutes later, the cars were half full, bringing home the night crews from O'Hare, sending early shifts into town to work coffee bars and diners. I found an empty seat and watched people sidle away from me. No one wants to catch poverty or grime from a stray homeless person. In my filth and tatters I looked worse than most.

I dozed my way downtown, changed to the Red Line, and dozed my way back north to Belmont. If someone was staking out my place I was past caring. I staggered the five blocks home and fell into bed.

24

Annoying the Giants

THE GUN HAD dug a deep bruise into my side when I tumbled from the boxcar. I'd be sore for four or five days, but if I was careful I'd be okay. Ditto for my left hip. The bruising there went down to the bone, so it would take longer to heal, but nothing was broken and none of the glass cuts in my arms needed stitches. Lotty dispensed that verdict at her clinic Sunday afternoon, her lips flat, her black eyes large with a misery that hurt me more than anger.

"Of course, being careful, taking it easy, those are concepts beyond you, as I know to my sorrow. Still, I understand what these glib radio psychologists mean when they talk about enablers." She put her ophthalmoscope away with a snap and turned to wash her hands. "If I would have the courage to stop patching you up, perhaps you would stop breaking yourself into pieces. You are foolhardy, which, in case you didn't know, means to be daring without judgment: I looked it up this morning. How long do you think you can go on this way? A cat has nine lives, but you have only the one, Victoria."

"You don't have to tell me; my body's doing it for you." I found myself shouting. "My arms are sore. My hamstrings ache. I can hardly walk across the room. I'm getting old. I hate it. I hate not being able to count on my body."

"So you are going to follow Joan of Arc into the flames before your body fails you and you have to admit you're mortal?" Lotty gave a twisted smile. "How old was your mother when she died?"

I stared, startled by the unrelated question, and subtracted dates in my head. "Forty-six."

"And she was ill for two years? It's a hard feeling, to know you will live longer than a mother who died young, but it is not a crime to do so," Lotty said. "You'll turn forty-four next month, won't you? You don't need to push yourself past the brink so that you burn up in the next two years. You could have found a dozen ways to learn whether Mr. Frenada was inside his building last night. Make that the intelligent use of your energy, figuring out how to conserve your strength for those times when using your body is your last resort, not your first one. Don't you think that's what your mother would want for you?"

Oh, yes, probably. Surely. My mother's intensity had a blast-furnace quality, but she didn't prize brute strength above finesse. She'd died of a metastasis from the uterus that became apparent after a miscarriage, when the bleeding wouldn't stop and I'd brought her pads and changed my own in terror each month for years, wondering when it would happen to me, when I would drain away from the inside. Perhaps Lotty was right. Perhaps I was draining myself from the inside out of some survivor's guilt. If that was the case, my mother most surely did not want that from me, but life.

Lotty insisted on taking me home with her. I wanted to make phone calls, see if Lacey Dowell knew where Lucian Frenada was: I hadn't been able to raise him at his home or shop when I tried before coming to Lotty's clinic. I wanted to talk to Murray about how he'd gotten word that Frenada was running cocaine. I even had a manic idea about calling Baldine and accusing him of engineering the dope stashes.

Lotty refused to listen to my impassioned plea for a phone—she pushed me to her guest room and pulled the jack out of the wall. I fumed for around thirty seconds, but the next thing I knew it was ten o'clock Monday morning and I was more hungry than angry.

Lotty had left a note for me: the doorman knew I was staying and had orders to let me back into the building if I went out for a walk. I should take it easy for a few days. The building had a sauna and a gym on the third floor—the spare key to her front door tucked into the envelope would open the gym. *Help yourself to fruit and bread. And, Victoria, for my sake if not yours, don't leap again without looking very carefully.*

After an orange and a piece of toast I went down to the gym. It was really only a small workout room, with weights and an exercise bike, but I was able to work off some of my stiffness. A half hour in the sauna sent me back to bed. When I got up again, around one, I made a hot meal out of eggs and fresh tomatoes. The calls I'd wanted to make yesterday didn't feel so urgent today, but I took the phone out onto Lotty's balcony and started with Mary Louise.

When I finished describing Saturday's debacle at my office, she said, "So you really did find drugs there. And if Lemour planted them, then you can't call the cops."

"I do have a videotape of Lemour in the act, which I guess I could take to the State's Attorney. Trouble is, I don't know anyone there personally these days, and anyway, I'm afraid Lemour might be able to make even that evidence disappear. If I thought Murray would or could do anything, I'd give it to him, but these days I'm not sure I can count on him. How about showing it to Terry Finchley?"

She hesitated. "I've got these children I'm responsible for. I can't put my life on the line for some case you're inventing."

I sat up with a jolt that made my side ache. "Mary Louise, where do you get off with that kind of statement? You were with me when all this started. In fact, if I remember correctly, it was your panic that made me wreck my car. Which has been impounded by the cops and may well never surface again. Exactly what about that am I inventing?"

"Okay, not making up," she muttered. "And I'm sorry about your car. If I had the money I'd repair it for you. But it's the same story with you every time. You can't bear to be scared or beaten, so if someone threatens you, you have to take them on, no matter how big they are. Terry warned me about that when I started working for you, he said he saw you do it over and over again and that no one's life is worth that much principle. And in this case you're trying to take on giants. Don't you see? Don't you know?"

I clutched the phone so hard my sore palms began to throb. "No. I don't."

"Oh, Vic, use your brain. That didn't take a beating Saturday night. You're trying to go nose-to-nose with Robert Baladine. Who's his best friend? Who got him that contract out in Coolis? And who can bury a body, no questions asked, faster than you can say 'Jimmy Hoffa'? Why didn't you take that nice little assignment Alex Fisher dangled in front of you?"

"What on earth? You yourself advised me not to

touch it. And if you think I want to be bought by some—"

"I know. You're too damned holy to be bought off by a Hollywood slimeball. One thing you'd better believe—I'm not putting Josh and Nate at risk. Thank God Emily's in France and I don't have to worry about her. If you keep poking at this hornets' nest, I'm resigning and flying out of town with the boys."

You can't quit, you're fired. That's the standard line in such cases, but I only thought it, didn't say it. When I cooled off I'd regret it—Mary Louise is good for my little operation. But I hadn't cooled off yet, and our good-byes were unfriendly. Especially after she said she didn't have time to help put my files back together. She had exams, she was doing some work for a law firm that might let her take an internship, she had the boys in summer camp, she couldn't possibly spend a week cleaning up the kind of wreck I was describing.

At first I was too angry to think, but I made myself calm down, hobbled around the apartment, studied Lotty's art collection. Including an alabaster figurine of Andromache that I'd recovered for her by the same methods she and Mary Louise were criticizing in me today. No, dwelling on that was only making me angry all over again.

I drank a glass of water and went back to the balcony to stare at the lake. At the edge, the line where lake meets sky, a cluster of sailboats looked like bits of white paper glued to a child's collage. I wanted to be on that remote horizon, but I had no way to reach it.

What didn't I see and know about Baladine? Of course it was Poilevy who got him that contract out in Coolis, you didn't have to be Sherlock Holmes's smarter brother to figure that out. But bury a body, no

questions asked, as Mary Louise had said, meant
Poilevy had mob ties in Du Page County. One of her
old pals must have warned her about him while I was in
Georgia—probably Terry Finchley.

It also didn't take a genius to figure that Detective
Lemour could do mob work on the side, not after what
I'd seen of him on Saturday. And he could do it in the
suburbs. Chicago cops were required to live inside the
city limits, but no ordinance forbade their moonlighting
in the collar counties if they wanted to. We'd had two
police superintendents with ties to the mob in recent
years, and I guess you have to start somewhere.

Lemour must be on Poilevy's payroll. No, not
Poilevy's. The House Speaker wasn't going to get his
hands dirty in a way that a reporter like Murray—like
Murray used to be—could uncover. Lemour was on
someone's payroll. But I already knew that. It was obvious Saturday afternoon when his unnamed boss had
phoned, told him to let me go.

What I couldn't make sense of was how all this had
mushroomed out of Nicola Aguinaldo's death. What
did Lucian Frenada know that mattered to Baladine or
Poilevy? Something about the Mad Virgin T-shirt dress
Aguinaldo was wearing when she died. Would Lacey
Dowell know? And would she tell me if she did?

I looked up the Hotel Trianon number. The operator
asked me to spell my last name, put me on hold for a
moment, and then said Ms. Dowell wasn't available.
Had Ms. Dowell returned from Santa Monica I asked.

"All I can tell you is that Ms. Dowell isn't available."
She hung up crisply.

I lay back on the floor. I'd become a non-grata person since talking to Frank Siekevitz in the Trianon's
security department last week. Had Lacey put me on

her index, or had Alex Fisher done it for her? I sat up and redialed the hotel and asked for Siekevitz.

"Vicki!" He was embarrassed. "I'm sorry, but the lady doesn't want to talk to you. She put it in writing."

"She did, Frank? Or did the studio?"

"That I can't tell you. But you don't want to go bothering her if the studio wants you to stay away, do you?"

"Actually, I do. I need to talk to her about something pretty important."

"Nothing's that important, Vicki, believe me."

"So it was the studio."

He gave an uncomfortable laugh and hung up gracelessly. I wanted to limp to the Trianon as fast as my trembling hamstrings would carry me, but Mary Louise's comments haunted me. What would running to the hotel do for me, anyway? Frank would stiff me harder in person, because the giants, as Mary Louise had called them, had left nothing to chance. They had threatened him or cajoled him.

The giants knew our strengths and weaknesses. I'd realized that Saturday night: they knew I would rise to the bait, that I'd be daring without exercising judgment. Joan of Arc, Lotty'd called me. What no one around me would believe was that I really didn't want to lift the siege of Orleans. I wanted to keep on doing nice little investigations for Continental United until I made enough money to fund my Money Purchase Pension Plan and bought me a little house in Umbria, where I'd make Orvieto Classico and raise golden retrievers.

In frustration, I turned on the television, looking for news, fearing actually to hear news about Frenada. The Global channel had local coverage at four. It was the usual tabloid stew of sex and violence: an overturned truck on the tollway with flames and car wreckage, Mrs. Muffet and Mr. Tuffet exclaiming that they heard the explosion, they thought my God it's World War III. Nothing on Frenada—or me, thank goodness.

When the ads started I turned off the sound, but after a truck climbed the Grand Canyon and a cleanser removed oily stains from a white blouse, a map flashed on the screen, showing a dotted line connecting Mexico and Chicago. Then Murray's face loomed over it. I hastily switched on the sound but heard only, "Tuesday night at nine. Chicago's hottest news, from the inside out, with Murray Ryerson."

After that I kept the station on for another half hour, watching a tedious rerun of some sex comedy and about twenty commercials, until the Mexico map finally reappeared. "Enterprise zones. The perfect route for small businessmen hoping to make it to the top. But sometimes those businesses are taking federal seed money and using it to grow cocaine. Go inside Chicago with Murray Ryerson and find out how Mexican immigrants are using such innocuous-seeming businesses as a uniform factory as a cover for drug deals. Tuesday night at—"

I switched off the set before the tag line ended. Joan of Arc or no, on my own against the giants or not, I couldn't lie here on Lotty's living room rug while Global used Murray to destroy Frenada's reputation. I started a reflexive finger on the phone buttons, about to call Murray and shriek at him, when I realized it would be one of those conversations that begin with "what the hell do you think you're doing" and end with both parties slamming the phone down.

I frowned for a moment, then went into Lotty's little home office. She's never felt the need to add automation to her home, but she has a typewriter. I'd used just such a primitive instrument until a couple of years ago. I scrounged in her drawers for a large envelope, typed LACEY DOWELL, TRIANON HOTEL. SCRIPT CHANGES. BY MESSENGER in caps across it on the diagonal. In the left corner I typed Global's Chicago address. It would be better, of course, if I had a laser printer and could manufacture something resembling their corporate logo, but this would have to do.

Dear Ms. Dowell, I wrote.

Do you know that on Tuesday night, Global television is going to run a story denouncing Lucian Frenada as a drug smuggler? Do you know why they want to do this? Do you approve? Finally, do you know where Mr. Frenada is? I am a private investigator who has been caught up willy-nilly in his affairs, and I am virtually certain that evidence against him has been manufactured. If you know any reason why the studio would do such a thing, I will wait downstairs to talk to you, or, if you prefer, you may call me.

I included my home and office numbers, put the note in the envelope, and sealed the whole thing with packing tape. I wrote a note for Lotty, telling her I was going home and would call her tonight, and rode the elevator down to the lobby, where I got the doorman to summon a cab.

25

Reaching Out To—A Friend?

No one bars you from an upscale hotel as long as you're properly dressed. I had the cab swing by my apartment and wait while I put on my wheat-colored pantsuit and some makeup. The midsummer heat continued as June inched into July; the rayon rubbed unpleasantly against my cuts and bruises, but the bellman inside the Trianon's entrance accepted the envelope and a ten with a respectful promise to see that it was taken up to Ms. Dowell's suite at once. I sat in an alcove off the main lobby, flipping idly through newspapers, but although the bellman assured me he'd hand-delivered my packet, no message came down for me.

Short of checking into the hotel, there wasn't any way I could get upstairs without Lacey's summons: the Trianon had someone stationed between the desk and the elevators to monitor traffic. I watched a discreet pantomime take place between the front-desk staff and the monitor, subtle nods allowing the blessed to pass into paradise. If I wanted to get upstairs, Lacey had to call me.

I read pages of Washington scandal, which I usually avoid; I read about the bodies hauled off the sidewalks after the weekend's drive-bys—which I also usually skip —and even the sad ending of an unidentified man in his late thirties who'd been pulled out of the water at Belmont Harbor, but no word came for me from on high. I was starting to feel frustrated, which made my sore muscles ache more ferociously.

Maybe after another night's rest a different way of probing at Frenada and Global would come to me, but for now all I had energy for was collecting my car—which I hoped was still sitting three blocks from Frenada's headquarters. As I pushed myself out of the padded armchair, someone I recognized sailed through the revolving door like the *Merrimac* descending on a wooden frigate. Alex Fisher had such a head of steam that she ignored the doorman holding the side door wide for her. She also ignored a younger woman who was running to catch up with her.

"I can't wait around for you," Alex snapped in a ringing voice.

"I'm sorry, Ms. Fisher, I was paying the cab." The young woman panted; she was pasty-faced and out of shape, probably from too many late nights dining on pizza while waiting for commands from the studio.

I had slipped behind a pillar to watch, but Alex was so wrapped up in her own business that not even a marching band could have distracted her. When the hall monitor tried to detain her, Alex jerked away and pushed the elevator call button. I was admiring her forthright tactics when Frank Siekevitz suddenly appeared at her side.

I couldn't hear what the security director said, but Alex announced that Lacey Dowell was expecting her, this was urgent, and would he get out of the way. Frank murmured something else, his posture so deprecating that I cringed. The hall monitor used a phone, and in another minute Alex and her satellite were allowed to pass.

I sat back down, hoping Lacey might decide I could help her after all, but when Alex and her attendant reappeared, no one had asked for me. I couldn't resist following Alex outside.

"Vic!" Her greeting was half surprise, half venom. "I thought you—what are you doing here?"

So Lacey hadn't told her I'd written to her: interesting. "Yeah, I know, I was supposed to be dead or in jail or something, but here I am. Lacey doing okay?"

"If you're trying to see her, you can't." Alex waved off a doorman offering her a taxi.

"She's not the only guest at the Trianon. I was having tea with my aunt. She's a permanent resident."

"You don't have an aunt who can afford this place."

"You haven't read the LifeStory report on me very thoroughly, Sandy," I chided her. "As a matter of fact I do have a rich aunt. Actually, I have a rich uncle. He's very big in the food industry. And his wife could afford to live here if she wanted to. By the way, where did you get the cocaine you planted on me?"

Alex became aware of her satellite, who was frowning in an effort to follow our conversation. She gave an unconvincing laugh and said she didn't know what I was talking about.

"It has that Hollywood feel to it, the kind of thing Gene Hackman would turn up in *French Connection Three*. Did you get Teddy Trant to talk to his screenwriters, have them come up with an absurd plotline, then turn it over to Baladine and his tame goons to act out?"

"Vic, why didn't you take that assignment I dug up

for you? It would have saved everyone a lot of grief."
Her green eyes were dark in the twilight.

"Was it a bribe or a distraction?" I asked.

"There are worse things on the planet than bribes. I
didn't remember you as so uncompromising in law
school."

"No, that was you back then," I agreed. "Hot politics and stubborn intransigence. If you weren't part of
the solution you were part of the problem. Although
maybe in that regard you haven't changed so much."

She bit her lower lip, swollen from collagen injec-
tions. "Well, you were always stubborn, that's for
damned sure. But you weren't ever right about everything. As you'll find out now if you don't back off.
Felicity, can you get a cab over here? We have a lot of
work to do tonight."

Felicity scuttled over to the doorman, who blew
grandly on his whistle. The lead car in the taxi line
pulled forward.

"Back off? From what?"

"Don't play the naive fool with me. I have you pretty
well pegged by now. Come on, Felicity. Are you waiting
for the Second Coming?"

"Poor Felicity," I said. "If her mama knew she'd be
working for you, Sandy, maybe she would have named
her Anxiety instead."

"And you know damned well that regardless of what
my *mama* called me, my name is Alex—Vicki." On that
shot Alex threw herself into the car, Felicity handed the
doorman a dollar, and the two of them took off.

I stood in the drive, watching the street long after
the cab's taillights had disappeared. I know I'm not
right about everything, but she'd made it sound like

something specific. Was it the same as the egg Murray was going to smear all over my smug face?

I was too tired and too sore to figure it out this evening. The doorman who'd taken in my letter to Lacey was urging me out of the drive and into a cab. I followed him meekly, although it was the fifth driver he whistled up who agreed to take me—when the first four heard the address I wanted, they shook their heads, willing to lose their place in line to avoid Humboldt Park. I didn't blame them, exactly, but I could understand why people on the West Side get so frustrated at being denied service. The guy who finally took me to my car barely waited for my feet to touch the street before screeching into a U-turn and heading back to the Gold Coast.

The Rustmobile fit into the neighborhood so perfectly that no one had removed the tires in the two days I'd left it there. The roar from the exhaust blended in with the vibrating low-riders. Definitely a better car for me than a Jaguar convertible or some other high-rent import. No one looked at me as I went back down Grand. I stopped in front of Special-T's front door. No lights shone tonight, but I wasn't going in for another look—I wasn't in shape to escape a second trap.

I parked several blocks from my apartment. Now that Alex could tell Lemour I'd surfaced, I needed to watch out for ambushes. No one was lying in wait so far; I stopped to chat with Mr. Contreras and the dogs. My neighbor had received the LifeStory report on Lucian Frenada that I'd mailed Saturday afternoon. I'd forgotten to tell him about it, but I explained its importance to him now.

"You want me to keep it for you, doll, I'll be glad to."

"Remember how you got shot a couple of years ago when you were helping me out? I don't want to involve you like that again. Anyway, I need to make a bunch of copies so I can get it into the public arena as fast as possible."

He protested his willingness to take on any punk his size or bigger, but I took the report upstairs with me. I wished there was someone I could talk to—about the LifeStory report, or the putative connection between Baladine and Officer Lemour, or even the story Murray was running on Frenada. I hadn't realized how dependent I'd grown on Murray over the years. This was the first major investigation I'd taken on that I couldn't discuss with him, or tap into his vast knowledge of local corruption. And I badly needed help. This wasn't even an investigation. It was some kind of demon's cauldron I'd fallen into. I was bobbing around with the newts' eyes and bats' wings, and I wasn't going to have too much more time to figure out the brew before I drowned in it.

I suddenly thought of Morrell. He didn't have Murray's local connections in politics, but he had an entree into Nicola Aguinaldo's world. Vishnikov vouched for him. And I didn't think anyone knew I'd been talking to him.

I looked up his home number on my Palm Pilot, but as I was dialing I remembered his own nervousness about talking on the phone. If BB Baladine was really riding my ass, he could have a tap on my line or even a remote device to pick up anything I said in my building. That might explain why I hadn't seen any obvious surveillance on the street: if they knew they could track me at home, they could jump me on my way out, without having to leave a man in place twenty-four hours a day.

I don't like having to be paranoid about everything I say and do, but I switched on a Mozart CD on my stereo and the Cubs on television and sat between them with my cell phone. It was hard for Morrell to understand me over the interference, but once he did he readily agreed to meet me for a drink.

If I was right about Baladine not doing on-site surveillance, then I could probably leave again as long as I was quiet about it. I waited until the roar from Wrigley Field rose to a fever pitch, both on the streets behind me and on the set in front of me, and slipped out my door in bare feet, carrying my sandals to avoid making noise on the upper landing. An hour later I was back at Drummers, in Edgewater.

When I described my exit to Morrell, making a comic story of it, he didn't laugh. "That's the trouble with living in fear of the cops: you don't know if you're being a fool or taking sensible precautions."

"My dad was a cop and a good honest man. And so were his friends. Some of them are still on the force."

I thought of Frank Siekevitz. My dad trained him. The three of us used to go to baseball games together. Siekevitz wept at my dad's funeral and vowed in a tribute that made others cry to remain true to Tony's principles. Now he was backing away from me because Global Entertainment had leaned on him.

Maybe that was what was really keeping me from taking my story to my dad's oldest friend on the force. I was afraid deep down that Bobby Mallory would turn away, too. Not bought—no one could buy him—but any man with six children and a dozen grandchildren is vulnerable. Of course, everyone has a hostage to fortune. If someone kidnapped Lotty, or threatened to hurt her—

"Where are you, Vic?" Morrell asked.

I jumped at his voice. "In a place where I feel terrified and alone. That's why I called you. I need an ally, and I need one who doesn't have an easy lever to pry him apart. Unless—do you have children or lovers?"

He blinked. "Are you asking me to risk myself for you because I'm alone in the world and no one cares if I die? Why should I do that?"

I felt my cheeks stain crimson. "No reason I can think of. Unless you think I could teach you something useful, like how to jump off a building onto a moving freight train."

"Probably not a skill I can use: most of the places I'm fleeing don't have buildings high enough to jump from. Anyway, don't you do financial investigations? Why were you jumping onto a train?"

I gave him as complete a rundown of the past two weeks as I could manage. He interrupted with the occasional question, but for the most part he sat quietly, chin in hand, dark eyes watching me.

"That's why I'm eager to talk to Nicola Aguinaldo's mother," I finished. "I need someone who can tell me who her daughter would run to—or from. Nicola worked for Robert Baladine, and he's definitely on the visiting team. Would she have gone to him and ended up being beaten or kicked for showing up? It matters terribly that her body's disappeared, and I'd like to know that Abuelita Mercedes really didn't bury it without an autopsy."

Morrell put a warning hand on my arm; I hadn't noticed the waiter hovering nearby. I ordered a double espresso and a little gorgonzola–pear pizza. Riding the rods Saturday night had taken away my appetite. I certainly didn't feel like drinking. No Philip Marlowe I, downing a pint of rye every time I got injured.

When the waiter had left I said, "When Nicola died she was wearing not a dress but a long T-shirt, a Mad Virgin T-shirt. I think Lucian Frenada made it, and that doesn't make a lot of sense to me, either. How did she get it after making her break from Coolis? They can wear civilian clothes in jail, but not that kind of flimsy minidress."

After the waiter brought our food, Morrell asked me what had happened to make me think someone might be monitoring my apartment. "The last time we talked you weren't very forthcoming. Now you're rattled and want to make me an accessory, if not an ally."

I grimaced. "You weren't Chatty Cathy, either. I was willing to let it go because I thought I could get information on Aguinaldo some other way. But I haven't been able to, and anyway, so much is going on I can't seem to focus on any one problem. And then, when I got back from an out-of-town assignment this past Saturday, I found that someone was trying to frame me in a major way."

I went into more detail about the dope I'd found in my office and the chaos I'd seen at Special-T Uniforms. "I haven't been able to get hold of Frenada since the phone call—which presumably didn't come from him at all. I did go to see Lacey Dowell today—which sent her hotfoot to Global's lawyer, instead."

When I finished, Morrell nodded to himself several times, as if digesting what I'd told him. "Abuelita Mercedes really doesn't have her daughter's body. If her assailant got the body released, it's probably been buried or cremated by now: I don't think we can expect to find it."

I agreed. "The jobs are county patronage; it would be easy for a man whose clout owed Baladine or Poilevy a favor to misdirect a body if that was required. I did talk to Vishnikov the other day, and he said he'd check to see whether the body was still there but had been mislabeled. Maybe if my pals know Vishnikov is mounting a major investigation, they'll tip their hands. But the person I'd most like to talk to is Abuelita Mercedes. I would dearly love to ask her about her daughter's acquaintances."

He shook his head. "You sound like dynamite right now, to be blunt. I don't want you leading some menace to her doorstep. She fled her old apartment because someone was asking after her. Remember? You told me that yourself, and she confirms it."

I ate a slice of my cold pizza. "What if they weren't from INS or the state? What if they were the people who killed Nicola, come to make sure she hadn't talked to her mother? No matter how much Abuelita Mercedes denied having heard from Nicola, they'd never believe her. Have you asked her yourself? If Nicola talked to her before she died, I mean?"

Morrell's lips twisted in a half smile. "Bryant Vishnikov warned me that you'd wear me out if I got involved with you. No, I haven't asked her that, and yes, I'll make time to get back to Señora Mercedes in the next day or two."

"Did Vishnikov tell you I'd consulted him about you as well? He didn't give me a character reading, though."

"Maybe there's nothing people need to be warned about when they meet me," he said with a sly smile.

"Or maybe too much to be covered in a single phrase. What does the C.L. stand for?"

"Good grief. Have you really been investigating me? I didn't think any record still existed of those initials. My parents didn't speak English, and they longed for America as for the promised land. They named me in the hopes I'd fit in when we finally got here and instead gave me something that got me beat up regularly. It would have hurt their feelings if I'd changed my name, so I use only my surname. Think of me as someone like Madonna or Prince."

I imagined lying in bed with him, whispering "Morrell" instead of—what name could have been that embarrassing? Maybe they'd named him for name brands, like Clorox and Lysol. I blushed at my fantasy and hurried back to business.

The list of things that needed doing depressed me. I was like a tetherball, gyrating erratically from one side to another, depending on who was punching me. My physical stamina was limited and my emotional energy was not much greater.

"There's one other thing I'd like to ask of you," I said abruptly. "I don't think it will wear you out, but who knows? I have a videotape of the police goons in my office. I'd like it taken to Cheviot Labs, to an engineer named Rieff who's been doing some work on Aguinaldo's dress for me. I was going to send it to him tomorrow, but I want copies made first. I'm too nervous about how much of my phone conversations may have been overheard. I'm thinking my assailant heard me talking to my client about my out-of-town trip and used the opportunity to plant drugs in my office. If they heard me leave a message for Rieff Saturday night they'll go to him, or intercept me, or do something to keep the tape from him. The other thing is a copy of a report on Lucian Frenada's finances. Global is going to slam him on—on Murray Ryerson's show tomorrow night, but I have evidence that he's not living in luxury off the drug business. I want a million photocopies so it's public."

"Fine." Morrell held out a hand. "I'll take care of those. What do you want me to do with the copies?"

"Of the videotape? One to my lawyer, the original to Rieff to see if he can pick up who Lemour was speaking to on his cell phone. One to Murray Ryerson. And the report on Frenada, that should go to all those people, and a bunch of reporters I know—I can make up a list for you."

"How'd you videotape Lemour when he had you cuffed?"

"Carnifice Security isn't the only high-tech player in the detective world." I told him about the video glasses as I scribbled a media list on the back of an old parking receipt.

"I once helped photocopy details of torture conducted by the Brazil secret police," Morrell said. "It was a project organized by the Archbishop of Rio. We had a terrifying time, sneaking into the office after hours to see the records, copying them, returning them without anyone getting caught out or squealing. We could have used glasses like those. You going to be okay getting home?" he added as the waiter brought a check. "You'd be welcome to stay with me—I've got a spare bedroom."

It was appealing, the idea of not having to worry about who might be lying in wait outside my door. Besides, there was my fantasy, lying with his long fingers on my body—on my sore body, but maybe he had a lover of some sex and wouldn't find an exhausted forty-plus detective sexy, anyway.

Lotty had almost been killed once, helping me in a crisis, and Mr. Contreras had been shot. Conrad had left me after a similar episode. I couldn't bear to have one more person maimed on my account, even one I didn't know well. I thanked him but turned my roaring Skylark south toward home.

26

If You Can't Swim,
Keep Away from Sharks

I HAD CALLED Lotty from a pay phone on my way home to tell her I was still alive and to ask her to phone me with only the most innocuous questions. She wasn't best pleased at being awakened—it was past eleven— and took in my request with a terse wish for me to stop being so melodramatic. Melodramatic and foolhardy. Those were hard words to take to bed.

When I left Mr. Contreras, he sent Peppy up with me for comfort. I hoped she brought enough that I could keep at bay my nervous fantasies about someone scaling the side of the building to break into my bedroom.

As I switched off the light the phone rang. I sucked in a breath, wondering what new threat might lie at the other end of the line, but I answered. "Warshawski's twenty-four-hour detective service."

"Miss Warshawski?"

It was a child's voice, high-pitched with its own nervousness. "Yes, this is V. I. Warshawski. What is it, Robbie?"

"I've been calling you and calling you tonight. I thought you'd never answer. First I was just going to tell you about BB's shoes—you know, you asked if any of them had horseshoe buckles or something, and I don't think so—but this is worse, it's about that man, that man they showed on the news. He was—" I heard a click and the line went dead.

I squinted at my caller-ID pad and dialed the number on it. It rang fifteen times without an answer. I hung up and tried again, making sure I'd entered the right numbers. After twenty rings I gave up.

One of his parents must have heard him talking to me and cut off the phone. I pictured the mad swimming Eleanor standing over the phone, listening to it ring when I called back. Or they turned off the sound and watched a light flashing red until I hung up, while Robbie protested, crying, his father mocking him for his tears and making him cry harder.

A week ago I might have driven out to the Baladine home, middle of the night or not. But only someone who had daring without judgment would do that. Or someone whose hamstrings weren't so sore that she couldn't run if she had to. Anyway, before leaping into action I should find out what man Robbie had seen on the news. There wasn't any local television coverage this time of night, but if it was important—or grisly— the radio would carry the story.

"It's midnight and hazy in Chicago, seventy-nine at O'Hare, eighty-one at the lakefront, going down to a low of seventy, with another muggy scorcher in store for us tomorrow. Sammy Sosa capped a sparkling June with his twentieth home run, the most in a month in major league history, but the Cubs dropped another one at Wrigley today, going two and eight over their last ten games."

I drummed my fingers impatiently through another update of the Starr chamber's slow grind; through the pious hypocrisies of the House Speaker and the

President's sincere bombast, through more mass murders in ex-Yugoslavia and riots in Indonesia.

"In local news, the drowning victim found late yesterday at Belmont Harbor has been identified as local Hispanic entrepreneur Lucian Frenada. It is not known when or how Frenada came to be in the water; the sister with whom he lived had reported him missing Saturday morning. Mrs. Celia Caliente says she does not know what would have taken her brother to Belmont Harbor, but that he was unable to swim. In other local news, accused killer—"

I snapped off the set. Lucian Frenada was dead. That's why he hadn't been answering his phone. I wondered how you got a man who didn't know how to swim into the lake. I wondered how long it would be before I joined him.

I pulled on a shirt and tiptoed into the living room. If Baladine had one of those fancy listening devices tuned on my building, could it pick up the faint tap of Peppy's toenails as she followed me? I slipped a finger between two slats of the blind and squinted at the street.

This part of Racine is close to the trendy bars of Wrigleyville, which means we get a lot of people trying to find parking. Even late on a Monday night, occasional knots of young men, made loudly cheerful by beer, swayed up the street. I stood for twenty minutes but didn't see the same people pass twice.

If I boldly went out the front door, collected my car, and drove to Oak Brook, would I be followed? And more to the point, what would I do when I got there? Climb the security fence on my quivering legs, get arrested for trespassing, try to claim I was responding to an SOS from a twelve-year-old boy whom his successful and beautiful parents would paint as emotionally unstable. Prone to self-dramatization. And maybe they were right. Maybe it was only my animus to Eleanor and BB that made me take their child seriously.

I tried the Baladine mansion one more time, but the phone still rang unanswered. I climbed back into bed, lying rigidly, waiting for the sounds of traffic, of crickets, of drinkers laughing their way up the street, to resolve themselves into menace. There is no worse feeling than not knowing if you are truly alone in your own home. To my surprise, when Peppy pawed at my arm to rouse me, it was eight-thirty.

I rolled over and looked into her amber eyes. "Woof. Sorry, old girl. Bruises and too much of whatever antiinflammatory Lotty gave me, and I even sleep through fear. Let's get you out and fetch the paper."

Ever since Peppy and Mitch learned that bringing in the paper netted a dog biscuit, they like to collect them for the whole building. This morning we were up so late that only my own *Herald-Star* was still on the sidewalk. Mr. Contreras sent Mitch out to join us, but Peppy drove him off with a serious growl and presented the paper to me, golden plume waving grandly. The encounter made me laugh out loud—a good thing, since the rest of the day was singularly lacking in humor.

I unfolded the paper in the vestibule outside Mr. Contreras's door. The *Herald-Star* put Frenada's death on the front page, under the headline DRUG LORD DROWNS.

Late yesterday, police identified the man pulled out of Belmont Harbor early Sunday morning as Lucian Frenada, owner of Special-T Uniforms in Humboldt Park. Frenada had become the subject of intense investigation by *Herald-Star* reporter Murray Ryerson, who taped an exposé on the use of Frenada's small business as a cover for a drug smuggling ring. This story will air tonight at nine on GTV, Channel Thirteen.

Police who raided Special-T late Saturday night discovered five kilos of cocaine inside the cardboard rolls used for shipping uncut fabric. While Frenada hotly denied any connection to the Mexican drug cartels, his bank accounts told a different story. Police speculate that he may have committed suicide to avoid arrest. Frenada grew up in the same Humboldt Park building as movie star Lacey Dowell, widely known by her fans as the Mad Virgin for her role in those movies. Dowell couldn't be reached for a comment on her old playmate's death, but studio representative Alex Fisher says the star is devastated by the news. (*Murray Ryerson and Julia Esteban contributed to this report.*)

The story ended with a tearful denial by Frenada's sister, Celia Caliente, who said her brother had no money and that it was a struggle for him to meet his share of the mortgage on the two-flat they jointly owned. The story ran with a photo of Lacey Dowell as the Mad Virgin next to a picture of her at her First Communion. Their irrelevance to Frenada's death underscored the titillative purpose of using them. *Buy this paper and get an intimate look at Lacey Dowell.* I thrust it from me with so much irritation that Peppy backed away in alarm.

"What's up, doll?" My neighbor had been watching me read.

I showed him the story and tried to explain why it bothered me so much. The one thing Mr. Contreras picked up from my incoherent rant was that Murray was framing Frenada. He didn't care whether it was because Global was feeding Murray the story or not—Mr. Contreras has always disliked Murray, even more than the men I date. I've never been sure why, and now, to my own exasperation, I found myself feebly defending Murray to the old man.

Mr. Contreras was pardonably incensed. "Either he's acting like a scumbag, no matter what the reason for it, or he's not. Don't go being his ma or his scout-master, telling me he's a good boy at heart, because someone with principles don't carry on this way, and you know that as well as me, cookie. He wants the limelight, he wants that TV show they got him doing, and he's looking the other way. Period."

Period indeed. I knew all those things were true, but Murray and I had been friends for so many years it hurt like any other loss to see him move away from me. Away from truth. I made a sour face at my own arrogance: I was hardly the avatar of truth.

Mr. Contreras was still fuming, hands on hips. "So whatcha going to do about it?"

"I'm going to work out and eat breakfast." I felt too defensive to share the rest of my morning's agenda.

I assured Mr. Contreras I wouldn't go to the park alone: Mitch and Peppy were happy to be my guardians. I did my stretches, then tested my legs with a modest run. I stuck my Smith & Wesson in a fanny pack. It bounced uncomfortably against my abdomen as I jogged, but the bruise in my side was still too tender for me to carry a shoulder holster.

I could only manage three very slow miles, but I was happy to be in motion again. While I jogged, I kept the dogs closely leashed, much to their annoyance. They kept tugging at me, testing the muscles in my side. I turned around frequently to see who was coming up on me, but we did a little circuit of the harbor where the cops had found Lucian Frenada without anyone trying to shove me off the rocks.

On the way back to the car I called Morrell from a pay phone. I started to ask him about the LifeStory report, but he cut me short.

"You're calling from a pay phone, but I'm on my home phone. I don't think you can take any chances with these people. There's a coffee shop two blocks north of where we ate last night. East side of the road. I'll be there in half an hour."

"Cops and robbers," I muttered to the dogs. "Or paranoids and orderlies. This is ludicrous."

Yesterday I'd accused Alex-Sandy of getting a Hollywood scriptwriter to devise the plot to frame me with cocaine in my office, but today I felt I was acting out a B movie myself, playing at spies, with a guy so nuts he wouldn't use his first name. I drove up to Edgewater and cadged a container of water for the dogs while I waited for Morrell. When he arrived, he looked more worried than wild, but who knows what face paranoia turns to the world. I asked if this charade was really necessary.

"You're the one who called me last night worried about eavesdroppers. As to whether it's necessary—that's the misery of this kind of situation. You don't know if you're being watched or making it up. The psychological toll rises so high that you almost welcome a chance to give in, just to have the uncertainty end. Which is why it's important that teammates keep each other's morale up."

I felt chastened and took the manila envelope he was

carrying with a mumbled thanks. "I know I came to you first, but it seems nuts to be playing James Bond in my own hometown."

He bent over to greet the dogs, who were whining for attention. "That's quite a collection of bruises you've got. They from your jump on Saturday?"

I hadn't had time to change out of running shorts and top. They revealed large patches of greeny purple on my legs and torso, as if Jackson Pollock had been spray-painting me.

"Well, you weren't running away from a phantom." He straightened up and looked at me, brown eyes somber. "I know living in Central America has distorted my judgment, and I try to correct for it when I come home. But you see how easily the lines between police and power get blurred, especially in a country like America, where we're always on full alert against enemies. After fifty years of the Cold War, we've gotten into such a reflexive posture of belligerence that we start to chew up our own citizens. When I come home I like to relax, but it's hard to put aside the habits that help me survive nine months out of twelve. And in this case—well, you did find drugs in your office. And Lucian Frenada is very dead."

Robbie Baladine's late-night call came back to me with a jolt. "There's something odd about that death. Can you call Vishnikov, ask him to do the autopsy himself? Just in case SMERSH did use some poison known only to Papua natives before putting Frenada into Belmont Harbor."

He grinned. "You'll be okay, Vic, as long as you can joke about it." He looked a little embarrassed, then added, "You have beautiful legs, even with all those bruises on them."

He turned hurriedly toward his car, as if paying a compliment might leave him open to a hand grenade. When I called out a thanks, he smiled and sketched a wave, then suddenly beckoned me over to the car.

"I forgot. Since we're playing at James Bond we need a more efficient way to keep in touch. Are you free for dinner tonight? Do you know a restaurant where we could meet?"

I suggested Cockatrice, part of the restaurant explosion in Wicker Park. It was walking distance from my office, where I hoped to spend the afternoon cleaning up files. First, though, I needed to run some errands.

27

Hounding a Newshound

Murray wasn't at the *Herald-Star,* but he rated a personal assistant now, so I got to speak to a human voice instead of a machine. When I told her I had important information on the Frenada story—and gave her enough details to convince her I wasn't one of the horde of nutcases who always have important information on breaking stories—she said Murray was working at home.

"If you leave your number, I'll give it to him when he calls in for his messages," she promised.

I told her I'd call back later and didn't leave a name.

I pulled on clean jeans and a scarlet top and took the Smith & Wesson out of the fanny pack. I balanced it on my palm, trying to decide whether to take it or not. In my present mood I might use it on Murray, but that was a risk he'd have to take: I felt more secure with the weapon. I put it in a leg holster, where I could get to it if I acted like a contortionist. The straps dug into my calf.

No one stopped me on my way to the Rustmobile. I kept checking my mirror on the way to Lake Shore Drive, but if I was being tailed it was expertly done. I detoured downtown to my bank and left a copy of the report on Frenada in my safe deposit box. Heading back north, I swung by Tessa's mother's palace on the Gold Coast long enough to leave spare padlock keys with the doorman so that Tessa could get into our building.

I didn't bother to look for parking on the streets near Murray, since there never is any. I left the Skylark in the alley behind his building, underneath a sign that said: WARNING, WE CALL THE POLICE TO TOW UNAUTHORIZED VEHICLES. Let them.

Murray lives in one of those six-flats with wood-burning fireplaces, tessellated marble floors in the entryways, and all the other stuff you get if you can afford a Mercedes convertible. The bells were brightly polished brass set into cherry paneling.

When Murray's voice came through the intercom, I pinched my nose and said, "Florist. Delivery for Ryerson."

We all imagine we're so special that an unexpected gift of flowers doesn't seem surprising. Murray released the lock and waited for me in his doorway. Sinéad O'Connor was wafting out from the living room behind him when I got to the second floor. The surprise in his face when he saw me did not seem to include delight.

"What the hell are you—"

"Hi, Murray. We need to talk. Is Alex-Sandy here?"

He didn't move from the doorway. "What do you think this is? A public library with regular visiting hours?"

"That's very good. I'll have to use that. Like the next time you come around unannounced with Alex Fisher-Fishbein to con me into framing someone for you. What did you say to her: 'Let's sprinkle some crumbs from the Global table in front of Warshawski, she's so perennially hard up she'll jump on them like a carp on live bait?' "

His face darkened. "I tried to do you a favor. Just because you're in some twenty-year-old catfight with Alex—"

"Darling Murray, when I'm in a catfight you see the gashes a jaguar leaves. But it's hard for even a jungle cat to do much against a shark. Are you her partner or her patsy?"

"I've listened to you mouth off a lot of bull to a lot of people over the years, but this is the most offensive thing I've heard you say yet."

"Did she tell you Global planned to toss my place? And did she mention whether they were sowing or reaping?"

His scowl got uglier, but he moved out of the doorway. "You'd better come in and tell me what happened before you go off half-cocked to Alex."

I followed him into the living room and sat uninvited on one of the couches. He picked up a remote gadget and shut off his stereo, a cute system about as thick as my finger, with silvery speakers like rockets tucked into the corners of the room.

He leaned against the wall: this wasn't a social visit and he wasn't going to sit. "Okay. What happened to your place?"

I eyed him narrowly, even though I know you can't read the truth in most faces. "Someone planted three—large—bags of coke in it while I was out of town last week."

"Don't bring it to me. Call the cops."

"I did that very thing. A specimen named Lemour, who apparently freelances for BB Baladine, or maybe

Jean Claude Poilevy, beat me and tried to have me arrested. That was when he couldn't find the stuff. And he knew exactly where it was supposed to be." I smiled unpleasantly and cut off Murray as he started to speak. "I ran a secret camera during the search."

His scowl didn't lighten, but a shade of doubt came into his eyes. "I'd like to see the film."

"So you shall. I'm having your very own copy made for you. And today, because we've been pals for a long time and I hate to see you turn into a fawning sycophant for the studio, I am hand-delivering to you the LifeStory report I ran on Lucian Frenada two days before Global decided he needed to be discredited."

Murray's eyes blazed with fury at my studied insult, but he snatched the envelope out of my hand and sat down opposite me. While he examined the report I looked at the mess of papers on the glass-topped table. He'd been fine-tuning his script for tonight when I arrived: even upside down it was easy to make out Frenada's name.

After a couple of minutes Murray dug out another report from the pile in front of him—his copy of Frenada's finances—and began a page-by-page comparison. When he finished, he flung both of them onto the table.

"How do I know you didn't forge this?"

"Feeble, Murray: the creation date is embedded in the report. What I want to know is what Frenada knew about BB Baladine—or Teddy Trant—that made the studio come after him."

"He was harassing—"

"No." I cut him off sharply. "He was not hanging around the hotel. He came there once, and Lacey met with him for an hour in her suite. Frank Siekevitz, the

Trianon's security chief, may be changing his tune now, but he told me that a week ago. I'll be honest—Lacey has refused to talk to me—but I don't believe that crock about Frenada harassing her. I think Global wanted me and Frenada both out of the picture. They'd give me so huge a fee for getting dirt on him that I couldn't speak against them—and he'd be discredited. I know nothing that could interest, or harm, the studio, so why they're riding me so hard I don't understand. Whether Frenada did is another matter, but one we're not too likely to find out at this juncture. But one thing I will stake my reputation on is that he was not in the drug trade."

Murray's full lips tightened in a thin line. I realized I wasn't used to seeing his mouth—in all the years I'd known him he'd covered it with his beard. His face looked naked now, with a kind of bewildered petulance replacing his anger. It made me uncomfortable and I felt myself softening—into his ma or his scoutmaster. Mr. Contreras's admonition came back to me and made me laugh.

"Yeah, it's really funny. Maybe I'll get the joke in a year or two," Murray said resentfully.

"I was laughing at myself, not you. What are you going to do with this?"

He hunched a shoulder. "Cops found five kilos of coke in his office Saturday night."

"Put there by the same hand that planted them on me. Unless you think I, too, am running drugs in from Mexico?"

"Nothing you do would surprise me, Warshawski. Although it wouldn't be like you to do something that actually turned a profit. Where is the stuff you found?"

"St. Louis."

"St. Louis? Oh. You flushed it."

The Chicago sewers flow into the Chicago River. To keep the lake clean, we reversed the current of the river so that our sludge—properly treated, of course—flows backward, into the Mississippi. I suppose eventually it reaches New Orleans, but our rivalries are local—we prefer to think we're dumping on St. Louis.

"In that case, you've got no proof. I don't know what to make of this report. It's the only thing that contradicts my story. It may be that new evidence came in between when you asked and when I did."

"In forty-eight hours?" I lost my temper again. "If you go on the air tonight with this slander against Frenada I am going to persuade his sister to sue the studio and you for every dime you have."

His anger flared up as well. "You are always right, aren't you? You have one flimsy piece of counterevidence and you come galloping in like some damned Amazon, quivering with omnipotent self-righteousness, and based on your say-so I'm supposed to abandon an investigation I've worked hard on. Well, take your story to the *Enquirer,* or put it on the Web. A lot of people out there love conspiracies. And unless Frenada's sister is a major enemy of yours, don't egg her on against the studio: Global breaks bigger people than Celia Caliente like crackers over soup."

"That what they're threatening you with?"

His face turned the color of Lake Calumet brick. "Get out! Get out and don't come near me again."

I got to my feet. "I'll give you a hint for nothing. The story on Frenada and Global isn't about drugs. I'm not sure, but I think it's about T-shirts. Mad Virgin T-shirts. We could have a nice little coup together—if Global didn't own you. I mean, the paper, of course."

He put a hand between my shoulders and pushed me

toward the door. When he slammed it behind me, I dearly wanted to put my ear to the keyhole to see if I could hear him on the phone: would he go straight to Alex? I was glad I thought better of it: as I started down the stairs his door opened.

I turned to look at him. "Second thoughts, Murray?"

"Just wondering if you were really leaving, Vic."

I blew him an airy kiss and continued down the stairs. At the bottom I wondered what I'd really gained from the encounter. It's a mistake to try to interrogate someone when you're angry. But at least that cut both ways with Murray this morning.

My car was still in the alley when I got there. One of the few pluses of a difficult day.

28

Friendly Warning

I WAS EXPLAINING to a woman from a temporary agency how to match invoices and case reports when the call came. "Collect for V. I. Wachewski from Veronica Fassler," the operator said.

I thought for a minute but couldn't place the name. "Sorry. I think she's mistaken."

"Tell her from Coolis, she met me at the hospital," a voice at the other end gabbled frantically, before we were cut off.

Veronica Fassler. The woman who'd had the baby and was shuffling along the hall chained to the orderly when Mr. Contreras and I left. So much had happened in the last week that I barely remembered the event. I wondered how she'd gotten my name and number, but that wasn't important—I'd been strewing my cards wholesale around the hospital.

"Oh, yes," I said slowly. "I'll accept the call."

"I been in line thirty minutes and there's people behind me still waiting. You asking questions about Nicola, right?"

Nicola Aguinaldo. Somehow I'd also lost track of her in the last few days.

"Did you know something about her?" I asked.

"Is there a reward?"

"The family doesn't have much money," I said. "If they could find out how she managed to get out of the hospital, it might be worth a hundred dollars."

"Out of the hospital? I only know how she went. On a stretcher. That ought to be worth a whole lot more than how she left."

"Female difficulties, I understand." I sounded prim.

"You call pounding a CO on the chest with your bitty fists and getting burned 'female difficulties,' you have a different body than me, miss."

"Burned?" Now I really was bewildered: I didn't remember seeing burn marks on Nicola's body, but there was no way of finding out now.

"You don't know anything, do you? With a stun gun. The CO's all carry them to keep order in the workshop. No one would've guessed they'd ever need one on Nicola."

"That's what took her to the hospital?"

"What about the reward, before you pry any further."

"Did you see the CO burn her?"

A silence on the other end told its own tale. Before the speaker could bluster into some lies, I said I thought that much information was valuable, probably worth fifty dollars.

She paused again, marshaling her tale, then said in a rush, "Nicola took the gun—the stun gun—from the guard, turned it on him, and he got so mad he gave her a lethal dose. Stuns the heart, you know, just like the electric chair, if they turn up the juice. So the guards thought she was dead and rolled her body out of the hospital themselves to make it look like she didn't die there. They wouldn't want an investigation. That's what happened."

"I like the story; it's a good one. But it's not how she died. Where shall I send the fifty?"

"Fuck you, bitch, I'm calling to help, aren't I? How do you know when you wasn't there yourself?"

"I saw Nicola's dead body." I didn't want to tell her what injuries caused the death, because then she'd embroider some story to account for them. I told her it would be worth another fifty to me if she could get me the name of someone at Coolis who'd known Nicola well.

"Maybe," she said doubtfully. "She didn't speak much English, but the Mexican girls didn't hang with her on account of she was from China."

I was startled, but then decided it was just garbled geography, not some unusual fact about Aguinaldo I hadn't heard before. "You said she got injured in the workshop?"

"You know, where we do prison work. She was in the sewing shop. My friend Erica, her roommate Monique was working there the day the CO took after Nicola."

"Maybe I could talk to her roommate."

"And let her get the reward money when I've done all the work? No thanks!"

"You'd get a finder's fee," I encouraged her. "The roommate would get an informer's fee."

Before I could push any harder, the line went dead. I called the operator to find out if she could reconnect me, but she told me what I already knew: you can call out from jail, but no one can call in.

I sat back in my chair. So the prison had lied about the ovarian cyst. Possibly had lied, if I could believe Veronica's tale. The idea of Nicola Aguinaldo attacking a guard seemed utterly improbable, but it was obvious when Veronica had started lying—when she blurted out the tale about the guards putting Nicola's dead body out of the hospital. Of course, she'd had a week to prepare a realistic story. You don't have to be behind bars to be a con artist, but the odds are more in your favor there. In my days as a public defender I'd encountered every variation of injured innocence known not just to man but to woman as well.

I needed more information on Coolis, on what Nicola had been doing the day before she went into the hospital. I'd have to make another trip out there, in my guise as a lawyer in good standing with the Illinois bar —which I am, but I wouldn't advise anyone to retain a lawyer who hadn't practiced in over a decade.

In the meantime I had more obvious tasks right in front of me. The woman from the temporary agency was standing next to me with a heap of computer printouts that needed sorting.

We were halfway through those when Tessa bounced in. She'd wrapped red beads around her locks and pulled them back in a kino cloth.

"What's going on around here, V.I., that you put up that ridiculous set of . . . ?" Her voice trailed away as she took in the chaos. "Good grief! I knew you were a bit of a slob, but this is way outside your usual housekeeping. Unkeeping."

I made sure the woman from the agency was clear enough on her work to leave her alone for a while and took Tessa into her studio to talk. She frowned when I finished.

"I don't like being so vulnerable here."

"Me either," I said with feeling. "If it's any comfort, I don't think my marauders would bother you."

"I want to get a better lock system installed. One

that's more secure than those padlocks you have out front. And I think you ought to pay for it, since it's due to you that the place was vandalized."

I expelled a loud breath. "You're going to choose it and I'm going to fund it? No, thanks. You chose a number-pad system that seemed relatively easy to bypass."

She frowned again. "How did they do that?"

I shrugged. "The pad itself hadn't been tampered with, so my best guess is with UV-sensitive ink. They spray the pad, then after you go in they shine an ultraviolet light on the pad. The keys you've touched are clean, see. Then they just have to try those numbers in different combinations until they get the right sequence. If that's the case we could reset the combination—but we'd have to remember to touch every number on the pad each time we went in. A magnetic card lock would be less vulnerable—but you have to remember to carry the card with you all the time. Anyone can break a padlock, but you have to stand there with equipment, which makes you more vulnerable to a passing squad car. Or to Elton. He's keeping an eye on the joint for us."

"Oh, for God's sake, Vic! An alcoholic street dweller!"

"He's not usually falling-down drunk," I said with dignity. "And his drinking doesn't stop him from using his eyes. Anyway, I'll ask Mary Louise to look into it. If she has time."

My voice trailed away into doubt. Mary Louise seemed more than just too busy to work for me right now. She seemed scared.

Tessa was too absorbed by her own needs to notice my hesitation. "Daddy thinks I should—we should—

get a system like Honeywell's, that notifies a central computer of an unauthorized break-in."

"Your daddy could well be right. But the guys who came in here wouldn't have triggered anyone's alarm system."

We thrashed it around inconclusively, until the woman from the agency came to get more direction.

I tried the Baladines a couple of times during the afternoon, but only got Rosario, the maid, who said, Robbie not home, Robbie away, Missus away. The third time I called I asked for one of the precocious swimming daughters. I remembered they had names like street signs, but it took me a while to come up with Madison and Utah. The intersection where bad deals are done.

I didn't introduce myself in case there was a parental warning out on me. Madison had seemed alarmingly forthcoming in her remarks when I was out there two weeks ago. She didn't disappoint me today.

"Robbie isn't home. He ran away, and Mommy's out looking for him. Daddy is furious, he says when he finds Robbie he'll make sure he toughens up, we've been soft on him too long."

"He ran away? Do you know where he'd go?" I hoped there was a sympathetic grandmother or aunt someplace who might stand up for Robbie.

That's why Eleanor had taken off, Madison explained, to go to her mother's in case Robbie was hiding there. "We're going to France on Saturday, and Robbie better be back before then. We're renting a castle with a swimming pool so me and Utah and Rhiannon can practice. Do you know we're having a swimming meet here on Labor Day? If Rhiannon beats me in the backstroke, I am going to be so sick. Robbie would never beat me, he's too fat, he can't do anything with his body. Like last summer when he fell over his feet playing football at our cousin's. He got his feet tangled up in his shoelaces. He looked so funny, me and my cousin Gail laughed our heads off. Robbie was up all night crying. That's something only weak girlie girls do."

"Yes, I remember," I said. "You didn't even cry when a fire truck ran over your cat. Or did you cry because the nice shiny engine had a smear on it?"

"Huh? Fluffy didn't get hit by a fire truck. That was Mom; she ran over her with the car. Robbie cried. He cried when she killed a bird. I didn't."

"You're going to be a credit to Dr. Mengele one of these days."

"Who?" she screeched.

"Mengele." I spelled the name. "Tell BB and Eleanor he has an opening for a bright young kid."

I tried not to slam the phone in her ear: it wasn't her fault her parents were bringing her up to have the sensitivity of a warthog. I wished I could take some time off to look for Robbie, but I had more to do here than I could figure out. Such as what to do about Veronica Fassler's call from Coolis. In the morning I'd take another trip out there, but for right now I could try to get the doctor who'd operated on Nicola Aguinaldo at Beth Israel.

Before calling the hospital I looked inside my phone to see if the folks who broke in had planted a bug in it. When I didn't find anything unusual in the mess of wires, I went out behind the warehouse to inspect the phone junction box. There I found that the wires had been stripped and clipped to a secondary set of cables, presumably leading to a listening station. I tapped on them thoughtfully. Probably best that I left them in place. It wasn't a sophisticated system, but if I dismantled it, Baladine would get something less primitive, harder to find, and harder to circumvent.

Back inside, I let Andras Schiff play Bach on my office CD. I don't know if those old spy movies are right, that radios block listening devices, but the *Goldberg Variations* might at a minimum educate the thugs—who knows? I sat next to the speaker with my cell phone and called the hospital. The woman from the agency stared at me curiously, then turned a huffy shoulder: she thought I was trying to keep her from listening to me.

Max Loewenthal's secretary, Cynthia Dowling, came on the line with her usual efficient friendliness.

"I can't remember the ER surgeon's name," I said. "I should, since it's Polish, but all I remember is that it had a hundred zees and cees in it."

"Dr. Szymczyk," she supplied.

When I explained what I wanted, she put me on hold and tracked down the report. Of course Dr. Szymczyk hadn't done an autopsy, but he had dictated information while he was working on Aguinaldo. He had described necrotic skin on the abdomen but hadn't mentioned any serious burn wounds. He had noted a couple of raw spots above the breasts that didn't seem connected to the blow that killed her.

Raw spots. Those could conceivably have been caused by a stun gun, so maybe Veronica Fassler hadn't been spinning a complete lie. I would bring fifty dollars for her with me to the prison in the morning.

I worked desultorily with the woman from the agency, but it was hard for me to focus on files. For some people, putting papers in order is a wonderfully soothing act, but I could make so little sense of the world around me that I couldn't make sense of my scattered papers either.

Late in the afternoon, as I was trying to remember what year and what file records about Humboldt Chemical belonged to, my office buzzer rang. I stiffened and had my gun in hand when I went to the front door. I was astounded to see Abigail Trant, her honey-colored hair and softly tinted face as perfect as when I'd met her two weeks ago. Her Mercedes Gelaendewagen was double-parked on the street outside. When I invited her in, she asked if I'd talk to her in her vehicle instead. I wondered briefly if she had been dragooned into acting as a decoy but followed her to her trucklet.

"Do you know that Robbie Baladine has disappeared? If you know where he is, can you send him home?"

I blinked in surprise but assured her I hadn't heard from him for several days. "Did Eleanor or BB send you to talk to me?"

She looked straight ahead, ignoring an angrily honking line of cars behind her. "I came on my own initiative, and I am hoping you will honor my speaking confidentially to you. We are flying to France with the Baladines on Saturday, along with the Poilevys, so Eleanor discussed Robbie's disappearance with me in a frank way, as it is affecting their travel plans. They both feel that you have encouraged Robbie to be disobedient. I don't know if that is the reason, but BB has been talking furiously about wanting to put you out of business or thoroughly discredit you in some way. Knowing something about his methods, I didn't want to call you—he might well be monitoring your phone calls. I think I told you when we met that he doesn't like to feel anyone is getting the upper hand with him: for some reason he thinks you are taunting him or undermining him in some way."

I gave a snort of mirthless laughter. "He's been making it almost impossible for me to run my business."

A car shot around her from behind, giving her the finger and a loud epithet. She paid no attention.

"I had suggested to Teddy that Global try to make use of your agency, that it would be a good thing to support local talent. But he said you refused to take the assignment."

My jaw dropped so suddenly that my ears popped. "You were behind that? Mrs. Trant—that was extremely gracious of you. The trouble is, the assignment as it came to me from Alex Fisher was to frame someone, a man named Lucian Frenada who was drowned over the weekend. I couldn't take it on."

She sighed. "That's so typical of Alex. I wish Teddy didn't rely on her advice so much—I think she often leads him astray."

What a good wife, letting herself believe her husband was the innocent victim of bad advisers. But I wasn't going to ride her: she had gone out on a long limb for me with no reason for doing so. I asked her what made her put in a word for me with her husband.

She looked at me for the first time. "Do you know that the only money I've ever worked for was exercising horses for people when I was a teenager? I love my life and I love my husband, but I've often wondered what I would do if he—and my own family—lost everything. Would I be able to cut my own path, the way you have? Helping you out is like—like—"

"A sacrifice to the gods to keep them from putting you to the test?" I suggested when she fumbled for words.

She flashed a radiant smile. "That's it exactly. What a beautiful way of phrasing it! But in the meantime, if you hear from Robbie, send him home. Even if he's not always happy there, his parents really have his best interests at heart. And I don't think you can win against BB. He's too big, and he has too many powerful friends."

I couldn't argue with that. I hesitated over my words before speaking again, then said, "Mrs. Trant, you've gone out of your way to help me. So I don't like putting you on the spot. But have you noticed whether any of— well, the men you see socially, BB or Poilevy for instance—would you notice if one of them had lost a medallion from a Ferragamo shoe?"

"What a strange question. I suppose that means you must have found one? Where, I wonder? Are you allowed to tell me?"

"In the street near where Nicola Aguinaldo—the Baladines' old nanny—died."

She smiled again but without the radiance. "It's not the kind of thing I notice, I'm afraid. Now—I'd better take off. It's an hour on the Ike this time of day, and we're entertaining some studio execs. I'll certainly pay special attention to everyone's feet tonight. Don't forget about Robbie, will you? He should be at home."

That seemed to be my exit line. I thanked her for her warning. And for trying to help my little agency. Maybe that was why Baladine hadn't murdered me, I thought as I went back into my office. Maybe Teddy had told him that Abigail would be upset if they killed me. She knew about the shoe, though. I was willing to bet my meager pension plan on it.

29

Help Me, Father, for I Know Not What I'm Doing

At FIVE-THIRTY I sent the woman from the agency home. I didn't want to pay overtime on a job that would take at least sixteen or twenty more hours to finish. And I wanted her to leave while enough commuters were filling the sidewalks that no one would shoot at her, thinking it was me.

Tessa was still working in her studio. She put down her mallet and chisel after I'd been standing in her line of sight for six minutes. Artistic geniuses can't break their concentration, I know. I told her I was worrying about her safety while Baladine was gunning for me.

"I'm going to take my computer home. It's the only thing I need from my office for the immediate present. And then I'll get word out that I'm not operating out of here. We could install a small video camera at the entrance concealed in one of your metal pieces; that would provide a record of anyone who broke in. For an extra five hundred or so we could even get little monitors so we could watch the entrance. And we could install a five-digit number pad with a breaker that froze it if someone tried more than three times in ten minutes to open it. With those you should be pretty safe."

She wiped her face with a used towel, leaving a film

of glittery dust on her cheeks. "Oh, damn you for being so noble, Vic. I was all set to chew your ass into tiny pieces. Now what am I supposed to do?"

"If you'd chew up BB Baladine it would be more helpful. I know everyone thinks I'm in this mess because I'm too impulsive, but honestly, all I did was stop to help a woman in the road."

"That means something to you, I suppose. Get me a video camera installed tomorrow, and a new number pad, and leave your damned computer here. By the way, my daddy is insisting that someone from his staff meet me when I leave here at night."

"Ah, that would be your mother's next candidate for the father of her grandchildren?"

She grinned. "She's hoping. His name's Jason Goodrich—sounds solid enough, doesn't it? He's one of those software whizzes who gurgle in code coming out of the womb."

"More to the point is whether the boy knows how to disarm a man holding an automatic. But if you're happy, I'm happy."

I went back to my office to call Mary Louise. When I asked her if she would have time to take care of the office security, she hemmed and muttered something about her midterms.

"Pete's sake, Mary Louise. This isn't asking you to go into the Georgia mud for a month. It would be a big help if you could take care of the setup. I don't want to discuss what I want on the phone, but I can come over tonight or tomorrow morning and explain it."

"No!" she snapped. "You're not to come anywhere near this place."

"What on earth is going on?" I was hurt more than baffled. "What have I done to you?"

"I—you—Vic, I can't do any more work for you. You take too many risks."

"You made it through ten years in the department, but I take so many risks you can't even go to the Unblinking Eye for me?" I slammed the phone down so hard my palm smarted.

Was I really more dangerous to work for than the Chicago police? I fumed, pacing the room. If she could go down dark alleys after drug dealers, why couldn't she at least go to the camera store and arrange for a video monitor for me? And all she'd say was she wasn't going to put the children at risk. As if I were asking her to use them as human shields.

I came to a halt by my desk. Of course. Someone had threatened the children. That was what had happened. My hand hovered over the phone, then I thought better of it. If BB was monitoring my calls, then he'd assume Mary Louise had squealed. Then he might really go after the children. I felt trapped, and horribly alone. I sat with my head in my hands, trying not to cry.

"Vic! What's wrong?" Tessa was leaning over me, her face lively with concern.

I rubbed a hand through my hair. "Nothing. I'm feeling sorry for myself, which is a disastrous indulgence for a detective. You taking off?"

"My appointed knight has arrived. It's time for me to go, or have my mother show up with the FBI."

She gestured toward the door and a man came in. He was tall and dark, almost as dark as Tessa herself, with fine-drawn features and the easy manner you get growing up with a lot of money. I could see why Mrs. Reynolds thought he looked like good husband material.

"Don't sit here brooding alone," Tessa said. "We'll

take you down to the Glow or some other place where you can be with friends."

I pushed myself upright. The soreness in my legs was fading, that was one thing to be thankful for—a tribute to my daily workouts, or maybe just my DNA.

"It's not such a good idea right now for you to hang out with me." I tried not to seem melodramatic, and sounded pompous instead. "Anyway, I'm going to see a priest, so I'll be in good hands."

"A priest?" Tessa echoed. "Vic! Oh, you're pulling my leg. Well, don't stay alone here too late, hear?"

I followed her to the door and watched her and her escort leave. He was driving a navy BMW sedan, an easy car to keep an eye on if you were tailing. Just as well I'd turned down a ride.

I watched the street through the small pane of wire-filled glass for five minutes or so. Who knew if I was under surveillance or not? I walked down to the corner, leaving the Rustmobile in the lot.

Elton was hawking *Streetwise* near the L stop. I stopped to buy a few; his red-streaked blue eyes looked at me with lively curiosity. "I see some dudes hanging around today," he whispered with hoarse importance. "*Streetwise*, miss, *Streetwise*, sir—read about the mayor and the homeless on Lower Wacker—they was driving some kind of late-model tan car, maybe a Honda. Fact of the matter they're driving down Leavitt now. Coming up behind you. *Streetwise*, sir, thank you, sir."

I scuttled up the L stairs, frantically fishing in my wallet for singles to stuff into the ticket machine. Below me the tan Honda stopped. I grabbed a ticket and ran up to the platform, shoving my way through a knot of commuters who swore at me for my rudeness. A south-bound train was getting ready to leave. I stuck a hand into the shutting panels, earning another yell—this time from the trainman—and watched the platform with a sick franticness until the doors hissed shut and we were under way.

I rode the train all the way into the Loop, where I got out and walked slowly around Marshall Field's, admiring the beachwear in the State Street windows and the garden furniture at the north end of the store. The setting sun made a mirror of the glass; I watched the people behind me. No one seemed to be paying me any special attention.

I climbed back up the L stairs and picked up the Blue Line outbound: I'd had a tiny inspiration while I was indulging in misery in my office. It took me to the California stop, in the heart of Humboldt Park. I walked the six blocks to St. Remigio's.

St. Remigio's was a Victorian brick monster, dating to the turn of the last century when Humboldt Park had a large Italian population. Whoever Remigio had been, his miraculous powers hadn't extended to protecting the building: the great arched windows in the sanctuary were boarded over, and the old wooden doors were fastened with massive chains.

Despite the lateness of the hour, small boys were racing after a soccer ball in the heavily fenced schoolyard. A stocky man with sparse white hair punctuated their screams with shouted directions in Spanish. After a minute or two he saw me at the locked gate and came over, asking in Spanish what I wanted.

"Ando buscando a el Padre." I stumbled through the phrase in my schoolgirl Spanish.

He waved an arm toward the back of the church and said something so fast that I couldn't follow it. Before I could ask for a repetition, two little boys ran over to tug at his arm and demand—as far as I could tell—a ruling on some dispute. I was immediately forgotten in the more important business of the moment.

I walked past the front of the church and found a narrow walkway leading to the rear. Chunks of pavement were missing, but someone had made a gallant attempt to spruce up the area. Scraggly rosebushes surrounded a dejected-looking statue that I assumed was St. Remigio himself. I picked an empty bottle of Four Roses from behind him and looked for a garbage bin. Finally, not wanting to present myself to the priest carrying a bottle, I tucked it into my handbag and rang a bell labeled FATHER LOU.

After a longish wait, when I was thinking the soccer coach might have been explaining that Father Lou was away, a harsh squawk startled me. I hadn't noticed the intercom to the left of the door.

"This is V. I. Warshawski. I want to talk to the priest about one of his parishioners." I didn't think I could explain my errand intelligibly at a shout through a speaker.

After another long wait, the dead bolt snapped back and an old man in a T-shirt and slippers stood in the doorway. His upper body and neck had the thickness of a weight lifter. He looked at me as if assessing whether to pick me up and throw me off the stoop.

"Father Lou?"

"Are you with the police or the press?" He had the gravelly voice of the old Irish South Side.

"No. I'm a private investigator—"

"Whether you're private or public, I won't have you digging around in that boy's past, trying to prove some slander about him." He turned back inside and started to shut the door.

I put out a hand to brace the door; it took all my strength to keep a big enough crack open for me to cry out, "I'm not slandering Lucian Frenada. I've been trying to stop the *Herald-Star* from running their story on him and drugs. I've been trying to talk to Lacey Dowell, because she knows something about the true reason he was killed, but she won't talk to me. I was hoping you might know something."

The pressure on the other side eased. Father Lou reappeared in the entrance, frowning. "If you aren't digging up dirt on Lucy, what's your involvement?"

"Please. Can we sit down? I can explain the whole story to you, but not standing out here in the heat with one foot in the door hoping you won't shut it on me."

"This is my rest time," the priest grumbled. "Everyone around here knows not to bother me from six to seven. It's the only way an old man like me can keep running a big parish."

That must have been what the soccer coach was trying to tell me—the priest is back there, but don't interrupt his nap. I was starting to mutter an apology when he added, "But Lucy's death—I can't sleep anyway. I might as well talk to you."

He led me into a wide dark vestibule. Despite his age he moved easily, his walk a graceful bounce. Dancers' legs, boxers' legs.

"Mind your step. I don't put lights on in the hall—have to save every nickel in a poor parish; don't want the cardinal shutting us down because we're too expensive."

Father Lou unlocked a small side room, furnished with the heavy remains of the previous century. Eight chairs with ornate legs stood primly around a heavy table. A blackened painting of Jesus in a crown of thorns hung over an empty grate.

The priest motioned me to one of the chairs. "I'm going to make tea. Make yourself comfortable."

I did my best in the wooden chair. The flowers carved into the back dug into my shoulder blades. I shifted forward. On the table a plaster statue of the Virgin smiled at me sadly. Her lips were chipped and the paint had flaked from her left eye, but the right one stared at me patiently. She was wearing a cloak of faded taffeta, painstakingly trimmed in handmade lace.

Father Lou returned with a battered metal tray holding a teapot and two cups as I was fingering the fabric. "A hundred years old, that lace, we have it on the altar, too. What did you say your name was?"

When I repeated it he tried to talk to me in Polish. I had to explain that I knew only a handful of words, gleaned from my father's mother; my own mother, an Italian immigrant, spoke to me in her language. At that he switched to Italian and grinned with delight at my surprise.

"I've been here a long time. Baptized Italians here, married Poles; now I offer the mass in Spanish. Neighborhood's always been poor; wasn't always this dangerous. Parish council suggested soccer. Seems to be good for the little kids, lets them run off some of that energy."

"But you were a boxer?" I was guessing, from his gait.

"Oh, yeah. I boxed for Loyola in the forties, then I found my vocation but kept boxing. I still run a club here. St. Remigio's remains the school to beat—gives the boys something to be proud of. We can't play football against those big suburban schools. We can't get enough equipment for eleven boys, let alone fifty or sixty the way they do. But I can outfit boxers. Lucy was one of my best. I was that proud of him."

His jaw worked. For a minute he looked like a tired old man, his pale eyes filming over, then he shook himself, an unconscious motion, shaking off one more punch.

He looked at me aggressively, as if to make sure I didn't try to pity him for his weakness. "The police came around suggesting Lucy was running drugs through his factory. They wanted me to spy on him. I told them what I thought of that. Then the papers and the television. Mexican boy makes good, so he must be selling drugs. All that innuendo—I saw what the *Herald-Star*'s been saying. This boy who drove an old car so he could pay his sister's children's fees here at Remigio? They couldn't leave him alone."

He stopped to drink some tea. I had some too, to be polite. It was light and flowery and surprisingly refreshing in the heat.

"When did you last talk to him?" I asked.

"He came here to mass once or twice a week. I'm thinking it was last Tuesday. He filled in as a server when he saw that the kid who was supposed to do it hadn't shown. They used to laugh at him when he was fourteen, when I talked him into coming here, do some training and serve at the mass—little altar boy, that's what they called him—but then he started winning boxing matches, and the tune they sang on the streets changed in a hurry.

"I'm getting sidetracked. I don't like to think about him being dead, that's all. It's easy to say people are with Jesus when they die, and I even believe it's true, but we need Lucy here. I need him, anyway. Jesus wept when Lazarus died—He's not going to condemn me for crying over Lucy."

He picked up the statue of the Madonna and twisted it around, smoothing the taffeta cape over her hips. I sat still. He'd speak when he was ready, but if I prodded him he might turn pugnacious again.

"So—he still came to mass. When he started his shop, Special-T, he could have gone someplace farther away, a safer neighborhood, but he liked to stay close to the church. Felt his life had been saved here. He went from being a lookout for the Lions, selling nickel bags, to citywide lightweight champ. Then my old school, Loyola, working nights at a downtown hotel to put himself through college, but he left those Lions and drugs behind for good when he boxed for me. I make it clear to all the boys: they can't get in the ring with Jesus and drugs at the same time."

There wasn't any hearty piety in his voice, just the facts. No one looking at those forearms, or the stern set to his jaw, could doubt Father Lou's ability to stand up to a gangbanger.

"Anyway, I'm thinking it was Tuesday, but maybe it was Wednesday, I can't be sure. But we had a cup of coffee and a donut after the service."

"Was he worried then?"

"Of course he was worried, all this—this crap about him and drugs!" the old man shouted, smacking the table hard enough to make the Virgin wobble. "And what's it to you, anyway?"

"If it's any comfort, I think someone was setting him up with the drugs." Once again I went through the long story of Nicola Aguinaldo, of Alex Fisher and the studio asking me to look into Frenada's finances, and the two very different reports on them.

"It's disgusting," Father Lou said, "disgusting that you could go pry into the boy's private business like that."

My cheeks grew hot. I didn't try to defend myself—I know it's a breach of privacy, and I wasn't going to give that pathetic adolescent bleat that everyone did it.

Father Lou glared at me, his jaw working, then said, "Still, I suppose it's a good thing you saw the accounts the way they really were. How could it happen, the report being changed like that, so that you get one version, that reporter friend of yours another?"

"I've thought a lot about that," I said. "That's one of the reasons I came to see you. You read from time to time about hackers trying to move money from a bank into their accounts; the security stops them when they try to take it out. I don't think it would be so hard for someone with a lot of sophisticated resources to break into a system and make more money appear than was really there. But what will happen if the user tries to withdraw it? If Lucian Frenada's sister is his heir, can you get her to try to take the money out? That will prove whether it's really there or just a shadow."

He thought it over. He didn't react quickly, but he was thorough, asking a series of questions designed to make sure Frenada's sister wouldn't be in any danger if she tried to get the money.

"Okay. I won't say yes or no tonight, but I'll talk to Celia in the morning. I want you to promise me you won't bother her. Are you a Catholic? Do you have a pledge that you honor?"

I shifted uncomfortably on the hard chair; my mother, fleeing Fascist Italy because of religion, didn't want that to define her daughter's life in the New

World. "I'll pledge you my word. When I give it I do my utmost to keep it."

He grunted. "I guess that'll have to do. And the other thing you wanted from me?"

I took a breath and said in a rush, "Lacey Dowell. She knows something about Frenada, about his shirts, why he made those Mad Virgin T-shirts and then pretended he hadn't. She won't talk to me."

"Magdalena. I never can think of her by that silly stage name. You think I can make her give up her story?" His full mouth twisted, whether in amusement or scorn I couldn't tell. "Maybe. Maybe. You being a detective and all, I suppose you know what fancy hotel she's staying in while she's in town. She sure avoids the old neighborhood, unless she's got a team of cameras following after her."

30

The Mad Virgin's Story

FATHER LOU WAS gone about twenty minutes. When he came back he said if I could wait he was pretty sure Magdalena would be along to the church sometime this evening.

I suddenly remembered Morrell, waiting for me at a restaurant on Damen, and asked for a phone. Father Lou took me into his study, a shabby but far more comfortable room than the parlor we'd been using. Boxing trophies were scattered about shelves stuffed with old papers. The desk, with a simple wood crucifix over it, was stacked with financial reports and old sermons. He didn't have many books; I noticed a collection of Frank O'Connor short stories and, to my surprise, one by Sandra Cisneros—trying to keep up with parishioners, he explained when he saw me looking at it.

He had an old black rotary phone, heavy and clunky to hands used to plastic Touch-Tones. He listened in unashamedly as I made my call—I suppose to make sure I wasn't going to set a mob heavy on Frenada's sister—but when he heard me ask the maître d' for Morrell he brightened.

"So you know Morrell," he said when I hung up.

"You should have told me that sooner. I didn't know he was back in town."

"He got thrown out of Guatemala," I said. "I don't know him well."

Father Lou had met him during the Reagan years, when American churches sometimes gave sanctuary to El Salvadoran refugees. St. Remigio's had sheltered a family that fled to Humboldt Park, and Morrell had come to do a story on them.

"Does a lot of good, Morrell. Not surprised he got thrown out of Guatemala. He's always covering underdogs of one kind or another. If you were meeting him for a meal I suppose you must be hungry."

He took me down a long unlit corridor to his kitchen, a cavern of a room, with a stove even older than the rotary phone. He didn't ask me what I wanted, or even what I wouldn't eat, but fried up a pan full of eggs with an expert hand. He ate three to my two, but I kept even with him on the toast.

When Lacey still hadn't arrived at nine, we watched Murray's show on a set in the parish hall. It was so old that Murray's face danced around in a wavy line of reds and greens. The report was subdued and lacked Murray's usual punch: he'd apparently been rattled by my information, however angrily he'd tossed me out this morning. Most of the report focused on the Mexico-Chicago drug route, with only ninety seconds on Lucian Frenada, "an up-and-coming entrepreneur whose untimely death means a lot of questions with no answers. Was he the point man for a drug ring, as the five kilos of coke found in his shop last week suggest? Was he murdered by associates he'd run afoul of? Or was he the innocent bystander his sister and other friends claim?"

Murray segued from that to footage of the shop, footage of the coke inside a bolt of T-shirting, and some old footage of Lacey and Frenada in front of the very church where I was sitting. "Father Lou Corrigan, who trained Lucian Frenada as the city champion light-weight boxer in this building, wouldn't talk to Channel Thirteen, either about Frenada or his other prizewinning student, Lacey Dowell."

He went on with details of Lacey's life, showed footage of his two-week-old interview with her, and closed with a summary that seemed lame to me. Father Lou was furious, but I thought it was a much more muted report than Murray would have made without my input. Of course, the priest had known Frenada for thirty years. It was a personal story to him.

We were back in his study, still thrashing it out over a second pot of tea, when the doorbell rang, a harsh, loud buzzing that fitted the priest's own voice. He pushed back from the chair and moved out to the hall on his light dancing step. I followed: if Lacey was bait in a Global trap I didn't want to be sitting under a crucifix waiting for it.

The star was alone, her cloud of red curls tucked inside a motorcycle helmet. No one would have known her in her nondescript jeans and jacket.

She put an arm around the priest. "I'm so sorry, Father Lou. Sorry about everything."

"Oh? And what do you have to be sorry for, miss? Something that you and I should talk about privately in a confessional?"

Her head jerked up and she squinted over his shoulder down the hall. When she saw me she moved away from Father Lou, and away from her sad drooping. "Who is that?"

"That's a detective, Magdalena," the priest said. "She's private, but she's got some questions about Lucy you would do well to answer."

Lacey turned toward the door, but Father Lou grabbed her left wrist in a businesslike grip and pulled her forward. "Your old playmate, and I have to call you to get you to come talk to me about him. That tells its own tale, Magdalena."

"Isn't this rather melodramatic?" Lacey said. "Midnight meetings in the church?"

"Why not?" I put in. "The whole of the last two weeks has been B-grade garbage. Did you talk to Alex Fisher about coming here? Is hers going to be the next knock on the door?"

"Alex doesn't know I'm here. She's making me nervous these days."

"This something that came on you suddenly after you saw the news about Frenada?" I demanded.

"Girls—ladies, I mean. Let's go sit down. More light, less heat."

Father Lou put a muscular arm around each of us and propelled us back to his study. He came up to about my nose, but I wouldn't like to test the strength in those arms. He poured cold tea into three cups and set the pot down with a firm smack on the tray.

"Now, Magdalena, you'd better tell me everything you know about Lucy's death." He spoke with an old authority over her.

"I don't know anything about his death. But—oh, I don't even know where to begin. I'm so confused."

She blinked tears away from her large blue eyes, but I didn't feel moved to pity, and Father Lou apparently didn't either. He fixed her with a hard stare and told her to save her dramatics for her movies. She flushed and bit her lip.

"What about the cocaine," Father Lou said. "Do you know anything about the drugs that were planted in his shop?"

"Planted? That isn't what happened." She shook her head. "I was shocked. I'd talked to Lucy at my hotel, oh, weeks ago, and he never breathed a word about it. Of course he wouldn't necessarily, but—but—it was unexpected, anyway."

"How do you know they weren't planted?" I asked. "Is that what Alex told you? After I wrote you that Global was doing the broadcast tonight?"

"How do you know—she didn't—" Lacey stammered.

"Alex?" Father Lou said. "Oh, the girl from Hollywood. Don't lie about this, Magdalena. If she talked to you about it, I want to know."

Lacey's wide mouth contracted into a sulky pout. "When I read this Warshawski woman's note, I called Alex. Don't bite me: I know her, and I don't know Warshawski from a pit bull. Someone like me gets a million people a day saying they have special news or they can protect me from some weird shit or other. I thought Warshawski wanted to scare me into hiring her detective services."

"That isn't implausible," I said. "But it doesn't explain why it rattled you so badly you had to call Alex about it. I wrote Ms. Dowell that Global was going to smear Frenada on television," I added to the priest. "I wanted to talk to Ms. Dowell about it. Since I couldn't get a phone call in to her, I wrote her and waited in the lobby in case she wanted to talk to me. Half an hour later Global's Doberman showed up, very agitated."

"What did she tell you, Magdalena?" Father Lou demanded.

"She—Alex—she came to the Trianon and told me it was true, she even showed me a photograph they had of a kilo of cocaine inside a fabric bolt Lucy brought in from Mexico." Lacey looked pleadingly at the priest. "If you think I wouldn't come here because I'm cold-hearted, you're so wrong. I didn't want to have to talk about Lucy with you if he was dealing drugs. You never could hear one bad word about Lucy. Not even when he was a lookout for the Lions when he was eleven. If you want to believe it was a plant, go ahead, but Alex warned me, warned me that Warshawski would try to get me caught in a smear campaign. And she warned me not to talk about it. It's one thing for Hugh Grant or some other male star to get in trouble with sex and drugs, but when a woman does it, especially one getting to be my age, she looks like slime. Alex said it could kill me if it got around." Lacey looked at me. "I suppose you were hiding behind the potted palm in the lobby."

"You took her word for it without asking anyone else?" Father Lou said. "Your old comrade, who saved you from getting beat up, and you didn't even question what a television show was going to say about him? Did you see what they did to him tonight, that boy who worked day and night to keep a roof over his sister's head after her husband was killed?"

"Alex had a photo," Lacey said, but she looked at her hands.

"That's true, Ms. Dowell," I said. "That's very true."

Lacey flushed. "She had a photo; I saw the cocaine in a photo."

"They set him up," I said. "You live in a world of doctored images; you know how easy it is to make a picture look like the truth. And how did you know the kilo in the bolt of cloth was even in Frenada's shop? But it's not the coke per se I care about. What I'm trying to understand is why they needed to shut him up. Was it something to do with the T-shirts? Why did he have a Mad Virgin T-shirt in his office?"

"It can't be anything about the T-shirts," she said. "That's not a story at all. Here's what happened. Lucy and I didn't stay close, but we keep—kept in touch. He sent me that story that ran in the *Herald-Star* about him two years ago, how he was the model of the up-and-coming minority entrepreneur. Then when we decided to shoot *Virgin Six* here, of course it was a big story. Lucy saw it. He wrote and asked if I would get the studio to give him a contract for some of the Mad Virgin T-shirts, a Chicago commemorative or something. So I told him I'd talk to Teddy Trant, which I did, and Teddy gave me a sarcastic brush off. And I let it drop."

"You were never a shuffler, Magdalena. You didn't care about Lucy enough to stand up for him?" The priest looked at her over the rim of his teacup.

"We were in the middle of a difficult contract cycle. I know—I should have thought more of Lucy, but I'm thirty-seven; in another few years unless I'm really lucky I won't be able to be a star. And anyway, Father Lou, I moved away more than twenty years ago." She held out her hands, the gesture she often made to her old lover halfway through the Virgin movies.

"But he made some shirts on spec?" I said.

"I guess he must have. Suddenly, the day before I was flying out, Teddy called me and asked for Lucy's number. He wanted to look at the factory or something."

"Then at Murray's party at the Golden Glow two weeks ago, why did you get so angry with Frenada?"

"Were you there?" she said. "Behind another potted palm or something? Teddy said he looked at Lucy's stuff. He said it wasn't up to Global standard. But Lucy claimed Teddy stole one of his shirts. I said that was nuts, we—the studio—manufacture zillions of them, why would Teddy steal one? Lucy threatened to make a scene right there, and I hate being humiliated in public that way. I had him thrown out. And then I felt terrible. I did, Father Lou, I really did. I called him and apologized and invited him up to my hotel for lunch. We talked and talked and he said one of the shirts he'd made really was missing. I couldn't get him to let it drop, so I told him I'd mention it to Alex, but really I thought one of his workers must have stolen it; it's the kind of thing people take."

"Yes, that is possible," Father Lou said. "What did you say to this woman Alex or to your boss?"

She knit her fingers. "I didn't see how I could say anything to Teddy. He'd already assured me he didn't have the shirt. He said something horrible about Lucy, anyway, and I had to remind him that I'm Mexican, too. But I told Alex and she said to stop fussing about it, if Lucy was missing a shirt she'd send him one. But of course that wasn't the point."

"What was so special about his shirts?" I asked. "The fabric? The picture?"

"Honestly, I don't know," she said, spreading her hands again. "I think Lucy was upset because Global didn't give him the contract, and it distorted his judgment."

"Where does Global make its spin-offs—shirts and dolls and whatnot?" I asked.

"I've never asked. All over, I suppose."

"Third World countries? America?"

She shook her head impatiently. "I don't know."

"You collect the royalties, but you don't ask for fear of what they'll tell you?" I said.

"I've sat here long enough with you thinking I'm a cockroach in the sink." She uncoiled her legs and sprang out of the chair. "I'm out of here."

Father Lou reached the door ahead of her and barred her way. "You can leave in a minute, Magdalena. I'm glad you came tonight. I think you'll sleep better, having told the truth, as I'm sure you've done.

"We're having the funeral mass tomorrow," he added, when she didn't say anything. "I expect you to be there. It will be at eleven. Lucy left his sister's children provided for—he had a life-insurance policy—but they could use another bit of cash to pay their school fees. And it would be a graceful gesture if you gave a scholarship to the school in his memory."

Her face was stormy, but after staring at the priest for a long minute she muttered agreement. He let her go. A few minutes later we heard a motor roar into life. Her motorcycle. I'd have to ask young Emily what kind of bike Lacey Dowell rode around town. I was betting on a hog.

Twenty thousand dollars to St. Remigio's instead of three Hail Marys? That's what it sounded like to me.

"I'm tired; I'd like to go to bed," he said. "Did she tell you what you need to know?"

I wasn't sure—I still didn't understand why the shirt

Frenada made was so important. And I wasn't as sure as Father Lou that I'd heard the truth. When I left the rectory I wondered how much time I had before I joined Lucian Frenada in a pine box. Maybe Father Lou would offer a funeral mass for me, heathen that I was.

31

A Day in the Country

EVERYTHING WAS MAKING me nervous. I was afraid to go home because I didn't know if someone would jump me. I was afraid to go to my car for the same reason. I was afraid to send Mr. Contreras down to my office to fetch the car in case Baladine had planted a bomb under the hood. In the end my nervousness made me angry enough that when I got off the L, I went home the direct way: up the sidewalk, into the front door. Nothing happened, and perversely enough that made me even edgier.

In the morning I took the train down to my office and threw a rock at the hood of the car. It bounced off. The car didn't blow up, but a couple of boys who were lounging across the street scuttled into the alley: it's scary to share the street with a crazy woman.

The woman from the temporary agency was waiting for me inside: Tessa had arrived unusually early and let her in. I got the woman started on organizing papers before calling the Unblinking Eye to discuss a surveillance system for the building. Since Tessa and I really had only one entrance to protect, we didn't need more than two screens, one for each of our work spaces. Although it was still money I didn't have, it wasn't as big a hit as I'd feared. The Unblinking Eye would do the installation in the morning and pick up their rental camera from me at the same time.

After that I buckled down at my computer, researching court cases, trying to find Veronica Fassler. It's a needle-in-a-haystack job: there's no index of cases by defendant. I tried to guess the year she'd been convicted, since she said she'd been at Coolis longer than Nicola Aguinaldo, and finally, with some luck, found her case, dating back four years. Fassler had been caught with five grams of crack on the corner of Winona and Broadway, and justice had followed its inexorable course of three to five years. A year for every gram. It seems odd that the U.S. is so reluctant to go metric, except in measuring the minute amount of crack it takes to send someone to prison.

I also did a search for information on Coolis. I had ignored stories when it was under construction, since I wasn't with the public defender any longer. I started with *Carnifice gets contract for new facility*. The *Corrections Courier* said it was *a novel idea, combining jail and prison in northwest Illinois, typical of the innovative approach to vertical integration that is Carnifice Security's hallmark*. Because of overcrowding in Cook and Du Page County jails, women arrested and unable to post bond would be housed in a special wing of Coolis. That way they could just move down the hall to the prison once they were convicted—since being in jail for a year or more while awaiting trial greatly increased your chance of conviction. If you couldn't afford bond you must be guilty, I guess.

Because you go from jail to trial, jails are supposed to be close to the courts—a condition obviously not being met at Coolis. An article in the *Herald-Star* described how House Speaker Poilevy overcame that little obstacle. The year Coolis opened, he held a special legislative session on crime. Fifteen of sixteen bills zipped through the state legislature that session. One designated a particular courtroom to be part of Cook County on Mondays, Tuesdays, and Wednesdays, part of Du Page on Thursdays, and split between Lake and McHenry on Fridays. A couple of public defenders from each county could carpool with the State's Attorney, spend a few nights in Coolis, and save the state the cost of busing large numbers of women from the jail to their local county court.

I could see why Baladine was so tight with Poilevy—the House Speaker worked Springfield as if it were legerdemain, not legislation he was engineering. What I couldn't figure out was where Teddy Trant and Global Entertainment came into the picture. The financial papers didn't shed any light on the problem.

The only story the *Wall Street Journal* ran had questioned whether Carnifice was making the right kind of investment in a women's multipurpose correctional facility. The *REIT Bulletin,* in contrast, praised the move highly and gave the project a triple-A rating for investors.

Women prisoners make up the fastest growing segment of the fast-growing U.S. prison population, the *Bulletin* said. A twelvefold increase in women in prison in the last decade . . . seventy-five percent with children . . . eighty percent commit nonviolent crimes—possession, prostitution . . . theft usually to pay rent or other bills, unlike men doing it for drugs or thrills.

I skimmed the stories and finished with *Model workshops in prison: Coolis is of, for, and by the prisoners.* Prison workshops in Coolis allowed prisoners to earn as much as thirty dollars a week manufacturing food

and clothes for consumption in the state prison system.
The computer produced a blurry picture of smiling inmates in a prison kitchen and two serious-looking
women operating monster sewing machines. Carnifice
had invested a lot of money in the workshops when
they built the prison; they lobbied unsuccessfully to
overturn an Illinois law that prohibited sales of goods
outside the prison system. In fact, that was the only bill
that failed Poilevy's special crime session.

"The labor unions have a stranglehold on this state,"
Jean-Claude Poilevy grumbled when he was unable to
muster the votes to overturn the law. "They make it
impossible for efficient use of industrial facilities in order to protect their own fiefdom."

While I waited for the articles to print, I logged back
on to LifeStory. I should have done this days ago, but
my cocaine adventures had put it out of my mind. I
wanted to see what kind of report I would get on Lucian Frenada this time around and contrast it with the
first. I pulled up my original report so I could double-
check the parameters I had specified.

When it came on the screen I thought I was hallucinating: instead of the modest bank accounts and two
credit-card balances I'd seen ten days ago, I got pages of
detail: bank accounts in Mexico and Panama; eighteen
credit cards with charges on each ranging as high as
twenty thousand a month for travel and jewelry; a
home in Acapulco and one in the Cote d'Azur. The list
went on and on in a mind-numbing fashion.

I was so bewildered I couldn't even think for a few
minutes. Finally I went to my briefcase and took out the
wallet of backup disks I carry between home and office.
I found the floppy with the Frenada report on it and

opened the file. The simple figures were the ones I'd shown Murray yesterday morning.

I sat bewildered for a long time before I could think at all. It slowly came to me that when the vandals broke into my office last week, they'd gone into my computer and altered my files. They'd somehow loaded bogus numbers into the LifeStory files and downloaded them onto my machine.

I wondered whether they had messed around with any of my other documents—altered my case records, my tax data—they could have done anything. Once again the sense of violation made me feel sick. Someone had helped themselves to what was almost an extension of my mind.

I'd started the day determined to drive out to Coolis to try to see Veronica Fassler as soon as I found her trial record, but I was too upset to deal with the prison system this morning. I wished I could find my old hacking buddy, Mackenzie Graham. He could have told me how someone had managed to screw around with the LifeStory data, but he was somewhere in East Africa with the Peace Corps these days.

I opened up several old case files but then decided I didn't want to find evidence of a stranger's hands and feet in my life. I zeroed out my disk. *Are you sure you want to do this?* The system asked me twice and then seemed to shrug its electronic shoulders. *Okay, but you will lose all your files.* I wiped it clean and reloaded the system from my backup disks, reloaded all my data, offering Mackenzie a million thanks for forcing me to the unwonted discipline of daily off-site backups.

I spent the rest of the day working assiduously with the woman from the agency. By five we had eighty-two neat piles of papers for which she could type folder labels in the morning. I told her what to do in the morning when the Unblinking Eye came to install our surveillance camera and monitors, then lugged my computer to my car and drove it home. I didn't know where to set it up that would be really safe, but my apartment was less vulnerable than the warehouse, because at least here someone was usually around.

I took my computer to the third floor and sat in my bathtub for half an hour, listening to Bach, trying to relax. It would have helped if I knew what my opponents wanted. Besides to drive me crazy with uncertainty. By and by I poured myself a whisky and went downstairs to see my neighbor. I wanted to persuade him to lie low until this miserable business had come somehow to an end. When he came to the door, I put a hand over his mouth and led him through his apartment to the back. A couple on the second floor was entertaining on the back porch. The reassuring clink of glasses and friendly laughter drifted down to us. Under its cover I told Mr. Contreras how someone had frightened Mary Louise into backing away from me and that I didn't want the same people terrorizing him.

"I don't want you to be a sitting target for BB Baladine," I whispered urgently. "What if he comes around trying to find who went with me to Coolis? For all I know they had a security camera taking pictures of us—I wasn't very bright. I bolted headlong into trouble without stopping to think. I'm worried I put you at risk as well. You were right not to want your name on the record."

"It ain't like you to scare easy, doll."

"It isn't very often that I come across a man who thinks bayoneting newborns is all in a day's work. Will you do me a favor and go to your daughter's until, well, until this Aguinaldo business gets sorted out?"

Of course he wouldn't. Aside from the fact that he and his only child had as much in common as a dog and a fish, he wasn't about to turn tail. Didn't I ever listen to him when he talked to me about Anzio?

"Listen!" I screeched, forgetting to whisper, so that the party above us momentarily grew quiet. "You were twenty-something at Anzio. You may have the will you had then, but you don't have the strength. And if this guy figures out the relationship between us, which he will if he puts any energy into the matter, then he'll know it was you with me at the Coolis hospital, not Nicola Aguinaldo's grandfather."

We argued for an hour, but all he would agree to was to deny any relationship with me if someone came around asking. Oh, Ms. Warshki, she lives in the building, but she's a young woman, we know each other to say hi coming in the door at night. Of course, if someone questioned the rest of the tenants, one of them was bound to say that the old guy and I were pretty tight. The woman on the ground floor, for instance, who complained about the noise the dogs made when I came in late. Or even the party above us tonight: Mitch and Peppy, bored with lying in the yard, went up to the second floor to investigate. I followed just in time to grab Mitch before he helped himself to a plate of hummus. Those neighbors certainly would remember Mr. Contreras and me barbecuing together in the backyard.

"Okay, I won't open the door to no one I don't know while you're away from home, but even if I ain't the guy I was at twenty, I can still look after myself without running off to Hoffman Estates like a scared mutt." That was the best I was going to get out of him.

Thursday morning I got up early, took the dogs for a long swim, and headed out to Coolis. Even though I wasn't stopping for lunch, without Mr. Contreras the ride seemed to take longer than it had last week. Still, I pulled into a visitors' lot at the prison a little before noon.

I had dressed professionally, in my wheat rayon trouser suit. The drive in the un-air-conditioned car had left my white shirt wet around the armpits and neck, but I thought the front still looked pressed and clean enough for my mission. I carried the briefcase my dad gave me when I graduated from law school. It's almost twenty years old now, the red leather worn pinky-white around the edges. To preserve it I use it sparingly, but today I needed to feel his presence in my life.

The prairie sun pounded on me as I walked across the asphalt to the first checkpoint. In the distance I could hear grasshoppers whirring in the high grasses, but in the prison compound no trees or grasses mediated the heat, which shimmered from the pavement in knee-high waves. The white stone was so bright that my eyes watered behind my sunglasses.

I stopped at the first checkpoint, held out my ID, explained I was a lawyer here to see one of the inmates. At the second my briefcase was examined for weapons. I waited forty minutes there for an escort to the prison entrance. The CO who finally came for me was a short, plump woman who joked with the guard but didn't say anything to me.

At the entrance the door slid slowly open on its pneumatic trolley. We then faced an inner door, which would open only when the one behind us had wheezed shut again. Inside, I was escorted to yet another guard station, where I explained my business: I was a lawyer, here to see Veronica Fassler.

I was sent to a waiting room, a small windowless space with plastic chairs on top of worn linoleum and a television mounted high on the wall. Oprah shouted down at me and the three other women in the room.

Two of the waiting women were black, the only faces of color I'd seen since entering the prison compound; all three stared ahead with the weary passivity of those accustomed to being of no account to the world around them. A corrections officer looked in periodically, I suppose to make sure we weren't stealing the furniture. When I asked her to turn down the volume, since none of us was watching the program, she told me to mind my own business and retreated again.

Around one-thirty the older of the black women was escorted to the visitors' room. Two more people arrived —a Hispanic couple, middle-aged, nervous, wanting to know what to expect when they saw their daughter. The white woman continued to stare stolidly ahead, but the second black woman began explaining the procedure, where you sat, what you could talk about. It was hard for the pair to follow her underneath the noise of the television. As she repeated something for the third time, the corrections officer returned to escort me to the warden's office.

CAPTAIN FREDERICK RUZICH, WARDEN, the plaque on the door announced. The CO saluted smartly; the captain dismissed her and invited me to be seated. Despite his military title he was wearing civilian clothes, a pearl tropical worsted with a navy tie. He was a big man; even sitting he seemed to loom over me. With his gray hair and eyes he looked almost colorless, certainly terrifying.

"I understand you want to see one of our prisoners, Miss . . . uh . . ."

"Warshawski. Yes. Veronica Fassler. She's serving a five-year sentence for possession and—"

"So you're familiar with her case. I wondered if you were coming out here on a fishing expedition." He smiled, but with so much condescension that it became an insult.

"No one comes to a prison hunting for clients, Captain. The legal-aid money doesn't even cover gas and tolls from Chicago. Do you take a personal interest in every lawyer–client consultation here at Coolis?"

"The important ones I do. Have you talked to Veronica's regular lawyer about her case? I would have expected him to be here with you or at least to call ahead to let us know a different arrangement had been made."

"Ms. Fassler asked to see me when she called my office. And her representation arrangements are with me, not between the prison and other counsel. Or between me and the prison."

He leaned his massive torso back in the chair, his hands clasped behind his head, the smile lurking at the corner of his mouth. "Be that as it may, we had orders to transfer her. She's in another part of the prison system. So you made your trip out here for nothing, Detective."

I stared steadily at his smirk. "It's true I'm a detective, Captain. But I'm also a lawyer, in good standing with the Illinois bar. Where was Ms. Fassler sent?"

"I wish I could tell you that, but I can't because I don't know. Carnifice Security sent someone in with a van and moved her and the infant yesterday morning, and that's all I can tell you." His gray eyes were transparent, like a guppy's, which made it hard to look at them.

"Why was she moved? She didn't know anything about it when she phoned me."

The superior smile lingered. "There's always a problem in the prison when a prisoner has a baby. The logistics are hard here. No doubt too many of the other inmates complained."

"What a humane place this is, where the women's complaints are taken so seriously by the staff." I was not going to let him goad me into losing my temper, but I couldn't help myself pushing on him a little. "But a man like you who likes to be in charge, I can't believe you just salute and say yessir when your bosses tell you to move out a prisoner to an unknown destination. Especially in a private prison, where it affects your bed count and your margins."

The smile hovered at the corner of his mouth. "Whatever you want to believe, Warshawski, whatever you want. How did the Fassler woman get your number to begin with?"

"Probably from the yellow pages. That's how most people find me."

"Wouldn't have been on your visit to the hospital asking questions about Nicola Aguinaldo, would it? When you came out with her—grandfather, was that what you called him?—making inquiries. Was that as a detective or as a lawyer?"

"When a lawsuit is threatened, it's usually because a lawyer's present."

"And usually someone with standing is present." His smirk turned into a full-fledged grin. "You claimed the man was the girl's grandfather, but she doesn't have a grandfather. At least not an American. And that was definitely an American you brought out here."

I clasped my hands around my right knee in a pretense of thoughtful relaxation. "Is your information about Ms. Aguinaldo's family from BB Baladine or the INS? It's hard for me to believe BB pays much attention to the families of the illegal immigrants he hires. Not enough to know whether an American serviceman might have been in the Philippines during World War Two and have a Filipina granddaughter."

Poor Mr. Contreras: he would have protested mightily if he knew I was imputing that kind of immorality to him. He might have had sex with a local woman in his army service days, but he wouldn't have left her alone with a child.

"If he cared so much about the girl I'm surprised he never tried to visit her here."

"Family relations are a never-ending mystery, aren't they?" I said affably.

"If this grandfather really exists I'd like to talk to him, especially if he's bringing a suit against the hospital." He wasn't sure whether to believe me or not, but at least his lingering smirk disappeared.

"If he decides to file the suit, the hospital's lawyers will be allowed to interview him for discovery. Until then, if you have any questions for him, you can direct them through me. By the way, it would lessen the chance of a lawsuit if I could get him more concrete information about what made you send Ms. Aguinaldo to the hospital in the first place, and how she was able to escape from what is clearly a tightly secured ward."

"The information I have from my staff is that she had female difficulties. You'd probably know more than me what that meant." The sneering smile played again around the corners of his mouth.

"Ovarian cysts or cancer, which wasn't present when the doctors in Chicago opened her."

That not only effectively destroyed his smile but caused him to forget himself: he blurted out that the body was missing, that no autopsy had been performed.

"You do keep a lively interest in your prisoners, even after death," I marveled. "It's true her body disappeared from the morgue before they could perform an autopsy, but the surgeon in the emergency room where she was sent did a detailed report on her abdominal cavity after he failed to save her life. He wondered if the peritonitis might have been caused by an ovarian or uterine rupture and looked specifically at those organs."

Of course I was making all that up, but it didn't matter. I was convinced that whatever had sent Nicola Aguinaldo to the hospital, it hadn't been an inflamed ovary. At any rate, for the first time since I'd come into his office, I'd made Ruzich uneasy. What was it he was afraid an autopsy would have shown?

"Why don't you let me see the model workshop where Ms. Aguinaldo was working when she took so ill she had to go to the hospital? If I can assure her grandfather that it's a safe environment, it might make him less inclined to sue."

He scowled, an ugly expression but easier to watch than his smile. "Definitely not. You have no reason to be involved in that part of my operation."

"Not even if that's where Ms. Aguinaldo's injuries occurred?" I suggested softly.

"She was not injured there, despite the wild rumors Veronica Fassler was spreading. Yes, Ms. Warshawski, we monitor all those phone calls. We have to. It's the best way to keep track of drug and gang traffic between the cities and the prison. I'm sorry you made that long drive for nothing, but there's nothing else for you to do here. Unless you'd like to come up with the name of another prisoner to pretend you represent." Ruzich pushed his intercom and demanded that a CO escort me from the building.

32

Midnight Caller

I TRIED TO think over what I'd learned from meeting
the warden, but the long wait I'd had before seeing him
meant I hit Chicago at rush hour. In the time I sat on
the tollway, it was hard to think of much of anything
except floating in Lake Michigan with a cold drink in
my hand.

They had moved Veronica Fassler as soon as they
overheard her conversation with me. Whether she had
been sent to another of Illinois' women's prisons or out
of state or was simply in solitary at Coolis didn't matter. What mattered was that Fassler knew something
about Nicola Aguinaldo's death that the prison didn't
want me to find out.

I couldn't force my mind beyond those elementary
deductions. When I got home, eager to get out of my
rayon trousers, it was hard for me not to bark at Mr.
Contreras, bustling into the hall with the dogs. Apparently the only effect last night's conversation had on
him was to make him redouble his vigilance as the
guardian of my gate.

I leaned against the railing, scratching the dogs' ears.
I couldn't very well embroil him in my affairs and then
refuse to talk to him, but while I told him about my day
my hot, swollen feet occupied most of my mind.

Partway through my recital, the woman who lives across the hall from Mr. Contreras opened her door. "I have a presentation to an important client tomorrow, and I don't need your dogs and your conversation going on in the background while I try to finish it. If you two have that much to say to each other, why don't you move in together? It would give the rest of the building some much-needed peace and quiet."

"Living together don't guarantee peace for the building," Mr. Contreras said, his color heightened. "Maybe no one ever told you, but when you and your husband or boyfriend or whatever he is get to shouting at each other, even I can make out every word, and my hearing ain't a hundred percent these days."

Before the quarrel could build, I pushed myself upright and said I needed to take a cold shower and change out of my business clothes. The woman muttered something that ended with "show some consideration" and slammed her front door shut. Mitch barked sharply, to say he didn't like her attitude, but I persuaded Mr. Contreras to take him inside and let me get some rest.

I lay in the tub for a long time, long after the grime of the drive and the prison were out of my skin and hair, trying to figure out what Baladine was up to. Maybe he only wanted to discredit me, possibly with a spectacular arrest for drug possession, rather than kill me outright, but in a way it didn't matter.

I couldn't keep on this way, not knowing where the next menace might come from. Whether Baladine was carrying on a war of nerves, or he wanted me dead or arrested, or all three, I couldn't run a business when I was afraid to be both in my office and in my home. I couldn't turn to my oldest friends for fear of jeopardizing their lives or families. Murray, who I'd worked with for so many years, was carrying a bucket for the other side this time. Mary Louise had been frightened into leaving me alone.

If only I could get the story together I might be able to find a way to make it public. It had something to do with Coolis and something to do with Frenada's factory, although how those two places came together on Nicola Aguinaldo's frail body I didn't understand. I needed to get in touch with Morrell and insist that he take me to Aguinaldo's mother before Baladine succeeded in whatever his plan was.

When I finally climbed out of the tub it was dark outside. I could hear the steady popping of firecrackers as people in the area geared up for the Fourth of July, coming up on Saturday.

When I was a child my father used to take me for a walk on the Fourth, telling me a thrilling version of the War of Independence, stressing the role of General Kosciuszko and other Poles in the American Revolution. My mother always followed my father's tale with a reminder that it was Italian explorers who found the New World and made it possible for the English and Poles to leave Europe.

In the afternoons we'd make a picnic with my father's pals on the force and my mother's vocal coach and his daughter. My mother would make my favorite dessert—an Umbrian rice pudding with currant jelly and sweet wine sauce—and I'd race around screaming with the other children, playing baseball and wishing I had a big family instead of just my one cousin, Boom-Boom.

I wondered what the Baladines taught their children

on the Fourth of July. Perhaps something instructive about free markets.

I took that bitter thought to bed with me. Despite my fatigue I couldn't relax. Coolis, Aguinaldo, Frenada chased through my mind, sometimes with Baladine in pursuit, sometimes Alex Fisher. I was just deciding I'd do better to get up and pay bills than lie churning over these profitless ideas when my front doorbell rang.

No one in Chicago pays calls at midnight if they have your well-being in mind. I pulled my jeans on and grabbed my gun from the closet safe before calling down through the intercom.

A voice quavered, "It's me. It's Robbie Baladine."

I stuck the gun in the back of my jeans and went downstairs. Sure enough, Robbie Baladine was standing, by himself, on the other side of the door. His plump cheeks were dirt-stained, and he looked exhausted. I opened the front door at the same time that Mr. Contreras came into the hallway with Mitch and Peppy: he probably thought Morrell was paying another late-night call.

When the dogs bounded forward to greet him, Robbie stood stock still and turned white. Yelling at the dogs to stay, I caught the boy as he started to crumple. I caught him before he hit the floor. His deadweight hit my low back and hamstrings like a pile driver.

"Put the dogs inside, will you?" I panted to Mr. Contreras. "And let's get this young man warm."

Robbie hadn't quite fainted. While my neighbor dragged the reluctant dogs back to his apartment, I helped Robbie to the bottom of the stairwell and made him sit with his head between his legs. He was shaking with suppressed sobs. His skin was clammy, his sweat acrid with the smell of fear.

"I'm such a weakling, aren't I, fainting at the sight of a dog," he gasped.

"Is that what happened? Mitch is a pretty big dog, and he took you by surprise. And you look done in. Don't worry about it."

Mr. Contreras returned with an old sweater and helped me wrap it around Robbie's shoulders. "This a friend of yours, doll? He needs hot cocoa. You stay here with him; I'll heat up some milk."

The door opposite Mr. Contreras's opened and the woman making the important presentation stormed out in sweat clothes. "Did you buy this stairwell to use as your living room?" she demanded. "If not, could you entertain upstairs so that people like me who work for a living can get some rest?"

Behind Mr. Contreras's door, Mitch took exception to our neighbor's hostility and let out a sharp bark.

"Think you can manage the stairs?" I said to Robbie. "If this woman gets any more excited she'll have a stroke, and then we'll be up all night carting her to the hospital and you'll never be able to tell me why you came or how you got here."

"I'm only asking you to show some consideration," the woman said.

I didn't think Robbie needed the added stress of me getting into a fight, so I bit back the various remarks that sprang to mind and concentrated on helping him up the stairs. When I turned my back on her, the woman gasped and ran back inside her apartment. It was only when we reached the second landing that I realized she must have seen my gun. I laughed a little to myself: that might be the last time she pissed to me about noise in the building.

We went slowly; by the time we reached my door

Mr. Contreras was huffing up behind us with a tray and three cups of cocoa. The old man is at his best in dealing with the halt and lame. I left him roughly coaxing Robbie to drink some cocoa while I took my gun back to my bedroom.

"You must think I'm pretty weird, coming here like this and fainting and everything," he said when I came back.

I pulled the piano bench next to the armchair. "I don't think anything about you, but I'm about to burst with curiosity. Your sister said you'd run away. How did you get to Wrigleyville?"

"Is that where we are? By Wrigley Field? I've been here with my dad." Some of the strain eased out of his face—if I lived in known territory it couldn't be as scary as he'd been thinking. "I came how Nicola used to—I took my bike to the bus and rode the bus to the train. But then I got lost trying to find you and I didn't have enough money for a cab or anything, so I've been walking and walking, I bet I've walked five miles. That would make BB and Eleanor delirious with joy if they knew I got that much exercise in one afternoon."

"Who are BB and Eleanor?" Mr. Contreras asked.

"Parents," I explained briefly. "Baladine's nickname at Annapolis was BB-gun Baladine."

"He loves it," Robbie said. "He's such a he-man, it proves it when people call him that. Only—only I'm not. He hates that. Or hates me; he wishes Madison and Utah had been the boys and me the girl, he said if I was a girl he could dress me in—in pink ruff—ruffles."

His teeth began to chatter. I moved over to the arm of the chair and forced some cocoa into him, giving Mr. Contreras a warning sign to keep quiet. I was afraid even a man as benign as my neighbor might appear threatening to this very tired child.

"You're exhausted," I said in a matter-of-fact voice. "You're probably dehydrated too, from walking so much. That's why your body is acting up on you. Everybody's does when they're overtired and then have to deal with a strange situation: it happens to me, which is how I know. Finish this cocoa before you try to say anything else."

"Really?" He looked at me hopefully. "I thought—thought it was only because I was a—all the names he calls me."

I supposed Baladine stood over him and called him a faggot or queer or other names that pass for insults with someone like him. "Name-calling is a horrible kind of torture, especially when it comes from your parents. It leaves you without any defenses."

He gulped the drink and kept a death grip on the cup as the best way to hold on to his wayward feelings. When he seemed calm enough to speak, I asked why he'd come to me.

"That was probably the stupidest thing of all, me coming to you, because what can you do? Only, when I saw he was going to send me to—to boot camp, I thought I couldn't take another time like that, like when they made me go to the camp for fat kids, that was horrible enough, but at least everyone else was overweight too, but boot camp, that's like when all the other kids get to haze you for being queer or different somehow. Like my cousins, when I have to go spend a month with them, they play football, they're supposed to toughen me up."

I blinked. "Is this a definite plan?"

"Oh, yes." He looked at me bleakly. "Don't tell me it's wrong to snoop in his briefcase, it's the only way I know what he's up to, and I saw the fax from this place in South Carolina—of course anyone who does anything with prisons or army stuff, they fall over themselves for a chance to help out BB and this guy, he's the head of this military school and they run a summer boot camp. So he faxes BB that they'll be expecting me Saturday night, I can start Monday morning. BB and Eleanor can put me on a plane to Columbia when they take off for France. Not that I wanted to go to France with those ghastly Poilevy twins and my sisters, watch them swimming all day long to get ready for Mom's swim meet. She's doing this thing for charity on Labor Day, and of course she wants Madison to beat everyone. But I'd rather clock Madison and Rhiannon Trant in the pool than go to military camp."

"But you disappeared two nights ago, didn't you? Where have you been in the meantime?"

He looked at his hands. "I hid out in our grounds. When BB and Eleanor went to bed I'd go sleep in the cabana. Only the gardeners found me this morning and I was afraid they'd tell Eleanor."

"Your folks are looking for you—that's how I know you left home. Do you think they would call the police, or will they rely on Carnifice's private security force?"

"I'm so stupid, aren't I, I didn't think about that," Robbie muttered. "I only thought I should get away as fast as I could. Of course if he wants me he'll sic his whole team on finding me. Not that he really wants me, but no one is supposed to outsmart BB Baladine."

"I think you're pretty smart," I said comfortably. "You hid out right under your parents' noses for two

days. You found me, and that's not so easy for a suburban kid who gets driven everywhere, to navigate a city
like Chicago at night.

"Here's the problem. I don't mind putting you up,
but your father is on my case in a serious way, and if he
came here looking for you I wouldn't have any way to
keep him from taking you: you're a minor child and I
have no legal relationship to you. Is there anyone you
can go to who would stick up for you with your dad? A
teacher, or an aunt? Your grandparents?"

He shook his head, miserable. "I'm like this really
weird person in my family. Even my grandmother keeps
telling BB he's too soft on me. If I ran away to her she'd
probably put me in handcuffs and take me to military
camp herself."

Mr. Contreras cleared his throat. "He could stay
with me, doll. I got that sofa bed."

Robbie turned white but didn't say anything.

"Is it the dogs?" I asked. "They look ferocious because they're huge, but they're pretty gentle."

"I know it's sissy to be scared of dogs," he whispered, "but it's one of the—BB—some of his clients
work with rottweilers, he thought it would be funny—it
made everyone laugh—Nicola, she tried to get the dogs
to leave and one of them bit her."

"What did he do?" My hand on his shoulder had
clenched reflexively into a fist, and I had to force the
fingers to relax.

"He brought them home with him. Also the handler.
It was kind of when he started running Carnifice. *This
will kill you or cure you,* that's what he's always saying
to me. So he sort of, well, he didn't really sic the dogs
on me, tell them to attack me, just to corner me, in the
family room, I was watching television, they stayed

there and stayed there and I—I couldn't help it, I had to go to the bathroom so bad—"

His shoulders started to heave again. I kept my arm around him but drank some cocoa myself to try to keep my own stomach from turning inside out on me. Family night at the Baladines. Fun for everyone.

"Now listen here, young man," Mr. Contreras spoke roughly. "I been a soldier, I been a machinist, I spent my life with men who could take your daddy apart and line up all his arms and legs in a row and not even work up a sweat, and let me tell you that is not how a real man acts, setting a dog on his kid."

"Damn straight," I said. "Why don't we bring the dogs up here for the night and let Robbie sleep downstairs with you? That way if BB shows up he'll get an earful of Mitch but no son."

Robbie cheered up at that. I helped him back down the stairs to Mr. Contreras's and held the dogs while he went inside. The old man said he reckoned Robbie could wear one of his pajama shirts to sleep in tonight and they'd get him some blue jeans and T-shirts in the morning.

"I know you're really tired, but could you answer one question for me before you go to bed?" I was unfolding the sofa bed while Mr. Contreras brought in clean sheets. "What were you wanting to tell me when you phoned me last week?"

He'd forgotten about it in the stress of his journey. That phone call to me was what made BB and Eleanor decide to send him to military camp, but it had lost its importance to him. He blinked his eyes anxiously, then suddenly remembered.

"You know that man who got pulled out of Lake

Michigan? I'm pretty sure he came out to see BB. With Mr. Trant, you know."

"Teddy Trant from Global? Are you sure?"

"Come on, doll. Boy's asleep on his feet. This will wait until tomorrow."

"You're right. Sorry, I wasn't thinking," I said, but Robbie, taking off his military shirt with a sigh of relief and putting on one of Mr. Contreras's violently striped pajama tops, said, "Of course I recognize Mr. Trant, and I'm pretty sure it was the guy I saw on television with him. He was really, really angry, but I couldn't hear what he said and, well, they kind of locked me in the nursery with Rosario and Utah. On account of Mom said I was—a little snoop—who'd go telling tales out of school. But I woke up in the middle of the night because they were standing under my window and Mr. Trant was saying that should solve the problem for the time being if only Abigail—Mrs. Trant, you know— didn't start getting helpful ideas again."

"Okay, Victoria. Boy's going to bed now. No more detecting tonight."

"Ms. Warshawski, thank you for letting me stay here, and you too, sir, only I'm sorry I don't know your name, and I'm sorry about the dogs, about making them leave. Maybe—maybe tomorrow I won't be so chicken around them."

I squeezed his shoulder. "Get a good sleep. Like the man said, tomorrow is another day."

It was only as I started back up the stairs that I re- membered my fears about BB bugging my apartment. I hoped I was wrong, but my stomach turned cold as I imagined what Baladine might do next.

33

Thrown in the Tank

LEMOUR ARRESTED ME as I unlocked my front door Friday afternoon. He flung me against the stone railing and yanked my purse from my shoulder. A Du Page County deputy sheriff who was with him tried to calm him down and was thrust roughly aside.

When Lemour had the cuffs locked, he flashed a warrant under my nose for the arrest of one Victoria Iphigenia Warshawski, acting upon information and belief that she did unlawfully and without the permission of the parents seize and hold against his will Robert Durant Baladine, a minor child not her own.

Mr. Contreras erupted with the dogs. Mitch broke away from him and launched himself at Lemour. The detective punched his head. Mitch yelped and huddled on the ground. Lemour started to kick him, but I threw myself between his foot and the dog. We went over in a heap of leash, detective and me, with Peppy joining in to mew worriedly at her son.

"That's it, Warshki," Lemour panted from the pavement. "I'm adding resisting arrest to the kidnapping charge. You'll be lucky if you're home in time for Christmas. And I'll have this dog put to sleep for assaulting me."

Homebound commuters began to crowd around to

see what the show was. One young woman said she thought it took a lot of nerve to beat a dog and then threaten to put it to sleep.

"He's obviously perfectly friendly and he's on a leash, aren't you, good doggy." She scratched his ears, carefully avoiding looking at me.

"Shut the hell up unless you want to be arrested for interfering with the police," Lemour said savagely.

She backed away as the sheriff's deputy once more muttered an ineffectual intervention.

My hands were cuffed behind me. I'd fallen hard on my side and lay there on the walk, the wind knocked out of me, my right cheek smarting from grazing the concrete. Mitch climbed to his feet and shook himself like a boxer who's taken a bad blow but is ready to go back in the ring. Peppy licked him anxiously. He's a big ugly dog, half black Lab, half golden Peppy, and I've never been crazy about him, but right now his attempts to grin, wag his tail, show there were no hard feelings, made my eyes smart.

I rolled forward onto my knees. Mr. Contreras anxiously helped me up, keeping one eye on Lemour, who was brushing concrete crumbs from his suit, his face patchy-red with rage. When he got to his feet the dogs started toward him.

"Mitch, Peppy! Stay!" I was gasping for breath, but the dogs for once paid attention and sat. "Get them inside before Lummox here loses his head completely and shoots them," I said to Mr. Contreras. "And take my handbag before this cretin steals my wallet. Can you call Freeman for me? Also, will you get a message to Morrell? I'm supposed to meet him for a picnic tomorrow. In case I can't get out on time, will you call and tell him? His number's in my electronic diary, there in my bag."

Mr. Contreras was looking so bewildered I wasn't sure he'd heard me, although he did pick up my handbag from where Lemour had dropped it. I started to repeat myself, but Lemour, furiously trying to straighten his tie, grabbed my arm and jerked me down the walk. He tried to throw me into the back of the squad car, but he wasn't big enough to get the right leverage. The Du Page sheriff's deputy took my left arm and whispered something apologetic as he pushed me behind the cage.

"Uh, Doug, uh, can you give me the key? I need to lock her to the seat, and she can't ride with her arms behind her."

Lemour ignored him and climbed behind the unmarked car's wheel. The sheriff's deputy looked at me uncertainly, but as Lemour started the engine he quickly shut the door on me and got into the passenger seat. Lemour took off so fast that my head banged into the metal cage.

Rage was building in me. I knew I had to keep it down. I was helpless—physically and in the situation—and if I let my fury ride me I'd give Lemour the opening he wanted to pound me into the ground. When he stopped at the light on Addison, I maneuvered my body so that I was sitting sideways in the narrow space with my legs stretched out across the width of the backseat. My shoulders were beginning to ache horribly.

The day had started so well, too. When I got back from swimming with the dogs, young Robbie was up and willing to make timid overtures to Peppy. Mr. Contreras prepared his breakfast specialty, French toast, and Robbie relaxed visibly as the old man urged seconds on him: perhaps it was the first time in his life his every mouthful hadn't been monitored and criticized.

I drove north to Morrell's place in Evanston. In the theme of Spy–Counterspy, I wrote out a note explaining my visit to Coolis yesterday and how imperative it was that I talk to Señora Mercedes. Morrell frowned over my message, then finally decided—whether because of my dogged determination, my impeccable logic, or my nice-looking legs—to take me to see Nicola Aguinaldo's mother. We rode the L, since that was the easiest way to check for tails, first in and out of the Loop and then over to Pilsen on the city's near southwest side.

When I met Abuelita Mercedes I realized I'd been carrying the unconscious stereotype of her title of "granny"—I'd been expecting an old woman in a kerchief, with round red cheeks. Of course, a woman whose daughter was only twenty-seven was still young herself, in fact only a few years older than I. She was short, stocky, with black hair curling softly around her ears and forehead and a permanent worry crease worked between her brows.

Tagalog was her first language, but she could get by in Spanish, which Morrell spoke fluently—although his was the Central American version, not always in sync with Filipino Spanish, he explained. Abuelita Mercedes's English was limited to a few social phrases, which she used upon his introducing us: *Señora Mercedes, le presento a la Señora Victoria.* He assured her that I was a friend worried about Nicola's death, as well as a lawyer committed to justice for the poor.

Sherree, Nicola's surviving child, greeted Morrell with an eager cry of *"Tío!"* but she chattered away in English to him. After a formal reception, with strong black coffee and little fried donuts, we began to broach the subject of Nicola's death.

With Morrell translating Señora Mercedes's Spanish and Sherree reluctantly assisting with a Tagalog phrase or two, Nicola's mother made her halting way through Nicola's story. She explained that she knew very little of what had happened to her daughter in prison. Señora Mercedes couldn't afford a phone, so it wasn't possible for her to talk to her daughter except at very wide intervals: she would get permission from a neighbor, often Señora Attar, to use her phone, so that Nicola could call collect on a prearranged day. But then it depended on whether she was able to get a letter in to Nicola or whether Nicola could get phone privileges on that day.

She had to write in Spanish, which neither she nor Nicola wrote well, since anything she wrote in Tagalog was automatically turned back. Even so, the Spanish letters were often sent back. Coolis, out in the rural white countryside, had only one or two Spanish-speaking guards, despite the large number of Hispanic inmates. They often refused to let Spanish-language mail in or out, with the excuse that Señora Mercedes could be providing gang information to her daughter.

Now that Sherree was in third grade she wrote English—very good in English—but Nicola hadn't written English well enough to send out detailed news.

When the baby died, oh, that was terrible. Señora Mercedes couldn't go to Coolis: she didn't have a green card, she didn't know what papers you had to show, and what if they arrested her when she was visiting her daughter? Then, too, everything cost money, the bus fare to Coolis, it was all too much. So she sent a letter in Spanish, Sherree sent a letter—the priest helped her write it in English, this was before Señor Morrell became a friend or he would surely have helped—but she never heard from her daughter again, she didn't even know if Nicola learned the news about the baby's death before she died herself, and now here was poor Sherree, no mother, no sister, father dead in the Philippines.

Sherree seemed to have heard this lament before. She frowned over the dolls she was playing with and turned her back on her grandmother as Señora Mercedes went into detail about the baby's death. The poor baby, the cause of so much misery, needing money for the hospital, causing Nicola to steal, but then, those employers, so mean, not letting her get away to be with her own baby in the hospital, not lending her money, it was wrong of Nicola to steal, but Señora Mercedes could understand why she did it. And then, five years in prison? When men who did far worse crimes were there for much less time? Here in America it was all terrible. If not for the money, for the chance to have Sherree get a good education, they would never stay.

We took a break to let Señora Mercedes recover her poise before I asked what I most wanted to know: about Nicola's work in the prison shop. That was good, her mother said, because she got paid two dollars and fifty cents an hour. It was for sewing, sewing shirts, and Nicola was very fast, her little fingers so—so nimble, yes, that was the word, the best on the floor, the bosses at the prison said. It was piecework, but Nicola was so fast she made the top rate.

What kind of shirts? I asked, but Señora Mercedes had no idea. Of course she'd never seen her daughter's work. Even if she had visited her daughter, she would not have seen her work. Shirts, that was all she knew. She pulled out a letter from Nicola to show me.

With Morrell leaning over my shoulder to help translate, I stumbled my way through the text, which had been heavily censored:

My dear Mama,

I am well, I hope you and Sherree and Anna are well and happy. I am working now in the sewing shop, where I can make very good money. We sew (*crossed out*), I make more than anyone else in an hour, the other girls are jealous. For a higher rate you can work the (*crossed out*), but it is too heavy for me.

You must not worry about me, even though I am small (*two lines heavily crossed out*). Señora Ruby is a sweet old lady who takes care of me, and now that people see she looks after me the big women (*crossed out*). The food is good, I eat well, I say my prayers every day. Please give many many kisses to Sherree and to Anna.

Nicola

Anna had been the baby's name. There were six letters in all, all Nicola had been able to send in fifteen months, and most of them with large sections excised. When we moved onto more delicate ground— namely, Nicola's love life—Señora Mercedes either knew nothing, or there was nothing to know. When did Nicola have time to meet a man? her mother demanded. She worked six days a week for those cruel people. She came home on Sundays and spent the day with her own children. Nicola worked, Señora Mercedes worked on the night shift at a box factory, all so that Sherree and Anna could have a good life. A man named Lemour? No, Señora Mercedes never heard Nicola mention him. And Mr. Baladine, Nicola's employer? Nicola didn't like him but the money was good and she tried not to complain. Sherree, busy on the floor with her dolls, didn't seem to have anything to add to the story.

We had been talking for two hours. Morrell took us down the street to a taqueria for lunch. Over burritos and fried plantain Señora Mercedes told me about the day that Nicola died.

"I didn't know she was dead until the next day. My own daughter. Because on Monday the marshals came and Señora Attar, a good woman even if a different religion and a different language, woke up and saw them before they could arrest me and Sherree. She told these officers I was her own mother. What a good woman! But of course I had to move away at once."

I interrupted Morrell's translation to ask for a detailed description of the men. There were two. And how were they dressed? In suits. Not in uniforms?

"What's the point?" Morrell asked, when I pushed for as accurate a description as possible.

"If they were state marshals, they would have been in uniform. INS, who knows, but these men sound expensively dressed. I don't think they were with the law, except the one unto themselves."

"*Qué?*" Señora Mercedes demanded of Sherree. "*Qué dicen?*"

Sherree refused to look up from the dolls, who she'd brought to the taqueria and that were now climbing on top of each other in a fearful tangle of arms.

"The lady thinks they were not with the law, but perhaps men who had an evil intention toward Nicola and her family," Morrell said in Spanish.

That was as far as we could take matters. Señora Mercedes had seen Señor Baladine drive her daughter home, perhaps four times during the years she worked for him, but he always stayed in the car, she had no way of recognizing his face. If he had been at her home the day before Nicola died, she didn't know. I would have to dig up photos of Baladine and Trant to see if Señora Mercedes recognized either of them.

We left the tacqueria with copious thanks for the señora's time. Morrell bought Sherree a frozen mango on a stick from one of the pushcarts we passed on the way back to their apartment. On the L north, Morrell and I went over the conversation from as many angles as we could but couldn't squeeze any more out of it.

As for Nicola's body, that, too, remained a mystery. Morrell said he'd talked to Vishnikov, who hadn't been able to track it down. Vishnikov had also reported on Frenada's autopsy: the man had died by drowning—the water in his lungs made that clear.

"Frenada was out at the Baladine estate the night before he died," I said. "Robbie Baladine saw him there. I'd love to know whether the water in his lungs came from a swimming pool or Lake Michigan."

Morrell pursed his mouth in a soundless whistle. "I'll ask Vishnikov. I don't know if it's too late or not—the morgue released the body to Frenada's sister yesterday afternoon. Now, since I've been a good collaborator, taken you where you wanted to go, found out what news there was to learn about Lucian Frenada, will you do something for me?"

"If it's in my power, sure."

"Join me for a Fourth of July picnic tomorrow. I'll supply the food. We can use the private beach up the street from me—I know one of the families who live there."

I laughed. "That task sounds well within my capabilities. Thank you."

I was still smiling when I got home and walked into Lemour's arms. It was a long time before I smiled that freely again.

34

Fourth of July Picnic

I SPENT FRIDAY night at the Rogers Park police station. When we got there I was fingerprinted and searched. Strip-searched while Lemour looked on. His eyes were glistening, his lips white with spittle. All I could do was hold myself aloof. The dissociation that all prisoners practice. I would become expert at it in the weeks ahead.

The police have rules governing interrogation, but if they breach them it's hard to do anything about it—especially on a Friday night before a holiday with your lawyer who-knows-where. I tried to insist on my right to phone counsel, but Lemour and the charge officer ignored me.

I was put in an interrogation room where I sat for hours, without water, while Lemour screamed meaningless questions at me. When would I confess to cocaine possession? How had I gotten hold of Robbie Baladine? Alternating questions and punches. Every now and then he would leave and a uniformed man would come in and say, *Tell him what he wants to know, honey; it will only get worse.*

At first I kept repeating that I would answer questions only in the presence of my attorney. I kept praying

for Freeman's appearance. Had Mr. Contreras understood my plea to call him?

After a time I stopped speaking altogether. Lemour's
fury mounted, until a final blow knocked me to the
floor. I'm not sure what happened next—the charge sergeant pulled Lemour out of the room and came back
for me.

"You sleep it off," he advised. "It'll look better in the
morning."

"What will?" I muttered through bruised lips. "The
charge of police brutality against Lemour?"

The sergeant took me to the station lockup, where
half a dozen other women were waiting. One of them
looked at me with shock that was half admiration.
"What'd you do to Lemour, girl, refuse to pay him his
shakedown? I seen him go insane more than once but
never nothing like he did to you tonight."

I tried to say something, but my mouth was too
swollen for me to speak. She banged on the cage demanding water. By and by a matron brought a paper
cup of tepid tap water. I swallowed as best I could and
sat down, gingerly rubbing my sore head and shoulders.
I tried to thank my benefactor, but only parodies of
words came from my bruised mouth.

I spent a sleepless night. One woman was chain-
smoking, the one next to me on the floor spewed curses
as the ashes floated on her, while a third roommate
moaned over the fate of her baby. Roaches paraded
across us all night. We were transients; they owned this
room.

In the morning a matron came into the cage, forcing
all of us to our feet. The lights in the room were too
bright, but when I shut my eyes the room around me
spun in nauseating spirals. I held on to the wall for

support and felt my stomach heave. I didn't want to throw up, not on myself, not in public, but I couldn't hold it in.

"Jesus Christ, you whores come in here with a load on and then foul up the cell. Come on, wash it off, put these on, let's get going."

I was cuffed to another woman who'd also been sick. We were taken to a tiny toilet where we cleaned ourselves as best we could. I put my head under the sink tap and let water run through my hair and mouth until the officer dragged me away.

"You there, Warshki, get moving."

"I need a doctor." I coughed hoarsely. "I have a concussion."

"You need clothes. Put these on. You're riding out to Coolis."

"Coolis?" I couldn't raise my voice above a whisper. "Not Coolis. Only arrested, not convicted."

The policewoman pulled me away from the sink. "You have a bad fall or a rough john or what last night? Put this shirt on."

The shirt was a bright yellow that made my eyes smart. On the back was stamped IDOC—Illinois Department of Corrections. "Your detective Lemour, he's got to be the roughest john in Chicago. This was all his handiwork. I'm not going to Coolis. I'm waiting for my attorney. Post bond."

"Look, Warshki, I don't have time for games. I got four girls to get on a bus, including you, and you're not in shape to do anything but say yes, ma'am. It's a holiday today, no bond court; your lawyer if he calls will be told where you are. Coolis has the overflow jail for Cook and Du Page County, and we are filled to the brim with all you girls turning tricks up and down the city, so you get a bus ride in the fresh country air, which is more than I'm allowed on the nation's birthday, let me tell you."

I put the shirt on. I didn't know what other choice I had. I had been so sure Freeman would be here this morning to post bail that I was too disappointed to react. Only four of us out of the cage were being sent to Coolis—did the others get a free pass, and if so, why?

The matron cuffed me back to my bathroom partner and marched us out to the street, where an old white bus painted with the Department of Corrections logo waited. Our escort exchanged a few jovial words with a guard as she handed us over to the state. I got my watch back and the six dollars I'd had in my jeans, but my keys were a potential weapon and were handed to the guard in a sealed envelope together with my paperwork.

Rogers Park was the last stop for the bus, which had picked up women from various lockups on the west and north ends of town. There were twenty-nine of us altogether. The guard pushed me into a seat, attached leg and hand shackles to me, connected them to a central pole, and signaled to the driver to take off.

As we lurched west to the expressway, the diesel smoke and the hard seats made my empty stomach heave again. A pregnant woman two seats in front and on my left begged the driver to stop, in halting accented English. No one paid any attention. She threw up, trying to cover her mouth with her manacled hands.

"Can you stop?" I called through my bruised lips. "There's a sick woman in here."

No response from the armed guard.

I shouted again. Several prisoners stamped their feet. A guard yelled through the loudspeaker that they would halt the bus and make us stand at attention on the side of the road for an hour if the noise continued. Everyone subsided, including me—I didn't want to be the one who made this group of women stand in the midday sun.

"Fucking assholes," the woman next to me muttered as the bus waited in line to get on the tollway. "Don't let you go to the john, then bounce you around hard enough to make you pee over yourself."

She wasn't talking to me, and I didn't answer. She'd kept up a stream of invective since the guard attached us. She was twitching, her eyes a telltale yellow. As the day wore on, flecks of spittle appeared around her mouth, but she couldn't stop talking.

At noon we halted for a rest stop at the place where Mr. Contreras and I had our picnic with the dogs two weeks ago. We were unshackled two at a time, the bathroom closed to the public while we were escorted in. It was hard to walk past the people stopping for food or walking their dogs, their jaws gaping, trying not to show how avidly they were staring.

We were given fifteen minutes to relieve ourselves and buy something at the vending machines. I used one of my six dollars to buy a can of juice, which I had to drink in quick gulps under the intense glare of a guard: they would confiscate any metal we tried to sneak onto the bus.

While we waited for the driver, some of the women exchanged small talk with the guards. When we were finally loaded back on, the smart talkers got to move closer to the front, away from the diesel fumes. I got to move closer to the back. My reward for trying to speak up for the pregnant woman.

It was three when the bus pulled in through the main

gates at Coolis. A heavily armed force supervised our unbuckling from the pole and emergence into the prison yard. I ended up behind the pregnant woman. She was small and dark, like Nicola Aguinaldo, and deeply ashamed of the vomit down her front. She tried timidly to ask for help but none of the guards responded. They were busy counting us and comparing lists. It was here that the sheep and the goats were separated—some bound for prison, some for jail.

"This woman needs help," I said to one of the guards near me.

When he ignored me I repeated myself, but the woman next to me hissed and stepped on my left foot. "Shut up. They only start over from the beginning each time they're interrupted, and I need to use the john."

A smell of urine now came from the pregnant woman and she began to weep. The guards ignored her and began the count again. Finally, when the heat of the sun and the long wait made me wonder if she might faint, they started calling us forward. My traveling companions disappeared one by one into the building. Another half hour went by. I badly needed a toilet myself, but they were taking us in alphabetical order. There were three of us left when they called me.

"Warshki."

I shuffled forward in my chains. "Warshawski, not Warshki."

I should have kept quiet—speech was their license to kill. They sent me back to wait, took "White" and "Zarzuela" while I compressed my thighs as best I could for the chains. And finally was called again. Not "Warshki" this time but "Warshitski."

At the door I was unlocked, printed again, sent under double escort to an interior room where I once again took off all my clothes, squatted, coughed, tried to remove myself from the burn of shame at my exposure, and the dribble of urine I couldn't help releasing. A guard barked me into the shower, where hair and a whitish film of soap covered the floor and sides. I was given a clean IDOC uniform, the pants too short on my long legs and riding too tightly in the crotch, the shirt big enough for three of me. At least it covered my waist so I could leave the pants unzipped.

On this far side of the gates my shackles were finally removed. A guard took me through a series of locked corridors to the jail wing. At five I joined the line to the refectory and had a Fourth of July special: hard-fried chicken, overboiled green beans, corn on the cob, and cooked apple slices on something that looked like cardboard. It was too tough to cut with the plastic utensils we were issued, so most of the women picked it up and ate it by hand.

I was eating the corn when I felt something on my leg. I looked down and saw a roach working its way toward my food. I smacked it off in revulsion, then saw that the floor and table were covered with them. I tried to stand, but a guard quickly came over and slapped me back down. Even though I hadn't eaten since the lunch Morrell bought me yesterday in Pilsen, I couldn't face the food. I kept flicking roaches, real and imagined, from my legs and arms until the guards were willing to escort us back to our cell blocks.

At nine I was locked in an eight-by-twelve room with another woman, a black woman young enough to be my daughter, who told me she'd been arrested for possessing crack. We were given bunk beds, metal frames bolted deep into the wall with a thin mattress, a nylon sheet, and a blanket on each. A toilet and sink formed out of a single piece of stainless steel was buried in the concrete floor. There is no privacy in prison—I would have to learn to perform intimate functions in the open.

Like the shower, the sink was caked with hair and mold. I didn't know how to get soap or cleansers to make it palatable to brush my teeth—but then, I didn't have a toothbrush either.

My cellmate was angry and jumpy and smoking heavily, which made my head ache. If I had to live with it for more than a day I'd ask her to stop, but it was the kind of request that could escalate into a fight in here, and I didn't want to be fighting other prisoners. My quarrel was most assuredly not with them.

I was exhausted, I was sick to my stomach, my shoulders were sore, but I couldn't sleep. It terrified me to be locked inside a room, subject to the whims of men —or women—in uniform. All night I lay rigid on a narrow mattress as prayers and shouts hurtled through the corridor. I am strong, and a skilled street fighter, but the misery and madness around me kept swooping toward mob hysteria. Like telephone poles dipping past a train, swooping down, veering away just as you were sure they would hit you. Every now and then I dozed off, but then a cell door would slam, a woman would scream or cry out, my neighbor would mutter in her sleep, and I would jerk awake again. I was almost happy when a corrections officer came around at five to rouse us all for breakfast and the day's first head count.

35

A Little Game on a Small Court

ALL DAY SUNDAY I tried signing up for phone privileges, but I wasn't able to get a time slot until Monday afternoon. All day Sunday I fumed uselessly about my incarceration. I was furious at being locked up—as were many of the people around me. The level of rage was so high that the building could have exploded at any time. Everywhere we went guards watched us behind double-thick glass, or behind TV monitors, tracking the furies and the fights before the corridors turned incandescent.

The calmest women were those who'd been in the jail wing for some months, waiting for trial. These were the people who either had been denied bail—or more commonly didn't have a thousand or fifteen hundred dollars to post it. For half a dozen or so women, this marked the second Independence Day they'd spent in jail. They had gotten used to the routine and were more or less at ease with it, although they worried about their children, their lovers, sick parents, whether they'd still have a place to live if they got off the charge that had brought them here in the first place.

A jail is a place where someone awaits trial. A prison is where you go if you've been convicted and sentenced. Coolis was the great experiment in combining the two places for cost-saving reasons. And while the jail was technically separate from the prison, one of the ways Carnifice saved money was by combining as many functions as possible. We jailbirds ate with the prisoners and used the same common room for recreation.

On Sunday afternoon a guard took me down there for my hour of recreation. It was a multipurpose room, with an exercise area separated from the entertainment unit simply by a difference in floor—green linoleum for the common room, bare concrete for exercise. The entertainment side included a television set attached to the wall and a long deal table with cards, checkers, and some jigsaw puzzles. A handful of women were watching some inane game show, turned to top volume, while three others yelled ribald insults at each other over a game of hearts.

I went to the exercise area to work the worst knots out of my shoulders and legs. The room didn't have much in the way of equipment, but it did have a basketball hoop and ball. I began shooting. At first my shoulders resisted and I had trouble making my hook shot, but after a while the muscles loosened up and I got into a rhythm. Shooting baskets is a narcotizing, private kind of routine. Dribble, shoot, retrieve the ball, dribble, shoot, retrieve. I began to relax for the first time since Friday afternoon. The blare of the television and the shouted insults of the women playing cards receded.

"You're pretty good." One of the women in front of the television had turned around to watch me.

I grunted but didn't say anything. I play most Saturdays through the winter with a group of women who've been together for fifteen years. Some of the young ones were in tough collegiate programs—I've had to get better to keep in the game with them—but mostly I play for the pleasure of feeling my body move through space.

"Play you one-on-one," she persisted. "Dollar a point."

"Play you one-on-one for nothing," I panted, not breaking stride. "I don't have one thin dime in my possession."

"No shit?" she demanded. "Your family, they haven't sent you nothing for a prison account?"

"No shit. Anyway, I only got here yesterday." I jumped up and pulled an errant shot off the backboard.

She got off the couch and came to stand next to me. Other women in the room urged us to a game: "Come on, Angie, she can give you a real game for a change." "No way, my money's on Angie." "Not me, I been watching Cream there, I put five bucks on Cream." I noticed my cellmate on the fringes of the crowd, shivering and rubbing her arms.

Angie snatched the ball away from me and posted up. I jumped as she shot and batted the ball down. She elbowed me hard in the side and grabbed the ball back, shot, and scored. When I rebounded she came in low, trying to head-butt my stomach. I twisted away and shot over her head. The ball caromed around the rim, then went through. She grabbed the rebound, kicking me savagely on the shin as she passed me under the basket. I went in below her guard as she was shooting and knocked her arms up in the air. She swore and gave me an undercut to the chin. I twisted away and grabbed the ball. We weren't playing for baskets but for dominance.

The calls from the sideline grew louder. Out of the corner of my eye I saw uniforms of the corrections officers on the fringes of the crowd, but I didn't dare take my eye off Angie or the court. My sore shoulders, my weak stomach, all that had to be put to one side. Shoot, grab, feint, duck, rebound, shoot again.

Sweat was blurring my eyes. Angie was a good athlete. She was strong, and she was some years younger than me, but she wasn't well-conditioned and she didn't have disciplined technique, either as a fighter or a player. I was keeping up with her and giving her back blow for blow. Moves I'd learned on the streets of South Chicago thirty years ago came to me as if I'd last been jumped on Commercial Avenue yesterday.

The crowd was beginning to roar every time I shot. That made Angie fight uglier but more wildly, and I had less trouble keeping the ball from her. I was driving to the basket when I saw light glint on metal in her hand. I dropped to the floor, rolled over onto my back, and scissor-kicked Angie's feet out from under her. When I jumped up to kick away her weapon, Angie was lying under the basket. A knife cut out of an aluminum can lay next to her.

The women in the crowd began a confused yelling, urging us on to fight. Some of them were Angie's followers, wanting a real brawl; others wanted me to put a stop to her once and for all: "Stick the knife into her now while she's on the ground," I heard one person call out. A guard stepped forward and picked up the knife, while another put a headlock on me. I knew how to break that hold, and with my adrenaline still high was about to, but remembered in time that I mustn't fight back. The guards carried stun guns on their belts; they had plenty of other weapons, not the least the power to keep me in Coolis longer than I wanted to stay.

"Bitch planted that on me," Angie muttered.

One of the CO's who'd been cheering loudest said he

was writing us both up. If you're written up in jail it adds to the charge sheet when you finally get your court date. If you're already in prison it can send you into solitary and deducts from your "good time" for early release.

As I stood motionless with my head under the CO's arm, facing Angie, who was similarly corralled, a woman spoke up from the middle of the crowd. Everyone in the room, CO's and inmates both, quieted down at once. The woman said that there hadn't been any fighting, just basketball, and where that knife came from she didn't know, but she could swear I hadn't pulled it.

"That's right," several voices affirmed. "You were there, Cornish, you saw. They was playing one-on-one. Angie musta tripped in her own sweat."

Cornish was another CO who'd been watching the game, if that's what you could call my outing with Angie. He asked the first speaker if she was sure, because if she was he wouldn't issue either of us a ticket on account of the holiday weekend.

"Uh-huh, I'm sure. Now I'm going to get me a pop. It's a hot day." She was a tall woman, with skin the color of toffee and thick graying hair pulled back from her head in a knot. As she moved toward the vending machines in a corner of the room, the crowd parted, like the Red Sea.

The guard who'd been clutching me let me go. A couple of women came over to slap my palm and tell me they'd been with me from the start. Others, perhaps members of Angie's gang, gave me an evil eye and some pretty inventive insults.

CO Cornish grabbed my arm and told me I needed to get back to my cell to cool down. And what was my name? Warshawski? "You're new, right, oh, in the jail wing. Then you shouldn't be down here for prisoners' recreation. Jail-wing recreation is in the mornings." I opened my mouth to say I'd been ordered down here at three, but shut it again. Don't trouble trouble, my mother always warned me, and trouble won't trouble you.

A woman CO, one of only two or three I'd seen since arriving, was appointed to escort me back to the jail wing. "Lucky for you Miss Ruby spoke up when she did. Otherwise you'd have found your bail request doubled for sure."

"Miss Ruby? Who is she?"

The CO snorted. "Miss Ruby thinks she's Queen of Coolis because she's been in prison a long time, at Dwight eight years before they opened this place. She cut her husband into little pieces and put him in different garbage cans around Chicago, claimed it was self-defense if you can believe that, but the judge didn't buy it and gave her thirty years. Now she's a churchgoer, and the lieutenants and some of the CO's treat her like she's holy. And she has a lot of influence on the young girls, so it doesn't pay to go up against her."

We had reached my wing. The CO signaled to the guard behind the control panel to let me through. She stood on one side of the airlock and watched it close around me. When the door on the other side opened to decant me onto my floor, she took off again.

The wing had a shower room in between the cell block and the guard station. I knew the guards had cameras trained on the showers, and they also could come in on unannounced inspection, but I needed to rinse off my sweat and blood: Angie had given me some pretty serious bumps. When you're in the middle of a fight—or game, for that matter—you don't notice the cuts and blows. It's only later, when the adrenaline is wearing off, that you start to ache.

I didn't have any soap. I had learned this morning that even the most basic toilet items like toothbrushes and shampoo had to be purchased from the commissary and that I had to have money deposited in a trust account at the prison before I could buy anything. It was a nice little racket, like a company store for sharecroppers. You're there, you're a captive market, and they can charge you whatever they damned well want. Even if my five remaining dollars would have covered the cost of basic toiletries, I was told I couldn't open my trust account until after the holiday weekend.

I dried myself with the threadbare square of gray toweling I'd been issued when I arrived yesterday and put my pants back on. They smelled pretty unpleasant, but at least they fit.

At five we were all ordered into our cells for a head count and then escorted down to the dining hall. I hadn't realized yesterday that you had some control over what went on your tray and that salads were available on request. Tonight I asked for a salad and extra bread and rolled lettuce up into a sandwich, which I ate while walking to the table. I tried to eat some of the overcooked meat and beans on my tray but still couldn't deal with the roaches. I suppose if I had to stay here any length of time I'd learn to overlook them, but I was still too finicky in my ways.

Within five minutes of my sitting down I'd been identified as the woman who "took out Angie." A woman across from me told me I'd better look out, Angie was one of the West Side Iscariots and they were panting for revenge. Another one said she heard from her girlfriend that I used karate to wipe out Angie and could I teach her how to do it. One woman, with a dozen braids done up in colored ribbons, said Miss Ruby told a lie to save my hide, but three others spoke up hotly.

"Miss Ruby never told no lie. She spoke the truth, she say Cream here did not pull a knife, and she say Cream and Angie just playing basketball, not fighting, which is the gospel truth, right, Cream?"

"It was the most physical basketball game I ever played," I said, which somehow satisfied her.

The woman with braids said, "No, it's true—Angie, she dissed Miss Ruby, stole her shampoo out of the shower, so Miss Ruby, she was lying in wait to teach Angie a lesson, that's why she stood up for the new girl. Even though she's white."

That started a hot argument, which raged as if I weren't there at all: was I white or Spanish or black? The one who'd nicknamed me Cream insisted I was black. With my olive skin and dark curly hair I could have been anything; since there were very few white faces at the tables, they assumed I was part of the majority culture, although most of them decided I must be Spanish.

"Italian," I finally explained. There was more argument, over whether Italy was part of Spain. I let it flow past me—I wasn't there to conduct geography lessons. In fact, I had a feeling that the less I flaunted my education, the better off I might be.

They also wanted to know how old I was, and when I told them, the one with the ribbons in her braids exclaimed I couldn't be, her mother wasn't that old and I looked younger than her mother. I realized with a jolt that the women around me were terribly young. Only a handful could have been my age, let alone as old as

Miss Ruby. Many didn't seem to be out of their teens, certainly not over twenty-five. They probably yearned desperately for their mothers, or some mother: no wonder they clung to Miss Ruby and argued jealously about who she favored and what she was doing.

I couldn't see Miss Ruby in the dining hall, but they put us through in three shifts of three hundred. Even if she'd been in my shift I might not have been able to spot her in the throng. When I asked after her, they told me she was probably eating in her room: women with enough money or status could buy special food from the commissary. They said it was so expensive most of them did it only for their birthdays, but there was almost always someone wanting to buy a meal for Miss Ruby.

My cellmate ate on the shift after mine, so I had the room to myself for forty-five smoke-free minutes. When she came in, I saw my prowess against Angie had affected her: she accorded me a nervous respect, and when I asked her not to smoke after lights out, she didn't wait for us to be locked in for the night but quickly stubbed her cigarette out on the floor.

Her nervousness made me aware that I was big enough and strong enough to seem menacing. It took me back uncomfortably to the year after my mother died, when I went wild on the streets of South Chicago. I had always been big for my age and I had learned early—partly from my hockey-playing cousin Boom-Boom, partly from experience—how to defend myself in the rough neighborhood where we grew up. But the year I was sixteen I roamed the streets looking for fights. It seemed as though after Gabriella died, I couldn't feel anything unless I was feeling physical pain. After a while even the biggest boys stayed away from me: I was too crazy, I fought with too much insanity. And then I was picked up, and Tony found out and somehow helped me get over it. But I'd felt that same surge of maniac rage on the court with Angie, and I didn't want it taking me over: I might be able to terrorize my jailmates, but I didn't like what it would do to me in the process.

I leaned over the top bunk and asked my roommate her name and whether she had a trial date. Solina, and no trial date yet. With a patient interest I wasn't really feeling, I pried her story out of her, got her to relax over the narrative of her babies, her mother, the father of the children, how she knew she shouldn't be doing crack but it gets hold of you, it's hard to let go of it, and all she wanted was a good life for her children.

At nine the loudspeaker interrupted us. It was time for the day's final count. We stood in our cells next to our beds while the CO's looked in, asked our names, checked them on a board, and locked us in for the night. Once again the hiss of the magnetic lock made my stomach turn over. I climbed to the upper bunk as the lights went out and prayed that Freeman would get a message from Mr. Contreras, track me down, and be waiting for me first thing in the morning with a check for my bail.

Fatigue finally pushed me into an uneasy sleep, in which I kept feeling roaches on my face and hands. Sometime in the night the slamming of a door jerked me awake. I heard a woman scream. My heart began to race again: I was locked up and could do nothing, for myself or anyone around me in peril.

I thought of Nicola Aguinaldo, lying in a bunk like mine on the prison side of Coolis. How much more helpless even than I she must have felt, with no lawyer to bail her out, no powerful friends, alone in a strange country, getting commands in a language she barely understood. At least in her last letter to her mother she had said that—I sat up in bed. Nicola had told Abuelita Mercedes not to worry, that Señora Ruby was taking care of her. Miss Ruby, the powerful protector of young inmates.

I'd been a fool to howl over the injustice of being sent to Coolis. I was right where I needed to be: in the heart of Carnifice territory, where Nicola Aguinaldo had last been seen alive. I turned on my side on the narrow bunk and fell deeply asleep.

36

Bail? Why Leave Such Cool Quarters?

When FREEMAN CARTER arrived Tuesday morning, he was appalled at my decision not to post bail. "I agree two-fifty is outrageously high: that's because it's Baladine and Carnifice. I couldn't get the judge to lower it. But Vic, there is every reason to post it and no reason to stay in here. Frankly, you smell awful and you look worse. That makes a hell of a bad impression on a jury."

"I won't smell so bad when you've deposited money into an account for me here and I can buy soap and shampoo," I said. "And I'm not going to stay in here until my trial—only until I find out what I want to know."

That made him explode. "You pay two hundred dollars an hour for my advice, which you proceed to flout, but I'm going to give it to you anyway. Get out of here. If you stay in here on some cockamamie scheme to rout out corruption in Coolis, you will be hurt worse than you have ever been before in your life. And if you then call on me to glue whatever's left of you back together, I will not be a happy man."

"Freeman, I won't claim my brain is in top gear right now. Being locked up is distorting, I agree. But for the last three weeks I've been ducking missiles that

Carnifice and Global Entertainment have been launching at me. I was sure you'd understand if you watched the video I asked Morrell to send you, the one showing Baladine's tame cop looking for coke he'd planted in my office. For once in my life I did not go out of my way seeking to make an enemy: they came and found me."

We were sitting in a special meeting room for attorney visits. It was utterly bare except for two plastic chairs separated by a table that was bolted to the floor. We had to stay in our respective chairs, or the guard watching us through a glass panel would remove me. Supposedly the room was soundproofed, but for all I knew they were taping everything we said.

When I talked to Freeman Monday afternoon, during my fifteen-minute slot for phone calls, I insisted he bring a camera with him to photograph the fading remains of Lemour's attack on me. He'd harrumphed a bit on the phone but came with a Polaroid. When he saw the marks on my face and arms, his eyes widened with anger and he took a dozen shots. He was already planning the complaint against Lemour, but it made him even less able to understand why I wanted to stay at Coolis.

I pushed my palms together, trying to marshal my words. "It all started when I stopped to help Baladine's ex-nanny three weeks ago. Until I find out why that matters so much to him and to Teddy Trant, I don't think there's going to be much left of me even if I do leave Coolis. The answer is here, at least the answer to what happened to the nanny, to young Nicola Aguinaldo. If I had money in a trust account and some bills for feeding the guards, I should be able to learn what I need to know about her in a couple of weeks. Maybe less."

He thought I was quixotic as well as insane, and he argued persuasively: I may have thought I wasn't going out of my way to needle Baladine, but why didn't I leave well enough alone as he'd asked me when he was dealing with the State's Attorney about my car last month? And prison was a destructive environment. It wore on you physically as well as mentally, warped your judgment and your ethics.

"You know that as well as I, Vic: you did your share of criminal pleadings in your days with the public defender."

"I know it from being here four days. I got entangled with the leader of the West Side Iscariots on Sunday and I've been watching my back ever since. I hate it here. I'm lonely. Even if the food wasn't horrible, the dining hall is so covered with roaches you have to keep brushing them off your legs while you're at the table; every time the locks shut on our rooms at night, my stomach twists up so hard I can't sleep; there's no privacy, even on the toilet." To my dismay I could hear my voice cracking on the edge of tears. "But if I let you bail me out, the only thing that will save me is to close up my business and hide out someplace. Even if my self-respect would permit that my finances won't."

"You can't convince me those are your only two choices, but I can't stay to argue. I have to get back to Chicago for a court appearance." He looked at his watch. "Anyway, you've already made up your mind to be pigheaded, so there's no point in my arguing with you. Tell me what you want, both in bucks and in permitted goods, and I'll send Callie over to your home to collect things. I've got an intern who can ferry things out here for you and do the basic paperwork on the money."

Besides the clothes I was permitted (two bras, two pairs of jeans, three underpants, five shirts, a pair of shorts, and a modest set of earrings) I told him what I most wanted was to see Morrell. "I want to see any friend who will make the drive—I listed Lotty and Mr. Contreras and Sal on my visitors' sheet—but will you ask Morrell to come out here as soon as possible? As far as the money goes, I'd like three hundred dollars put into a prison trust account."

I picked my words carefully for the rest of my request. "I know it's a felony to bring cash in for someone in prison, so I'm not going to ask you to do it. If I could get four hundred dollars in bills, though, it might come in handy. Will you mention the idea—and the risk —to Lotty?"

I wanted money in hand in case I needed to bribe some CO's or inmates or both. In theory, there was no cash at Coolis: you got issued a photo-ID card with a computer chip when you were admitted. Any money in your account was programmed onto the chip and then deducted when you used the card, whether in vending machines, at the commissary, or doing laundry. The idea was you wouldn't have gambling or bribing or drug sales if you kept out the cash, but in my four days here I'd already seen plenty of bills changing hands— and not always very secretively.

Freeman frowned and said in his most austere tones that he would speak to Lotty, but only to advise her of the felony nature of my request.

He finished making notes in his quick, tiny script and packed up his papers. "Vic, you know my steadiest advice as your counsel is for you to post bail and come home. If you decide to listen to me, a call to my office will get someone out here on the instant."

"Freeman, before you go, do you know why I'm here? I mean, instead of at Cook County? Was this some shenanigan of Baladine's?"

He shook his head. "I have to confess I wondered about that, but once you were arrested, even with Lemour involved, you moved out of Baladine's orbit. The simple truth is, Cook County is always filled to capacity, and on the Fourth they started splitting at the seams. Women arrested at precincts on the far North or West Sides were automatically shunted out here. Anyway, Baladine is out of the country. He's taken his family on some exotic vacation."

"I know: to the South of France. Is Robbie with them? I don't know what became of him after I left the house on Friday morning."

Freeman told me that Baladine had wrested Robbie from Mr. Contreras in the middle of the night Saturday. The old man ("He's been living with you too long," Freeman said in an unnecessary aside) had tried to hold off a warrant from a Du Page County sheriff's deputy. He only gave in when Robbie said he couldn't stand it if they arrested Mr. Contreras; he would leave if the sheriff promised not to hurt the old man. Robbie's father had taken him to South Carolina, to boot camp, before flying out to join the Poilevys and the Trants with the rest of his family in the Pyrenees.

"I tried to talk to Baladine, but his staff wouldn't give me his number overseas. They say he left strict orders that even though he has the kid back he's not doing a deal with you," Freeman added.

"Freeman—if they don't know I'm here don't tell

them. If anyone asks, let them think I posted bail and am lying low."

He gave me a queer smile, half loving, half exasperated. "As you wish, Donna Victoria of the Rueful Countenance."

He tapped on the window to let the guard know we were finished. I was searched, the guard spending more time than necessary on my bra, and taken back to the jail wing. Now that I was alone I felt unbearably desolate. I lay on my bunk, a strip of towel over my eyes against the light, which stayed on from 5:00 A.M. until lights-out at nine, and let myself give way to misery.

37

In the Big House

THE NEXT FOUR weeks were the hardest of my life. I hunkered down and tried to learn the ropes at Coolis—how to avoid being beaten up by my sisters in chains, how to butter up the CO's without having to have sex with them, how to keep myself busy enough that the pervasive helplessness and boredom wouldn't drag me so far down I couldn't function.

I wanted to talk to Miss Ruby, to thank her for her help on Sunday, but mostly to find out what she could tell me about Nicola, and about getting work in the clothes shop. I let everyone I talked to know that I'd like to meet her, but except for a couple of times in the dining hall, where the CO's kept us firmly in place at the table, I didn't see her after that first day.

Freeman's visit did bring a material change in my physical comfort. True to his word, he sent his intern out with money for my account, along with my clothes allotment. The intern had a stack of legal documents for me to read and sign. In the middle of them was a letter from Lotty. She begged me to post bail in lines of such loving concern I was hard put to stick to my resolve about staying, but in a postscript she added, *I helped Freeman's secretary pack your clothes and mended various tears.*

"She especially wanted you to know about a hole in the waistband to your shorts," the intern said primly.

Lotty was no seamstress. When I got back to my cell, I surreptitiously picked apart an inch of the waistband seam. Tightly folded bills almost matched the khaki of the fabric. I pulled out a twenty before stitching the seam shut again—it was the safest place to store money, and washing wouldn't hurt it any.

With my prison trust account set up, I was not only able to buy a toothbrush and soap at the commissary but also some cleanser to scrub out the sink–toilet unit in my cell. The cash I would keep for bribes, once I knew to whom and how to administer them.

Except for being able to buy overpriced, poor-quality shampoo and soap, my first trip to the commissary was a disappointment. The women around me had talked about what they planned to do on their expeditions as if their weekly thirty-minute trip was an outing to Water Tower Place. I suppose the women found the trips exciting because they made a break in the routine. They were also our main contact with the outside world, which we could experience through magazines like *Cosmo* or *Essence*. *Soap Opera Digest* was also popular.

Besides magazines and toiletries, you could buy canned or packaged food, cigarettes, and artifacts made by inmates throughout the Illinois prison system. A large number of male inmates seemed to like to embroider. We could get handkerchiefs, place mats, head scarves, even blouses with intricate designs of birds and flowers, brought in from Joliet and points south.

Also available were Mad Virgin T-shirts and jackets —the average age of the prison population was, after all, Lacey's target audience, and many of the inmates were fans. Curious, I inspected the labels. They read *Made with Pride in the USA*, so I didn't think Nicola Aguinaldo had bought the shirt she died in here. The commissary also stocked spin-offs from other Global favorites, including Captain Doberman and the Space Berets, which women liked to buy for their children.

On my first outing I bought cheap lined writing paper—the only paper the commissary carried—and a couple of ballpoint pens. When I asked the clerk if they had plain paper or roller-ball pens, she snorted and told me to go to Marshall Field's if I didn't like the selection here.

When I got back to my cell, my roommate, Solina, apathetically watched me scrub the basin. She had been at Coolis only a week longer than me, and the fact that the sink was filthy when she got here meant it wasn't her job to clean it up.

"We'll take turns," I said, my voice bright with menace. "I'm getting it spick-and-span, and that means tomorrow, when it's your turn, it will be easy for you to clean up."

She started to say she didn't have to obey orders from me, then remembered my prowess against Angie and said she'd think about it.

"We can control so few things in here," I said. "Keeping the place clean means at a minimum we can control the smell."

"Okay, okay, I already got the point." She stomped out of our cell down the hall to watch television on a small set belonging to an inmate who'd been awaiting her trial date for eleven months.

I had to laugh to myself, picturing the friends who've complained about my slovenly housekeeping over the years—they'd be astounded to find me laying down the law on hygiene to my roommate.

Besides making it possible for me to bathe, Freeman had also delivered my message to Morrell. On Thursday near the end of my first week, I got summoned to see him in the visitors' room.

My arrest had stunned him. He hadn't even known about it until he saw a paragraph in the *Tribune* on Sunday—Mr. Contreras, never fond of communicating with the men in my life, had been too rattled to call Morrell. Like Freeman, Morrell talked to me persuasively about all the reasons to leave Coolis, but unlike Freeman, he could see a point to my staying.

"Are you learning anything helpful?"

I grimaced. "Not about Nicola, so far. About the way people without power turn on each other because they feel too helpless to see who's really to blame for their day-to-day misery—I'm learning way too much about that."

I leaned forward to talk more privately, but an alert CO made me back away the requisite arm's length—if we touched, Morrell might pass drugs to me. After five minutes of glaring scrutiny the CO decided I wasn't trying anything too heinous and turned her attention to another inmate. Only a handful of women got visitors on weekdays; it was hard to speak privately.

"There's a place called the Unblinking Eye where you can get a particular kind of watch–camera," I said in a prison-yard mumble as soon as the CO turned her attention away. "If you buy one for me and bring it on a Saturday or Sunday when there's a mob here, we ought to be able to make a switch."

"Vic, I don't like it."

I smiled provocatively. "I don't think they'll do anything to you if they find you with it—except bar you from visiting me."

He gave an exasperated sigh. "I'm not worried about that but about you, you fool."

"Thanks, Morrell. But if I ever manage to get into the clothes shop, I may see something that I should document. And frankly, there's plenty else to record here between the inmates and the guards."

Morrell gave me another quizzical look and said he'd see what he could do. He switched the talk to neutral matters—my neighbor, who was so distraught at the idea of me behind bars that he wouldn't make the trip to see me. He gave me news of Lotty, of the dogs, of all the people whose welfare I cared about and couldn't attend to. He stayed an hour. I felt a wrenching desolation when he left. I went down to the rec room, where I shot baskets for an hour, until I was wet with sweat and too tired to feel sorry for myself.

When I went back upstairs to shower, the CO at the entrance, a man named Rohde, seemed to react oddly. He looked at me, then got on the phone. I had to wait five minutes before he let me in, and then it was only when two other CO's joined him. I wondered if they had somehow monitored my conversation with Morrell and were going to put me on report, but Rohde watched me go past the guard station without saying anything. Still, he seemed to have an air of suppressed excitement about him, and he was joined behind the double-glass walls by the other two men. The video cameras were trained on the shower rooms as well as all other common areas, but I had already figured out which shower head cut the camera angle so that it could only catch me if I stood directly under it. If he'd called his buddies for a peep show, I figured I knew how to avoid providing it.

I was jumped almost before I got into the shower room. Two women, one from the front, one from the rear. Rohde's manner had put me on guard, otherwise they might have destroyed me. I dropped my supplies and towel and kicked, all in one motion. I was lucky; my foot caught the woman in front square on the patella, and she grunted and backed away.

The one behind me had my left shoulder in a steel grip. She was pulling me toward her. I gasped—she had something sharp that sliced across my right shoulder. I hooked my feet around her ankles and used her own force to catapult her forward. The wet floor made it hard to get a purchase and I slipped and fell with her. I chopped across her right wrist before she could recover and forced her to let go of her weapon.

The one I'd kicked was closing in on me. I rolled over on the moldy floor and got up into a crouch. She flung herself at me before I could kick the weapon away. She had her hands around my neck. I held on to her shoulders for leverage and swung both knees into her stomach. She squawked in pain and let go of me.

The woman with the weapon was behind me again. I was winded; I'd already been working out for an hour and didn't know how much longer I could keep fighting. When she lunged at me I ducked. It was the wet floor that did the rest. She lost her footing, scrabbled to gain it, and careened so hard against the concrete wall that she stunned herself. Her partner saw her fall and suddenly shouted for help.

The guards appeared so fast I knew they must have

been on their way as soon as the woman knocked herself out.

"She jumped me! She jumped Celia, too, and knocked her out!"

Rohde grabbed me and held my arms behind me. Polsen, the CO who'd joined him at the video monitor, stood nearby but didn't touch my assailant.

"Nonsense," I panted. "Celia is lying there with something in her hand that gave me this cut on my neck. And as for you, whoever you are, if you were waiting to take a shower, where the hell is your towel or your soap? As you two CO's know, because you were watching all this on your monitor."

"You stole them from me."

"Those are my things on the floor there. Where are yours?" I demanded.

At that point CO Cornish appeared. He was the fairest-minded of the CO's on our wing.

"You fighting again?" he asked me.

"The woman on the floor there cut me with something when I came into the shower room," I got my story in quickly. "She still has the razor or whatever she used in her right hand."

The woman was beginning to stir. Before Rohde or Polsen could move, Cornish bent over and pulled a strip of metal from her.

"She belongs on the prison wing. As does the other one. I'm putting all three of you on report. Warshawski, if I catch you in one more fight you're going into segregation. And you two, off you go to your own quarters. How did you get in here, anyway?"

Rohde was forced to let me go. He and Polsen escorted my assailants off the floor. Cornish looked at my neck and told me to go to the infirmary for a tetanus

shot. It was the closest he was going to come to acknowledging that I'd been jumped, but it eased the injustice of the whole situation slightly.

"I'd like to wash off first," I said.

Cornish waited in the hall while I picked up my
shampoo and towel from the filthy floor. I took off my
shirt and bra and washed off under the shower most
remote from the video monitor. Cornish took me in an
elevator down to the basement, which I'd never seen,
and waited while I got my shot. The woman on duty
put some antibiotic ointment on the wound in my neck.
It hadn't gone deep enough to require stitches, which
was fortunate, since she didn't have the equipment to
put me back together.

Cornish took me back to my cell and told me to be
very careful where I walked at night. Everyone on my
wing seemed to know about the attack. In fact, they
seemed to have been warned away from the showers
when I came up from my workout.

"You're in trouble now," Solina said, gloating.
"Rohde's fucking one of the Iscariots. He got those two
to jump you out of revenge for Angie. And he put
money on them."

When we stood at attention for our predinner head
count, Rohde handed me a ticket. He had written me
up for instigating a fight that injured two other inmates.
My hearing would come in a month, after the captain
had reviewed the charge. Great. Now Captain Ruzich
would realize I was one of his inmates. As I studied the
ticket I got my one gleam of hope: Rohde had put my
name down as *Washki*. Maybe the fact that none of the
CO's could pronounce my last name, let alone spell it,
would save my butt.

Miss Ruby stopped me after dinner and told me she

was disappointed in me, that she didn't think fighting was the right way to solve my problems inside. "The women tell me you're old enough to be a mother to most of them. This isn't the way to look after the young ones or set them an example."

I pulled down my T-shirt to show her the oozing wound in my neck. "Should I have turned the other cheek until I was cut to ribbons?" I demanded. She gave a snort that was half a gasp but wouldn't stay to discuss the point.

After that I began to wonder if the attack in the shower would make it impossible for me to learn anything about Nicola. I even began to wonder if Baladine knew I was here, if he'd e-mailed the warden from France and told him to stage the attack. Only the realization during the next few days that none of the CO's treated me any better or worse than the rest of the inmates made me decide that was a paranoid fantasy.

The fight in the shower grew as it was told around the prison. I had moves like you saw in the kung fu movies. I had given the two Iscariots subtle blows that stunned them and then pulled a knife to finish them off when the guards intervened. Some of the women wanted to attach themselves to me as a protector, but others, especially the real gangbangers, thought they wanted to fight me. I managed to talk my way out of several confrontations, but it added to my tension to have to be on my guard during recreation time or in the dining room. Any time I saw signs that anger was about to spill over into combat, I'd leave the area and return to my cell.

Fights were always breaking out, over things that might seem trivial to you if you'd never had this experience, the experience of being crammed behind bars with a thousand other people, without privacy, at the mercy of whatever whims the guards might feel that day. Someone stole someone else's body lotion, or pushed in front of her in line, or spoke disrespectfully of a relative, and fists and handmade weapons flashed out in an instant.

People also fought over clothes. You got a replacement bundle only every five years in prison, so a torn shirt or lost button mattered terribly. Women paired off as lovers and had lovers' quarrels. Various street gangs besides the Iscariots marked territory and tried to control such things as the flow of drugs.

After my fight in the shower room, my roommate became more nervous around me than ever. At least fear made her cut down on her smoking and made her halfheartedly clean out our sink every few days, but I learned she had begged for a transfer, terrified that I would jump her in the night.

Her attitude changed dramatically on my second Thursday, when I returned from my workout to find her bunched up in bed howling with misery.

"Caseworker is trying something with my children," she screamed when I asked what was wrong. "Moving them to foster care, saying I'm unfit; even if I get out of here I can't keep them. I love those children. No one can say they ever went to school without socks and shoes. And that caseworker, did she ever come watch me cooking dinner for them? They eat a hot meal every night of the week."

"You don't have a mother or sister who could take them in?"

"They're worse off than me. My mother, she's been high since the year I start first grade, and my sister, she's got eight children, she don't know where they're at from one end of the week to the next. My aunt down in Alabama, she'd take them if I send them, but the caseworker won't listen to me about my aunt. And who will give me money for my children's bus fare if the caseworker's against me?"

I leaned against the wall—of course we didn't have a chair. "You could write again, showing that you have a proper home for them to go to and pledging your willingness to go into rehab as part of a plea bargain."

She looked at me suspiciously. "What do you know about plea bargains and rehab? And how can someone like me who can't afford a lawyer, how can I get into a rehab program? You think they grow on trees for poor people? The only rehab for someone like me is doing time."

I sidestepped how I knew about things like plea bargains and concentrated on how she could find one of the few remaining publicly funded drug programs. The good programs have long waiting lists, of course. I wondered whether Solina was a serious addict who would promise reform to get out of prison time but not really try to quit: drugs were readily available in Coolis, as in many jails and prisons, and some of her more violent mood swings, with periods of agitated withdrawal, told me that Solina had found her way to an in-house crack supplier. But drafting a letter for her would give me something to do, besides shooting baskets and occasionally practicing my singing.

Solina was touchingly awed by the finished letter. We didn't have access to computers or typewriters, but I printed it carefully for her on the cheap lined paper available in the commissary. She read it over and over, then took it down the hall to the cell where she spent most of her day and showed it to the group around the television. A number of inmates studied law books in the library and filed complaints and appeals for themselves or their friends, but most came to Coolis with such minimal literacy that they couldn't put their learning into appropriate language.

The word of that letter and my special knowledge spread fast: over the weekend, women began visiting my cell with requests for letters—to the State's Attorney or their public defender, to different welfare agencies, the children's caseworkers, the employer, the husband or boyfriend. If I would write they would get me anything I wanted—cigarettes, reefer, coke, crack, I didn't do drugs? Then alcohol, chocolate, or perfume.

If I didn't accept payment I'd look like a patsy or a phony. I said I'd write a letter in exchange for fresh fruit or vegetables—much harder to come by in Coolis than drugs.

It was my letter-writing that really saved my hide in Coolis. The women I helped began constituting themselves into an informal set of watchdogs, warning me when trouble was lurking.

My letters also began to make it possible for me to ask questions about Nicola and the clothes shop.

38

Prisoners in Cell Block H

WHETHER YOU WERE in jail or prison, if you were at Coolis for more than two weeks you had to work. A woman lieutenant named Dockery, who was strict but considered fair by most of the inmates, made up job rosters. The newest arrivals got kitchen or cleaning duty, the lowest paid and least popular. Kitchen duty, as far as I could make out, had to be the worst, working with grease and heat and heavy pots, but cleaning the showers and other common rooms would come a close second.

The most coveted jobs were in telemarketing and hotel reservations. The pay was the best and you didn't have to lift anything heavy. But that kind of work only went to prison inmates. In management's eyes, those of us in jail awaiting trial wouldn't be around long enough to go through the training—or, more to the point, for our names to move to the top of the long waiting list for the cushiest jobs.

Of course what I was most interested in was the clothes shop. When I was in line at the dining hall or working out in the rec room, or in my cell writing letters for women, I kept trying to find someone who worked there or who roomed with someone who worked there. Everyone had a different story about it, and no one wanted to work there.

"But I knew one woman, Nicola, she wrote her mom that the pay was really good," I said one day in the rec room when several women were watching me shoot baskets.

They didn't play themselves, but they were hoping someone who did play would show up—watching and betting on games was a popular pastime. One of the women asked who Nicola was.

"She was that girl from China who ran away," one woman said.

"She wasn't from China, it was some other place over there, like maybe Japan," someone named Dolores chimed in.

"Philippines," I suggested, jumping up for the ball as it banged off the rim. "I know her mother, and she said Nicola wrote she was really happy to have a job in the clothes shop."

"Of course, if she wrote it in a letter home," Dolores snorted. "They don't let you say nothing bad about it, or it won't get past the censors. One woman, she worked there, she was crying all the time, they treat you too rough there."

The third woman said they only took foreign girls in the shop; they worked them to death and then brought in more foreign girls as replacements.

"Oh, don't be stupid," Dolores said. "They use foreign girls because they know foreigners won't complain in case their children get deported."

"Yes, but don't you remember Monique? She was from Haiti, and she said the back room was foreign girls on death row. They're all in segregation, and the

CO's bring them over in the morning in a locked van to work and then take them back at night."

It was a startling notion, but I said I didn't think there was a death row at Coolis.

"Maybe not," the friend said stubbornly, "but still, there's something spooky over there. Maybe it's because they don't let Americans work there. It's all Mexicans and Chinese and—where did you say Nicola was from? Uh-oh—Polsen's looking at us queer; better go to our cells for head count."

This last she muttered out of the corner of her mouth in the prison mumble everyone mastered in their first few days. CO Polsen was always looking at women "queer," when he wasn't outright touching or threatening to touch us.

Polsen was one of the CO's that I tried to avoid, but of course the guards had enormous power in our lives. If they took a dislike to you they wrote you up—gave you a ticket, which could result in anything from a loss of commissary privileges to a stint in segregation. Women they liked they brought gifts for, ranging from better cosmetics than you could get in the commissary to drugs. But the women they liked had to pay a price for that attention. Rohde, sleeping with one of the Iscariots, wasn't the only CO having sex with the inmates.

One of the hardest things to take during my time at Coolis was the constant sexual harassment. It was verbal, it was physical, it was incessant. Many of the CO's, not just Rohde, put their hands on your ass when you were waiting in line for dinner. When they searched you after you had a visitor, they would linger a long time on your breasts. I had to learn to hold myself very still, very aloof, not act on the impulses of a lifetime to break an arm or separate a rib. If I saw something blatant I tried to photograph it with my wrist-camera, but it was the language as much as the behavior that was demeaning. It was hard to accept the abuse passively, and it fueled both my rage and my fear.

Morrell brought me the wrist-camera from the Unblinking Eye on my second Sunday in Coolis. In the crowd of women and children in the visitors' room, we managed to exchange my wristwatch for the camera model. I now had a watch that could take pictures, although I hated seeing mine go out the door with Morrell—my father's mother gave it to him when he graduated from the police academy fifty-five years ago.

The tiny camera had cost over fourteen hundred dollars. Freeman was paying my bills while I was locked up, but I wondered how I'd ever pay him back—my prison time wasn't a good advertisement to clients.

At least the camera made me feel a modicum of control over the crazy world I was inhabiting. I started taking pictures of some of the worst outrages I saw, but I would have needed the video model I took to Georgia to capture the verbal abuse.

"Looking good, Cream," CO Polsen said as I came into the rec room a few days later. "Like to see you in shorts. I bet that pussy of yours has seen plenty of action, so I'd fit right in."

I moved past him without breaking stride or looking at him: Polsen had constituted himself an enemy, and right now the only defense I could come up with was to pretend he didn't exist.

The problem had really begun over my fight in the shower: he'd been watching on the monitors and felt cheated by my taking out my assailants before anything serious got under way. But his hostility was exacerbated the night after I got my camera, when I was running a load of laundry. The laundry room lay beyond the rec room, so I was watching TV with some of the women while I waited on my clothes.

Polsen was one of the CO's on duty. He abruptly called Dolores out of the room. The sudden slackness in her face and her dragging posture as she obeyed made me get up a few minutes later and follow after her into the laundry room.

Polsen was behind the door trying to pull down her jeans. Dolores was struggling to keep them up, hissing, "No, please don't do this, please don't do this, I'll tell the lieutenant," and he was laughing and saying she was dirt, no one believed her lies, but that if she did say something, he'd see she got into segregation so fast it would make her head spin. I had been practicing with my wristwatch and used it now, wishing I could tape him as well. Polsen looked up and I turned quickly and moved my clothes out of the washer. He let go of Dolores, who ran from the room back toward the prison wing. Polsen gave me a look that liquefied my hamstrings.

When I returned to the common room, the women in front of the television shrank from me: they all knew why Polsen had called Dolores away, and they had watched from the shadows the byplay that took place when I went into the laundry. None of them wanted Polsen to think they supported me.

Back in my cell I wrote down a verbatim account of Polsen's language and what I'd seen, with the date and the time. I interleaved the pages with a copy of *Cosmo*, which I'd bought at the commissary as a cover for my notes. When Freeman's intern came out the next day to tell me my trial date was set for the last week in September, I managed to slide the magazine to her in a flurry of exchanging documents. I asked her to take the magazine away with her and keep it for me. I wasn't sure what use I'd make of my notes, but I didn't want to leave them in my cell—we'd already been locked down twice for searches in my short time at Coolis.

Before she left, the intern asked if I was ready to post bail. It was hard to say no, but I wanted to get a look at the clothes shop. I said I'd give it one more week before throwing in the towel.

I was pretty sure at least one CO was going into rooms on our wing after lights out—it was the only explanation I could think of for the banging doors and cries that sometimes woke me in the night. But none of the women ever said anything. There were several pregnancies in the prison, I noticed, among women who had been inside for over a year—in one case six years.

When I asked about it during my letter-writing sessions, the women clammed up. One of them whispered to me in line at dinner later that someone named Cynthia spent a year in solitary for filing a report on a CO who raped her. The prison said she made up the charge to try to shorten her time. After that, people were more afraid than ever to complain. Usually, too, if they got you pregnant they gave you drugs. "They say, oh, your cycle out of balance, you take these. Then you sick for three days, a week, and you lose the baby."

Chemically induced abortions, in a country that banned RU-486. How enterprising of the Department of Corrections. I wondered who made the diagnosis and who dispensed the drugs, but we had gotten our trays and my informant scuttled across the floor to join her friends.

If Polsen decided to come into my cell after lights-out, what would I do? The thought made me lie tense in bed that night and for some nights after.

39

An Audience with Miss Ruby

At the start of my third week I was assigned to a kitchen shift, a miserable job, especially in summer. We lugged fifty-pound pots of food between stove and steam table, carried out mounds of refuse, slipped in grease on the filthy floor, got covered with burns from careless cooks flinging hot food around. The work paid sixty cents an hour. My coworkers were sullen and sloppy and made it harder to keep from getting injured.

The only job action available to Coolis workers was refusal to work. This led to a ticket, and enough tickets sent you to solitary confinement, but usually after your stint in segregation you got a new work assignment. Turnover was high in the kitchen, but I couldn't afford time in segregation, so I grimly kept at my post.

"This isn't a vacation resort," the CO in charge would say if a woman complained of a burn or a sore back. "You should have thought of that before you thought a life of crime was fun. You're not here for your health, but to learn a lesson."

I had already learned that such medical care as existed was hard to come by. When a woman had hot grease spilled down her arm, the CO in charge of the kitchen upbraided her for crying over nothing. The next day she didn't come in to work; I learned from the comments of the other women that her arm had become a mass of pustules in the night. She had been treated by the in-house "doctor," a CO who had studied prenursing for a year at the local junior college before getting into Coolis.

The stench of the overboiled food and the sight of roaches and mouse droppings took away most of my appetite; if it hadn't been for the fruit my clients brought me I don't think I would have eaten. After a week in the kitchen I was so exhausted it was hard to remember why I'd decided to stay in jail instead of posting bail. I was lying on my bunk Friday night, trying to make up my mind whether to call Freeman and ask him to bail me out on Monday, when Solina came in to say that Miss Ruby had sent word over that she wanted to see me.

On my first day at Coolis, Cornish had sent me back to my cell with a reprimand because jail inmates were supposed to use recreation facilities at a different time than the prisoners, but I'd learned early that was a regulation the CO's enforced only if they wanted an excuse to write you a ticket.

The main reason I hadn't seen Miss Ruby in the rec room since Independence Day was her work schedule. She had one of the cushy jobs, the phone reservation desk for the Passport chain of motels and rental cars. While most prison jobs ran from nine to three, the reservation lines had to be staffed twenty-four hours a day. She'd been on the noon-to-six shift, and I hadn't known to look in the rec room for her in the mornings.

A day earlier I'd written a letter to Rapelec Electronics for a woman, explaining why she was not able to take part in her job-training program and requesting that an opening be kept for her in September. The woman paid me with a box of six local tomatoes, the best food I'd eaten since my arrest. I took two of them as an offering and went with the woman who'd brought the message from Miss Ruby; Jorjette had grown up with one of her granddaughters.

It took some doing to get the guards to let Jorjette and me into the rec room in the morning. CO Cornish, on duty that morning, worked closer to the rules than Rohde or Polsen did on the afternoon shift. Jail inmates didn't have recreation privileges until 3:00 P.M.

"Vic going to show me her basketball shot," Jorjette whined. "You know everyone say she the best, she beat Angie. And we got kitchen duty in one hour; we gotta go now if we're going at all."

"We could do it another time," I said. "Although another time I probably won't have any tomatoes. Do you grow them yourself, Cornish?"

I held one out for him to look at. He admitted that gardening was his hobby but that his tomatoes hadn't ripened yet.

"You have one hour down there, girls," he finally said, accepting the tomato as he signaled to the man behind the bulletproof glass to release the lock on the jail-wing door.

When we got to the rec room, a woman CO I didn't know was on duty. She was watching Oprah with a handful of women on the couch. Miss Ruby sat in the middle of the group, her iron-gray hair freshly cut and curled, shell earrings three or four times regulation size in her ears.

Her eyes flicked at Jorjette and me when we came in and pulled up chairs nearby, but she gave no sign of noticing us until Jorjette approached her during a commercial break and asked nervously how Miss Ruby was doing today.

Miss Ruby inclined her head, said as well as anyone could in this heat, too hot to go outside, but she longed for a breath of fresh air. Jorjette said, well, it was pretty hard on everyone but she knew Miss Ruby's joints suffered real bad in the heat. Maybe she'd like a nice fresh tomato, to remind her of the fresh outdoor air?

"Cream here brought it for you special."

Miss Ruby accepted the tomato and jerked her head toward the far end of the deal table. The CO stayed on the couch watching Oprah, and the handful of other women left us alone: Miss Ruby wanted privacy, Miss Ruby got privacy.

"I can't make up my mind about you, Cream," she said when we were seated. "Are you a fighter or a Good Samaritan? First you beat up a couple of gangbangers, but now I hear you spend your spare time writing letters for the girls. Some of them think you're an undercover cop."

I blinked. Of course in a way that was the truth, but I didn't know Miss Ruby and I couldn't trust my secrets to a stranger, especially one who seemed to be plugged in to the gossip pipeline as thoroughly as Miss Ruby was.

"If I'd known my life history mattered here, I'd have written it up on the bathroom wall," I said. "I was arrested same as everyone else."

"And that would be for what crime, I wonder?"

"You know the sad old story about the man who leaves his wife for a cute young thing? And the first wife, who worked hard and put him through school and scrimped so he could build his business, she gets left with the shirt on her back and not much more? And he gets the kids, because how can she give the kids a decent home when she doesn't have any money and she has to be out at work all day?"

"I heard a bunch of versions of that story in my time." She kept her eyes straight ahead, talking in a prison mumble out of the corner of her mouth.

"My twist on it is I figure the guy for about the meanest bastard in Chicago. So I take the oldest child. A boy, who's overweight and sensitive, and Daddy likes to beat on him, make him cry, then beat on him some more for crying like a girl. Daddy had me arrested for kidnapping."

"Uh-hunh. And you couldn't make bail. Everyone says you got a real lawyer, not a PD. Not to mention, of course, your fancy education that lets you write all those letters."

"Guy's got a lot of important friends. The judge set bail at a quarter of a million. If your friends ran a financial check on me they could tell you why I couldn't pull together that much money overnight."

"And how'd you learn to fight like you do, taking out two big women in the shower?" she demanded. "Not to mention Angie, which I watched you do."

"Same way Angie did," I said softly. "On the streets of Chicago. Ninety-first and Commercial to be exact. But I was lucky. My mother wanted me to have an education, and she made me study when the other girls on my street were getting pregnant or doing drugs."

Miss Ruby thought this over. "I don't know whether to believe you or not. But I hear you've been asking questions about a young woman who used to be here. I hear you've been saying you want to talk to me about her. And so here I am, talking to you, wondering how you know her and if that's the real reason you're at Coolis."

I sidestepped the comment. "I never met Nicola Aguinaldo. I know her mother. Señora Mercedes is grateful to you for looking after Nicola."

"Hmm. She's not very grateful in person."

"She doesn't have any money. And she doesn't have a green card. She's afraid to come out here in case they inspect her documents and report her to INS, and she can't write in English. But Nicola's last letter to Señora Mercedes brought her great comfort, because Nicola told her mother you were keeping an eye on her."

Miss Ruby inclined her head slightly in acknowledgment. "And how did someone like you come to be friends with Nicola's mother?"

I smiled. "I didn't say we were friends, but that I know her. Before my own arrest I was trying to help Señora Mercedes find out what happened to Nicola. You know that she died?"

Miss Ruby gave another brief dip of her chin.

"All the women say you know everything that happens in this prison. I want to know what happened to Nicola. How did she get to the hospital?"

"If you're not a cop yourself, they put you here to talk to me." She spoke with finality but didn't try to move away from me.

"Cops don't give a rat's toenail for who killed a poor little girl who didn't even have a green card to her name."

"So who did put you in here?"

"You know who Robert Baladine is?" When she shook her head no, I explained that he owned Coolis and that Nicola had worked for him before she was arrested. "He's the man I was talking about, and he's got way more power and money than I ever will. He likes the idea of me being locked up in his prison."

She finally looked at me directly, thinking over my story, which had the unusual virtue of being mostly true —even if it might leave her thinking Baladine was my ex-husband. "Nobody knows what happened to Nicola. I heard a lot of different stories, and I don't know which is true. The CO's said she had female difficulties and went into the hospital, where she ran away. Someone else said she got tangled up in one of the big machines in the clothes shop and got killed and the guards were scared they'd be punished for not turning the machinery off in time, so they dumped her body in Chicago. And some girls are saying she beat up on a CO, which is silly, because she wasn't much bigger than a minute, let alone those men."

"She actually died in Chicago," I told her.

Miss Ruby liked having inside information, more than a whole bushel of tomatoes, and she questioned me closely on Nicola's death. After I told her what I knew—omitting how I'd come on Nicola to begin with —I asked how she came to take Nicola under her wing.

"Too many of these girls here don't have any respect for any other human being on the planet. Nicola came from a country where old people are treated with respect—someplace near Japan, which is probably the reason why. She saw how my shoulders and neck bother me after talking on that phone for six hours, and she used to rub the knots out for me. Of course I tried to help her in a few little ways myself."

While Miss Ruby talked, I wondered if perhaps Nicola had never made it to Coolis Hospital. Maybe Captain Ruzich had her taken to Chicago directly from the prison. No, that didn't work—the floor head at the hospital's prison wing clearly had known about Nicola. Unless she'd been primed to say Nicola had been on the ward when she wasn't?

"I need to find someone who will tell me what went on in the shop the day Nicola left here. Or I need to get a job working over there."

Miss Ruby grunted. "You can't get girls to talk about what goes on in the clothes shop. Of course everyone around here is more or less scared, the guards can take away your commissary privileges or your phone calls or put you in seg. But the girls in the clothes shop, they don't talk to anyone. And of course, for the most part they don't speak English anyway."

"So if I wanted to get into the clothes shop, I'd have to be a foreigner."

"First, you have to lose at your trial. The jail girls, they get kitchen duty and other ugly stuff, but they don't ever get the jobs that pay anything decent."

"I really need to see the inside of that shop," I said, looking across the room. CO Polsen was in the doorway, eyeing me in a way I didn't like, but I willed him out of my mind. "How much would it cost, and who could arrange it for me?"

"What's your real business here, Cream?" Miss Ruby asked softly.

I continued to look ahead, speaking as she did, out of the side of my mouth. "I want to see Robert Baladine destroyed. If I can learn what happened to Nicola, I may find a way to make him . . . well, sorry he ever crossed my path."

"If revenge is what you want to eat for dinner, you're going to get yourself a bad case of indigestion. It never pays, believe me, Cream. I tried that meal for a lot of years, before Jesus showed me a better way."

She paused, as if waiting for me to say amen, sister, or ask for her conversion story, but even for her help I couldn't pretend to a faith I don't own.

Disappointed at my lack of interest, she finally said, "No one wants the jobs in the clothes shop; the stories on how they treat the girls over there are too unpleasant. So I never heard of anyone bribing her way in before—usually they're crying to get out. And most of them sleep and eat together, too. So if you want to get in, well, Lieutenant Dockery, she's in charge of the work details, and no one ever gave her a bribe in their life: she's strict but fair. But Erik Wenzel—he's in charge of the shop—he's another kettle of fish. And he's not a CO, he's some manager they hired, like they do for my reservations work—someone who knows how the job is supposed to be done. Give me a day or two. I'll see what I can find out."

She tapped my arm with a manicured finger. "You don't know how to behave here, Cream. Maybe you're the toughest bitch on your block in Chicago, but that makes you a challenge to the CO's: they want to break you. There are no secrets in Coolis. And the CO's know them, too. There's always some girl willing to tattle to them in exchange for some favor, a better work assignment, or real makeup—you notice how most of the girls here are black, but the makeup in the commissary is made for whites? Which, by the way, you can wear with your skin, but most of us can't. So if you can come up with some carmine nail polish and lipstick for me, it would make me move faster on your strange request.

"Anyway, what I'm trying to tell you, Cream, Troy Polsen is a bad man, but don't go beating him up. The satisfaction you'd get wouldn't be worth it. You'd land in segregation, and you'd never get out of it, so you'd go to your trial in prison clothes, and you know how that will look. Watch yourself, Cream."

Polsen yelled to Jorjette and me that we were due in the kitchen. "You're not on vacation here; move those lazy buns."

"Exquisite manners," I murmured. "It's either that or the cuisine that keeps me coming back. I appreciate the warning and the offer of help, Miss Ruby. I don't want to look a gift horse in the mouth, but . . ." I let my voice trail away suggestively.

"Why am I helping you? You don't need to know everything about my life." She smiled suddenly. "This I'll tell you for nothing: I have a big bone of curiosity. My mama always said it would be the death of me, but I want to know what goes on in that shop myself. I have to spend another eight years in this building. I hate there being stuff about it I don't know."

Polsen came over and yanked me roughly to my feet. "Come on, Princess Di, they want you at Buckingham Palace."

As he shoved me toward the corridor I couldn't help wondering if my own bone of curiosity would be the death of me.

40

Sewing Circle

*M*ANNACCIA!*"* I SWORE. *"Puttana machina!"*

My fingers had once more slipped on the stretchy fabric so that the armholes puckered up. While I used the little clippers to pull the threads out, I flexed my shoulders, trying to ease out the knots in my neck as well. None of the women around me stopped or looked up. They were tied to the whirring machines, working on jackets and leggings, their fingers moving so fast the movement of arms, fabric, and needle was a blur of motion.

"Hey, you, Victoria!" Erik Wenzel suddenly stood in front of me. "I thought you said you knew how to run this machine. *Sabes usar esta máquina.*"

When they spoke Spanish, the men always used the familiar form of *you.* I said in Italian how insufferable Wenzel's manners were, then added in Spanish, *"Sí, sí, se usarla."*

"Then act like you can *fabricar.*" He snatched the shirt from my fingers, ripping it in two, and slapped my head. "You've destroyed this shirt so it can't be used. *La arruinaste!* It comes out of your pay. *No te pago por esta!*"

It had taken almost my whole four hundred dollars cash to get here; so far all I'd learned was that in a prison shop the foreman can do whatever he damned well wants. Miss Ruby managed somehow to spread the money among CO Rohde in the jail wing, his counterpart in the prison wing, and one of Erik Wenzel's subordinates who put together the work rosters for the clothes shop. She told the man that I was a fragile immigrant far from home and she thought kitchen work might kill me. Miss Ruby got a Revlon lipstick and compact, and they weren't easy to come by either.

I hoped I never had to depend on sewing to pay my bills. I thought it would be a cinch to run one of those machines, and I thought it would be a holiday after the misery of working in the prison kitchen, but after four days all I had to show were a permanent knot in my shoulders and neck, bruised and bleeding fingers from getting in the way of the needle, and three dollars and twenty-four cents in earnings, which wouldn't be paid into my trust account until the end of the week.

We got paid by the piece: nine cents for T-shirts, which were the easiest to assemble, fifteen cents for shorts, thirty-three for the heavy denim jackets. Some of the women were so fast they could make nine or ten jackets an hour. One of my neighbors was turning out thirty-two T-shirts an hour.

When I started, one of the women was detailed to show me how to assemble a shirt. She put one together at lightning speed, unwilling to slow down her own production to show a newcomer the ropes. I had followed her moves as best I could. By the end of the second day, I had worked out how to do eighteen an hour, but of those only ten or so met the quality-control standards; the ruined ones got deducted from my pay. And if Wenzel was angry at a woman—as he was with me—he would deliberately destroy a garment and then deduct the cost from her pay. One thing about prison labor: there is no shop steward or Labor Department to take a grievance to. If the foreman is pissed off at you and wants to spit at you or slap you or destroy your output, there's not a lot you can do about it.

In a twist of irony, we sewed little tags into the shirts that read *Made with Pride in the USA*. So I had learned one thing—that the shirts in the commissary were made in the prison, although the ones we sewed were all plain white. Maybe they were shipped to one of the men's prisons for the Mad Virgin or Captain Doberman to be embroidered onto them.

In an adjacent room, women operated heavy shears to cut out the pieces to the garments we were sewing. A pair of runners went between the cutting room and the sewing room, bringing us the raw materials for construction.

We got two ten-minute breaks in our six-hour shift, with half an hour in the dining hall, but most of the women except the smokers preferred to work through their breaks. As Miss Ruby had said, the crew here were all foreign, primarily Hispanic but with a handful of Cambodian and Vietnamese women.

Also as Miss Ruby had said, most of the women in the clothes shop were housed together. They arrived in a group in the morning, were escorted to the dining hall or commissary in a group, and were taken off together to a separate floor at night. I hadn't been moved over to their quarters, but I was closely monitored now by the CO's. So closely that I decided I had better speak only Italian, or my fractured Spanish, from now on, even in my cell.

My withdrawal from English made Solina and the

crowd begging for letters at first tearful, and then furious. In revenge, Solina started smoking heavily in the cell, as if hoping to provoke me into yelling at her in English instead of Italian. She fell asleep each night with a cigarette burning on the floor beside her, when I would climb down to make sure it was out—I didn't want to go through everything I was enduring only to suffocate in a cigarette fire.

It seemed absurd to think that I could fool the CO's into thinking I wasn't really an English speaker, but I hoped to keep the pretense in place long enough to learn something about Nicola's end. CO Polsen was the likeliest to get me into trouble. When he was on duty in the afternoon, responsible for taking me over for recreation after my work shift ended, he showered me with foul language. When he did that, I treated him as if he were part of the ambient air, but if he tried touching me I would shout loudly—still in Italian—and keep shouting until I could move away from him to a public space. It wasn't a great defense, but it was the only one I could think of. I hoped I learned something useful soon, because I didn't know how much time I'd have before either the women or Polsen decided to take me apart.

In the shop I trailed around with the smokers during our brief breaks, trying to ask them about Nicola or about the clothes—where did they go when we finished them? Illinois law said that anything manufactured in the prisons had to be for prison consumption, but I'd never seen any of these plain shirts or jackets for sale in our commissary. And our—or at least my coworkers'—output was enormous.

It was the size of the production, and the fact that no English speakers were working in the shop, that kept me going, despite my hacked-up hands and the fury that the foreman Erik Wenzel kept unleashing on me.

The other thing that kept me going was a room down the hall where our goods were sent when they were done. Every hour Wenzel and CO Hartigan, the subordinate who'd taken my money from Miss Ruby to give me my assignment, collected our output, inspected it, wrote on a card how much was usable, and stacked the finished goods on a giant trolley. One of the Cambodian women pushed the trolley down the hall to the next room.

My second morning, during the smoking break, I sauntered after her. When the door opened to admit the trolley, I saw a kaleidoscope of lights, machines, and people. Before I could look more closely I was flung hard to the ground. I rolled over, ready to kick my assailant. I actually had my legs scissored, pulling in to strike, before I remembered myself. Wenzel stood over me, his face red with fury, and ordered me back to the workroom in a mix of English and Spanish. His Spanish wasn't any better than mine, but it included an array of crude words for female anatomy that startled me. He wrote me a ticket, my third since coming to Coolis. My tickets could get me put in segregation at any moment, since they were all for offenses that could be construed as physical assaults.

My glimpse into the room had been so fleeting, I couldn't make sense of what I'd seen. How secret could it be if the Cambodian women were allowed into it? Yet my coworkers were so fearful of talking about it that it must be very secret indeed. The only women who worked back there had been given life sentences—that was all I could glean. No one ever talked to them—they were housed in a separate part of the prison.

When I persisted in trying to ask about the room the next morning, the smokers backed away from me in a cluster, as if I were a wolf going after a flock of pigeons. CO Hartigan was a heavy smoker himself; the women eyed him nervously when I talked to them.

"Tu preguntas demasiado," one of the women finally whispered to me when Hartigan had gone into the cutting room to deal with a machine that had stopped working. *"No sigas preguntando por Nicola.* Do not keep asking about Nicola. She learned that her baby was dead, and she wanted to go to Chicago to bury the child. Of course no one would let her leave, but she was mad with grief and began pounding on Wenzel with her tiny hands. He and Hartigan shot her with those guns of theirs that fire electricity, and then they laughed and made sport with her. Now, ask nothing more. For us she never existed, and the guards will punish you severely if they know you are inquiring about her. And they will punish me if they think I remember her."

Her hoarse Spanish was hard for me to follow, but before I could ask her to repeat anything she flinched and tried to duck back into the workroom. CO Hartigan grabbed her arm and then one of her breasts, which he twisted until she gasped in pain.

"You're not talking out of turn, are you?" he asked the woman. "Remember: we know where your little boys are. *Sabemos donde son tus niños.*"

Her eyes were streaming and she spoke pantingly. "Only tell woman, she no have money, no get my cigarette. She lazy, not working, why I think she pay back someday?"

I knew her quick wits were protecting herself, not me, and the look she gave me was one of loathing. Hartigan let her go and slapped me for good measure: I was a lazy cunt, he said, and they weren't going to give me a free ride forever.

Once again I controlled myself in the nick of time. Rage and helplessness were so bottled and boiling inside me, I knew I had to leave Coolis soon; even if the guards didn't harm me I was destroying myself. If I didn't learn something soon that I could use against Baladine, I would forfeit my only chance to understand what was going on in the clothes operation. I had a pretty clear picture at least of why Nicola had gone to the hospital, even if I didn't know how she'd died in Chicago, but it wasn't anything I could use to get her killers arrested.

I didn't want to think about what might have lain behind the woman's phrase that the guards "made sport" with Nicola. I only knew I had to move fast before either my language fraud or my ineptitude with the sewing machine landed me in trouble. How fast I'd have to move was made clear to me on my return to the jail wing that afternoon, when I got a summons to see a visitor.

Morrell stood up on my entrance, an old-fashioned courtesy so remote from the mores of Coolis that I blinked back tears. It was a Thursday; as always midweek, the visitors' room was almost empty.

Morrell squeezed my fingers, a fleeting pressure that the CO in the room overlooked. "You need to leave as soon as possible, Vic."

I agreed, thinking of the abuse I was enduring, and started to detail some of the language and actions of the CO's and the work shift managers.

Morrell cut me short. "That's appalling, Vic, but that isn't what I mean. Things have come unraveled on the outside. Since Baladine left Chicago shortly after your arrest, he apparently didn't know what had happened to you. He's coming back from Europe tomorrow. He knows—or will know when he lands—that you're here. And while you're in Coolis he has the power to have you treated more harshly than you want to imagine."

I shivered involuntarily. "How do you know this?"

He gave a glint of a smile. "I'm a journalist, I have press credentials. I've started being very attentive to Alex Fisher at Global, told her I'm working on a book about the security business."

To my chagrin I felt a stab of elemental jealousy. In the midst of my potpourri of misery and fear, I was picturing the contrast between Alex, with her clear, smooth skin and Rodeo Drive wardrobe, and my own bedraggled condition. Like seducing Murray wasn't good enough for her, she had to take Morrell, too. I muttered something farouche about her being able to make sure he got a good movie deal for his book.

"In that case I'd better get a contract before she reads it. She thinks highly of you, by the way, and says it's a pity your stubbornness gets in the way of your success. I've told her you were out of town, vacationing until your trial, and I don't think she's double-checked that news. And since she's extremely busy, she's been happy to palm me off on her poor overworked assistant. Who's not sophisticated enough to keep news to herself. Like the urgent e-mail Baladine sent Alex yesterday demanding to know your whereabouts after making bail. It will take them this long"—he snapped his fingers—"to learn you're in here. Have you found out what you wanted to know?"

I shook my head. "I've learned some things, but not enough. It seems reasonably clear that Nicola died of injuries she got here, although I don't think I can ever prove that. There's some reign of terror that goes on with the women in the clothes shop where she worked —the foreman today threatened the children of a woman who was talking to me. Whether that's random —there's a lot of vile abuse that goes on here, most of it sexual assault—or whether there's something specific they don't want the women talking about, I don't know. It's mighty peculiar that the only women who work back there can't speak English."

Morrell tapped the table impatiently. "Vic, do I have your permission to go to Freeman and tell him to bail you out as fast as possible? He might be able to appear for you in a Chicago court tomorrow instead of waiting through the weekend."

I rubbed my face, overwhelmed with a desire to lay my head down on the table and cry my heart out. Everything I'd been doing seemed so futile, ever since the night I'd stopped to help Nicola Aguinaldo. My career was in shambles, I was demoralized from my weeks in Coolis, I didn't know any more than I had a month ago about why BB Baladine was gunning for me.

"Yeah, tell Freeman to bail me out. I don't have much time left in here before everything comes unglued for me in here, anyway. Everyone on the jail side knows I speak English, that I was even writing legal letters for some of the women. It won't be long until that word gets over to the creep who runs the clothes shop, and then I'll—well, the best-case scenario is I'll be assigned back to the kitchen."

"Vic, I don't know whether you're heartbreakingly gallant or only out of your mind, but you're worth a dozen of Alex Fisher, with her stock options thrown in besides. Don't do anything too foolish before Freeman can post bail." His lips brushed the back of my hand and he was gone.

CO Polsen wasn't on duty; the woman guard patted me down in a perfunctory way and sent me to my cell to be counted before dinner. I brushed the back of my hand against my cheek. I had one last chance to learn something tangible at Coolis. I don't know if it was gallantry or insanity that was driving me, but the only plan that came to me made me so cold that I lay shivering under my blanket while Solina and her friends marched in formation to the dining hall.

41

Photo Op

IN THE MIDDLE of the night, when I couldn't sleep, I wrote a letter to Lotty. A light in the corridor came through the grated window at the top of our door, projecting a small grid of light on the wall behind our toilet, enough for me to make out the shape of my words on the page without being able to read them.

I wanted Lotty to know how important she'd always been to me, since my student days at the University of Chicago when I'd been not only young but rawly unsophisticated. She took me under her wing and taught me basic social skills I'd missed growing up in a rough neighborhood with a dying mother. Somehow over the years she'd moved from being a kind of fulfillment of my mother to a more equal friend, but she'd never lost her importance for me.

If I am foolhardy, daring without judgment, *I wrote,*
it isn't because I don't love you, Lotty. I hate to bring
you grief, and if I am seriously injured you will grieve.
I don't have an answer to the conundrum. Not the old
masculine swagger that I couldn't love you as much as
I do if I didn't love honor more. Something more restless drives me, a kind of terror that if I don't take care

of things myself I will be left with a terrible helplessness. More than anyone I've ever known, you've kept
that helplessness at bay. Thank you for your years of
love.

In the morning I quickly put it in an envelope without reading it over. On my way to breakfast I handed it
over to CO Cornish for the outbound mail.

The condemned woman's last meal: cornflakes, pow-
dered orange juice, watery coffee, a piece of soggy
toast. At nine, CO Cornish brought me to the gate of
the prison's work wing. There we were counted again
and marched down the hall to our assignments. One
group was escorted to the room of phone banks, where
Miss Ruby and other well-spoken inmates took hotel
reservations for families crossing America on their summer vacations. The rest of us were taken farther down
the hall to the sewing room. We stood at attention
while we were counted for a third time, this time by
Wenzel and Hartigan, and then sent to our machines.

Before I could start on the pile of pieces I had left
over from yesterday, Hartigan grabbed my arm. "You!"
he spat at me in English. For one heart-stopping minute
I thought maybe Baladine had already tracked me down
and given orders to treat me in some unspeakable way.

Apparently it was only my ineptitude as a seamstress
that made Hartigan grab me. In a graphic mix of Spanish and English he explained I was being demoted to a
cutter. The pay there was a flat dollar-thirty an hour,
did I understand?

"*Comprendo*," I said through lips thick with anger.

For the next three hours, with one ten-minute break,
I stood in the cutting room, pinning stencils to thick
stacks of cotton, then holding the stacks in position as

automatic shears sliced through them. It was back-breaking work, made harder by Hartigan's periodic eruption into the room to yell, *"Vamos, más rápido!"*

All last night as I had lain sleepless on my bunk and in the morning as I moved the heavy plastic stencils onto the fabric, I kept rehearsing in my mind what I wanted to do. My chance came at lunchtime. We were allowed to put aside the stencils and turn off the shears just as the Cambodian woman gathered up the previous hour's sewing output onto the trolley. While everyone else moved into formation for lunch, I followed the trolley down the hall in the other direction. As people chattered and milled around stretching their sore arms, neither Wenzel nor Hartigan noticed I was going the wrong way.

The Cambodian woman rang a buzzer in the door. When it opened I followed her inside. In the confused medley of light and noise that greeted me, I couldn't make anything out at first: giant machines, women in Corrections Department smocks, the ratcheting of conveyor belts. It was a major production plant. I moved to a conveyor belt carrying T-shirts.

Lacey Dowell's face stared up at me. Her red hair was artlessly tangled, her lips half-parted in a mischievous smile. The smile was repeated half a dozen times as shirts passed in front of me on the belt. Hot lights overhead made me start to sweat; I realized they were there to dry wet ink—two women operating a giant press on my right were stamping decals onto shirts the Cambodian woman was unloading from the trolley. At a second belt facing me, another pair were stamping Space Beret insignia onto denim jackets.

At the far end of the belts other women pulled the garments off, folded them, and fed them to someone operating a commercial iron. Another pair laid ironed clothes in boxes. I watched in frozen fascination, until a shout behind me galvanized me. I began snapping the stem of my wrist camera, taking pictures as fast as I could, of Lacey's face, of the belt, of women pressing decals onto shirts and jackets.

A man grabbed my arm, yelling, "What the hell are you doing in here? Where did you come from?"

I darted away, trying to snap a picture of the machines themselves, of the workers, of anything where I could get a clear view. The man who'd yelled out at me began to chase me. I ducked under a conveyor belt and skittered on my hands and knees toward the entrance. The women feeding shirts to the iron stopped working and huddled against a wall. Clothes began to pile up and then fall to the floor.

My pursuer tripped on the T-shirts and bellowed for backup. CO Hartigan came through the door on the run. Jackets and shirts tumbled from belts and got tangled in the machinery. Sirens howled and the clanking machines ground to a halt.

I ducked under Hartigan's outstretched arm and pushed open the door, with some foolish hope of pretending I'd gotten turned around and ended up in the room by mistake. Wenzel was on the other side of the door. He seized my arms. I slid my legs around his ankles and with the fury that had been boiling in me for a month, took his feet out from under him. He fell backward, still holding me, but his grip loosened as he fell, and I pulled away, rolling on my side and coming up in a crouch.

Hartigan was facing me, pulling a gun. I twisted away, then suddenly lost control of my limbs. I was shot through the air as from a cannon and careened headfirst onto the pile of jackets. I couldn't breathe. I couldn't move. The skin on my chest stung. My legs were wet, and I smelled urine and burning cloth. My arms and legs jerked spastically.

Hartigan stood over me, a smile of exultant sadism on his face, and lifted one large booted foot. I managed to wrench myself sideways just before he kicked me. His boot sank savagely into my ribs, and then into my skull.

When I woke I was in a dark room. My head pounded violently. I tried to lift a hand to feel my head but I couldn't move my arms. My ribs ached and my stomach heaved. I shut my eyes and passed out again.

I felt a hand on my arm and someone saying, Is she alive? I wanted to pull my arm away but I still couldn't move it. I was alive, someone else confirmed, but I wasn't going anywhere, they could take off the manacles.

"Someone like her will fool you, Hartigan," the first voice said. It belonged to CO Polsen. "Wenzel has a concussion from the blow she gave him. Leave her chained up, that way you'll be sure."

It was the fall, I wanted to say. I took his legs out from under him and he fell. But my jaw hurt and I couldn't speak. Later someone brought me water. I was so grateful tears spurted out the sides of my eyes.

My cousin Boom-Boom had dared me to climb the crane, I tried to tell my mother. And why had I done it, she demanded in Italian. *Do you need to do everything that crazy boy does? What are you trying to prove, that you're a cat who has nine lives?* My father told her to let me be, I had a concussion and two broken ribs and that was punishment enough. *And my punishment,* my mother shouted in English, *if she's taken from me in*

*one of these crazy exploits you and your brother laugh
at, I will never survive it.*

I thought it would be safe now to open my eyes,
because my father would be smiling down at me, but
when I opened them I was in a cell—not the one I
shared with Solina—one with a single bed in it. I heard
a sharp snap. The pounding pain had subsided to a
muted throb and I could move my head. I saw the door,
with a window in the top and an eye bulging as it
peered at me. There was a second snap as a shutter slid
across the window, leaving me once more in darkness.

I kept dozing off into phantasmagoric dreams, where
I was eight or nine or ten, with my mother as she made
me practice scales until my arms hurt so much I begged
her not to make me do music anymore, or with Boom-
Boom at a Fourth of July picnic where the fireworks
made my head ache and tears run down my cheeks. The
fireworks smelled, too, like some kind of horrible un-
cleaned toilet.

The snapping shutter roused me periodically. I could
move my arms now, but the pain in my ribs and gut
was so great I didn't move them much. I was alternating
between drenching sweats and chills so violent they
caused a rattling at my feet. I thought my bones were
clanking, but when I tried to sit up to look at my feet,
the pain in my stomach stabbed me brutally. I cried out
and lay back down. Once when the shutter opened I
had a flash of awareness: my legs were manacled together. It didn't matter—I was in too much pain to
walk anywhere. I shut my eyes again.

Someone asked again if I was still alive. I knew the
voice, but my mind floated off. She's not in good shape,
a second man answered. She stinks, the first voice said.
She'll be in back, Polsen, you won't smell her once you

get her inside. Wenzel can't drive; you'll have to come along. Put on some gloves and a mask. Change her shirt; we don't want to get into the mess we had with the other one, having to come up with a clean shirt because this one's got burn marks on it.

CO Polsen. He was tearing off my shirt; he was going to treat me the way he had that other woman, and I was powerless to stop him. I would not cry I would not give him the satisfaction I would not cry when he touched the raw skin on my breasts. I was jerked upright, and the pain across my abdomen was so ferocious I blacked out. Then I was sick and my father was carrying me, but he was too rough, he was hurting me, my head and my stomach.

"No, Papa," I begged. "Put me down."

That made him laugh, and I cried for my mother but she couldn't hear me. When he finally put me down it was on something hard, not my bed. *"Mio letto,"* I sobbed. *"Voglio mio proprio letto."* He slapped my face and shut the door on me, and I remembered it hurt his feelings when I spoke Italian, because he didn't speak it himself. "I want my own bed," I repeated in English, but it did me no good, he started shaking the room from side to side so that my sore ribs and stomach bounced against the hard floor.

I kept passing out. I would come to when an extra-fierce jolt flung me against the floor. At some point the jolting stopped and the door opened. I had another brief moment of clarity: I was in a panel truck, lying on packing cartons. A couple of men approached me. I couldn't protect myself as they seized me. They tossed me on the ground and slammed the van door shut. Polsen called me a stupid cunt and said this would teach me to mind my own business and then they left me on

the ground and returned to the truck. The back door
swung open as they drove off and several boxes
bounced onto the road.

I saw now how Nicola Aguinaldo got out of prison
and made it back to Chicago. And died.

42

Slow Mend

I LOOKED UP and saw the machine that made decals ready to push into me. My arms were manacled to the bed and I couldn't lift them to guard my face. A man leaned over me. I didn't want CO Polsen to know I was scared, but I couldn't help crying out. The man called me "cookie" and seemed to be weeping. I shut my eyes and fell back asleep.

The next time I woke I realized the machine was the arm holding an IV drip. I wasn't wearing manacles but had lines running into both arms and an oxygen tube in my nose. A woman was feeling my left wrist. She had on a yellow sweater and smiled when she saw me watching her.

"You're all right, you know. You're with friends, so don't worry: you're not in prison and you're going to recover."

I looked at my wrist. It was empty. I didn't have my watch, my father's watch that he'd worn for twenty-five years.

I croaked something and she said, "Your watch didn't come over from the hospital with you. I'll ask Dr. Herschel about it."

This seemed so disastrous to me that I began to cry. The woman in the yellow sweater sat down next to me and wiped my eyes, since I was having trouble moving my arms. The fingers on my right hand were in splints, but both my arms were so sore it seemed like too much work to lift them to wipe my eyes.

"We'll do everything we can to get your watch back to you. Now that you're awake I want to see if you can drink something. You'll recover faster if you can start to eat on your own. As soon as you drink a bit of this, I'll call the hospital about your watch." She cranked the bed up, and I swallowed something sweet.

I croaked again.

"You're in the Grete Berman Institute. Recovering from your injuries."

I knew I had heard of the Grete Berman Institute, but I couldn't remember what it was. I went back to sleep, puzzling over it, but after that I began recovering, drinking more each time I woke, staying awake for longer intervals. Sometimes the man who called me "cookie" was there, and I finally remembered it was Mr. Contreras. I tried to smile and say something so that he'd know I knew him and appreciated his being there; I could just manage to say "Peppy," which made him start to cry again.

Once when I woke, the woman in the sweater handed me my father's watch and helped me strap it onto my wrist. I was relieved to have it back but still felt upset, as if I were missing something of even greater importance. The woman in the sweater urged me to drink miso broth. I was getting stronger—in a few days I'd be able to have rice, and then I'd be strong enough to remember what was troubling me.

I was too tired to think. I gave up worrying about the watch and drifted between waking and eating and struggling upright: the wound in my abdomen made sitting up an exquisite pain. It was only three days, in fact, between my first waking up and my shaky progression from bed to chair and a tour of the hallway, but the pain and the painkillers stretched time's passage in odd ways.

On the day that Mr. Contreras helped me into a chair so that I could eat my rice and watch the Cubs, Lotty came in. Sammy Sosa had just hit his forty-sixth home run, but Mr. Contreras muted the television and with rare tact left us alone.

When Lotty saw me out of bed and in a chair, she burst into tears and knelt with her arms around me. "Victoria. I thought I was going to lose you. Oh, my dear one, I am so thankful to have you back."

Close to her I could see how much gray was in her hair; for some reason that made me cry as well. "I thought you would chew me out."

She blinked back her tears. "Later. When you're strong enough to fight back."

"She mustn't have too much agitation, Dr. Herschel," the nurse said.

Lotty pushed herself to her feet. Despite the gray hair, she still moved with easy agility. I smiled foolishly at her. She didn't stay long but the next evening she returned with Morrell. The two together told me my story.

A state trooper had found me on the Belmont exit ramp to the Kennedy around three on Sunday morning. The boxes that tumbled out of the back of the truck when CO Polsen drove off had saved my life: a motorist, swerving to avoid them, noticed me lying in the road and called the cops. The state troopers rushed me to Beth Israel, where Dr. Szymczyk—the same surgeon

who'd been on call the night I found Nicola Aguinaldo
—patched me together.

I had been luckier than Nicola on several counts.
When Hartigan kicked me, I'd managed to twist away
enough so that my ribs took the main force of his blow.
He had badly bruised my intestine and I had developed
a severe infection, which accounted for my fever, but
when the state trooper found me, the wound had only
just begun to perforate the peritoneum. Nicola already
had such advanced peritonitis when I came on her that
she didn't have much chance for survival.

And then, unlike Nicola, I was in good physical condition and I was used to defending myself, so that despite the jolt from the stun gun—which was what
Hartigan shot me with—I was able to shield myself
from the worst of his blows. I had apparently managed
to put my hands over my head, so that the kick that
knocked me out broke the fingers in my right hand but
didn't do serious damage to my skull.

"You were lucky, Vic," Lotty said. "But you also
don't have the habit of victims."

"But how did I end up here instead of in the hospital? The Grete Berman Institute is for torture victims,
isn't it? That isn't really me."

"I didn't think you should be moved from Beth Israel
until you were more stable, but Morrell persuaded me
that the man Baladine could get access to you in a hospital if he was looking for you. I wanted to bring you to
my home, but the Berman Institute is secure and fully
staffed, so I finally agreed to let you be moved here as
soon as you were out of surgery. But besides that,
you—" Her voice cracked and she steadied it. "You
were in a helpless situation, at the mercy of the law,

shot with an electric weapon, beaten, and then chained to a bed. I think you were tortured, Victoria."

"She needs to rest now, Dr. Herschel," the nurse intervened.

Over the next several days, as I got back on my feet and began to get some exercise in the Berman Institute gardens, Morrell put together the rest of the story for me. He had called Freeman Carter when he got back to Chicago from Coolis that last Thursday, urging him to try to get me a bail hearing in Chicago on Friday; Morrell told Freeman he was worried that Baladine might not let me survive the weekend. Freeman was skeptical at first, but Morrell managed to persuade him.

Freeman spent all day Friday shaking up the judicial system trying to find me. It was three on Friday afternoon before the head of the circuit court granted Freeman permission to post my bail in a Chicago courtroom and have me released that afternoon instead of making us wait until a circuit judge rode out to Coolis on Monday.

At that point, although no one outside the prison knew it, I was already chained to a bed in the segregation wing, with a rising fever. Freeman couldn't get anyone at Coolis to admit to my whereabouts and finally was told that they lacked the administrative personnel to process my release after 5:00 P.M. on Friday, that Freeman would have to come back on Monday.

Freeman went to the state appellate court and got an emergency writ requiring my immediate release. The prison then told him I had faked an injury at my work station and they had put me in the hospital. On Saturday, as my fever rose, they played a shell game with Freeman, passing him between the prison and the hospital, each saying the other had possession of my body.

Of course neither Freeman nor Morrell knew what discussions took place at the prison end of things, but the most likely guess was that the staff panicked. Perhaps they thought I might die, and Freeman was making it clear they would face intense scrutiny if they didn't produce me in good shape. They probably figured they could repeat what had sort of worked for them with Nicola Aguinaldo: dump me in Chicago—where I'd either be hit by a car or die of my wounds—and put out word that I had managed to escape. Morrell showed me the *Herald-Star*'s report.

PRIVATE EYE, HELD ON
KIDNAPPING CHARGE, FLEES COOLIS

For the second time this summer, a woman managed to run away from the experimental jail–prison complex operated by Carnifice Security in Coolis. This time, though, the hue and cry is much louder: the woman in question is notorious in Chicago, being private eye V. (Victoria) I. (Iphigenia) Warshawski. Warshawski had been arrested on charges of kidnapping the son of Carnifice chief Robert Baladine and spent a month in the jail wing at Coolis after failing to post bail.

She was not an easy prisoner, Warden Frederick Ruzich said, often getting involved in fights with other inmates and ignoring orders from corrections officers, whose job includes trying to smooth the adjustment for women new to the Coolis system.

How Warshawski managed to escape may never be known. Her body was found at the foot of the Belmont ramp to the Kennedy. Although she is still alive, she suffered severe brain damage and may never speak again. Dr. Charlotte Herschel, Warshawski's physician at Beth Israel Hospital, says Warshawski is able to breathe on her own, which gives them hope for some partial recovery. She has been moved to a nursing home, but Dr. Herschel declined to tell reporters where.

Warshawski is best known for the work she did in tracking down the murderer of social activist Deirdre Messenger last year, but her successes in investigating white-collar crime have earned her respect from many quarters in Chicago, including the Chicago Police Department.

Robert Baladine, the president of Carnifice Security, is angry at lapses in security at the Coolis complex, which have made escape begin to seem like a routine matter for the inmates. He promised a thorough investigation of security measures at the prison. Illinois House Speaker Jean-Claude Poilevy (R–Oak Brook) says the legislature granted a number of tax breaks to Carnifice to get them to take on the women's prison and expects them to live up to their side of the bargain. (*See Murray Ryerson's story on Page 16 for a summary of Warshawski's most notable cases.*)

The story included a map of Illinois, with a blowup of the northwest corner showing the town of Coolis, the prison, and the roads running to Chicago.

I put the newspaper lethargically to one side. I didn't even care what Murray had to say about me. I had remembered recently what was troubling me about my watch, and it left me feeling so futile that it was affecting my recovery.

"That mini-camera that got me these wounds—it's

disappeared," I muttered to Morrell. "I don't know if they took it off me when they put me in segregation or if it just got lost at the hospital, but it's gone."

Morrell's eyes widened. "V. I.—they were supposed to tell you when they gave you back your father's watch. I have it. I took it to the Unblinking Eye to get the pictures developed. I didn't mention it because they keep telling me not to get you excited, and I thought you'd bring it up when you were ready to look at the pictures. They'll be ready in another day or two."

After that I felt giddy with relief. "Did you and Lotty really think I might never talk again, or was that wishful thinking?"

Morrell grinned. "Alex Fisher from Global kept pumping me, so I thought I'd play it safe. When I told Freeman what she and I said, he thought it was such a good idea that he put it out in a press release. The only people who know the truth besides him and Dr. Herschel are Sal and of course your neighbor. Dr. Herschel thought it would be intolerably cruel to Mr. Contreras to imagine you in such straits. And it gives us some wiggle room to figure out what to do with Baladine and Global Entertainment."

Yes. Baladine and Global Entertainment. I wanted to do something about them, but right now I couldn't imagine what. My first week at the Berman Institute I was too tired and too sore to think about what I'd been through. As I grew stronger physically, I was bewildered by my wild mood swings. At one moment I'd be euphoric over my escape and the knowledge that I had managed to smuggle out pictures; the next I'd see a stranger coming toward me and think it was one of the corrections officers, Polsen or Hartigan. I'd start feeling unbearably helpless, as I had in Coolis, and would find myself moving away as fast as I could, my legs wobbly, as if I expected to be hit again with fifty thousand volts of electricity.

The institute treated many people who had been held longer and in greater duress than I. I felt guilty for taking up room that someone from Rwanda or Guatemala could have used, but the psychologist who met with me twice a week told me the institute didn't see it that way.

"Do you think our doctor shouldn't treat your broken hand because someone else has breast cancer and needs more intense medical attention? You deserve to make the best recovery you can from your experience."

"But the other people here didn't choose to be tortured," I burst out. "I chose to stay at Coolis. If I'd followed my lawyer's advice and made bail, none of the rest would have happened."

"So you blame yourself for your misfortunes. But many of the people here torment themselves in the same way: if I had not gone back to my home that morning, if I had followed my mother's wishes and gone to see her, if I had not signed that petition. We wish we had power over our fates, and so we blame ourselves when something goes wrong. You wanted to stay in Coolis to try to understand what happened to a poor young woman you tried to help. I think that was noble. And you cannot blame yourself for the fact that men—and women—with unlimited power over the lives of others used that power in very sadistic ways. If Coolis were run along humane lines—well, your young friend would not have died to begin with."

I tried to accept his advice, but my dreams were still so shocking that I often dreaded going to sleep. I knew if I could only rest properly, I would recover more rapidly.

"What will help you sleep?" he asked the next time we talked.

"If I could stop feeling so humiliated. I know I can't shut down Coolis. I can't change any prison anywhere in America. All these degradations will go on and on for any woman who lands there, the sex talk and the rape and whatever else. The law makes it almost impossible for a woman to lodge a complaint, and even if she does, the guards have so much power they can stop her voice."

Freeman Carter was filing lawsuits for me—one against the Chicago Police Department for the violence committed against my person and against my office by Douglas Lemour. The other was against the Illinois Department of Corrections for my injuries there. Bryant Vishnikov was studying the OR films of my injuries and thought he might be able to prove they'd come from a particular set of boots. Such as those of the man Hartigan out at Coolis.

"But these cases will take years to work through the courts," I told the Berman psychologist. "By that time I could be out of business and too broke for a settlement to help me. I want Robert Baladine to pay a price now for siccing his bent cop on me and for having me arrested on a trumped-up charge. I want that cop out of the force, and I want Baladine publicly exposed. And of course I need him off my back if I'm ever going to run my business again." Miss Ruby had told me if I wanted to eat revenge it would give me indigestion, but it seemed to me passivity was making me sicker than revenge ever would.

The psychologist didn't exactly endorse my wish: he told me he thought it was helpful to imagine a recovery of my own power and see where that left me.

A recovery of my own power meant I needed to recover my physical fitness. I began working out in greater earnest. Four weeks after I was found on the expressway, I ran a wobbly mile, but after that my strength grew measurably every day. On the Thursday before Labor Day, as the El Niño heat finally subsided into a bearable warmth, I felt ready to move on.

43

Planning Session

I'D DECIDED IT was time to move on, but I wasn't sure where to go. My own apartment would leave me a sitting duck as soon as Baladine learned I'd surfaced. For the same reason, I resisted Lotty's invitation to come home with her: I'd rather be killed than endanger her life one more time in one of my exploits.

It was Morrell who suggested that I spend a week or two in Father Lou's rectory. I kept asking him to make sure he'd discussed it with Father Lou and that the priest understood the potential risk; Father Lou in the end sent me a terse note saying I was welcome as long as I didn't smoke. The kids around the school were used to strange families moving in and out as the priest offered refuge to people who'd been evicted or were seeking sanctuary; they wouldn't blow my cover through idle chatter around the neighborhood. And so the Friday before Labor Day I moved from the modern, warmly furnished rooms of the Berman Institute to a narrow bed under a crucifix and a bathroom holding a badly stained tub and toilet. It was still a big step up from Coolis.

During the weeks I was healing, Morrell or Lotty came to see me almost every day. Lotty brought flowers that well-wishers, believing I was in a brain-damaged stupor, sent to her office. Darraugh Graham, my most important client, sent a miniature orange tree and a note that said if I ever felt able to get back to work he was eager to continue to do business with me. I was touched, and relieved as well, although Morrell, collecting mail from my office, found an ominous number of letters from clients canceling my services. (*We find a large firm such as Carnifice better meets our security needs at this time. . . .*)

Mr. Contreras visited me regularly while I was at Berman. Once he learned he could bring Mitch and Peppy, he'd bundle the dogs into the Rustmobile and drive down, careful to follow Morrell's instructions to keep anyone from tailing him. The dogs helped my recovery. When I ran around the gardens behind the institute with them, I started feeling more like myself.

A bouquet of anemones came with a note from Abigail Trant, wishing me a speedy recovery from all my ailments. After her surprise visit the week before my arrest, I wasn't exactly startled, but I was very pleased.

I saw Mrs. Trant's name in the papers from time to time, especially as the swim meet Eleanor Baladine had organized drew near: the *Herald-Star,* in its new role as shill for Global Entertainment, actually treated the event as front-page news. The meet was to raise money for several children's programs dear to Abigail Trant, Jennifer Poilevy, and Eleanor Baladine. The three women were photographed around Eleanor's pool, looking like beauty queens in their sleekly fitting swimsuits. Tickets were a thousand dollars; anyone with a child under thirteen who wanted to compete should get in touch with Alex Fisher at Global.

Another evening Lotty arrived with an outsize bouquet of scarlet and gold flowers and a letter from Murray Ryerson.

Dear Vic,

I can't believe you're really lying in a stupor. Half of it's denial, and the other half is my sources: they can't find you in any of the nursing homes in the area. So maybe Lotty Herschel will bring you these flowers and my letter.

I'm sorry you were arrested. I'm sorry you spent time in the big house. I don't know how you got out without posting bail, but my compliments: that took some doing. I'm sorriest of all I blew up at you over Frenada's finances. I don't know who or how that strange data got into his LifeStory report, but it was bogus. When his sister tried to access one of the accounts, it turned out there was nothing there. For reasons I haven't been able to find out, Carnifice may have wanted to discredit Frenada. At any rate they certainly have the technical wizardry to plant phony data on Frenada.

Anyway, I want you to know that I tried to do the right thing. I tried to tape a follow-up to my show explaining that I had received erroneous information about Frenada. The station wouldn't allow the tape. I tried to print a story in the *Star,* but the editor blocked it. I've been asked to take a vacation for a few weeks to see if "I can regain a sense of proportion."

If you're alive and well, give me a call. On the other hand, if you're really in danger of your life, V.I., I wish I could see you to tell you I'm sorry. And beg you not to die. I don't think I could keep working in Chicago if you weren't part of the landscape.

Murray

I pinned one of the flowers to my blouse and danced around the Berman gardens with it. I had a moment's euphoric impulse to phone Murray, to relieve his own anxiety. We had worked out some amazing stunts together in the past. But I couldn't afford to take risks right now, even for an old friend. Murray's course this past summer had been too rocky for me to trust him based on one letter.

The day I heard from him was the same day that Morrell brought in the pictures I'd taken at Coolis. There were thirty-three: I hadn't had time to shoot the whole roll. A few showed scenes in the jail, like the time CO Polsen was trying to pull down Dolores's jeans, or the pustular burn on the arm of a woman in the kitchen. Where I'd had time to focus, however surreptitiously, the quality was good enough to make out detail.

Many of the two dozen I'd taken in the back room were blurred because of my nervous flying around the space, but there was one clear shot of Lacey's face on a T-shirt, with a man in an IDOC uniform standing behind it. I had two shots of women operating the stamping machines. And somehow, at the end, I'd photographed Hartigan standing over me with the stun gun pointed down at me. I didn't remember taking it; perhaps his shooting or kicking me had inadvertently clicked the shutter. He was foreshortened by my lying on the floor, with his head, bloated and shining in sadistic pleasure, looming larger than his body. The gun appeared in one corner.

Looking at the picture made me start to sweat. I had to take a walk around the Berman gardens before I could sit down again with Morrell. I felt embarrassed by my weakness.

"What do these pictures show, Vic? Besides the idea of a certain amount of sadism in the prison, I mean."

I'd had a lot of time to think during my recuperation, and I spelled it out slowly, putting the events in order as much for myself as for Morrell. "A prison is a great place to run a factory. Labor is cheap and it's captive: you never have the danger that a union will form or that anyone will protest work conditions. Even if you're paying the workers more than you would in Southeast Asia, you still save money because you don't have any capital costs. The state provides the physical plant. The state buys the machinery. Shipping to the world's biggest market is cheaper than from Thailand or Burma, especially if you're close to the main shipping routes out of Chicago. So Coolis started producing shirts and jackets for Global Entertainment."

He frowned. "It sounds disgusting but not a reason to try to kill you for finding it out."

"Illinois law. You can only make things in prison for sale in the prison system. Baladine and Teddy Trant at Global are good friends. When Baladine started running Carnifice Security and got the bid to build and run Coolis, the two of them probably saw what great potential there was in the captive workforce. The two men are very tight with the Speaker of the Illinois House. Poilevy ran a special legislative session exclusively on crime a couple of years ago. I think he probably promised Baladine that for enough money sprinkled around the right way he could overturn the law, but labor balked. Usually they do pretty much what the Speaker says, but they wouldn't budge on this one, because they'd face a rebellion from the rank and file if they undercut real jobs in the state."

Morrell fiddled with the photographs. "I still don't get it. Did Baladine have his nanny arrested simply to send another body to the prison factory?"

"No. That was one of those things. Nicola was arrested for stealing. She was tried, and sentenced, and ended up in the clothes shop because she was small with quick little fingers and because she didn't speak much English and the prison tries to keep discussion of the operation to a minimum. They intimidate the women who work in the clothes shop and try to keep them separate from the rest of prison population. I discovered early on that women were scared to work in the clothes shop, even though they could make better money for piecework than they could at some of the other gigs.

"Then Nicola learned her little girl had died of asthma, the same little girl whose hospital bills put her in so much debt that she stole the necklace to begin with. She wanted to see the dead child herself and bury her, and they laughed at her. She lost her head and pounded her little fists on this guy's chest—" I flicked my middle finger against Hartigan's face. "He shot her with a stun gun. He kicked her. Her intestine perforated. They shut her in segregation, then they got scared and sent her to the hospital. I'm guessing the hospital said she needed expensive surgery to fix her up and even then she might well die. They thought if they dumped her body near her apartment, they could pretend she'd run away and been killed at home."

My voice became drier and drier, more and more impersonal as I tried to keep from feeling anything about the narrative. Morrell put a hand in mine, giving me a chance to draw away if I wanted to: it's one of the things they train you in at the Berman Institute. Let people have plenty of room to get away if they're nervous about being touched. I squeezed his fingers gratefully, but I needed to get up, to be in motion. We went back to the garden and talked while I restlessly moved around the late-flowering bushes.

"When they got Nicola to Chicago they saw that the stun gun had singed her shirtfront. In case the medical examiner noticed the burn holes during an autopsy, they stripped off her clothes and put on a Mad Virgin T-shirt—I'm pretty sure one that Lucian Frenada had made on spec for Global."

I explained to Morrell what I had learned about Frenada and Trant the night I'd been at Father Lou's, right before my arrest, that Frenada had made some shirts for Global and had argued both with Lacey and Trant over what became of them.

"He claimed Trant had stolen one, and Lacey laughed it off. I did, too—why would a Global boss steal a shirt when he could get a dozen of them free anytime he wanted? But the ones Trant could get all had a label reading *Made with Pride in the USA*, a kind of *Arbeit macht frei* label we had to sew into the necks of the T-shirts we made. Why they wanted a Mad Virgin T-shirt on Nicola I don't know—maybe Trant had a crazy idea that they could finger Frenada for the murder if anyone was asking questions. Everything they did had a B-movie feel to it; it was just the thing that a studio executive would come up with. Or maybe it was Alex Fisher's idea.

"When they thought I was dying they took my damaged shirt off in the cell and put on another one. They made some comment about it at the time. Even though I kept blanking in and out, I was aware of what was going on, although at the time, it didn't make sense."

Before my arrest, I had wondered if Frenada had something to do with Nicola Aguinaldo's death, but during a wakeful night at Coolis I remembered the sequence of conversations we'd had. It was when I asked him how a shirt he made came to be on her body that Frenada suddenly became quiet, then hung up on me. The night that Robbie saw him in Oak Brook, Frenada had gone out to confront Trant and Baladine. The trouble was, I couldn't prove that Baladine killed Frenada— I could only guess it. I asked Morrell if Vishnikov's autopsy had turned up anything unusual.

"Oh, that's right: we've had so much else to talk about I forgot about that," Morrell said. "Frenada definitely died by drowning. Vishnikov says he had a blow on the side of the head that could have come from slipping on the rocks by the harbor—he got it before he died, and that might have been why he went into the water. Other contusions had appeared postmortem."

I scowled. "He was out at the Baladine estate the night he died. Robbie saw him there and later overheard a most suggestive remark from Trant, something about that taking care of the problem. I think they drowned Frenada in the pool and carted him off to Lake Michigan, but I guess that didn't show up on autopsy."

Morrell shook his head. "After you asked me to go back to him, Vishnikov did a really thorough study of every organ in the body, but he says there's no way to prove whether he drowned in fresh or chlorinated water."

I started shredding the wilted flower in my button-hole. "If I can't pin something substantial on that bas-tard, I'm not going to be able to work again. I can't prove he killed Frenada. I can testify to someone some-where about the shirts, but I can't prove they're running a factory out in Coolis either. That is, I can't prove they're selling the shirts and jackets and whatnot out-side the prison system, not without a huge amount of effort."

"What would it take to prove it?" Morrell asked.

"Oh, the grubby kind of detective work we used to do in the days before we could check everything out on-line. Watching for service vans like the one that carted me off, follow them, see which ones contain Global products, where they get dropped off. You could proba-bly bribe the drivers and shorten the process, but it would still take weeks. And then there'd be hearings, and somehow during that time I'd have to come up with money to live on, not to mention money to fund the investigation. It would be easier if I could get Baldine to confess."

Morrell looked at me in astonishment. "You don't really think you could do that, do you? That kind of guy won't. His self-image, his need to be the top dog—"

While he was talking I was imagining the way Baldine had come after Frenada and me: trying to plant cocaine in both our shops, arresting me for kid-napping, planting phony data on the Internet about Frenada's finances. Baldine wasn't just a high-tech op-erator; he liked to get his hands dirty. But I began to see a way in which I could use his technology to make the

confession happen. Was I going to be foolhardy once
again? To be daring without judgment? In a way, I
didn't care. I had been through the fiery furnace; I had
been badly burned, but I had survived. No harms that
befell me in the future could be as bad as the ones I had
already endured.

"I have an idea." I interrupted Morrell abruptly.
"But I'm going to need a little help."

44

Diving in with the Sharks

THE BALADINE INVITATIONAL swim meet drew a respectable crowd. Morrell dropped me twenty yards from the front gate. It stood open but was protected by uniformed members of Carnifice Security's private security division. I joined a line that spilled into the road, standing between a couple of small girls arguing over a gym bag and two well-coiffed men discussing baseball. We crawled forward as guards checked tickets with a handheld scanner. They ran the scanner over my media pass and looked into my briefcase but saw only videocassettes and a notebook. Another man handed out maps and programs. He directed me toward the pool, where a special tent had been set up for media, with refreshments.

"And you can use the bathroom off the kitchen, ma'am. The public and swimmers are using the facilities in the cabana."

It felt good to be called "ma'am" by a member of the Carnifice organization. I thanked him genially and mingled with the crowd going up the drive. I wasn't exactly in disguise, but hoped that a wide-brimmed hat and the fact that no one expected to see me would protect me. I skirted the drive, clogged with SUV's and the occasional actual car, and moved around to the back of the house, where the crowd was thicker.

In the media tent I got the press packet marked for Morrell but ducked back outside before I had to get into idle chitchat with anyone. Alex Fisher's hapless assistant was there; I didn't want her questioning me on where Morrell was. Besides, I had recognized several reporters I knew, and it would take only about three sentences before they'd realize it was my face behind the big hat and sunglasses. I planned to talk to them all soon enough, but it would be disastrous if they saw me now.

Thirty-two children were entered in the contest, I read in my packet. The meet was divided into different heats for children of different ages and abilities. Swimming was scheduled to start at one, but the Carnifice and Global sponsors had plenty of entertainment lined up for both before and after. Lacey Dowell was supposed to make an appearance, and the first three Virgin films were being shown in a tent behind the garage.

The event had grossed sixty-seven thousand dollars to be shared by three charities dedicated to children with disabilities, inner-city children, and children's athletic programs. Carnifice Security and Global Entertainment had each contributed ten thousand dollars. It was a nice mediagenic event, and plenty of media was swarming about.

"Jennifer! They want us inside in five minutes to do a press conference."

It was Eleanor Baladine, speaking so close to me I jumped. She was on the other side from me of a large shrub with spiky leaves. I sipped my Malvern water thoughtfully and kept an eye on the flash of turquoise linen, which was all I could see of her.

"I'm annoyed with Abigail," Eleanor continued. "She says Rhiannon got tired of swimming when we were in Limoux and doesn't want to compete. I wish she had said something before we had the programs printed: I tried telling her how bad it looks for one of the organizers to withdraw her own daughter from competition. I thought it was ridiculous the way she kept running off with her daughter to Toulouse for little shopping trips, as if they were girlfriends together. My girls were in the pool six hours a day and loved every minute of it."

"But you're so intense, Eleanor," Jennifer Poilevy said. "Not everyone has your drive. Of course your girls inherited your competitive spirit. It's a shame about poor Robbie, but I do wish you and BB had brought him to France with you. He might have kept the twins from terrifying me with their climbing and jumping. Half the time we were there, I was scared they were going to be brought in on stretchers."

"We certainly never have to worry about that with Robbie," Eleanor said dryly.

"Eleanor—there you are." Baladine had come up to the women from the other side of the house. The sound of his voice woke in me such a frenzy of hatred and of helpless rage that I had to move away before I blew my cover by leaping through the shrubbery and strangling him.

Before I got out of earshot I heard Baladine say, "Did your sister say anything about visiting Robbie at Camp Muggerton on Friday? Major Enderby called to say the boy's Aunt Claudia took him out for dinner and got him back after lights-out."

My stomach jumped. I hadn't expected the camp commandant to check up on a family visitor. That meant I had to move as fast as possible.

I scurried past the media tent into the kitchen, since the bathroom we media folk were allowed to use was there. Rosario the nanny was washing glassware while caterers assembled monstrous platters of shrimp, mushroom tartlets, and other delicacies. The contrast to the kitchen at Coolis, where roaches crawled over congealing piles of grease, and women swore at each other as they lugged dented pots around, made my anger start to boil again. When a waiter offered me a tray of salmon tartare with a perfect circle of caviar in the middle, I turned him away with more fury than manners.

The bathroom stood next to a swinging door leading into the body of the house. I pushed on it—anyone could make a mistake—and a Carnifice guard sprang to life in the hall beyond. He saw my green media badge and said, "House is off-limits to guests, ma'am. If you're looking for the bathroom it's next to this door. And don't you want to be at the press conference? It's starting in two minutes."

I murmured an apology and slipped into the bathroom. The first swim heat would start immediately after the press conference. It was the one for the littlest children, in which the Baladines' younger daughter was competing. Both Eleanor and BB would be at the pool for that, or at least Robbie had seemed to think so. "They'll both want to see the girls beat everyone else, or if they lose, BB and Eleanor will want to show them everything they did wrong. They love that kind of stuff."

He told me that at dinner Friday evening. When he came into the visitors' room at Camp Muggerton on lagging steps, his head down, I felt an uncomfortable parallel to the visitors' room at Coolis, but when he saw me his face lit up.

I had been afraid he'd blow my cover out of surprise, but after a moment's confusion he said, "Oh, I thought —oh, it's you, Aunt Claudia."

Over chicken and mashed potatoes at a diner in Columbia, he begged me to take him away. I wished I could but told him that would put real teeth into his father's kidnapping charge and I might not manage an acquittal.

He started crying, apologizing between sobs, but Camp Muggerton was a miserable place, the hazing was horrible, he couldn't get anything right, he was always last at everything. And they were on strict orders about his diet, did I know that?

I knew that—Major Enderby had stressed it when I was sent to his office for a visitor's pass. The major was pleased to see a family member paying a visit: most of the boys were home for the holiday weekend, and young Robert felt left out, having to stay in camp, but Commander and Mrs. Baladine thought it better he not be put in the way of the temptation of a big party. I gave my most dazzling smile and nodded gravely when the major told me Robbie was not allowed fat or sweets of any kind—so no Big Macs and shakes, ma'am.

I said that Robbie's weight was a trial to the whole family and everyone wondered where it came from. Certainly not my sister's and my side, although Commander Baladine's mother had been a plump little woman.

I told Robbie about the conversation while helping him decide whether he wanted caramel or chocolate

sauce on his sundae. He had lost weight, his soft chub-
biness replaced by something worse, a kind of gaunt
hunger.

"You've lost weight too, Ms. Warshawski. Was that
because of being in jail? Was jail as horrible as this
camp? You don't want ice cream?"

I'm not much of a sweets eater, but I got a cone to
keep him company. As we ate our ice cream, Robbie
sketched a plan of the Baladine house for me—where
Baladine's study was, where the controls for the house
security system were, and where the surveillance cameras were trained. I had explained I wanted to know
because it had to do with Nicola's death.

"But I want to use the information to—well, in part
to get your father to stop trying to destroy me and my
business, and in part to pay him back for the miseries I
endured in the prison he runs. I want you to think carefully before you betray your parents to me."

His tear-streaked face contorted in angry hurt.
"Don't start preaching the Ten Commandments to me
like they do here. I know I'm supposed to honor my
father and mother, but how come they never think of
me? It's like there's something horrible wrong with me,
I know they wish I'd disappear on them, I wish I could,
I wish I was strong enough to kill myself."

I gave him what awkward consolation I could—not
that deep down his parents really loved him, but that
deep down he was a fine and unusual person and that
he needed to hold on to that idea. After we had talked
for a time, I was relieved to see him start to look happier. I asked him if he wanted more time to think over
what I wanted to do, but he said it was fine with him, as
long as Utah didn't get hurt.

"She's kind of a brat, but I like her."

"I don't think anyone's going to get hurt. Not physi-cally, anyway, although I'm hoping your father may have to find a new job, perhaps in a different city. That may be hard on your mother."

He ate another ice cream while he helped me draw up plans of the interior of the house. Afterward we sat and talked, about life and what could lie in store for him after he outgrew Eleanor and BB. I hadn't noticed the shadows drawing in on the town; we were going to be late for taps. I bustled Robbie into the rental car and drove like mad for the camp.

Before dropping him at the guardhouse I gave him a handful of twenties. "This is enough for bus fare from Columbia back to Chicago, if you decide you can't stick it out here any longer. Sew it into the waistband of your shorts, but for pity's sake, don't use it until I know if your dad is going to drop the kidnapping charge. Or until after my trial, whichever comes first."

The escape hatch seemed to breathe a little bit of optimism into him. I apologized to the guard for mak-ing my nephew late and begged him not to blame Rob-bie: I had gotten lost, and that wasn't the boy's fault. I had thought another dazzling smile would take care of matters, but now here was Major Enderby calling the Baladines to tell them Aunt Claudia had violated lights-out.

I waited in the kitchen bathroom until I heard the loudspeaker heralding the start of the swim meet. The bathroom had a second door, locked right now, that led into the maid's room. It took about fifteen seconds to pick that lock. I moved quickly, in case Rosario was getting a break while the swimming started, only stop-ping for a moment in front of a tin icon to the Virgin of Guadalupe, which was nailed over the prim single bed.

I whispered a little plea for protection, although perhaps the Virgin would feel that not even Baladine's iniquities warranted protecting an intruder.

The back stairs led to Utah's and Madison's bedrooms and their playroom. On the other side of the playroom was a hall leading to Baladine's home office. I studied the location of the monitoring cameras in the bedrooms, playroom, and hall on my pencil map and ducked around the lenses, creeping into Baladine's office on my hands and knees.

Robbie said the system was voice- and motion-activated. My hands and knees rustling on the carpet wouldn't turn it on, but a cough might.

Inside Baladine's office, I crawled along the edge of the room and came to the desk from behind. Lying flat, I stuck up an arm and found the switch for his in-office video monitor and turned it off. I got to my feet and held my breath. After a couple of minutes, when no security guards appeared, I relaxed enough to look around.

I found myself listening tensely for noise. The house was well soundproofed, and the cheers from the pool came through as only a faint echo. I might have half an hour; I needed to control my nerves and make the most of it.

The room held everything a manly man wanted in his home office, from the buttery black leather couch in a window alcove to the electronics on the zebrawood desk, which included a shredder, a fax, a scanner, and a videophone.

I switched on the computer, covering my hand with a Kleenex—I thought it would be impossible to explain away rubber gloves if someone came in on me. The system came up and asked for a password. Baladine's ship number was what Robbie thought his father would use. When that didn't let me in I tried the name of the ship. Bingo. To get into Carnifice files I needed another password. I tried the ship ID again, but the machine preferred his service dates.

I called up the home-security system and set the hall camera to appear in a split screen of the computer. That would give me a little advance warning if Baladine was coming. I checked the doors on the far side of the room. One led to a closet, another to a bathroom, and a third to the far hallway.

I logged on to the e-mail server and called up the list of clients. Five of my own former clients had little stars by their names; Darraugh Graham had a question mark. I had memorized what I wanted to say and typed quickly, nervously proofreading and correcting my text. Did I want to send to the entire recipient list? I did.

Next I typed in my own media list and composed another message. When I'd e-mailed my media list I breathed more easily. I deleted all the messages, both from the out-box and from the trash file, so that Baladine wouldn't know from looking at his mailbox that someone had been using the server. Even if he found me now, I'd done enough to cause him some discomfort.

Just as a precaution I copied his home-security file onto a floppy, copied his client list onto another floppy, then, while I was still logged on to his network, started looking through his in-box for any messages that might be about me.

The searches had taken too much time. I was sweating, wondering if I'd better pack up and go, when I saw Baladine and Alex Fisher appear on the hall camera. I turned off the machine, grabbed my floppies, and dived into the closet at the back of the room. My heart was pounding so hard, I thought the closet door must surely vibrate in rhythm with it.

The two came into the room, talking in such low tones all I could make out was the murmur of their voices. Sweat began soaking my shirtsleeves as I imagined a telltale floppy or tissue alerting them to an intruder.

I didn't know whether to laugh or scream when I realized that Baladine and Alex hadn't come up to look at his computer, but to grab time together while Eleanor was focused on the pool, although I had one bad moment when Baladine spoke loudly enough for me to hear, saying he didn't remember switching off his office camera. After twenty minutes of frenzied thrashing on the leather couch and the murmured endearments of one barracuda for another, a hand grasped the closet doorknob.

It opened a crack, but Baladine said, "No, no, my dear, bathroom's the other door—that's just a supply closet."

Alex, sloppy Alex, didn't close the door all the way. "I need to get back downstairs, BB. I just got beeped— that means Lacey Dowell's limo is coming up the drive, and Teddy will want me on hand for her. She's been temperamental since Frenada died, and we don't want her going off half-cocked to some reporter."

"Like Ryerson?" Baladine said.

"Ryerson was a newspaperman from day one. I shouldn't have let him persuade Teddy he could handle television—he was in way over his head. Although we still haven't found anyone who can handle that 'Behind Scenes in Chicago' segment. Anyway, as the man said, enough of this lovemaking—on with your clothes."

"Want to see the replay on television while you dress?"

"You have a camera back here? God, I thought Teddy Trant was infatuated with his body, but not even he videos himself in the act."

"I'm infatuated with your body. This is so I can watch it over and over."

"Right, BB. I'll take that. I don't need to see myself on the Net, and you're just the kind of guy to make that kind of use of a tape."

They had a few more minutes grappling, with Baladine laughing and then cursing at her for being a damned bitch. I wasn't an Alex fan, but I hoped that meant she'd wrested the tape from him. Then a sound of hand on flesh and a furious outburst from Alex. I put my eye on the crack in the door. Baladine had Alex's left arm twisted back and was putting pressure on her wrist. Her face was contorted in pain and she dropped the tape.

He laughed and said, "I thought you'd see it my way, my dear. But don't worry, I won't share you with the Internet. The world at large can't appreciate you the way I do."

She swore at him but finally left when Eleanor phoned up to say Lacey was here and they were trying to find Alex. The door shut behind her. Baladine washed off noisily in the bathroom, humming "Anchors Aweigh." In another minute he was gone as well.

By then I was so shaken that I was tempted to quit with what I had—but I didn't know when I'd ever have another chance like this one. I turned off his personal camera again and went back to the computer. Shutting it off without exiting properly had made it unhappy; I had to wait an extra five minutes while it examined all its files. While it cycled through itself, I looked around for the tape he'd just made. He'd left it on the bathroom sink. I shrugged and slipped it into my pocket.

Finally I got back to Baladine's e-mail server and went to his in-box. In June, on the date I'd been in Georgia, I found someone calling himself *Shark* at AOL reporting on *successful drop-off.*

Subject out of town. 3 packs of Colombian Gold successfully deployed in location 1, 4 others at location 2.

My stomach so tight that my incision started to ache, I copied all of Baladine's correspondence with Shark. I logged off the Web and went into his data files to search for any material about me, or Shark. I found his detailed report from LifeStory and reports on the surveillance of my apartment. These files identified Shark as D.L. Not that I needed an acronym to tell me it was Douglas Lemour, but I was pleased that Baladine hadn't felt a need for real secrecy.

As recently as three days ago, D.L. reported a cruise around my neighborhood to make sure I hadn't surfaced. He was also looking at Lotty's place off and on *as the safe house the subject usually chooses.* I scrolled quickly through the rest of the file and came to an expense report. Five thousand dollars to D.L. for security work. It didn't seem like enough of a payoff for the amount of misery he'd caused me.

My heart was starting to beat too hard to focus on the screen. I copied the file and shut the system down. It was high time I was gone.

On a shelf in the closet where I'd waited out Alex and Baladine, he kept cassettes from the video monitor. After his byplay with Alex, I was curious to see them. I pulled one from the last month Nicola had worked here, another from six months previously. I peeled off the labels, stuck them on the blank cassettes I'd brought with me, and put the blanks in the empty slots.

I was halfway down the hall when I remembered Frenada. I counted dates frantically on my fingers. Even though I didn't have a third blank to use as a replacement, I ran back to the study and took the tape for two weeks before July Fourth. As I was leaving the second time, I remembered to switch Baladine's vanity recorder back on. I hurried down the hall again, through the girls' playroom, past acres of Barbies and stuffed animals, and down the stairs to the kitchen. I stopped briefly in Rosario's room to thank the Virgin of Guadalupe.

I'd been upstairs ninety minutes—nerves had made it seem even longer. I slipped outside and down the drive without anyone stopping me. Morrell was waiting for me at the bend in the road. His face was pinched with anxiety, but I felt lighter-hearted than I had in months.

45

Fugitive

MORRELL ARRIVED EARLY the next morning with the papers and a couple of cappuccinos—Father Lou breakfasted on sweet tea and bacon sandwiches and didn't keep coffee or fruit in the rectory. I'd already been up for a few hours when Morrell arrived. Game-day nerves, I suppose.

Father Lou had been up for hours, too. He started Labor Day as he did every day, with mass. This morning he startled me considerably by asking me to serve, since none of the children in his acolytes group had appeared. When I told him I'd never even been baptized, he grunted and said he supposed some hairsplitter would consider that a barrier, but would I at least keep him company by reading the lesson.

I stood in the Lady Chapel of the enormous church and read from the book of Job about how God desires humans to see the light. As Father Lou began the prayers for the mass, he prayed first for the souls of Lucian Frenada and Nicola Aguinaldo, for the working people of Chicago, for everyone who worked hard and had little to show for it. Along the way he surprised me by asking for light on my enterprise, to see whether it was good to let it prosper. I thought again of Miss

Ruby, warning me that revenge didn't make a good meal.

At the end of the mass I stood in front of a wood statue of the Virgin of Guadalupe, stubbornly arguing my case in my head. Even if it was revenge, didn't I have a right to live and work in this town? I said as much to Father Lou while he fried bacon in the cavernous kitchen.

He grunted again. "Not saying you don't, my girl. Turning the other cheek isn't the only advice Our Lord gives people. Just saying you need to remember you're not Almighty God sitting in judgment on Robert Baladine. Not why I asked you to read the lesson, though—wasn't trying to teach you a lesson." He laughed heartily at his little pun. "I wanted some company. It's a big cold church to celebrate mass in by myself."

Morrell's arrival cut the theology discussion short. He dropped the papers in front of me with a coffee and a bag of Michigan peaches.

"Triple Crown, Warshawski. All three Chicago dailies, not to mention the gorilla from New York."

I snatched the stack from him. The gorilla was on top and began with its usual rotund phrases.

CONFUSION REIGNS
AT CARNIFICE SECURITY

Oak Brook, Ill.— The Illinois prairie in this upscale community west of Chicago has been replaced by smooth sod and cool white marble, but inside the Carnifice office tower, life is anything but placid on

this Labor Day. Robert Baladine is emphatically con-
tradicting an e-mail message received by Carnifice clients yesterday announcing his resignation as chairman
and CEO of Carnifice Security, while his staff scurries
to explain how a third party could have breached the
security provider's own defenses to post messages on
Mr. Baladine's e-mail server.

These messages bear the unmistakable "finger-
print" of Mr. Baladine's personal e-mail address.
They say, in part, that impending publicity about alleged misconduct at the Coolis correctional facility
that Carnifice runs is forcing Mr. Baladine to resign
(*see Page C23 for the complete text of the e-mail received by Ajax Insurance in Chicago*). The misconduct is an alleged use of the Coolis correctional
facility to manufacture T-shirts and jackets for the
Global Entertainment company. This is in violation of
Illinois law, which forbids sale of prison manufac-
tures outside the state prison system. Congressman
Blair Yerkes (R–Ill.) has called for a complete investigation of the prison to see whether there is any truth
to the allegation. "I have known BB Baladine since we
hunted together as boys, and I utterly repudiate the
suggestion that he has lied."

In the meantime, more disturbing to Carnifice clients is the possibility that an outsider could penetrate
Carnifice's own computer. It means that confidential
—often highly volatile—data entrusted to the security
firm is at risk for dissemination across the Web. As
Ajax Chairman Ralph Devereux said, "From our
standpoint, we're left with two equally unpleasant
possibilities: either Robert Baladine is lying about his
resignation, or a hacker has been able to bypass all of

Carnifice's security measures. Either way, the instability of the company's head honcho leaves us wondering whether Carnifice is the right company to handle our most private matters."

Various papers and television stations also received e-mail from the Carnifice server, describing the manufacturing relationship between Carnifice and Global at the Coolis prison site. Because the source of the report could not be verified, it is not clear whether the information is accurate or whether it comes from a disgruntled Carnifice employee. Efforts to view the prison shop have been rebuffed by Coolis authorities, but state lawmakers are demanding an inquiry.

Mr. Baladine would not return phone calls to this paper, but Global Entertainment spokeswoman Alexandra Fisher says Global is considering the possibility that a local private investigator with a grudge against Baladine may have perpetrated the vandalism. The investigator, V. I. Warshawski, spent a month at Coolis after Mr. Baladine had her arrested on kidnapping charges. Although Ms. Warshawski escaped with what physician Dr. Charlotte Herschel calls brain-threatening injuries, Ms. Fisher says no one actually knows the detective's whereabouts. Finding the solo investigator is Carnifice Security's first priority. (*See Page B45 for coverage of some of Ms. Warshawski's investigations into industrial espionage.*)

Father Lou was reading the report in the *Sun-Times*, which gave the story the most attention of any of the Chicago papers. The *Herald-Star*, as a Global paper, ran a one-paragraph story in the business section that sounded as though there'd been a brief snafu in the Carnifice e-mail server. The *Star* didn't mention the

Global T-shirt connection at Coolis. The *Tribune* ran a half column in the middle of Marshall Field's big Labor Day advertising spread.

"So now what?" Morrell asked when I'd finished reading. "Wait for the Carnifice clients to drop like flies and come running to Warshawski Investigative Services for help?"

I made a face. "They're busy doing damage control at Carnifice. And the CEO of Warshawski et cetera had better surface if she wants any clients. I think the next thing is a media show. For which we need secure space. That, I think, will get BB so furious that he's likely to come for me in person. I want to put together a little tape of all my bits and pieces of pictures. Make some bullet-point slides—everyone feels they've gotten real information if you give it to them in bullet points. And I want a VCR so I can watch Baladine's home videos. He was taping himself having sex with Alex Fisher yesterday. It struck me as funny that the guy keeps his old home-security tapes, so I took three."

Father Lou stared at me in disgust. "Man photographs himself having intercourse? Did the girl know?"

"She tried to get the tape from him, but he wouldn't let her." I didn't feel like explaining that I had it now. I wasn't sure what I was going to do with it.

"Got a VCR in the school you can use," the priest said. "I'm still not sure whether you're doing the right thing, not sure I should encourage you since you stole the tapes you want to look at, but the man Baladine seems to do people a variety of harm. Set it up for you, then I have to meet with members of the parish council. Got a bunch of kids coming, cleaning out the crypt before school starts tomorrow. Parish picnic this afternoon. Lots to get done."

I ran down to my room and picked up the tapes I'd taken from Baladine's closet yesterday. The three of us walked through the church to a door that connected to the school. The dark vaulted space was full of life as a group of boys shouted to each other behind the altar: "Bet you it's full of bones." "Yeah, Carlos here is going to faint when he sees one of those arms coming after him, ain't you, man?"

Father Lou interrupted them with a good-natured shout that they needed to be more afraid of him than of any bones and he'd be back in a minute to make sure they were clearing out the old hymnals. He undid the dead bolt and led us into another long unlit hallway. He walked quickly in the semidarkness. Morrell and I kept tripping on things like loose tiles as we tried to keep pace. Father Lou took us up a back staircase to the school library. There he reluctantly decided he needed light to see what he was doing and turned on one dim desk lamp.

When he saw that Morrell and I knew how to set up the VCR, he went back downstairs to see how his hooligans were doing in the crypt. I started with the tape for the week that Frenada died.

We got a series of disconnected frames from the voice-activated system of Rosario waking Utah and Madison, of Eleanor starting work with them in the pool and then turning off the camera. And then Frenada was poolside with Trant and Baladine. The little red date in the corner identified it as June 26, the night Frenada died. Trant said he understood Frenada was telling people that he, Trant, had stolen a T-shirt and he was tired of hearing about it. Baladine must have turned the camera off at that point because the next scene was the following day with Rosario in the nursery.

I sat back in my chair. "No proof, but very suggestive," I said to Morrell. "Let's get some copies of this before I send it back to the Baladines."

He grunted agreement, although he pointed out there wasn't enough there to get Baladine arrested, let alone convicted. I agreed and put in the first of the Nicola tapes to see if it might give us something more concrete.

The tape was dated about six months before Nicola's arrest for theft. We watched Nicola waking Utah and Madison, a sleepy Utah clinging to her nanny while Madison chatted vivaciously about the many things she was doing better in at school than anyone else. We saw Eleanor and BB kissing briefly as he left for the office on a "don't know how late I'll be tonight, sweetheart" line and Eleanor in the nursery adjuring Nicola not to baby Utah. "She's almost three. It's time you stopped carrying her everywhere." When Nicola said brokenly that she didn't understand, Eleanor told her not to play stupid and plunked Utah from Nicola's arms onto the floor. Utah began to howl. As soon as Eleanor left the room, Nicola picked her up and began soothing her in a language I didn't know, presumably Tagalog.

It was unnerving to watch Nicola Aguinaldo alive, even in the grainy production of the home video. She was petite, so small that next to Eleanor Baladine she looked like a child herself. In Eleanor's presence she became as waxen as one of the children's dolls, but alone with the little girls she grew more relaxed. Robbie came in and began playing with Utah. He spoke Spanish to Nicola, who teased him about his accent and got him to laugh back at her. I had never seen Robbie happy. Talking in Spanish to him, Nicola became vivacious, almost beautiful. Eleanor called up to say the school bus was there.

The tape covered a two-week period. Scenes broke off abruptly as people either moved out of camera range or turned off the camera. A conversation Eleanor was having with a gardener ended suddenly as Baladine called Nicola to his study. We watched her enter and stand with a face drained of expression. When she quietly took off and folded her clothes, she seemed to treat it as the same kind of chore that putting away Madison and Utah's clothes was. Baladine himself did not undress. It was unbearable, and I couldn't watch. When Morrell heard me crying he switched off the machine.

"I can't show that to a roomful of reporters," I muttered. "It's too indecent."

"Do you want me to watch the other reel and summarize it for you?" he asked.

"Yes. No. I think I'd better see for myself."

The second reel was similar to the first, except for the scene in Baladine's study. This time Nicola was begging for money for her child's hospital bills and Baladine was telling her impatiently that he paid her a good wage and that she had a hell of a nerve to try begging for money on a made-up story. Nicola offered herself to him and he laughed at her. It was a scene of such agonizing humiliation that I finally left the library to pace the school corridor. When I came back, Morrell had finished the tape and rewound it. Father Lou had slipped into the room while I was walking around.

"There wasn't anything on it about the necklace or her arrest. We'll have to imagine that part," Morrell said.

"That poor child," Father Lou said. "What a crucifixion she endured. That man, her boss, he's the one you're after?"

I was as sweaty and depleted as if I'd run a marathon and could only nod.

"I still don't know if you're doing the right thing or not, but I'll help you out. Let you use the library here for your press conference."

I blinked. "But, Father, you know—Baladine not only has a lot of artillery at his disposal, he's not afraid to use it. Women and children don't mean anything special to him. I couldn't possibly guarantee your safety, or the safety of the school. Unless . . ."

"Unless what?" Morrell said sharply when I didn't finish the sentence.

"Unless I get Baladine to come to me first. Before we lay the case out to the media. Especially since we can prove Frenada was at his pool the night he died. If I bring him to me, I won't have to lie here tensely waiting for him to make some kind of move."

"No," Morrell said. "Putting your head on the block for him to chop off is nuts. You know Freeman Carter would give you the same advice."

I scrunched up my mouth in a monkey face. "More than likely. But I'm tired of walking around in terror. Ever since he sicced Lemour on me in June, I've had to watch every step I take, and my time in Coolis has only made me more nervous. If I let him know I've got these tapes and the tape he made of him and Alex, I think he'll come get them. And if I leave the church, he won't do it here where the kids will be in danger."

"Your press presentation is your best route," Morrell said patiently. "Bringing that much publicity not just to his Coolis operation but to his use of a Chicago police officer to plant drugs in your office will force Baladine to stop harassing you. Probably force his board to make him quit, too."

"Abigail Trant told me that he can't stand the notion of being bested. I saw it—or heard it—yesterday: he was furious when Alex got the tape from him. He hurt her to get it back: it wasn't a game to him. There's no telling what he might do."

"Think about it overnight," Father Lou suggested. "Offer a special intention at mass in the morning. Do some manual labor in the crypt. Nothing like hard work to clear the mind."

So Morrell and I spent the rest of the morning in the chamber underneath the altar, shifting old boxes of hymnals that Father Lou had decided the church would never use again, digging out the costumes the children wore in their Christmas pageant, and uncovering an actual reliquary that the Italians who built the church a hundred years ago had brought with them. This caused an explosion of nervous ribaldry from the boys working with us.

I hadn't resolved matters by three, when Father Lou called a halt to our work so that the boys could attend the parish picnic. Nor did a nap while Morrell joined them in a baseball game in Humboldt Park bring any special vision. I still wanted to call Baladine and tell him I had his videotapes: something like a childhood taunt—come catch me if you can.

The problem remained where I would be when I issued the taunt. At the church I endangered Father Lou and his schoolchildren. In my own home there were Mr. Contreras and the other tenants. Tessa's studio ruled out using my office. And he might be so berserk that he'd go after someone like Lotty out of sheer terrorism, even if I wasn't near her.

All evening long, as Morrell and I worked on my presentation—preparing the photographs in order, figuring out what video sequences to show of Lemour in action against me, where to put Trant and Frenada with Baladine at his pool, discussing whether to use any of the Aguinaldo footage, typing up camera-ready copy in St. Remigio's school computer lab—Morrell and I debated the question. At midnight, when Morrell left with the material—he was taking it to the Unblinking Eye in the morning for production—I was no nearer a solution.

I went to bed and fell into a restless sleep. It was only an hour later when Father Lou shook me awake. "Old man's at the door with a kid and some dogs. Says he's your neighbor."

"My neighbor?" I pulled on my jeans and jammed my feet into my running shoes and sprinted down the hall, Father Lou following on his rolling boxer's gait.

I looked through the peephole at the figures on the doorstep. Mr. Contreras. With Mitch, Peppy, and Robbie Baladine. My heart sank, but I told Father Lou it was, in fact, my neighbor.

"With the kid whose father had me arrested the last time he ran away to me."

Father Lou unscraped the dead bolts and let them in. Mr. Contreras started speaking as the door opened. All I caught was, "Sorry, doll, but I didn't want to use the phone in case they was tapping my line," before the dogs overwhelmed me with their ecstatic greeting and Robbie, painfully thin and grubby, started apologizing: "I know you said to wait until I heard from you, but BB called."

Father Lou shut the door. "Okay. Into the kitchen for tea, and let's sort this out one voice at a time. These dogs housebroken?"

"Where's the car?" I asked, before Father Lou pushed the dead bolts home.

"Sorry, doll, sorry, it's out front, you want me to move it?"

"It needs to go away from here. It's very identifiable, and if Baladine is scouring the city for me, he'll find it."

"Rectory garage," Father Lou said. "Filled with old junk but room for the car. I'll show—what's your name?—Contreras the garage. You take the boy into the kitchen. Put on the kettle."

Robbie and the dogs bounded down the hall with me to the kitchen. Robbie was trying hard not to flinch from Mitch, which seemed more heartbreaking than anything else about him.

"I'm sorry, Ms. Warshawski," he whispered, "but they figured out you weren't Aunt Claudia. They were going to lock me in the punishment barracks. I didn't know when I'd ever get out. And I thought if BB did something else bad to you because you came to see me, I'd have to kill myself. So I ran away. But now I see he can put you in prison no matter what I do."

"Sh, sh, *poverino*. It's okay. You're here, let's deal with that. Tell me the story when Father Lou and Mr. Contreras get back; that way we'll all get the same version and you'll only have to tell it once."

When the two men came in, the kettle was boiling. Father Lou made a large mug of cambric tea for Robbie and black tea with sugar for himself. I poured more hot milk into a mug for myself.

Mr. Contreras impatiently waved away refreshments. "He showed up about an hour ago, doll. He's

done in. I didn't know what to do—like I say, I was
afraid to use the phone—but I figured if they had any
kind of watch on the place, it wasn't good to leave him
there. I guess I could have gone up to Morrell, but all I
thought was, you'd be in real trouble now if that creep
Baladine—sorry, son, I know he's your old man—"

"Let's have it from the beginning, and short," Father
Lou said. "Have to say mass in a few hours, don't want
to stay up all night."

As short as any story involving Mr. Contreras could
be, it boiled down to this: the camp commandant had
summoned Robbie and questioned him about my visit.
Robbie stuck to the story that I was his Aunt Claudia,
his mother's younger sister, but the commandant revealed he had talked both to BB and to the real Claudia
Sunday night after the swim meet. All Robbie could do
was insist that I was Aunt Claudia. The commandant
said Robbie would be sent to the punishment block for
a few days until Eleanor arrived in person to talk to the
commandant.

"During reveille, while everyone stands at attention,
I snuck off. It was only this morning, but it seems like it
must've been a year ago. I ran in a ditch alongside the
camp and got out the back way and hitched into Columbia. Then I used your money to get the bus to Chicago, but I didn't know where to go except to your
apartment. I'm awful sorry, Ms. Warshawski; if this
means BB sends you back to jail for kidnapping, I don't
know what I'll do."

His eyes were dilating with fear and exhaustion. Father Lou cut off a hunk of bread and smeared it with
butter.

"Eat that, son. Cross that bridge when you come to
it, but if you stand up in court and tell your story like a

man, no one will send her to prison. Time you were in bed. You've had too long a day. You can sleep in in the morning, but you go to school in the afternoon. What year you in? Seventh grade. Get you a uniform—have extras for kids too poor to buy 'em. Worry about everything else later."

Father Lou looked a bit like Popeye, but his voice had the authoritative reassurance that children respond to. Robbie calmed down and followed me docilely to a bedroom near mine. I pulled clean sheets from a shelf and made up the narrow bed.

I heard a barking and yelping in the kitchen and ran back down the hall to find that Mitch had made himself into a hero: he'd emerged from the pantry with a rat in his mouth. Father Lou said in that case the dogs could stay the night. As an afterthought he offered Mr. Contreras a bed, too.

The priest stomped off to bed, leaving me to make up another bed for my neighbor. When he said good night, Mr. Contreras handed me a paper bag. "I been holding this for you since the day you was arrested, doll. I figure you might need it now."

It was my Smith & Wesson, which had been in the handbag I'd flung to Mr. Contreras the day Lemour came to get me.

46

In the Church Militant

MITCH HAD CAUGHT another rat and was barking with joy. "That's a good boy," I mumbled. "Now be quiet and let me sleep."

I put out a hand to pet him and woke up when I was stroking air and the barking hadn't stopped. I pulled on my jeans again and picked up the Smith & Wesson.

I'd gotten used to finding my way through the rectory in the dark and went down the hall in the direction of Mitch's voice. He and Peppy were trying to get into the church from the rectory passage. When they heard me they ran to me and pawed at my legs, trying to get me to open the door leading into the church.

Peppy, scratching on the door, only made impatient grunts in the back of her throat, but I couldn't quiet Mitch enough to listen for sounds from the church. Finally, I clamped his muzzle shut with my left hand, but he thrashed so violently that I still couldn't hear anything. I was trying to picture the geography of the buildings, wondering how to get around to the rear, when Father Lou materialized behind me.

"Think it's your man in there?"

"I don't know. You get many gangbangers breaking in at night?" I whispered back.

"Usually know better. Could call the cops, but it

takes them an hour to show around here. Hold the dogs. I'm opening the door into the church, want to see what's going on without animals running wild in the sanctuary."

He undid the three massive locks to the church door and went inside. Mitch was whining and straining to be after him, and even Peppy was pulling on my arms in angry protest. I'd counted to a hundred, figuring I'd go to one-fifty before I plunged after the priest, when he slipped back through the passage.

"Think they're coming in through the school. Fourth-floor windows don't have bars—must've scaled the wall somehow. I'm going outside to holler them down."

"No!" I let Mitch go. He scampered into the church and made a beeline for the door that connected the nave to the school. "If it is Baladine, he may have someone outside to pick off anyone who leaves the building. If he's coming in through the school he's probably hoping for a surprise attack, but it could still be a feint designed to draw us—me—outside."

There wasn't any light; I felt rather than saw the priest scowling. "Old coal passages connect church, school, rectory through the crypt. Keep them locked to stop the kids horsing around down there. I can come into the school behind him through the basement. Know my way in the dark, you don't, you stay here. Don't want any shooting in the church; do your best if they come in. Calling the cops on my way; hope they get here sometime before we're all dead."

By tacit consent we left Mr. Contreras asleep. Father Lou went down the hall to the kitchen, and I went into the church. I didn't know what time it was, but it was still too early for any light to come in through the church's dirty east windows. The red sanctuary lamp gave off the only light. I fumbled my way to the sanctuary, trying to orient myself by the lamp and by Mitch, who was barking sharply at the door to the school.

I bumped into Peppy and almost screamed. She wagged her tail against my legs. I clutched her collar and let her guide me. At the steps to the altar I could follow the altar rail toward the raised podium used for sermons on formal occasions.

When we finally reached Mitch he had gotten tired of his frenzied assault on the door and was lying on his haunches. I felt his raised hackles when I touched him, and he jerked his head impatiently away from my hand. The door was too thick for me to make out the sounds he was hearing on the other side. I took it for about five minutes, then retraced my way to the altar. A massive wood and marble carving rose behind it. When I worked my away around to the back, where the crypt entrance was, the altarpiece itself blocked most of the glow from the sanctuary lamp.

The trapdoor to the crypt was unlocked. I climbed stealthily down the narrow spiral stair, Peppy following me on uncertain feet. She mewed unhappily, and I hoisted her down after me one step at a time.

At the bottom I was in a well of such intense blackness that I had no way of orienting myself. I risked the switch at the foot of the spiral stairs. It showed me the passages that I'd overlooked when I was working down here this morning, one on the north to the rectory and another opposite that connected to the school. I flicked off the light and made my way through the south door to the school basement.

Clutching Peppy's collar, I let her guide me again,

until she found a staircase. We crept up, pausing after each step to listen. I heard the humming of machinery, but no human sounds. At the top I pushed open the door. Father Lou had come this way earlier and left it unlocked.

We were in the school kitchen; a streetlight made it possible to see the big stoves and refrigerators. I went through a swinging door into a hallway and suddenly could hear voices. Keeping my hand on Peppy, now more as a warning to her to be silent than because I needed her navigation, I moved toward the sound. Father Lou was outside the door that led from the school into the church.

"If you thought your son was with me you'd have knocked at the door like an honest man," Father Lou was saying. "You're breaking into a school. I don't know what valuables you thought a poor school in a neighborhood like this has, but I have you red-handed, and the cops will take it from here."

Baladine laughed. "A police detective is stationed outside. If the cops ever show up, he'll tell them he's got the situation under control. I'm sure there would be a lot of mourning in the neighborhood over your death, but wouldn't you rather get out of my way than die defending that stupid Warshawski woman and my tiresome son?"

My stomach tightened at the sound of his voice, at the reckless superiority of it. At first I thought Baladine was alone, and I was willing to risk a shot, but as my ears and eyes adjusted I realized he had at least two other men with him. I could make out only their ghostly shapes, but Father Lou's bald head reflected what light there was. He was the short ghost whose arms were perhaps pinned by two larger wraiths. Baladine was behind him. I lowered my gun; I couldn't possibly get a clear shot.

"I know you got into the school building from inside the church, Padre," Baladine said in the same patronizing voice, "because my man has the outside covered. So be a good fellow and let us into the church, and I promise you'll be alive to say mass in the morning."

"Jesus wants me tonight, tonight's when He'll get me," Father Lou said. "If not, not your decision, young man."

Baladine laughed. He was making a smart-alecky comment back when I heard a worse sound than Baladine's voice: a muffled outburst on the other side of the door. I couldn't make out the words, but the cadence told me Mr. Contreras had woken up. He wanted to know what was going on, did Mitch have someone cornered on the other side? He was fiddling with the bolts.

In the instant that everyone's attention slackened, Father Lou gave one of his captors a punch that knocked him over. I yelled at top volume to Mr. Contreras to leave the door alone and sped back down the hall to the basement stairs. I saw a red marker dancing on the floor, trying to find me. For one crazy moment I thought it was another sanctuary light. Then a gun spat fire at me as the red marker danced after me. Baladine had a laser sight. A death marker, not sanctuary. It terrified me so much that I hurled myself through the swinging door into the kitchen, Peppy running with me. In the light from the streetlamp I found the stairs and stumbled down them so fast I tripped over my feet and ended in a heap at the bottom. Behind me a shot echoed along the hallway. I prayed it hadn't hit Father Lou. Or Mr. Contreras.

Peppy landed on top of me. We scrambled to our feet in a confused mess of dog and woman and moved as fast as possible toward the crypt. Behind me I could hear doors slamming as the pursuit looked for the exit I'd taken, and then I saw a flashlight finger on the stairwell. It gave me the view I needed of the basement. I was heading away from the crypt door. I righted myself, called Peppy to me, and managed to get us both inside. I slid the bolt home as another shot sounded.

My legs were shaking as I climbed back up the spiral stairs. Above me the church was still dark, but when I got to the top I could see a light bounce along one of the aisles. I waited behind the altar. I was trying to figure out from the sound what was going on, when I heard Baladine's voice.

"Warshawski? I've got the priest and the old man. Come on out. Your life for theirs."

"Don't do it, doll." Mr. Contreras was panting. "Don't do it; run for help, I been around plenty long enough. Shouldn't have opened the door, anyway."

I slipped around the edge of the altarpiece, keeping low so that the altar itself shielded me from sight. I made my way to the old preaching tower and climbed up into it. From there I could see that the light in the aisle was coming from a flashlight. It was hard to see what lay behind it, but Father Lou and Mr. Contreras seemed to be attached to each other. One of Baladine's thugs had a gun trained on them. I couldn't hear or see Mitch.

"Your quarrel's with me, Baladine," I called. "Let the men go. When they're safely inside the rectory, I'll come out."

The flashlight swung around in my direction. Baladine couldn't see me, but he shone the light along the altar, the laser sight dancing behind it.

"Go open the front door to the church," he finally said to his henchman. "Lemour can come in and earn his keep, since the priest knocked out Fergus. This place is too big to search alone. Don't try anything, Warshawski: I'll shoot your friends at the first wrong move you make."

The underling went down the aisle and scrabbled with the heavy locks. I didn't know what to do next. Peppy was crying to join me in my turret, and Baladine said irritably that he thought they'd shot the damned dog. The red laser sight moved around the sanctuary, trying to pick out a warm target, but the turret was between Peppy and him. He himself was shielded by one of the pillars, or I would have risked a shot at him.

"Aren't there any lights in this damned place?" It was Lemour's reedy voice coming in to the body of the church. "What do you need me for, boss? Hunt out the Warshki bitch? Turn on the lights and we'll get her in no time. Drabek, go in the back and find the switches. I'll cover the altar."

Under cover of Lemour's voice, I slipped out of the little turret. I had chosen it because I could shoot anyone who came close enough to me to attack it, but I realized it was a stupid hideout: all my friends would be dead while I defended myself, and then I'd run out of bullets and die as well. I got down on my hands and knees and crawled down the center aisle until I came to the pews. Making sure the safety was on, I stuck my gun in a jeans pocket and slithered along the floor toward Baladine. I wished I could have ordered Peppy to stay at the turret, but she was anxiously following me.

"I know you're back there, Warshawski, I can hear you. Come out on the count of five or the first bullet goes into the old man."

"It's okay, cookie, don't give up, I can take it, just don't hold it against me that I let the guy in. You know there's never been anyone like you in my life, all seventy-nine years, and I ain't having you take a bullet just so I can see eighty."

Baladine savagely ordered him to be quiet, but the old man was either beyond paying attention or deliberately trying to give me cover. He started recounting the first time he saw me, I was wearing a red top and cut-offs and going after a gangbanger, street punk, but nowhere near as bad as this bastard, pardon his French.

Baladine smacked him, I think with his pistol. When Mr. Contreras fell silent, Father Lou began to sing, in a loud, tuneless voice, a Latin chant. I risked getting to my feet and running toward Baladine. He had one hand on the flash, the other on the gun pointing at Mr. Contreras's head. He was yelling at Father Lou to shut up or be killed when I got behind him and savagely chopped the back of his head.

He dropped the flashlight. His knees buckled, and I grabbed his right arm with all my might. He wrenched his arm free and his gun went off. A window shattered. Father Lou stuck out a foot and kicked the flashlight away, and I grappled with Baladine in the dark. Lemour shouted at the henchman to get the damned lights on, he was going to take care of Warshki once and for all.

Baladine was trying to twist his arm around to get a shot at me. I stayed behind him, pinning his left arm so

he had only his gun hand free: if he wanted to fight he'd
have to drop the gun. He jabbed backward with his gun
arm. I stuck my knee in his back and pulled his left
shoulder toward me. He dropped the gun, which went
off again, and pulled me close to him, bending to flip
me over his head. I held on and we landed on the floor
together. I lost my grip in the fall and he straddled me,
his hands locking around my throat. I brought a knee
up to his groin. His hold slackened enough for me to
get a breath and to try to pull my gun from my pocket.

In the dark next to me I heard a deep angry growl
and felt a heavy furry body lean against me. Baladine
gave a loud scream and let go of my neck. I wrenched
away from him and bounced to my feet. I kicked out as
hard as I could, not able to see him in the dark. I kicked
high, wanting to miss the dog. My foot connected with
bone. Baladine fell heavily against me. I backed away,
ready to kick again, but he wasn't moving. I must have
knocked him out. I scrabbled under the pew and picked
up the flashlight.

Mitch was lying across Baladine's legs. Mitch, bleeding but alive. I couldn't take time to figure out what had
happened, how he'd bitten Baladine—I had Lemour
and his partner to deal with. I shone the light briefly on
Father Lou, but he and Mr. Contreras were handcuffed
together, with their arms behind them. I couldn't free
them now.

Father Lou shouted a warning: Lemour had picked
his way through the pews to my side. I hurled the flashlight into his face and ran back toward the altar.

A bullet whined and smashed into the altarpiece, and
I smelled smoke. I ran behind the altarpiece. Lemour
fired again, this time in front of me. Light flooded the
building, and I was blinded. Lemour, running toward

me, was blinded as well. He tripped across the open trapdoor and fell headlong down the spiral stairs. Glass splintered as he crashed to the bottom.

I braced myself, waiting for the henchman to come after me, when a fireman appeared behind the altar. I thought at first I was hallucinating, or that Baladine had dragooned the fire department along with the police, and lifted my gun.

"No need to shoot, young lady," the man said. "I'm here to put out the fire."

47

For Those Who Also Serve

THE GUNSHOTS WOKE me and I saw the door to the church was open, so I snuck in. I heard everything but I didn't know what to do, because BB was saying he had a cop to cover up for him. Then I thought, well, if the church was burning, the fire department would come, so I set fire to a newspaper in the kitchen and called 911 and told them the church was on fire. Then I was afraid I was really going to burn down the building. Is Mitch going to be okay? What did they say at the vet?"

We were sitting in the rectory kitchen, drinking more cambric tea as Father Lou and I tried to clean up the sodden mess the firemen had left behind.

"Robbie, you're a hero. It was a brilliant idea, but next time you don't have to set fire to the kitchen—they can't tell downtown if the place is really burning up or not." I laughed shakily. "Mitch is going to be okay. The vet said he took the bullet in his shoulder, not the heart, and even though he lost a lot of blood he should make it through."

Peppy had stayed at the emergency vet to be a blood donor for her son. After the firemen finished putting out the kitchen fire, they'd gotten an ambulance for the wounded. Mr. Contreras and Baladine had both been carted off to County Hospital, although Mr. Contreras was protesting it was only a head injury, he'd survived worse than that at Anzio.

Detective Lemour was in the morgue. He'd broken his neck when he landed on the reliquary at the bottom of the stairs. The remaining two men from Carnifice Security had been carried off by a squadrol that the firemen had summoned. One of the officers driving the squadrol had been a student at St. Remigio's six years ago. He was horrified at seeing his priest in handcuffs and was happy to accept Father Lou's version of events: that Baladine had broken in with his two thugs, and that Lemour had died trying to rescue the priest.

"Saves trouble," the priest said when the policeman had left. "Hard to get the cops to believe one of their own is bent. If Baladine denies the story when he recovers, he'll have a lot of explaining to do, why Lemour was with him."

The firemen helped me carry Mitch out to their own car. They gave Peppy and me a ride to the emergency vet and even stayed with me to bring me back to the church an hour later.

"Six o'clock," Father Lou announced now. "Mass. Want to serve, young lady?"

I started to remind him I wasn't even baptized, then saw his fierce look and shut my mouth. I followed him back down the hall to the church. Robbie trailed behind us. There was broken glass in the side aisle, and a piece of St. Veronica's arm had been shot off the high altar, but the church looked remarkably placid in the daylight.

I went into the vestry with Father Lou and watched him robe. He told me what vessels to bring and just to do as he said and I'd be fine. I walked behind him to the

Lady Chapel, where a half dozen women waited, teachers going to mass on the first morning of school.

Father Lou bowed to the altar and turned to the women. "I was glad when they said to me, let us go to the House of the Lord."

48

Meet the Press

THIS PHOTOGRAPH IS a close-up of a bruise on my abdomen. A forensic pathologist says he can identify at least the make and size of the boot that made it. There will be a trial, I'm suing the person who kicked me, and I'll make an identification in court, so it doesn't matter now whether he burns the boot or cleans it. The point is, I'm alive, and I can make the identification."

The eleven people whose papers and broadcast stations had decided to send them to St. Remigio's looked at each other with a kind of incredulity that said, is this what she dragged us out here for? I smiled at them, I hoped engagingly. When they had come into the school library where Morrell had set up the screen and the projector, they'd mobbed me, wanting answers to all kinds of questions, ranging from what I knew about Baladine's injuries to where I'd been since getting out of Coolis. I promised they could ask me anything when I finished my presentation.

Murray Ryerson, looking both belligerent and sheepish, was the only one who hung back from the group swarming around me. He said he knew I couldn't be dead, I was too much of a grandstander for that, then planted himself in a corner and made a big play of studying his own paper when I started speaking.

In the back of the room Father Lou sat with a couple of squarely built men whom the priest identified only as being from his parish council, there to help out if the need arose. Also in the back were Mr. Contreras with Mitch and Peppy, Lotty and Max, and Sal. Neither Mr. Contreras nor Mitch seemed any worse for their night in the church, although Mitch had a large bandage wrapped around his belly and shoulder. He was sitting up, grinning crazily at anyone who wanted to pet him. Morrell was off to one side, operating the projector.

It was a week after Baladine's assault on the church. We had decided to go ahead with the show, because there were too many open-ended issues. Baladine was going to recover, and he was already trying to make a case that he had used some fancy equipment to scale the side of the church school, break in through the fourth-floor windows, and attack the priest simply in order to get his son back. I wanted my version in as many hands as possible.

"I'm starting with this picture because in a curious way it's the crux of a difficult case involving Global Entertainment, Carnifice Security, and that perennial chestnut, Illinois politics. I'm alive, talking to you, but another young woman, who received what I believe are identical injuries, was not so fortunate. Nicola Aguinaldo died in the early hours of June seventeenth from a perforated intestine. Her body disappeared from the medical examiner's office before an autopsy could be performed."

We had made a still of Nicola smiling, from a frame of the home video where she'd been talking to Robbie. I explained who she was, using a slide with bullet points, how she'd landed in prison, and how I'd inadvertently found her.

"I don't think we'll ever know what became of her body: her grief-stricken mother was denied the chance to bury it. But my guess is that a political appointee of Jean-Claude Poilevy at the county morgue removed the body on Poilevy's orders so that no one would be able to see what kind of boot kicked in Nicola Aguinaldo's abdomen."

I nodded at Morrell, who clicked up the slide of Hartigan standing over me with the stun gun. The audience gasped with shock.

"He was about six foot two, perhaps two hundred, two-twenty pounds. She wasn't five feet tall and weighed maybe ninety pounds. She didn't have too much of a chance against him. I managed to take this picture with a hidden camera seconds after I'd been shot with fifty thousand volts from a stun gun, right before I was kicked into insensibility." I held up my right hand, which was in a kind of brace; I'd reinjured the fingers fighting Baladine. "Two of my fingers and five of the small bones in the back of my hand broke as I tried to protect my head."

I heard another intake of horrified breath but continued with my presentation in a dry, academic voice. It was the only way I could speak without giving way to emotion. I went through the details of Nicola's daughter's death, what I'd been told by the women at Coolis about Nicola's desperate grief and how she'd pounded on the guard's chest when they laughed at her plea to be allowed to attend the baby's funeral. I couldn't look at Mr. Contreras; he was so upset that I knew my own composure would crack. I heard Peppy whining by his side with shared misery.

Morrell put up another slide. This one had a red flashing header reading *Speculation! Speculation!* We'd decided to use that to separate fact from guesswork. I told them I was guessing that Nicola was dumped on the Chicago streets in the same way I was.

"What takes some of the guesswork out of this is the fact that the guards changed my shirt before they took me out of Coolis. I was concussed, manacled, and running a high fever and not able to defend myself; they tore off my shirt and put on one that wouldn't show the scorch marks from the stun gun." I stopped for water, remembering Polsen touching the burned skin on my breasts. "They made a comment about not making the mistake they had before, where they had to change the victim's shirt in Chicago, so they had clearly done this before. It's just a guess that Nicola Aguinaldo was the person they'd done it to.

"Now here comes more speculation, and mighty interesting it is. The shirt they put on Aguinaldo had been made by Lucian Frenada. You may remember Mr. Frenada's name: his dead body was found floating in Lake Michigan right before the Fourth of July. Everyone who isn't brain-dead knows Frenada was a boyhood friend of Lacey Dowell, because Global has been trumpeting that information on television and in the *Herald-Star* for two months. They grew up together right here at St. Remigio's." I glanced at Murray. He was studying the floor.

Beth Blacksin from Channel 8 interrupted with a question about Lacey, and several other reporters jumped in. I ignored them and explained how Frenada had gone to Lacey and asked for a chance to make some of the Global Entertainment spin-off products.

"Money in movies isn't just made on the screen. When your kid has to have that Captain Doberman

T-shirt or those Space Beret action figures, the cash registers at Global are ringing. Mad Virgin shirts are very popular with young teens—they're one of the first movie spin-off items to find a huge marketing success with teenage girls. Oversize denim jackets are another hot seller in Global's Virginwear line.

"When Nicola Aguinaldo's body was found, she was wearing one of the T-shirts that Lucian Frenada made as a demo for Teddy Trant at Global. You all remember the party at the Golden Glow back in June, when Frenada came and Lacey had him thrown out? He was demanding to know why Trant had stolen one of the shirts. Global didn't want to work with him, but Frenada was highly suspicious that Trant might be going to copy some of his workmanship. Of course everyone thought Frenada was trying any tactic he could to get Lacey to influence Global into buying from him: why would a studio head, who could pick up a Mad Virgin T-shirt anytime he walked into his office, go to the trouble of stealing one from a small Humboldt Park entrepreneur?

"But I believe that is exactly what Trant did. He was at Frenada's shop on the Tuesday night right before Nicola died. That's a fact. This next is a guess, but I believe that in some crazy scheme, maybe caused by watching too many of his own movies, Trant stole one of Frenada's shirts to put on Nicola, so that if any questions were asked about her death he could direct attention away from Coolis, from Global, and toward an innocent bystander."

The room was in an uproar. I went back through the argument, ticking off the points on the slide that highlighted them.

When they seemed to be caught up with me, I went

back to Baladine and his fury with me. How Global first tried to bribe me by hiring me to frame Frenada, and when I wouldn't play, how Baladine began hounding me, culminating with planting cocaine in my office.

I played the video I'd made in my office. The group was firing so many questions now that I had to play it three times before I could go on.

"I don't know if Baladine wanted me dead or discredited—" I began, when Murray piped up unexpectedly from the back of the room.

"He was spinning around. I don't think he could possibly have told anyone he wanted you dead, but when some of us at the *Star* caught wind of the discussions going on about your involvement in the case, we —uh, made it as clear as we could that if anything—uh —well, a lot of people in Chicago would want to know why you got—uh—hurt. Also, I got the idea that someone high in the Global organization was lobbying for you, although Al—my contacts there—never said who it was. Anyway, I have a feeling—I was not involved in any discussions about you—but I think he—Baladine— thought discrediting you was the viable route. I didn't know about the drugs. And I was as amazed as everyone else here when you were arrested for kidnapping. And then, why on God's green earth you didn't post bail—" He broke off midsentence. "I guess you were being Wonder Woman again. Take us to the limit one more time, Warshawski."

I blushed but went on with my presentation. "As far as Frenada goes, I think they wanted him dead: he was starting to complain to too many people about Trant taking one of his sample Virginwear shirts. They thought they could discredit him with drugs; they planted some in his shop and planted some data on the

Web trying to show he was a high roller. I'm afraid it was something I said that sent him hotfoot out to Oak Brook to try to confront Baladine and Trant the night of June twenty-sixth."

Morrell ran the footage of Frenada with Baladine and Trant at Baladine's pool. He stopped it to make sure everyone noticed the date embedded in the film.

"This film doesn't prove that Baladine and Trant killed Frenada, but it does put the three men together the night Frenada died. Lucian Frenada had told me he couldn't compete with Global's current suppliers because his labor costs were too high. He also had other overhead that someone running a factory in a prison doesn't have to deal with. The state of Illinois paid for the machines that Global gets to use. The state of Illinois pays the rent on the space for the Global factory. You can't get lower production costs for this kind of operation, even if you go to Burma, because you can't beat free space and machinery. And you have a labor force that can never go on strike, never balk at the working conditions, never complain to OSHA or the NLRB. It's a beauty for the bottom line in these days of the global economy."

There was another barrage of questions about the Global–Carnifice shop. "You've been most patient to listen to me for such a long period," I finally said. "There are only a few more things I want to say. All summer, as Baladine and Trent were boxing me in, I kept wondering what was so important about Nicola Aguinaldo that they needed to find someone to take the blame for her death. It wasn't she they cared about, but their manufacturing scheme. It had been operating smoothly, no questions asked, for several years; they didn't want some outsider poking into Nicola's death to upset it.

"Maybe you're wondering how they could run that plant as long as they did with no one noticing. For one thing, they were well connected to the Illinois House Speaker, who's got a lot of power, in and out of Springfield.

"For another, we all assume that whatever goes on behind those iron bars is protecting all us law-abiding citizens—sorry, all you law-abiding citizens; I'm out on bail facing a felony charge." People laughed more loudly than my little joke merited—they needed some kind of release from the horrors they'd been hearing.

"Some of what goes on may be nasty, but as the corrections officers said to me and my sister inmates many times—like when a woman wasn't allowed medical care after getting a major burn on her arm in the kitchen"—I nodded and Morrell flipped up a slide of the arm—"Coolis isn't a resort. Inmates aren't on vacation. We law-abiding citizens don't necessarily want prisoners rehabilitated, but we sure do want them punished. And they get punished in carloads full of discipline."

I finished with the slides I'd taken of CO Polsen assaulting Dolores in the laundry room. The only sound in the room now was Peppy, crying to be allowed to come to me.

"This kind of thing is a daily occurrence. I witnessed it, I was humiliated in similar ways myself. Women have no recourse against this kind of abuse. Illinois law has no serious provision for removing abusive guards or for disciplining them. It can take over a year for a woman prisoner complaining of rape or battery to get a

court hearing. During that year she can be put in segregation. She can be repeatedly assaulted. And if her case
is found to be without merit, then she is cattle fodder
for the corrections officers. That's daily life at Coolis.

"I understand Robert Baladine sent around an
e-mail, offering to resign. I don't know if it's true or
not, but if it weren't for the fact that Lucian Frenada
was—probably—killed in an effort to cover up the
Global manufacturing operation, I'd think Baladine
should resign not because of Frenada but because of the
degradation of prisoners that goes on hourly in a prison
that his company built and runs for the state of Illinois."

I'd lost my dry composure. I sat down, shivering, my
teeth chattering. Morrell was at my side to put a jacket
around my shoulders. Murray had stepped forward
along with the rest of the team in the room, but when
he saw Morrell behind me, he turned on his heel and
left.

Lotty and Sal and Mr. Contreras applauded vigor-
ously, and Mr. Contreras finally let Peppy come up to
me. I sank my hands gratefully into her gold fur and
tried to calm down enough to answer other questions.

What the reporters most wanted to know, besides
their fascination with sex in the prison, was how
Baladine came to be injured.

"He says he needed to break into the church to get
his son back. I believe Father Lou has made a sworn
deposition that Baladine never approached him about
his son. Indeed, Robbie arrived at the church only a few
hours ahead of his father, who could have phoned or
come to the door the way most people might. But someone watching my home apparently saw him arrive,
tailed him here to St. Remigio's, and then called

Baladine for instructions. He chose to approach his son in this highly unusual way, and a police officer is dead as a result."

One of the Carnifice Security men who'd been in the church last week had decided to do a deal with the State's Attorney. No one in the State's Attorney's office cared much about Lucian Frenada, or Nicola Aguinaldo—or me. But Father Lou was a local legend. For forty years, any policeman who'd ever boxed grew up knowing him. An assault on him in his church was more than blasphemy. So the guy Father Lou had knocked out, after realizing that the cops were more interested in finding out exactly what punch the priest had used on him than in sympathizing with him, turned on his boss and his partner and told the cops the story of his watch on my building, of seeing Robbie arrive on foot, of calling for instructions.

"Isn't the dead officer the same man who was in your office with the cocaine?"

I smiled. "You'll have to ask the department about that one. I never actually saw the man who died at St. Remigio's: everything took place in the dark."

"And what about Baladine?" Beth Blacksin from Channel 8 asked. "I hear he's undergoing shots for rabies because your dog bit him? Is he suing you?"

"You have it backward," I said. "I'm giving my dog Mitch a series of rabies shots in case Baladine infected him. No, seriously, he shot the dog and thought he'd killed him, because the dog tried to stop him from chaining Father Lou to my old friend and neighbor Salvatore Contreras. When Baladine was strangling me, Mitch somehow made a supercanine effort, dragged himself up on his weak legs, and dug his teeth into Baladine's ass. If Baladine chooses to sue me, my lawyer is looking forward to cross-examining him, but we'll cross that bridge when we get there."

Regine Mauger, the *Herald-Star*'s gossip columnist, got up to demand what right I had to vilify the Trant family. Abigail Trant was a lovely woman who was doing an enormous amount of good for needy Chicagoans, and Regine thought I should be ashamed for attacking her husband in this way.

I didn't tell her I had called Abigail Trant myself the day after the fight in the church. After her efforts to help me, she deserved advance notice of what I was going to say about her husband. She asked only if I was sure. And I said, not about everything but about Trant's being with Baladine and Frenada the night Frenada died. And about the production of Global spin-offs at Coolis.

She didn't say anything else, but two days later she came to see me—again without warning, leaving the Gelaendewagen double-parked on Racine. She was as exquisite as ever, but the skin on her face was taut with tension.

"Rhiannon and I fell in love with France when we were there this summer. I'm taking her back to Toulouse. I've found a wonderful school she can attend there. I don't know what Teddy will do, because I don't know what Global will do when they hear your report."

She hesitated, then added, "I don't want you to think I blame you in any way for—for—the collapse of my marriage. I think the time will come when I will be grateful that my eyes were opened, but right now I can't feel much but pain. There's something else you deserve to know. Teddy came home the night of Global's television debut with the emblem missing from one of his

Ferragamo loafers. Maybe it's weak of me, but the day you asked about the emblem I went home and threw out the shoes."

She left abruptly on that line. I didn't think Regine Mauger needed to report any of that in her coy little phrases.

Mauger and some of the others continued to harangue me. Lotty came forward and announced that as my physician she was declaring an end to my stamina: I was recovering from serious injuries, in case they had forgotten. The group looked suitably abashed and packed up cassette recorders and other equipment. Morrell gave each person a copy of the videotape and slides. The two men sitting with Father Lou grunted and got up to escort the reporters out of the building.

"Now what?" Sal asked when they had gone.

"Now—" I shrugged. "Now I try to patch my business back together. Hope that enough people buy my version of events that some of the misery at Coolis will end, even if no one is ever arrested for Nicola Aguinaldo's murder."

"And what is Robbie going to do?" Sal asked.

I grinned. "Eleanor came to pick him up on Wednesday afternoon. He ran into the church screaming that he was claiming sanctuary, that he would chain himself to the altar and go on a hunger strike. That should have thrilled her, but it only made her angrier. She finally worked out a deal with Father Lou that Robbie could stay on as a boarder and go to St. Remigio's. Father Lou said that for a donation to the St. Remigio scholarship fund and money to repair the damage to the altar, he was willing to tell the state to drop the trespassing charge against Baladine."

Watching Father Lou blandly extort a fifty-thousand-dollar pledge from Eleanor Baladine had been one of the few joyous moments of the past few months. She had arrived at St. Remigio's with her lawyer, convinced that she was going to browbeat the priest with threats of additional charges of kidnapping, as well as of assault against Baladine—man coming to claim his son is set on by dogs, rabid detectives, and other scum. She left without her son and with a signed undertaking to support him at the school. The sop to her pride was Father Lou's grave statement that boxing would make Robbie a truly manly man, and that he, Father Lou, would personally oversee her son's training.

"The funny thing is, Robbie actually wants to learn to box," I told Sal. "This boy who couldn't learn to swim or play tennis to please his parents runs wind sprints every morning after mass."

I'd moved back home, of course, but for some reason I found myself getting up early every day and driving over to St. Remigio's for the six o'clock mass. Robbie or one of the other St. Remigio boxers would serve. Father Lou gruffly announced I could read the lesson as long as I was there. All that week, as I made my way through the book of Job, I thought about the women at Coolis. If there was a God, had He delivered the women into the hands of Satan for a wager? And would He appear finally in the whirlwind and rescue them?

Scar Tissue

MY VINDICATION BY the Chicago press was something of a nine-day wonder. Clients who'd left me for Carnifice called to say they'd never doubted me and they would have assignments for me as soon as I got off the disabled list. Old friends in the Chicago Police Department called, demanding to know why I hadn't complained to them about Douglas Lemour; they would have fixed the problem for me. I didn't try to argue with them about all the times in the past they'd told me to mind my own business and leave police work to them. And Mary Louise Neely showed up one morning, her face pinched with misery.

"Vic, I won't blame you if you feel like you can never trust me again, but they called to threaten me. Threaten the children. The man who called knew the exact address of Emily's camp in France and told me what she'd eaten for dinner the night before. I was terrified and I felt trapped—I couldn't send the boys back to their father, and I didn't know what else to do with them. I thought if I told you, you'd go riding off half-cocked and get all of us killed." She twisted her hands round and round as if she could wash off the memory.

"You could be right." I tried to smile, but found I

couldn't quite manage it. "I'm not going to sit in judgment on you for being scared, let alone for trying to look after Nate and Josh. What hurt was the way you were judging me. Claiming I was running hotheaded into danger when I was fighting for my life. I had to go into the heart of the furnace to save myself. If you could have trusted me enough to tell me why you were withdrawing from me, it would have made a big difference."

"You're right, Vic," she whispered. "I could have gone to Terry about Lemour; maybe it would have stopped him from trying to plant the coke on you or from beating you when he arrested you. I can only say —I'm sorry. If you're willing to let me try again, though, I'd like to."

We left it at that—that she would open the office back up, get the files in order, take preliminary information from clients while I continued to recuperate. We'd give it three months and see how we felt about the relationship then.

I kept trying to go back to work myself, but I felt dull and drained. I had told the psychologist at the Berman Institute I would sleep better if I stopped feeling so humiliated. By rights, taking care of Lemour and Baldine should have solved my problems, but I still was plagued by insomnia. Maybe it was because my month at Coolis sat like a bad taste in my mouth, or maybe it was because I couldn't stop blaming myself for staying inside when I could have made bail, as if I had deliberately courted what had happened to me. There were still too many nights I dreaded going to sleep because of the dreams that lay on the other side.

The night after my press presentation I'd invited Morrell home with me, but when he started to undress I told him he would have to leave. He took a long look at me and buttoned his jeans back up. The next day he sent me a single rose with the message that he would respect my distance as long as I felt I needed to maintain it but that he enjoyed talking to me and would be glad to see me in public.

The knowledge that I could choose, that Morrell at least would not force himself on me, made sleep come a bit easier to me. I went to a couple of Cubs games with him as the season wound down—thanks to tickets from one of my clients—and saw Sammy Sosa hit his sixty-fourth home run, invited Morrell to my Saturday afternoon pickup game in the park, ate dinner with him, but spent my nights with only the dogs for company.

I kept busy enough. I made endless depositions with attorneys for the state, attorneys for the CO's I was suing out at Coolis, attorneys for Baladine, attorneys for Global. I even had a meeting with Alex Fisher. She thought it would be a good idea if I toned down some of my statements about Global and Frenada.

"Sandy, the reason I call you Sandy, which you hate, is that it's the only thing about you I ever liked. You were a pain in the ass in law school. You wanted to be a firebrand and take the message about racism and social justice to the proletariat, and I made you uncomfortable because I was that odd phenomenon in an upscale law school—a genuine blue-collar worker's genuine daughter. But at least you were who you were—Sandy Fishbein. You didn't try to pretend you were anything else. Then you went off and found capitalism, and had your nose and your lips done, and cut off your name, too."

"That's not what I came to talk to you about," she said, but her voice had lost its edge.

"And another thing. I have a tape of yours. Baladine made it during his swim meet."

"How did you get it?" she hissed. "Did he give it to you?"

I smiled blandly. "He doesn't know I have it. It's yours, Alex. It's yours the day I get concrete evidence that Global has fired Wenzel, the man who managed the Coolis shop, and that he is not working elsewhere in your organization. And the day that Carnifice lets CO Polsen and CO Hartigan go. Without placing them elsewhere."

Her wide lips were stiff. "I have little influence on Global's day-to-day operation, and I do not work for Carnifice."

I continued to smile. "Of course not. And it doesn't look as though Baladine will be at Carnifice much longer, anyway, at least not if the report in this morning's papers can be believed. Between his sending that e-mail announcing his resignation and all the publicity we've generated this week, his board is pressuring him to step down. And Jean-Claude Poilevy, who's always been a survivor, is backpedaling as fast as he can scoot. He says Baladine operated a for-profit shop at Coolis completely without his knowledge, and he's shocked at the tales of sexual abuse in the prison. I think Carnifice would welcome the chance to fire a couple of low-level employees. If they let Polsen and Hartigan go, they can make a big press pitch on how they're cleaning house."

"I can't promise anything, of course."

"Of course not. By the way, you're not the only woman Baladine taped on that couch. He also took advantage of his kids' ex-nanny, the one who died. Not a nice man to be around."

Her throat worked as the implications of that struck

her. She started to ask me what I'd seen and then swept out of my office without saying anything else.

I'd thought about trying to use the Aguinaldo tapes as counters to get Baladine to drop the kidnapping charge, but I hated to exploit her in death as she had been in life. And I was sure by now I could beat the charges in court. In fact, six days later when my trial date came up, the judge dismissed all the charges. He made a stern statement to the effect that he didn't know why the state had charged me in the first place, but since the parents were not present to offer any explanation about why they'd called the police, he couldn't begin to speculate on their underlying rationale. At any rate, the arresting officer was dead, and that was the end of it. A real whimper after all that banging.

When I got home I found a hand-delivered envelope from Alex including copies of the termination orders for Wenzel from Global and Polsen and Hartigan from Carnifice. The three were fired for misconduct in performance of their duties and were not eligible for workers' compensation. I sent Alex her tape but kept the other three in a safe deposit box at the bank.

A discreet report in the paper the next day said that Baladine was suffering from exhaustion brought on by overwork and that the Carnifice directors had accepted his resignation while he received medical care in Houston. His wife was moving to California with her daughters to enroll them in a premium swim program while she took a job coaching the University of Southern California swim team. Good old Eleanor. She sure hated hanging with losers.

And still I couldn't sleep at night. I finally decided I had to go back to Coolis. I had to see the place, to know it had no power over me.

They were harvesting corn as I drove west the next morning. The bright greens of summer had given way to drab tans in the groves along the Fox River, but the weather still held an unseasonable warmth.

As I approached the prison, the place in my abdomen where Hartigan had kicked me tightened. I was coming here of my own free will, a free woman, but the sight of the razor-wire fences made me start to shake so badly, I had to pull over to the side of the road.

Morrell had offered to come with me, but I wanted to prove I could make this journey on my own. I wished now I'd taken him up on his offer. I wanted to turn around and head back to Chicago as fast as I could go. Instead, I made myself drive inside the front gate to the visitors' parking lot.

The guard at the first checkpoint didn't give any sign of recognizing my name. He passed me on to the next station, and I was finally admitted to the visitors' waiting room. It was CO Cornish who was assigned to escort me from there to the visitors' lounge.

He tried to greet me jovially. "Couldn't stay away, huh?"

I grunted noncommittally. I had filed a suit against the Department of Corrections for inflicting grievous bodily harm, and against Polsen and Hartigan by name. Cornish would probably be called as a witness; I didn't need to alienate him.

Miss Ruby was waiting for me in the visitors' lounge. "So you made it out, Cream. Made it out and now you've come back. You're a kind of hero around here, do you know that? The girls know it's because of you they kicked out Wenzel and Polsen and Hartigan. They closed that T-shirt factory too, but I suppose you know that."

I knew that. A report in this morning's financial section announced that Global was returning their sewing operations to Myanmar. I guess it made me happy to know that the Virginwear line was now being made by inmates in Myanmar's forced labor camps instead of inmates in an Illinois prison.

"They're still making things here, but not for Hollywood anymore, so production is way down. It's hard on the women who got let go; they don't speak English and they can only get work in the kitchen now, which doesn't pay as well. But I think they appreciate not having to work in that atmosphere over there. Everyone was too scared all the time. So I guess you are a hero, at that."

"You sound bitter. I didn't set out to be a hero."

"No, but you were undercover. I asked you point-blank and you lied. You might have told me when you came to me asking for help."

"I really was arrested. Just as I told you, because Robert Baladine accused me of kidnapping his son. The cops sent me out here because I got arrested on a holiday weekend. I decided to stay to try to find out what happened to poor young Nicola. I didn't dare tell a soul. Not just to protect myself: you have a lot of influence here with the other women, and even the guards mostly treat you with respect, but you're here and you're vulnerable. I didn't want harm to you to haunt me for the rest of my life."

She thought it over and finally, grudgingly, decided maybe I hadn't abused our relationship. I stayed to tell her the whole story, the story I'd given to the press. She liked having an insider's look at the news, and she especially enjoyed hearing about my confrontation with Baladine and Lemour at St. Remigio's.

"Girl like you who took on Angie and the Iscariots, you were plenty tough enough to go up against a bent cop. Glad to hear about it. Glad to know about it."

Before I left, I handed her a little bag of cosmetics I'd brought with me, buried under a stack of legal documents that hadn't been searched thoroughly. CO Cornish watched me but didn't try to intervene.

"Revlon! You remembered. Moisturizer, cleanser, new lipstick in my favorite color—you're a good woman, even if you did come to me under false pretenses. Now, since it turns out you're really a lawyer and a detective and all those things, maybe you'll write one of your famous letters for me. I've done fourteen years, that's already way over average for murder in this state, but I've got eight more to go. See if you can help me on my parole. I'd kind of like to see my granddaughter before she's a grandmother herself."

I promised to do what I could. Back in the parking lot I stood with my hand on the car door for a long time before opening it. The car was a late-model green Mustang, a replacement for both the Rustmobile and the Trans Am. Freeman had tried to get me back my beloved sports car, but the police first claimed they couldn't find it and then finally had to admit they'd pretty well trashed it. Luke went to the police pound to look at it, but the Trans Am was way beyond even his miraculous fingers. Freeman was suing the city for me to try to recover the price of the car, but I figured I'd be seventy before that case came to judgment.

Lacey Dowell had given me the money for the Mustang. She'd given me enough money that I could probably have bought a used XJ-12 convertible, but that was a fantasy, not a car for a working detective who has to use her wheels in the grime of Chicago.

Lacey came to see me at the end of the filming of *Virgin Six*. Father Lou told her that I'd solved Frenada's murder and that even though Trant and Baladine would never be arrested for it, she should know that the two men had killed her childhood playmate.

"I told them at Global that I couldn't work with Teddy anymore, that I'd stop production if he had anything to do with the movie. I guess I'm still a big enough star that they cared. They sent Teddy to Chile to head up their South American operation. But I understand from Father Lou that you put in a great deal of work on the case and never got paid. In fact, he told me you were badly injured as the result of your investigations. So I felt I should pay your fee, since Lucy and I were old friends, and we swore a pact when we were ten to help each other in the face of every danger. I didn't do too well by him this year: the least I can do is thank you for looking after him for me."

The check was for forty thousand dollars. Enough to take care of the bills that had mounted while I was out of commission. Enough for a car with only six thousand miles on it. Enough to pay some of Freeman's fee. Money made from T-shirts sewn by women in prisons here or abroad. It was in my hands, too. I could have turned it down, but I didn't.

I got into the car when the guard came over to see what the matter was. I sketched a wave and headed back to the tollway.

When I reached the city I drove to Morrell's place in Evanston. I tried to tell him what I'd been thinking as I drove home.

He cupped my face in his long fingers. "Vic, look at me. You set an impossibly high bar for yourself to jump. When you run into it, you bruise yourself and then blame yourself for the injury. You have to live in the world. It's the unfortunate reality of being alive. Even a monk who abjures the world and the flesh gets his clothes and food provided by someone who's willing to do the dirty work for him.

"You can't save everyone or fix every broken part of this planet. But you do more than most. If Lacey's money comes in part from sweatshops, you still brought some relief to women in prison here in Illinois. And that bastard Hartigan, who kicked you—he's likely to go to prison himself. Even if it's not for the murder of Nicola Aguinaldo, there's a measure of justice there. It's true Trant and Baladine are walking around, but Trant lost his marriage and it looks as though the studio is demoting him in a serious way. You said Lacey told you they're sending him to Chile.

"And look at Robbie Baladine following Father Lou around like a duckling. Share some of his joy in life. You've earned it, you brought it to him. Okay?"

"Okay," I whispered.

I spent that night with him and a number of nights after. And if my sleep was still disturbed, if the images of terror still sometimes woke me, at least I had the comfort of a friend to share my journey.